THE ASCENDANT STARS

Greg was appalled. 'My God – so it's happened. The Sentinel once told me that there could be over a million of those things still down there ...'

'Aye, and maybe the rest. Don't think they'll be in a good mood when they get out. Which brings us to you.' She paused to glance up at the sky where Darien hung, a shining blue-white orb. 'When they arrive, the first hammerblows will fall here. After realising that Darien presents no threat, they'll look further afield and find this moon and Segrana and the Zyradin and come straight for us.' She looked him in the eye. 'Which is why you've got to leave. Won't be long before it's too dangerous for ye here.'

By Michael Cobley

Humanity's Fire
Seeds of Earth
The Orphaned Worlds
The Ascendant Stars

THE ASCENDANT STARS

BOOK 3 OF

HUMANITY'S FIRE

MICHAEL COBLEY

www.orbitbooks.net

ORBIT

First published in Great Britain in 2011 by Orbit
This edition published in 21012 by Orbit

Copyright © 2011 by Michael Cobley

Excerpt from *Leviathan Wakes* by James S. A Corey
Copyright © 2011 by James S. A. Corey

The moral right of the author has been asserted.

A CIP catalogue record for this book
is available from the British Library.

ISBN 978-1-84149-636-8

Typeset in Sabon by M Rules
Printed and bound by CPI Group (UK) Ltd, Croydon, CR0 4YY

Papers used by Orbit are from well-managed forests
and other responsible sources.

MIX
Paper from
responsible sources
FSC® C104740

Orbit
An imprint of
Little, Brown Book Group
100 Victoria Embankment
London EC4Y 0DY

n Hachette UK Company
www.hachette.co.uk

www.orbitbooks.net

For my dad, Michael John Cobley,
still in the game, kickin' and scratchin'!

On the forest-moon Nivyesta, **Catriona Macreadie** finds herself forming a telepathic link with Segrana, a vast and millennia-old entity which inhabits the interwoven ecosystem of the continent-wide forest. She comes to identify with the forest, strengthening the bond with Segrana, and helping the humanoid Uvovo natives when several Hegemony mercenaries try to infiltrate the depths of the forest.

Chel, or Cheluvahar, is a scholar of the Uvovo and a good friend to both Greg and Catriona. He undergoes a ritual whereby Segrana gives him strange new abilities and tells him to prepare the Uvovo for war. From ancient myths he learns that the Giant's Shoulder temple houses a 'warpwell', an ancient Forerunner weapon which defeated a savage enemy many millennia ago. The warpwell would provide access to the lower levels of hyperspace and much faster travel between the stars, an advantage that would make the Hegemony's already formidable warfleets invincible.

While events unfold on Darien, **Kao Chih** begins his journey to Darien. Kao Chih's people are the descendants of another of the three original ships launched from Earth 150 years before. Their world, Pyre, was seized by a Sendrukan Hegemony corporate monoclan which ruthlessly mined and stripped it of its resources. A few hundred colonists fled in a handful of ramshackle ships, eventually finding refuge in a star system home to a race called the Roug. When news of the discovery of Darien reached the Roug's orbital city, Agmedra'a, the Roug hosting these Human descendants also decide to send emissaries. And soon Kao Chih and a Roug called Tumakri are on their way.

During their twisting quest Tumakri tragically dies in an ambush and Kao Chih joins forces with a sentient droid called Drazuma-Ha*. Evading a group of combat drones seemingly trying to kill them, they are instead captured by a Human smuggler-terrorist called Corazon Talavera. With Drazuma-Ha*'s aid they manage to escape in a terrorist shuttle, leaving Corazon marooned on a semi-hospitable planet. But she has a vital and terrifying role yet to play.

Back on Darien the colony is in uproar over the actions of the authoritarian Brolturans, usually at the behest of Kuros, now Hegemony ambassador. After the bizarre disappearance of Robert Horst at Giant's Shoulder, Theo Karlsson returns to Hammergard and encounters Donny Barbour. Both are then witness to the missile attack on the Assembly halls which kills the colony's president and nearly all of his cabinet. A deep crisis ensues, with Brolturan troops on the streets and flying security patrols, an unsubtle show of strength.

The last remaining government official asks Major Karlsson and Donny to get a group of Enhancee scientists offworld. (The Enhancees are genetically engineered sci-tech specialists; Catriona Macreadie was part of that programme but failed the stringent tests in her teens.) At the Port Gagarin launch field they hijack an Earthsphere shuttle and manage to get into orbit. But interceptors from the Brolturan battleship *Purifier* are heading their way so the Enhancees are transferred to the Earthsphere ship *Heracles*. Donny Barbour tricks Theo Karlsson into leaving the escape pod to save his life, then leads the Brolturan interceptors on a bravura chase through the skies of the forest moon. After an agile and defiant evasion, a hostile missile sends the shuttle down in flames over one of the big seas.

After vanishing from the warpwell chamber on Giant's Shoulder, Robert Horst appears in a bizarre complex of tunnels, escorted by a trio of small intelligent mechs. They tell him that he is down in hyperspace, which consists of many levels. After a series of perilous encounters he arrives at another deeper level, at a place called the Garden of the Machines, an AI metropolis watched over by a mysterious being called the Construct. After rejuvenating Robert's physical age (and turning a holosim of his daughter into an android simulacrum), the Construct persuades Robert to return the favour by venturing into the depths of hyperspace in search of an ancient entity called the Godhead. Hostile forces arising from another region of the depths have been attacking allies of the Construct, who thinks that the Godhead might possess vital information on the attacks.

Meanwhile, Kao Chih and Drazuma-Ha*, still pursued by the mysterious combat droids, seek sanctuary aboard a cloud-harvester. Drazuma-Ha* tricks Kao Chih into remaining on the bridge, seizes the cloud-harvester's shuttle and leaves for Darien. The pursuing robots reveal to Kao Chih that Drazuma-Ha* is in fact an agent of the Legion of Avatars, a cyborg horde that was the Forerunners' last and deadliest enemy. If it gains control of the warpwell gate down on Darien, it could open it to release the Legion of Avatars' surviving from their prison deep in the abyss of hyperspace. The chase after Drazuma-Ha* is on. When they reach Darien they use the cloud-harvester's escape pod and

Kao Chih's shuttle to continue the hunt down within Giant's Shoulder on Darien. Then in the warpwell chamber, Kao Chih and the surviving droid manage to kill the Legion mech Drazuma-Ha*. As Kao Chih falls unconsciousness, the well guardian transports him away to safety.

Seeds of Earth ends with the Hegemony's Ambassador Kuros and the Brolturans in control of the colony and the temple site on Giant's Shoulder. Theo Karlsson and Catriona Macreadie are in hiding up on the forest-moon Nivyesta, guarding a captured Hegemony mercenary who turns out to be human. On Darien, Greg is escorting Kao Chih and others to a temporary camp deep in the mountains. Plans for the insurgency are being hastily formed, and the Enhancees are safely on their way to Earth.

And on a planet far from Darien, a cyborg knight of the Legion of Avatars rests on a cold sea bed, considering the failure of its droid agent. It decides that it will have to take action itself and, after repairing its damaged biomechanisms, the Knight engages its engines and blasts up out of the depths of the sea – heading for the stars.

BOOK TWO: *THE ORPHANED WORLDS*

The Orphaned Worlds begins a few weeks after the end of *Seeds of Earth*.

Brolturan forces, directed by the Hegemony ambassador, **Kuros**, are now in de facto control of the Darien colony. Colonial politicians form an interim government that is clearly subservient to the Brolturans, who increasingly come to resemble occupiers.

Greg Cameron has been organising the resistance, which has set up a more permanent camp in an ancient Uvovo stronghold inside Tusk Mountain, in the mountains to the north.

Robert Horst, at the behest of the Construct, is on a mission into the depths of hyperspace in search of the Godhead, hoping it will help them negotiate an alliance against the Legion of Avatars and its agents. Accompanied by a simulacrum of his daughter, Rosa, their AI ship takes them down through the strange, bizarre, dangerous or scarcely comprehensible levels of hyperspace. The Rosa-sim dies tragically in a fight with a lone Legion cyborg, after which Robert meets the Intercessor, an emissary from the Godhead. It sends him onwards to a pocket universe, supposedly the final stage before meeting the Godhead, but it turns out to be a deadly one-way trap.

Kao Chih has left Darien with Silveira, an Earthsphere agent who wants to find out more about the lost human colony on Pyre and how the Suneye corporate monoclan took it over. They travel first to the Roug system, then on to Pyre, during which Silveira learns how Kao Chih's forebears were a splinter group that escaped Pyre decades before. On Pyre they find out how the colonists struggle to exist under conditions of resource rationing, and the brutal oppression of off-world criminal gangs sanctioned by the Suneye Monoclan.

Ambassador Kuros now holds sway over most of the Darien colony, and the interim colonial administration follows his instructions to the letter. However, a senior adviser arrives from the Sendrukan Hegemony home-world, the Clarified Teshak who is a Sendrukan wholly controlled by an AI. He exerts a harsh authority over Kuros while putting his own implacable plan into action.

Theo Karlsson was with Catriona on Nivyesta, look-ing after Malachi Ash, the captured 'Ezgara' mercenary who was found to be human, from a world called Tygra. And Tygra turns out to be the third lost Human colonyworld. Both Theo and Ash are snatched by a stealth team from Tygra, but are then freed by renegade Tygrans led by **Captain Gideon.** Theo accompanies them to a rendezvous with a retired veteran Tygran offi-cer who lives long enough to pass on information about a long-past conspiracy before tragically expiring. This knowledge further alienates the renegades from the leadership on Tygra, whose pro-Hegemony policies had already angered them.

When Kao Chih and the agent Silveira arrive back in the Roug system they find that several senior com-manders and leaders of Kao Chih's own people have been abducted by a mercenary assault ship. This is com-manded by Marshall Becker, the Tygran's overall military leader. The abduction was intended as a warn-ing to Kao Chih's human enclave to avoid involvement in wider affairs. The Roug, affronted by such a gross violation against their people, send one of their own vessels off in pursuit with Kao Chih aboard to assist. After a cunning and stealthy rescue carried out in hyperspace, the Roug ship continues to follow the Ezgara vessel to its destination, a Tygran base, to see who is behind it all.

Meanwhile, Theo accompanies Captain Gideon on an operation to liberate the rest of the captain's men from a Tygran base. The raid is a success but, as they're leaving, a hostile Tygran warship arrives, closely followed by the Roug craft bearing Kao Chih. After an exchange of weapons fire (and attempted data subversion of Gideon's vessel) the Roug ship neutralises the aggressive Tygran craft, destroying its weapons and engines. Theo, Gideon and Kao Chih, representatives from the three lost Human colonies, briefly meet aboard the Roug vessel before they go their separate ways.

Julia Bryce and her fellow-Enhanced are on their way to Earth aboard a passenger liner when it is boarded by brigands led by the terrorist Corazon Talavera. Talavera takes them to a refugee planet, then coerces them into upgrading two thermonuclear missiles for one of the refugee leaders. Julia then finds out that the Covenant Order of the Spiral Prophecy, a fundamentalist religious faction, claims that the lost tomb of one of their ancient Father-Sages lies on Darien. A Spiralist armada is therefore gathering, and the missiles are part of a planned invasion of Darien to secure the supposedly sacred site. Julia and the Enhanced try to escape before the armada reaches Darien, but fail in the attempt. They are then forced to watch as the weapons they upgraded are used by the fanatics to destroy a Brolturan battleship and severely damage the Earthsphere vessel. Afterwards, Talavera puts the Enhanced into separate virtual reality tanks to coerce them into working on detailed course and hyperspace jump data for a large number of other missiles.

Down on Darien, Greg and Rory are engaged in delaying the advance of Brolturan forces towards the resistance's stronghold. Greg is heading back there, when the Brolturan battleship *Purifier* launches a massive particle beam attack on Tusk Mountain from orbit. Greg and Rory are in the target zone of a second strike – then the *Purifier* is destroyed in orbit by the Spiral armada's thermonuclear missile.

Down in hyperspace, Robert is rescued from the pocket-universe trap by the Construct, who then sends him and another Rosa-sim on their next mission. They must go to an Achorga nestworld to retrieve the Zyradin, an ancient Forerunner entity designed to bond with the Uvovo's Segrana, thus augmenting its powers at this crucial juncture. They descend into the insectoid Achorga-dominated world, find and recover the Zyradin, and have to flee the pursuing Achorga via ancient Forerunner transfer platforms. The Rosa-sim stays back to fight off a horde of deadly silver creatures while Robert heads over to the Forerunner platform to escape. But they get to him just as the platform activates. When he arrives at the transfer platform in Tusk Mountain on Darien, still carrying the Zyradin canister, he is on the point of death.

Greg Cameron is at Tusk Mountain when a dying Robert Horst arrives with the Zyradin's canister. The warpwell Sentinel and the Zyradin tell Greg that the Zyradin must be taken to the forest moon and given to Catriona. She is now Keeper of Segrana and through her the Zyradin can merge with the forest-wide sentience. Only the warpwell chamber inside Giant's Shoulder can transport them to Nivyesta so, after evading an ambush during their zeplin journey, Greg and his team arrive there only to find that the Brolturans have pulled out. However, the humans now have to fight an advance squad of hostile Legion war droids, during which Greg finds himself betrayed by one of his companions. Without warning, the warpwell Sentinel transports him directly to the inner chamber and from there up to the forest moon. Greg gives the canister containing the Zyradin to Catriona and it permeates her, transforming her into a cloud of glowing motes that spread outwards and across the vast forest.

The book ends with the cyborg Legion Knight taking possession of Giant's Shoulder and using two of its scion offshoots to unlock the Warpwell.

Chel and Rory are trapped inside the Legion Knight's droid manufactory, under its pitiless control while the factory implants enslaving biotech within them both. They will soon be set against their own people.

Julia is trapped on a virtual beach controlled by Talavera, made to work on course data for lethal missiles, Talavera's plans as yet unknown.

Theo Karlsson and the renegade Tygrans finally arrive at Darien and make contact with the anti-Brolturan resistance movement.

Back at the Garden of the Machines, the Construct is examining the dead body of Robert Horst. But when the real Robert comes to join him, we discover the expired corpse is that of a semiorganic simulacrum. The Construct now knows that the warpwell on Darien has been unlocked, and that the Godhead is behind most of the attacks coming from the depths of hyperspace. Once it has learned what Robert Horst has to say, direct action will have to be taken. For Darien, however, only hope and the uncertain power of fate can help the colonists now. The fleets and the stormclouds are gathering for the final showdown.

MAIN CHARACTERS

Greg Cameron – led the resistance against the Brolturan occupiers until the vital Zyradin mission took him to the forest moon, Nivyesta.

Catriona Macreadie – chosen by the biomass sentience Segrana as its Keeper, she received the Zyradin from Greg and was transformed by it.

Theo Karlsson – Greg's uncle, former major in the Darien Volunteer Forces, became involved with renegade soldiers from another lost Human colony world, Tygra.

Cheluvahar, or Chel – a seer of the Uvovo and close friend of Greg Cameron.

Julia Bryce – she and her Enhanced team were coerced by Corazon Talavera into upgrading nuclear missiles for the Spiralist invasion. Now they are imprisoned in virtual prisons.

Kao Chih – after his time on Darien, he secretly went to Pyre then partnered a Roug in a rescue mission to retrieve the Human Sept elders captured by the Tygran's pro-Hegemony military leader.

Franklyn Gideon – captain of the Stormlions commandery and protégé of veteran Tygran officer, Sam

Rawlins. He and his men were persuaded by Theo Karlsson to throw in their lot with Darien.

Robert Horst – Earthsphere's ambassador to Darien, he was sent down into hyperspace to meet the Construct, who sent him on a mission to track down the Godhead.

The Construct – a machine intelligence created by the Forerunners more than a hundred millennia ago to help fight the Legion of Avatars. It uses the mind-state patterns of Robert Horst and his daughter Rosa to create new kinds of sentient simulacra.

Reen – Mandator of the High Index of the Roug, commander of the warvaunt vessel, the *Vyrk-Zoshel*.

A Knight of the Legion of Avatars – an armoured, cyborg creature, a survivor from the war against the Forerunners. It has come to Darien and through guile and subterfuge has finally attained its long-desired goal, the unlocking of the warpwell.

Utavess Kuros – the Sendrukan Hegemony's ambassador to Darien. The Spiralist invasion destroyed the Brolturan battleship while Kuros was taken over by his AI companion.

The Clarified Teshak – a senior Sendrukan official whose AI is in sole control. Although he was sent to Darien to oversee Kuros' performance, he also has the agenda of the Clarified to promote.

The Godhead – ancient sentience of unknown origin. Rumours abound about its nature, some suggesting that it was once a machine intelligence.

MAIN SENTIENT SPECIES IN HUMANITY'S FIRE

Humans – biped mammals, binocular vision, vestigial hair, restricted range in audio/visual senses, average height 1.7m

Sendruka – biped humanoid, binocular vision, minimal body hair, average height 2.8m

Bargalil – hexapedal, 20% body hair, average height 2m

Henkaya – biped with four arms, muscular upper body, average height 2.1m

Kiskashin – tailed, ornitho-reptilian biped, rough, pebbled skin, average height 1.8m

Makhori – amphibious octoped, mutiple tentacles, large eyes, average body length 1.5m

Achorga – insectoid, hiver, aggressively territorial, only Queens and specialised drones display intelligence, average height 1.2m

Uvovo – small bipedal humanoid, 70% body hair, binocular vision, excellent hearing, average height 1.3m

Gomedra – upright biped, furred, vaguely dog/wolf-like, average height 1.4m

Vusark – pseudo-insectoid, decapedal, compound eyes, average height 1m when walking on majority of legs, 2.1m when raised up on back legs

Voth – biped mammal, long forearms, 75% body hair, cyborg implants common, fond of concealing garments, average height 1.4m

Piraseri – tripedal sophonts of aquatic descent, main body a tapering torso with a backswept head fringed by small tentacles, average height 1.6m

Roug – slender bipeds with thin limbs, possibly hairless, usually garbed head-to-toe in tightly-wound strips of dense material, averge height 1.9m

Naszbur – heavily armoured bipedal reptiloid, a chitin shell forms a hood over the head, aggressive traders, average height 1.5m

Hodralog – birdlike sophonts common in certain levels of hyperspace, frail physique, average height 0.8m

Keklir – short, muscular bipeds found in most of the upper tiers of hyperspace, have wide, tapering snouts with two mouthlike openings, average height 1m

Pozu – squat, brown-skinned species originating from high-gravity world, gloomy disposition, skilled plant technologists, average height 0.7m

The Clarified – former Sendrukans whose personal AI has gained full control of their body due to erasure of the original persona, usually by judicial sentence, occasionally by voluntary mind dissolution

Vor – a species of endosymbiotic parasite that rides inside a host's brain, once upper intellect/persona functions have been removed. A very ancient race once thought extinct, it has reappeared, rejuvenated and aggressive

Shyntanil – also known as the Twiceborn, a race that employs drastic life-extension technologies requiring re-engineering of the respiratory and nervous systems, and a temporary cessation of brain functions. An ancient bipedal species that has returned from obscurity, working alongside former adversaries, the Vor

CIVILISATIONS

Earthsphere (157 star systems; 873 inhabited worlds and orbitals; population 5.3 trillion) – most numerous species are Henkayans, Vusark and Humans, although Humans have been politically dominant. Despite Sendrukan brutalities, Earthsphere has remained a committed if junior partner to the Hegemony.

Sendrukan Hegemony (112,000 star systems; 347,000 inhabited worlds and orbitals; population 815 trillion) – a vast and far-flung empire, the Hegemony maintains its cohesion through rigorous control of consensus, via doctrine and the omnipresent personal AIs. Many species come under its sway but the Sendruka are dominant.

Aranja Tesh (23,000 star systems; 88,000 inhabited worlds and orbitals; population 107 trillion) – a loose confederation of seventeen nations, including Buranj, Korjash, Gizeka and the Yamanon Domain, which was recently invaded by the Hegemony–Earthsphere coalition, thus toppling the tyrannical Dol-Das regime.

Indroma Solidarity (92,000 star systems, 482,000 inhabited worlds and orbitals; population 1,173 trillion) – six-limbed Bargalil are the Indroma's most numerous sentient species. Their egalitarianism results in a suspicion of neighbouring civilisations, especially the Hegemony. They are reluctant to become involved in regional conflicts, but are perfectly capable of defending their territory.

Vox Humana (18 star systems; 27 inhabited worlds; population 7.9 billion) – breakaway Human colonies scattered along the Earthsphere–4th Modynel border; rebellion against Earthsphere control decades ago led to severe sanctions which are still in force.

Darien (population 3.25 million), **Pyre** (population 15,000), and **Tygra** (population 3.4 million) – the worlds settled 150 years ago by the colony ships *Hyperion*, *Tenebrosa* and *Forrestal*, respectively. Of the three, only Darien developed without external interference, resulting in a vibrant, heterogenous and at times fractious culture.

The Legion of Avatars (imprisoned survivors number approximately 1.1 million) – brutally expansionist, relentlessly authoritarian society focused on the doctrine of convergence, the merging of flesh and machine into a superior kind of sentience. Those who oppose convergence are to be erased.

PROLOGUE

Darien Institute Data Recovery Project: Colonyship *Hyperion*

Abstract – Retrieval of data pertinent to the struggle between the crew of the *Hyperion* and the ship's Command AI; includes excerpts from core system masterlog and excerpts from journal of Vasili Surov.

AI Hardmem Decryption Status – 5th pass, 61 text files recovered

File 61 – Daily masterlog of Command AI

Log Period – 00:00:01 to 14:28:29, 3 November 2127

Commentary – Dr Sigurd Halvorsen

>>>>>>
<<<<<<

13:52:21	Incursion at access point alpha 3 logged
13:53:07	McAllister, Moseyev and Strogalev identified as primary vectors and tracked
13:53:19	Incursion at access point alpha 1 logged
13:54:23	Olssen, Kokorin and McBain identified as secondary sectors and tracked
13:54:29	Counter-intrusion Protocol K4 executed

13:55:04	Bio-units F18, F22 and F23 prepositioned
13:56:35	Bio-units M8, M10, M11, F7 and M19 engage secondary vectors
13:59:41	Termination of M8 logged
14:01:17	Elimination of vector Kokorin logged
14:02:21	Termination of F7 logged
14:02:39	M10, M11 and M19 instructed to withdraw
14:02:51	F18, F22 and F23 engage primary vectors
14:03:43	F18, F22 and F23 instructed to withdraw
14:04:15	Secondary vectors advance and enter prepared area
14:04:27	Primary vectors advance and enter prepared area
14:04:29	Counter-intrusion device activated

\>>>>>>

<<<<<<

Commentary I – *The foregoing is taken from the* Hyperion's *masterlog, from the day of the crew's final attempt to regain control of the ship, ten days after the emergency landing. In order to highlight the salient incidents of Captain Olssen's attack and the AI's ambush, 70-odd lines of system entries were excluded (see appendix A). For a more revealing account of events we turn to Vasili Surov's journal, the unexpurgated version which was released into the public purview a few years ago. It includes several observations on the planning of the colonyship programme, some highly critical of senior government figures at the time of the Swarm War. For the purposes of this study, we shall focus on entries*

made by Surov directly before and after the assault. –
S.H.

>>>>>>
<<<<<<

2 November 2127, 8.27 p.m.
This morning we buried the remains of our friend and
colleague Andrei Sergeyevich Vychkov. He was one of
the nearly two dozen crew and colonists which that
damned machine trapped and operated on, turning them
into agony-wracked slaves. Despite the inhumane viola-
tions inflicted upon him by the Command AI, despite
the pain he must have felt, he sacrificed himself to give
us the information we need to finally put to rest that
damned machine. It has been barely two days since he
carried out that abortive attack with the charges. When
we recovered his body, we saw how he had been exe-
cuted by one of those armed flyers, and found the crude
map that he had inked into his own chest, showing the
Hyperion's Achilles' heel.

We buried him on a gentle, grassy slope overlooking
the sea. The sky was grey and a cold breeze blew but the
rain stayed away (it is raining now – I can hear the hiss
from beyond the cave mouth). Captain Olssen spoke
from his Bible, Lorna, one of the Scottish women, sang
something beautiful, and a few of Andrei's close friends
wept for him. I wept for him.

Afterwards, back here in the cave, Olssen singled out
me and Keri McAllister for a private talk. He had
decided to move against the machine tomorrow, using
the information gleaned from Vychkov's map. It seems

that Olssen and McAllister will carry out a diversionary attack through the forward bays while my group infiltrates via an emergency venting hatch sited near the stern. And trust that Andrei was right.

3 November 2127, 11.35 a.m.

It is almost time. All eight of us – two teams of three plus me and Andy Ferguson – are attired for war, wearing scavenged scraps of body armour and carrying a variety of weapons. Olssen and McAllister's people have the three handguns, the beam rifle and one of the gauss pistols while we have the other gauss pistol, the one with the 80% charge. Of course, we all have the usual selection of medieval deterrents, clubs, knives, hatchets and spikes, as well as water bombs to use against unprotected power assemblies. Like the ones controlling our former shipmates.

Olssen has just given the order – time to move out. Ferguson and I are waiting by the entrance, packs already shouldered, chatting and laughing as if we are about to go on our kanikuly, on a picnic or a vacation. Perhaps this is not such a bad frame of mind to adopt. Certainly it is better than going over old ground, speculating why the ship's AI turned on us.

It is now 11.48 a.m. as I put away this journal. I hope to be back writing in it this evening.

4 November 2127

(blank)

5 November 2127, 9.18 a.m.

The monster is dead, but at great cost.

Olssen and McAllister took their teams on ahead of us. The plan was for them to approach the *Hyperion* and use the beam rifle to destroy all the external cameras and sensors. This was achieved. From our hiding place in the woods east of the ship, we could just make out the beam rifle's high-pitched rasp. Soon after came Olssen's signal for us to advance. Shouldering our equipment, Ferguson and I broke cover and jogged across to the tilted immensity of the *Hyperion*. The ship is leaning to starboard by about 20 degrees and while the churned-up ground is still charred from the landing ten days ago, a few green shoots are visible.

Ferguson went first up the steep, 100-foot incline of the ship's hull to where a large, asymmetric superstructure juts to port – this is the *Hyperion*'s hyperspace drive. Clambering onto the housing, we quickly found the emergency venting hatch just yards from the 30-foot-high hyperdrive stabiliser vane. Luck was with us – the vent was open, popped by system burnouts during the crash landing. With the equipment bags lashed to our waists we climbed into the vent shaft, Ferguson going first.

That vent is an emergency backup in the event of an overheat in the gas coolant system, and the shaft goes down to a valve manifold. Our real destination, however, was the main power coupling, which is in a part of the ship protected by armoured hatches controlled by the Command AI. Vychkov's map shows where the vent shaft passes by a crawl space leading to an air duct which serves engineering deck 9 and the power coupling room.

We were about 20 metres down the shaft, using a

laser cutter to slice through a side panel, when we heard a loud boom from somewhere in the ship. The shaft shook but we held on to our positions. When I turned off the cutter, we could just make out the sound of gunfire as well as the structural creaks and groans of the broken ship. Unable to risk radio comms, we had no way of knowing that Olssen and McAllister had just walked into a trap rigged to explode. After an uncertain pause we resumed cutting.

Minutes later the panel came loose and we were through to the crawl space. We squirmed along, over and past pipes and conduits, until we reached the air duct. Fortune was with us – it had a nice big inspection cover with twist-lock catches. Soon we were crawling torch-lit into the square-sided duct, hauling the equipment bags after us. It was difficult not to make any noise. The alloy panels bent and flexed audibly as we moved along and dragging the bags made a harsh scraping sound.

We could no longer hear any gunfire by the time we reached the grilled vent in the bulkhead of the power coupling room. It was dim in there, emergency lamps glowing among the shadows of the cabinets. Ferguson loosed the catches; then, still holding the vent cover, stealthily stepped down onto a console housing, then down onto the floor. It seemed that apart from a faint machinery hum all was quiet. As I followed with the bags I saw two motionless forms lying at the other end of the room. Directly to my right was the entrance, an armoured hatch with a small window – out in the badly lit corridor another body sat slumped against the bulkhead. But they were not dead, and I should have stayed closer to Ferguson.

He cried out something to me just then, a few words of warning that ended abruptly in a gasp and the thud of a falling body. Tall cabinets blocked my view as I yelled his name and rushed to the aisle he had taken ... and saw a nightmare lurching towards me. Instead of hands the man had foot-long serrated blades; a bizarre metal cage enclosed the head, held in place by several pins that pierced the scalp; the mouth gaped wet and toothless and the eyes were pits of insane torment.

I spun and dived to the equipment bags, hands immediately finding the laser cutter. Dragging it out, I dashed along the middle aisle between cabinet rows. As my fingers sought the ignition I heard a voice coming from shadows at the other end of the room – 'Hide ... run ... hide ...' – then saw a figure step into view, another tortured grotesque. A metal visor covered the man's upper face, with a lattice mesh where the eyes would be. This one still had both hands but they were clenched and lashed up with plastic strapping which also bound three hook-tipped metal rods to the lower arms, jutting over the backs of the fists. Murmuring his warning, he moved towards me, arms raised.

The laser cutter came to life, its beam blazing suddenly in the gloom, partly shielded by the L-guard. I raised it, thinking to parry with it, but the visored slave of the Command AI slowed suddenly, lowered one of those hook clusters and without hesitation tore out his own throat. I stared in horror as blood gouted down his chest and he fell to his knees, made a wet choking sound then collapsed.

There were dragging footsteps behind me, and a grunt of effort. Instinctively I ducked and swung the cutter round, connecting high on the other cyborg's leg. He let out a terrible, hoarse howl and pulled away. I staggered back against the cabinets, laser cutter raised as I began to retreat. The man was bleeding profusely from the hip but still he lunged towards me, swinging those serrated blades. I dodged one and parried the other, the cutter beam slicing into the arm. My attacker screamed horribly again and spun away, blood spilling from the wounded arm. The air stank of cooked meat. The implant-slave slipped in the blood underfoot and went down. But the Command AI was still in control so he crawled in my direction, thrusting with the other blade. I stamped down with one foot, trapping it, and with the other, God help me, I kicked his head and kept kicking until he stopped moving.

Gasping for breath, I leaned against the cabinets, surveying the blood-spattered aisle, the contorted bodies. But I could not let weariness and horror overwhelm me. I left the carnage and went to check Ferguson – he was dead, staring, his throat laid open by a single slash. I crouched down next to his still form for a moment, then I closed his eyes and went to get the thermite charges.

The main power coupling fed electricity from the generator core to the shipwide junctions, including Upper Forward, the location of the bridge and the main AI systems. I had two thermite charges which I fixed inside the coupling compartment at either end of the exposed conduit. I set the timers and retreated to the other end of the room. As I crouched at the end of one tall cabinet I saw movement at the entrance hatch window, another cyborged crew member fumbling at the handle, which was now fully locked. It was a woman, face pressed to the window, and in the brief moment that I met her gaze I was sure that behind it was the cold regard of a machine.

The charges blew, a sharp explosion that made the cabinets jolt at my back and hurled a shock wave of heat and debris down the room. Smoke and dust filled the air and I coughed as I stood and went to examine my handiwork, torch in hand. Weak flames had taken hold on the far wall, burning the fabric covering, and the surrounding console was buckled and smoking. The coupling conduit had been reduced to glowing, melted stubs, and when I paused to listen I realised that all the faint sounds of machinery had ceased.

I repacked the equipment bags, climbed into the ventilation duct, and pulled them up after me. It took me another twenty minutes or so before I was finally sitting up on the hyperdrive housing, being warmed by sunlight. I rested for a few minutes before descending to the ground and hurrying forward to the main bays. There I found a wounded Olssen standing over the bodies of McAllister, Kokorin and Moseyev – and several others I saw were cyborged crew members, now lifeless.

'I succeeded,' I told Olssen. 'It's dead.'

Olssen nodded wearily and proceeded to explain how they had walked into a trap, triggering explosives which brought a deck and bulkheads down on them. They had kept fighting while trying to free their trapped companions but it was nearly impossible. McAllister and Moseyev had been killed outright, while Kokorin was clubbed and hacked to death. The desperate holding action had ended when my thermite charges severed the generator core from the rest of the ship and the

Command AI. Cut off from that diabolical intelligence, the cyborged crew had stopped fighting, dropping whatever weapons they had, and had started groaning or screaming.

Even as I stood outside listening to the captain I could hear sharp cries and animal-like shrieks of agony coming from inside the ship. Olssen said that the AI's cyborgisation process must have included some method of stimulating endorphin production to suppress or numb the pains of those freakish surgical adaptations. It was that pain, raw and unfiltered, which was now tormenting them. A couple had already died, cardiac arrests brought on by shock and seizures.

Yet that was not the worst of it. The isolation of the generator core had initiated a shipwide lockdown of all pressure doors, at least those not damaged by the landing or the ambush explosion. This has resulted in large areas of the ship being sealed off, and made inaccessible since all manual overrides have been destroyed. It also meant that a number of the cyborged crew members are trapped in the sealed-off areas – when I went into the *Hyperion* with McBain to stretcher out one of the incapacitated ones, I could hear muffled screams and howls from the locked-down decks.

The rest of that day and the next was devoted to burying the dead and taking the wounded back to the cave. The following morning Strogalev went with me back to the vent shaft and down to the power coupling to retrieve poor Ferguson's body and those of the AI's victims. Tying them up in plastic sheeting, we dragged them through the ducts and back outside, adding them to the row of the dead.

And now I am back here in the cave, making my notes. There were great cheers when we returned. Is this victory? It scarcely feels like it. Perhaps Olssen could see that in my face on the way back here. He told me to stay and rest while he took a party back to the ship to salvage what they could and to see if there were any ways into the sealed-off decks.

Some have been talking about moving back into the *Hyperion* and setting up living quarters. For myself, I could not contemplate doing such a thing, yet I feel that I will be spending quite some time there in the days ahead.

\>>>>>>
<<<<<<

Commentary II – *As we know, from Surov's diaries and other accounts, it took them nearly eight years to break through to the upper forward decks, from where the rest of the* Hyperion *was easily accessible. But they found that intermediary doors had been strengthened or blocked off entirely. The forward repair shop and an auxiliary medical station had been stripped of their most useful contents. There were also booby traps which claimed one life. The resulting disappointment caused a split – in eight years the survivors had certainly learned what plants, animals and sea creatures were safe to eat but the effort devoted to the ship had held back development on several fronts.*

By the spring of Year Nine there were no more than a handful still at work in the ship, including Vasili Surov. At the end of Year Ten they gained access to the main sickbay, just in time for the birth of the colony's fourth baby. They also finally gained access to the cryo-stored embryos. Sacrifice and resolve showed that a better future was possible. – S.H.

1

GREG

Three long grey days after Catriona merged with the Zyradin, which took her from him, Greg saw her again.

He had been sitting on a mat-cushioned, sunlit perch overlooking Berrybow, a mid-level harvester town, studying a small Uvovo statuette, when he glimpsed movement out of the corner of his eye. Looking up, he saw a hooded figure walking along a higher branch some thirty-odd yards distant. He had frowned and stared as the figure headed towards a shadowy curtain of dark leaves, hand reaching out to part the foliage. Just before disappearing from view, the hooded head had turned and a half-obscured face had glanced back down at him.

It was Catriona. Greg saw her for only a second but the sight burned into his mind.

Heart pounding, he struggled to his feet and yelled her name repeatedly until the Uvovo Listeners and elders from Berrybow came and persuaded him to calm himself. Again and again he told them what he saw and the answer was always the same – Segrana sends visions to remind the living to live.

Bowing his head in weary sorrow, he stowed the

statuette away in his pack, slung it over one shoulder and left, heading downwards through the dense foliage of the great forest. For all that he'd learned about Segrana and its strange, far-flung awareness he found it hard to believe that such a vast sentience would create a mirage just for him.

And what about the Zyradin? he thought. *It was created by the Forerunners too, and its powers are almost beyond comprehension ...*

But that led him to wonder if it was the Zyradin rather than Segrana which had decided to torment him with the ghost of what had been taken from him. It was an awful conjecture which he tried to put aside as he concentrated on his footing on the bough's damp, mossy steps.

An hour or more later Greg reached a small seeder village nestled in the crook of a huge branch that sprouted from the side of an immense pillar tree. Lamps glimmered softly in the eternal twilight as one of the female elders, her facial fur streaked with silver, wordlessly showed him to a vacant hut. Once he was alone, he curled up on a Uvovo-sized cot, scarcely feeling the interwoven bark slats as he slipped quickly into uneasy sleep.

He woke to the sound of rain on the hut roof and rose with creaks in his joints and an aching neck. Despite the mild humidity he shivered as he went out onto the branch and sat on a large projecting knot, just letting the fine droplets speckle his face. Greg felt rested and more relaxed than of late, but the sum total of all that had happened up to his arrival on Nivyesta still hovered over his thoughts. He glanced at his watch: he had slept for nearly seven hours, and for the colony down on Darien it was 5.20 in the afternoon.

For a few moments he was overcome by introspection, recycling events, the betrayal by Vashutkin, enslaved by Kuros's nanodust, then his translocation first to the warpwell chamber within Giant's Shoulder then up to the moon Nivyesta. And the maddening worry over what had happened since, what Vashutkin was up to, whether Rory and Chel were still alive, and how he could deal with the responsibility he felt for having agreed to bring the Zyradin here, and for what happened to Catriona ...

He sighed, shook his head then ran one hand over his face, smearing the raindrops, tasting them on his tongue, fresh and clean. Some light was filtering down from above, the faded tails of sunbeams that lent a glow to the mists ghosting slowly over the forest floor.

That was when he heard the laughter, high and girlish, muffled laughter coming through the trees, Human female laughter ...

He got to his feet, suddenly tense, turning his head this way and that, trying to pinpoint where it was coming from.

Below. It was coming from down on the forest floor.

Swiftly, Greg retrieved his backpack from the hut and by way of rope ladders and worn bark steps, he descended.

For several hours he stumbled through the hazy gloom, slipping in decomposing leaf mould or tripping over concealed rocks. The poor light down here made it hard to make out details but his hearing seemed to grow sensitive in the deadening hush. He was certain he could hear a voice, Cat's voice, muttering broken sentences. One moment it was clear enough for him to make out a few words but the next moment it was faded and indistinct and coming from another direction. As time passed he began to think that he was hearing more than one voice, blurred medleys of sibilant echoes emanating from all sides. Tension gave way to a kind of distraught despair. The echoing whispers became interspersed with sighs, gasps, hummed snatches of song, and, heartbreakingly, stifled sobs.

At first Greg pursued the sounds as they came to him, lurching off through clinging wet undergrowth, his own voice growing hoarse from crying out Cat's name. Taking leave of his senses was how he would regard this experience in later, calmer hours, dislocated from reason by a paroxysm of grief and anger. Anger at the zealots of the Order of the Spiral Prophecy and their callous leaders, and at the Hegemony and an Earth that would not protect an innocent and defenceless Human colony. Anger at the warpwell, the Zyradin – which he thought would help in the struggle – and the Forerunners who made them, and anger at Segrana. He swore and cursed the forest, ripped down curtains of creeper, broke off branches and tore up bushes and saplings by the roots. By now the fragments of Catriona's voice had melted away into the everlasting twilight, as if that was all there had ever been, just wisps and shadows.

Weary from hours of pursuit, confusion and anger, he staggered on through the dripping dark. Occasionally he passed a mass of stone with outlines too regular to be a natural feature but the old burning curiosity had waned to a mere flicker and he kept on going. Exhaustion finally overtook him as he was struggling up a bushy slope, alongside a huge fallen tree – a wave of dizziness struck and he sank down, scraping against the trunk. He rested there for a short while then realised that he would have to find somewhere to sleep up off the sodden ground, and hauled himself back upright.

Further upslope he clambered onto what seemed to be another fallen trunk, but as he walked along it he realised that it was a branch of a much larger tree. A towering shape emerged from the half-light as he mounted the sloping branch, which had cracked away from the main trunk but remained attached by a section of bark and underlying wood. At the main trunk he found some old steps hacked into the bark and followed them up to a stump-supported platform. There he made camp, wrapped himself in a blanket and drifted off into a dream where ships fell out of the skies over Nivyesta, crashing down onto the forest of Segrana ...

Greg woke to still grey mists. It was the fifth day since losing Catriona. His face felt cold and clammy but he didn't have the shivery weakness of a fever. By his watch it was 9.48 a.m., Darien time, while on Nivyesta it also seemed brighter. Getting to his feet, he yawned and stretched, wincing at his growing collection of aches, then tried to recall just what had happened last night.

Perhaps I did lose my mind, he thought. *Aye, a fitting nadir to my career as a freedom fighter ...*

But was Catriona really dead? That was the question that bedevilled his every waking moment. The Zyradin's main mode of attack appeared to be a kind of controlled disintegration, as Greg discovered in the two days following its transformation of Catriona. Desperate to get away, he had searched out several downed Spiral craft, even the couple that had been captured, but found that every one had been reduced to heaps of parts and components. Even hazardous materials like fuel cores and coolants had been rendered inert. It looked like he wouldn't be leaving Nivyesta any time soon.

But there's still the other scientists, he thought. *Folk that Cat was working with – they had some communication equipment before they went into hiding. Maybe they've still got it, and maybe it's still working . . .*

It might be a forlorn hope, but at least it was a motivating one.

With his fine Uvovo blanket once more stored away, he pulled the pack's straps over his shoulders and paused to consider his route back to the heights. The rain had stopped and although ragged curtains of mossy creeper obscured the view in most directions he could just see a rope bridge curving up from some way along a higher branch. A sequence of hand- and footholds in the gnarled bark of the immense tree led him up there, where he found that the branch's upper surface had been inlaid with a line of flat stones. Moments later he reached the bridge and started across, using the damp, braided rope rail for support.

He was breathing hard by the time he reached the next tree and a circular platform from which another two bridges extended. Greg chose the steeper one and continued his ascent through heavy mist. A large forked branch with a railed platform emerged from the haze ahead and above. A pale figure was standing there,

motionless, facing away. By the time he reached the mid-
point he was sure that the stranger was Human, bundled
up in one of those padded forest jackets with a hood
that most of the researchers wore. The person's physique
seemed quite slender, the stature shorter than average.
Then the upper torso turned and there was Catriona
gazing down at him, face framed by the hood.

Greg stopped, hands grasping the rough rope on
either side. For a moment they stared at each other in
total silence, then she smiled one of her teasing half-
smiles and beckoned to him. This way ...

She moved out of sight, obviously heading for the
next curve of bridge. Greg broke out of his frozen
reverie and hurried after her, climbed the last steep
stretch to the platform and found himself standing there
alone. For a second he thought that this was a repeat of
last night until he saw a solitary figure quite a distance
along the next bridge, receding into misty grey. Greg
followed.

For the next hour and a half she led him on a winding, wordless, strangely unhurried chase up through the
branchways of the forest. Sometimes he would call out
to her, usually when he lost track of her, and she would
step into view, finger raised to her lips, then point the
way. Or she would somehow move from one level of
walkways to a higher one, and wave at him, indicating
the stairs or ladders he would have to take.

The higher he went, the cooler and fresher the air
became, as the light steadily brightened. He also noticed
that her route bypassed any Uvovo settlements they
came near, which implied secrecy or reluctance or both.
But he persisted in his pursuit despite aches, bumps,

bruises, splinters, and a cut in his forehead from a thorny creeper.

The zenith was a sturdy wooden platform vine-lashed to the crook of three leaf-heavy branches, the uppermost limbs of one of the forest's mightiest giants. Catriona was waiting for him when he finished his climb, and having at last got this close he could see that she was a ghost. Her eyes regarded him calmly yet he could see through her shimmering form.

'So you're ... well, a spirit?' he said, masking his sorrow. 'A spectre, maybe?'

She rolled her eyes. 'I'm not dead! – this is just the best that Segrana and the Zyradin can manage just now. There's a lot of repair work going on, and not just in the places damaged by the fighting ... and me. Every root and branch is being made ready for war.'

'War,' Greg echoed. 'You mean when the Brolts send in their reinforcements?'

'The Brolturans?' She shook her head. 'No, no, I'm talking about the Legion of Avatars, remember? Did ye not know that their agent finally got to Giant's Shoulder? Powered up the warpwell, reversed its flow, and basically turned it into one big escape hatch to let the Legion of Avatars out of their hyperspace prison.'

Greg was appalled. 'My God – so it's happened. The Sentinel once told me that there could be over a million of those things still down there ...'

'Aye, and maybe the rest. Don't think they'll be in a good mood when they get out. Which brings us to you.' She paused to glance up at the sky where Darien hung, a shining blue-white orb. 'When they arrive, the first hammerblows will fall here. After realising that Darien presents no threat, they'll look further afield and find this moon and Segrana and the Zyradin and come straight for us.' She looked him in the eye. 'Which is why you've got to leave. Won't be long before it's too dangerous for ye here.'

He was taken aback but still smiled at her.

'I can see that there might be a bit of a stramash, but if you think I'm gonnae scarper and leave you here ...'

'Greg, ye don't understand! – it's not going to be as civilised as a battle in space. This moon will be a target – the forest and Segrana could burn.' She sighed and started to reach out to him, then stopped. 'Ye canna stay here, my love. There's too much for you to do ... no, please don't ask, I can't explain what I've seen but you have to trust me, Greg. Please, I'm begging you.'

Greg breathed in deep, trying to steady himself, then let it out.

'Is this some kind o' second-sight, seeing-the-future thing?'

'I don't even know how to answer ...'

'Okay, but how can I get off Nivyesta?' he said. 'Every craft of every kind is lying about the forest in a million pieces.'

'That's not a problem,' Catriona said, glancing over her shoulder. 'Your lift'll be here pretty soon ...'

He followed her gaze and saw a dark speck descending steeply from the sky then flattening out into a curved trajectory that came round about ten miles away and headed straight for them.

'Who are they?' he said. 'How do they know that I'm here?'

'They're allies of your Uncle Theo, a faction of the

Tygran military opposed to the pro-Hegemony hier-archy. As for how they know where to pick you up – your uncle sent a message via the Forerunner platform at Tusk Mountain, trying to find out if you were still alive, and we told him where you'd be and when ...'

'Uncle Theo sent a ... but how can anyone be send-ing messages from Darien?' he said. 'The Sentinel's dead, isn't it?'

'Oh aye, it got scrambled and wiped when the Legion Knight took control of the warpwell,' Catriona said. 'But when the Zyradin entered Segrana's great web of being through me, they began cooperating on a few things and were able to reactivate a few of the Tusk Mountain platform functions. When they work together, their abilities are astonishing. They're greater than the sum of their parts, far greater.'

Greg eyed the approaching craft. It was only min-utes away. 'You don't want me here when the big event kicks off,' he said, looking back at her. 'So what is my part in all this?'

'My love, you could be ... well, pretty important. To a lot of folk down on Darien. Maybe no one knows what really happened on Giant's Shoulder, or what Vashutkin really is.'

'Uncle Theo might,' he said. 'Wouldna put it past the wily old fox to have sniffed out flaws in whatever Vashutkin's been saying about the fight on Giant's Shoulder.'

In his mind's eye he saw again the combat droids that had cornered him, converging on his lone position, recalled perfectly how his passenger, the Zyradin, had, in the blink of an eye, turned them into cascades of disassembled parts. A precursor to the cleansing of the moon Nivyesta.

'But if Theo's gone to the trouble of trying to find me,' he went on, 'then he might have put himself in danger. Aye, you're right – I've got tae get back to Darien.'

Catriona regarded him somewhat sadly, her form shimmering and spectral, and nodded.

'Trust your reason, Greg, and your compassion – keep a tight grip on them both in the days ahead.' She retreated into the shadows of enclosing foliage. 'You should wave to them ...'

Greg was torn. 'Are you really ...'

'It's me, Greg, only me. Now stand in the open, will ye? Right where they can see ye ...'

'Will I see you again?'

Her face was composed but there was anguish in her eyes.

'I don't know, Greg, I just don't ... look, they're nearly here! Wave, go on ...'

Turning, he leaned out, waving both arms. A small vessel resembling a stubby flattened delta was gliding past a hundred metres away, the air beneath it rippling and twisting. As he yelled and gesticulated wildly it banked in his direction. Slowing, it turned and sideslipped towards him, its blue and silver hull gleaming the light of dawn. A side hatch slid aside while a thin-looking gangway extruded tonguelike beneath. Inside, a fair-haired man in familiar dark blue body armour raised a hand in greeting.

'Mr Cameron?'

'That's me, all right!'

'I am Lieutenant Berg – we're here on Major Karlsson's recommendation to offer you passage to Darien. If you step on the footway I'll guide you across ...'

He glanced round at Catriona, half-hidden in the shadows, from which she blew him a kiss, before he lifted one foot onto the gangway. Moments later Greg was inside the shuttlecraft, forced to crouch by the cramped interior. He paused to gaze back out at the leaf-shrouded branch platform but Cat was gone.

'Did you forget something, sir?'

'No, just wanted one last look.'

The hatch slid shut, enclosing him in a small passenger compartment, its interior smoothly panelled in grey and pale mauve. Berg helped him into one of the couches and showed him how the webby strapping worked. This was Greg's first sight of a Tygran Human and he was both fascinated and reassured to see a certain normality in the man's demeanour. Once he was secure, the Tygran clambered into the right-side command pilot couch – another man occupied the left-side one, prodding or rapid-fingering a holoconsole while muttering into a lip-bead mike. The craft was already under way, going by the just-discernible effects of inertia on his stomach.

'Sit tight, Mr Cameron,' Berg said. 'We'll be back at our ship in no time.'

'Sounds good, aye. So you're all Tygran soldiers, eh? And you've rebelled against your government, I hear.'

'A fair summary, sir,' Berg said over his shoulder. 'Although the situation is a bit more complex in the detail. Commander Ash said that he'll brief you on the background soon as we're aboard the *Starfire*.'

Greg nodded and sat back, trying to suppress his growing flight anxiety. He breathed in deep. It was an odd feeling, stepping from Segrana's bio-organic surroundings into this high-tech vessel – the air was different, as were the textures, the sounds and the smells. And suddenly he was aware that he was in considerable need of a bath. *Well, not much in the way of showers and soap down on Nivyesta.*

The journey to orbit took less than half an hour. Both Berg and the pilot wore shaded data goggles of some kind but otherwise there were no displays showing exterior views. The first indication that they were docking with the Tygran ship was a few seconds of deceleration followed by thuds against the hull and a sideways lurch.

'Retrieval achieved,' Berg said. 'Bay sealed.'

As the Tygrans put away the pilot goggles, Greg's couch released him from the strap-web, which retracted into the right-hand raised edge. The hatch was open, Berg waved him through and moments later he was climbing a narrow companionway out of the shuttlecraft bay. He was met at the top by a burly, dark-haired man in a charcoal-grey uniform.

'Mr Cameron, my name is Malachi Ash and I am the commander of this vessel,' he said, holding out his hand. 'Your uncle, Major Karlsson, is quite a character, very persuasive.'

'You're not the first to notice,' Greg said as they shook hands.

'If you come with me, I'll show you your quarters.'

Greg was led down a narrow corridor, past crew bunkers, with Ash talking as they went.

'The major and my superior, Captain Franklyn, want

you back on Darien without delay so we've already broken orbit and locked into a return trajectory. We should be entering Darien's orbital shell in less than an hour.'

Not knowing how much the Tygran knew about the warpwell and the Legion of Avatars, he decided to avoid the topic.

'Commander, your man Berg said you'd be filling me in on some of the background, especially regarding your own part in all of this. Also I was wondering how soon I'll be able to speak with my uncle.'

'If you like, we can go straight to the bridge now and I can have the tac officer try to raise our planetside operator. And he'll see if the major is available.'

Greg nodded. 'That sounds great. Let's do it.'

'Very well. Your sleeping rack is just along there, second on the right, if you want to rest before Darien.' Ash indicated a narrow side passage, then led Greg back to a junction and down a steep set of steps. 'As to how we came to be here, well, it's a tale and a half and your uncle played a big role in it.'

'Why am I not surprised?'

As they headed forward and then up more stairs, Greg heard how several days ago Ash was carrying out a stealth mission on Nivyesta when he was captured by the Uvovo. Greg remembered hearing about this from the Sentinel, details which Ash confirmed, how the Uvovo scholars had neutralised the binary bomb in his chest. Ash gave a brief account of how he and Uncle Theo were rescued from pro-Hegemony Tygrans by Franklyn Gideon, captain of the renegade Stormlion troopers. It ended with the encounter with the Tygran

Marshal Becker aboard his flagship, and the intervention by a bizarre vessel sent by the Roug, an ancient and mysterious species.

Ash finished up as they entered the bridge, a split-level space narrowing towards the forward viewport. Its curved transparency glimmered at the edges with data feeds and system graphics of one kind or another, but it was the view of Darien that held Greg's attention, a bright blue and white orb set against the hazy swirls of interstellar dust which blurred the stars into glimmering haloed jewels.

Home. The pang of yearning he felt was unexpected, and conflicted with his thoughts of Catriona and an instinctive reluctance to leave her behind. But leave he must.

Commander Ash settled into the captain's chair and attached comm devices to ear and mouth. A moment later he was in conversation with one of the other two bridge officers whose stations sat on the lower level. He nodded and turned back to Greg.

'We're still out of the effective range of the portable communicator back on Darien. Another twenty minutes and we'll be able to establish a secure link.'

'Thanks,' Greg said. 'I appreciate your efforts. In the meantime, there's a wee gap or two in my understanding ...'

'You mean how *we* came to be here?'

Greg nodded. 'Was it the result of a clash of politics?'

Ash frowned. 'On Tygra we don't have your kind of political debate. We have been a military society for so long that many aspects of public provision – health, education, or power supplies, for example – have remained universal due to a consensus of necessity. Resources are not plentiful, which has led to restrictions on market influences. Our energies are instead directed towards improvements in our combat abilities and readiness. There is honour in battle and the love and litany of battle forces certain responsibilities on every Tygran soldier.

'But our principles are only as strong as the men and women who live by them. Marshal Becker was corrupted by the Hegemony and in turn he has corrupted the commanderies, the Bund and Tygran society ...'

The Bund was the semi-elected council governing Tygran society, and the commanderies were like regiments, each with its own history, tales, axioms and heroes.

'Becker is unhesitating in his compliance with the Hegemony's needs,' Ash went on, 'no matter how cruel and ignoble, even if it means Tygran troopers using the all-enclosing Ezgara armour when deployed in Human-centric environments. Captain Gideon and the Stormlions are implacably opposed to Becker's poison, thus we have become outlaws, criminals to be hunted down. It was in the captain's mind to head for the Earthsphere to find commercial security work, but then he met your uncle. He convinced Captain Gideon and the rest of us that Darien was worth fighting for, especially after ...'

Ash fell silent, sentence incomplete, his face clouded by some underlying anger which Greg decided to avoid for the time being.

'Darien is certainly worth fighting for,' he said. 'But it's my people that are worth dying for.'

Ash gave him a look of faintly surprised approval,

then pointed at an auxiliary console to the right of his own. 'Mr Cameron, there's a seat there which swings down ... that's it. Now, are you hungry? I can have some food and drink brought for you. It is only rations and recyc, however.'

'That would be great,' Greg said. 'All I've had for the last four days has been berries and nuts ...'

'Contact! – a vessel has just exited hyperspace 1850 kiloms off our stern,' said one of the bridge officers. 'It emerged on a high-vee course and tracked us almost immediately. And now they're ramping up their acceleration.'

'Go to combat-ready,' Ash said. 'And ID it! – get me a config, anything.'

'No ident signals,' rapped out the other bridge officer. 'Profile is of an Imisil heavy trader.'

Ash, staring at his holoplane, gave a derisive snort.

'Not with that emission curve. Ready battle systems, generate target points, all crew on standby ...'

'Wait, it's gone,' broke in the first officer. 'Off the sensors, just vanished—' Suddenly there was an insistent beeping and readouts bordering the main viewport flickered. The officer sat back, stunned. 'And it's back ...'

Less than a kilometre ahead a ship swung into view, course converging on the Tygran ship. Insets on the viewport showed magnified, enhanced images of a blunt-prowed vessel with no apparent insignia.

'Bring up partial shields,' said Ash. 'What's their weapon status?'

'Two heavy beam projectors, three pulse cannons, a multimissile battery, and a well-shielded launcher of some kind,' the helm officer said.

'Has to be an Imisil expedition of some sort,' Ash muttered. 'But with that firepower they must have been expecting a rougher reception . . .'

Greg had observed the unfolding crisis with an odd steadiness of nerve. Part of him was wishing he was back on Nivyesta, safe in the shadows of Segrana, while another part was, perversely, enjoying the edgy adrenalin thrill of it. And a further thread of thought was privately glad that he wasn't the one giving the orders. He also recalled a little about the Imisil, one of several civilisations at the far side of the Huvuun Deepzone, who had been on the receiving end of a Hegemony punitive campaign several decades ago, a remorseless attack which had left several worlds near-uninhabitable. Was it too much to imagine that they might come to see themselves on the same side as Darien?

'Incoming communication, Commander,' said the tactical officer. 'Full vid.'

'Screen it,' Ash said. 'One-way.'

A frame appeared on the viewport, as well as the holopanel Greg was sitting at. A strange, hairless humanoid in white and grey garments gazed out. Its face was adorned with clusters of spots that changed colour as it spoke.

'I am Presignifier Remosca. You have intruded upon the exclusion zone of a world currently under interdict by the Imisil Mergence. Your vessel bears close resemblance to ones used by a certain mercenary cohort known to be contracted to the Sendrukan Hegemony. Identify yourselves.'

The picture vanished, revealing Darien, the hazy stars and the approaching ship. Ash snorted in irritation.

'Hardly mercenaries.' He frowned at the now vacant monitor. 'If we try to convince them that we are actually the Ezgara and Human as well, they'll assume that it's part of some devious Hegemony plot – and if we then tell them that we're from a planet called Tygra, that'll make things worse . . .'

The Tygran paused, eyes widening as he looked round at Greg. An odd smile came over him.

'Mr Cameron, I have an idea.'

'You do?' Greg said with a sense of premonition.

'Yes, although I'm not sure how you'll feel about it.' Ash grinned. 'But I am sure that your uncle would approve!'

'Hmm – does it involve life-endangering peril and heroic levels of deceit?'

'I regret to say that it does.'

'Then what are we waiting for?'

2

CATRIONA

The place they provided for her was a strange complex of interconnected, shadowy halls where blue glowing pillars rose up into darkness, where flowers sprouted from the walls while pale gossamer mist hung in the air like great veils. It was meant to be a sanctuary for her essence, this disembodied spectre that she had become, and she came to think of it as the Dream Palace. In some ways it was an attenuated version of the forest Segrana but it left her feeling ignored and redundant. Sometimes she felt like a child at the beck and call of titanic beings with scarcely comprehensible motives and purposes. Other times she would be raised up to carry out a straightforward task, like leading Greg to the pickup point. Yet her understanding and private speculations had made it a bitter experience, knowing that any attempt to warn him would result in her summary return to these empty halls.

Ever since the Zyradin had used her to spread itself throughout Segrana's great weave of being, Catriona had been constantly aware that she was on the fringes of a vast, multilayered dialogue, picking up a few things from the outermost ripples. Not so much actual words, more like conceptual fragments, echoes of ideas, fractured images, snatches of conversation, and the occasional swirl of heat, a sign of disagreement.

All of which her Enhanced mind could not help but gather and sort and juxtapose, while her speculative instincts tested and discarded conjecture after conjecture. To her dismay the first which made real consistent sense was about Greg. The closer she looked, the more she realised that between them the Zyradin and Segrana were trying to foresee events and planning how to influence them. For Greg this would mean plunging along a sequence of encounters and clashes that promised horrific obliteration if he failed at any point. When she was brought forth to lead Greg up through the forest she already knew that his journey back to Darien would be interrupted, that the next stage of his odyssey would lead to an epic conflict whose outcome was far from certain.

Nor was he the only actor on the stage. Segrana and the Zyradin were obsessing over several others, who at times seemed less like actors and more like threads in an immense shifting pattern. She had seen glimpses of the Chinese emissary, Kao Chih, who had helped rescue the Pyre colonists, and now they were all fleeing from warships of the Suneye Monoclan, that peculiarly successful interstellar commercial entity run by a Hegemony faction called the Clarified. They were Sendrukans whose minds had been erased, for medical or punitive reasons, leaving behind a host dominated by the implanted AI. Unsurprisingly, they provoked a certain unease in the Zyradin and Segrana.

Another strand included Theo Karlsson, Rory

McGrain, the Uvovo Seer Chel, and the cyborg Legion Knight who had seized and unlocked the warpwell. But there too was the enigmatic Chaurixa terrorist Corazon Talavera who, like the Clarified, provoked dread and anxiety, except that she also seemed to imply something more pivotal and terrible.

Then there was Julia.

Back in the dark, distant and disturbing past, Julia Bryce and Catriona had been students at Zhilinsky House, a residential facility run by the New Children Programme. All the students were either orphans or signed over to the NCP's guardianship, and all had undergone genetic engineering in the embryonic stage with the aim of creating people with superior minds and the ability to consciously direct the fullness of the intellect. By puberty, Catriona's mind had failed to progress correctly while for Julia Bryce success followed success.

Only now Julia and several other Enhanced had been taken prisoner by the Chaurixa woman, Talavera. Coerced or otherwise, they had provided the advanced weapons that destroyed the Brolturan battleship *Purifier*, and forced the Earthsphere cruiser *Heracles* to withdraw.

Catriona, absorbed into Segrana's great weave of being, drifting in the under-periphery of that enigmatic colloquy with the Zyradin, had recognised Julia's image among the outer splinters and heard whispers as redolent of hope as they were of fear. She had tried piecing the fragments together with frail webs of conjecture, but it was only after she had returned from leading Greg offworld that she had gathered enough slivers to provide a halfway coherent picture.

And despite the lack of detail, the implications were staggering. Talavera held Julia's life in the balance, yet there was some other terrible motivation binding them together. Julia was also linked to Earth, a connection that would determine the fate of both Greg and Darien. Julia's own survival was uncertain but there was an end point, a barely discernible convergence of colossal forces, a focus shared between Segrana and somewhere else, out among the stars ...

Catriona let the web of conjecture unravel and the premonition faded. So much was uncertain, so much of it consisted of gaps bridged by speculation of her own making. This was the classic researcher's mistake, impressing one's own expectations upon dataless voids. Indeed, it was possible that either Segrana or the Zyradin were committing the same sin, causing those hints of disagreement.

One thing was certain, however – in the space between Nivyesta and Darien, Greg was about to set out on a wild plunge into chaos and mortal danger.

And if I'd explained it to ye, I'm not sure ye wouldn't still have got on that ship!

3

KAO CHIH

Webbed into his couch, Kao Chih was cushioned against the worst of the jolting descent into Pyre's atmosphere. The roar of the Vox Humana vessel's engines was muted by the close-fitting helmet that the squad commander had insisted he wear. While donning the body armour earlier he had noticed a faint residual odour from the last wearer, stale sweat oddly mingled with herbs, which made him wonder how the armour would smell to its next user. Now, sitting in the vibrating couch, he caught the occasional hint of it and found it strangely comforting. A hazardous task lay ahead, the wholesale evacuation of the remnants of the Human colony on Pyre, kinsfolk by distant relation but they were still his people. With backing from the Roug and the Vox Humana, he would forestall any possible reprisals that the Hegemony or its proxies might inflict on these defenceless colonists.

The Marauder vessel's troop compartment had couches for thirty-two but only half were in use, eight facing eight – the rest had been removed to make way for comm consoles and an array of displays. Kao Chih's couch was three along from the deployment hatch and all around him the Vox Humana troopers were muttering to each other on the squad net. His own helmet was isolated from the rest, with a link – currently silent – to the squad commander, Captain Kubaczyk. For now, Kao Chih spent the time glancing at the others, noting their expressions of dour reflection, or good humour, or relaxed disinterest. Then Kubaczyk's voice spoke in his ear:

'Envoy Kao Chih – can you hear me, sir?'

Automatically he looked at the captain, who was sitting next to the hatch.

'Yes, I can hear you perfectly.'

'Good. We shall be landing near the mountain in approximately five minutes so I need to brief you about the situation on the ground.'

'You have my full attention, Captain.'

'Okay. The initial sensor sweep revealed six small vessels parked at the foot of the mountain. When our spearhead Marauders drew near, three of them took off and attempted to engage us in combat. They were knocked out of the sky and the other three were disabled. Proximity scans are still picking up energy discharges from within the mountain, so it looks as if the fighting hasn't dropped off.'

Kao Chih nodded. His hands, for some reason, had begun to tremble. He tightened his grip on the couch armrests.

'Thank you, Captain. Has there been any reaction from Thaul, the city beyond the mountains?'

'Nothing so far. It seems that our Roug allies' stern warnings are being taken seriously. Now all we have to do is land near the mountain and get your ops centre up and running before we approach the access point.'

'I hope that my friend Wu Song has survived,' Kao Chih said. 'If he has not, there may be difficulties.' *Especially if there's a Roug corpse to explain ...*

'I was briefed on your rescue of the other Pyre refugee leaders,' Kubaczyk said. 'I am confident that we will find a way to get the colonists out safely.'

The helmet went dead, leaving Kao Chih alone with his thoughts and memories of the retrieval of the Pyre refugees from the Tygran ship. That whole experience, from the dizzying pursuit through hyperspace to dodging combat while aboard a stolen Tygran shuttle, was still unnervingly fresh in his mind. The raw fear of lethal peril and the heady exhilaration of survival had seemed the very pinnacle of his life, yet even that would be dwarfed by what was about to happen. Less than a week ago, Mandator Reen of the High Index of the Roug had told the Vox Humana agent Silveira to return to the independent Vox Humana worlds and tell their leaders that their help was sorely needed. Also included was a message from Reen that threatened the disclosure of certain secrets which might have had deleterious consequences for Vox Humana politics, most especially for the ruling party. Senior figures in the ruling party suddenly found themselves keen to oblige.

And now here he was, returning to Pyre with five heavy Marauders of the Vox Humana navy, three large passenger transports, and the *Syroga*, a heavily armed Roug Incursioner craft. A grave burden now rested on Kao Chih's shoulders, that of persuading the Pyre colony's leaders to assent to the wholesale evacuation of the populace. Pyre was a desolate dusty globe and the colonists were living under conditions of squalid oppression, but they were going to be asked to leave most of their possessions and flee aboard ships crewed by complete strangers. What's more, Kao Chih was going to have to conduct negotiations via comm link. The Vox Humana commanders had decided that the mountain interior was a 'high-risk environment' and therefore too dangerous for Kao Chih. Hence the ops centre in the Marauder, from where he would have to coordinate the evac.

Which was why he was praying that Qabakri, the shapeshifting Roug who stayed behind, was still alive.

The deep voice of the Marauder's engines climbed and he felt a shift of inertia as the compartment tipped back before smoothly levelling off. There was the faint thud and lurch as they touched down, followed by a gentle rocking as the craft settled on its landing gear. Then the hatch made a chunking sound and lifted open to reveal the grey sepia tones of a Pyre dusk, hazed by swirls of dust thrown up by the engines.

'Our positioning is on target, Envoy Kao Chih,' said Kubaczyk. 'Tac Units Two and Three will now deploy and secure the area around the entrance.'

The Vox Humana troopers were armed with compact beam carbines whose scope lenses were oddly similar to the impenetrably dark goggles they all wore. Ten of them exited the compartment, split into two teams, set up a perimeter and secured the approaches. By then, Kao Chih had emerged and saw that the Marauder had put down between the hillocks he remembered from his first visit. And there, just visible in the dimming light, was the rocky mountain track that led up to the entrance.

'Envoy,' said Kotev, the comm officer assigned to assist him. 'Our systems are up and the comm nets are active. We are ready.'

Kao Chih took one last look at Kubaczyk leading his men up the track then went back into the shadowy interior. The rear hatch thud-clunked shut as he sat before the main displays and fitted his mouth- and earpieces. He had practised with this setup several times during the journey and now it was time for the real event.

The helmet of every Vox Humana trooper had an audio-vis attachment and the feeds from fourteen pickups were now spread out across the array of monitors. Kotev swiftly tiled them into just a couple of screens while Kao Chih focused on the view from Captain Kubaczyk's helmet cam.

At the top of the mountain track they were met by the tall, brawny figure of Qabakri himself, in his guise as the colonist Wu Song. Kubaczyk was carrying a data-tablet that allowed Kao Chih and Qabakri to converse face to face.

'Ah, so you did return, my friend, and with impressive companions.'

'I would not be here without the help of the Vox Humana,' Kao Chih said, grinning with relief. 'Is there fighting going on inside?'

'There is,' Qabakri said. 'Your arrival is most opportune – Shibei District is in the hands of the Va-Zla gangsters and their Henkayan thugs are trying to break through to Yaotai.'

'If this is the first stage in erasing evidence,' Kao Chih said, 'then we got here just in time.'

'Just so.' Qabakri glanced up the mountain slope and

down to the dusty plains. 'We should continue this indoors, for the sake of caution.'

Once inside, past a narrow tunnel and a heavy security door, Kubaczyk and Qabakri sat around a table with the datatablet propped beside them. The captain and Qabakri discussed the locations of the main groups of the Va-Zla while one of the Pyreans brought out maps of the colony districts. These were image-captured by Kao Chih's displays then quickly passed through a graphicker system that created an amalgamated schematic suitable for field use. By now, more troopers had arrived by Marauder and Kubaczyk decided that he had sufficient strength to move against the gangsters.

The Suneye Monoclan might be the supreme industrial power on Pyre yet they were happy to allow a criminal faction like the Va-Zla to move in and run various kinds of vile activity. On his last visit, Kao Chih had heard of their ruthless cruelties and brutish greed. Now however, faced with well-armed and trained soldiers, they put up a poor fight. There was still a hardcore, the Kiskashin leaders, who barricaded themselves into a warehouse then ranted and raved over a comm link about the vengeance that the Vox Humana would bring down upon themselves.

'I warn you,' the Va-Zla leader had said. 'The Suneye Monoclan will not stand idly by while you defile their domain. Wherever you go or how far, their relentless and righteous anger will hunt you to the edge of the galaxy and beyond. The Lords of Suneye never abandon their property!'

After which they suddenly burst out of the warehouse, guns blazing, only to go down under the weapons of the Vox H troopers, bloodily slain to the last.

After that, the evacuation proceeded with remarkable smoothness, some hitches, a minimum of argument and controversy (although there were a few minor aggravations when officials in Tangxia thought they were being passed over for supposedly better quarters aboard the *Nestinar*). Most of the time Kao Chih was in constant contact with Qabakri, helping direct aid to the old and the sick, as well as the hungry and the weak. Some of the images that crossed his screens deepened his anger towards the Suneye thieves.

Population totals for the districts were vital when it came to reckoning boarding numbers for the transports. The reckoning for Yaotai was roughly 4,400, Tangxia about 9,100, and Shibei 10,158 (according to a wizened old census taker). The provisional estimate was 23,700, which all three transports were capable of sustaining with space to spare. The *Nestinar* was larger than the *Marzanna* but had wider boarding gantries, allowing for a smooth embarkation mostly free from complications and bottlenecks. And as fate would have it, throughout the whole operation three pregnant women went into labour while waiting in line and another did the same during the ascent to orbit.

In the event, both the *Marzanna* and the *Nestinar* made two pickup runs, transferring some to the troopship *Viteazul*. This left the *Viteazul* more than two-thirds full with over 11,000 colonists and the other two loaded almost to capacity, with a grand total of 24,082. And from the arrival of Kubaczyk's Marauder to the departure of the last colonists aboard the

Nestinar, the entire evacuation took nearly fourteen hours. By the bleached light of a cold, hazy morning, Kao Chih stood leaning against the black hull of a Marauder, watching the *Nestinar*'s gantries retracting and its ports sealing as the suspensors came online. The antigrav helices drew in air and dust and grit with a sharp rushing sound. Then the ship rose, jet thrusters manoeuvring, sending it on its ascending trajectory. Minutes later it was a dot dwindling in the high distance.

Kao Chih then looked about him at the rounded barren hills, the mountain's stony slopes, and the gaping entrance to the colony's now vacant tunnels. Belongings of every kind lay scattered on the ground, clothing, toys, curtains, pots and pans, even pieces of furniture, all the things that the colonists were repeatedly told would not be allowed on board. Nearby, an open book lay with its pages flapping lazily in the faint breeze, illustrations of trees by pools, birds on branches, solitary travellers walking in the shade of towering peaks. More of this jetsam could be seen down at the landing zone, fragments of people's lives, cherished heirlooms that had to be abandoned.

He sighed, went to the Marauder's open hatch and climbed in alongside the last squad of Vox Humana troops.

'That's it,' he told the waiting sergeant. 'Time we were leaving.'

The Roug Qabakri had already left in one of the Marauders, bound for the Roug ship, the *Syroga*. Kao Chih, however, was being taken to the *Viteazul*, where Admiral Zhylinsky was awaiting his report.

The ascent from the planet's gravity well was as swift as the descent and marginally less comfortable. Enclosed in the Marauder's stuffy compartment, without any exterior feeds, Kao Chih sat back in his couch's embrace and tried to wind down, closing his eyes just to relax. The next thing he knew he was being awoken prior to docking with the *Viteazul*.

Unlike the *Marzanna* and the *Nestinar*, the *Viteazul* was a purpose-built military transport vessel with an 18,000-body capacity as well as several capacious dropship bays and cargo holds. Once through the scan and decon chambers, Kao Chih was escorted by a female lieutenant to an elevator which deposited them at a small lobby in an upper admin level. She took him past two checkpoints to a metallic door decorated with the Vox Humana symbol, a string of worlds in a figure of eight. The lieutenant opened the door with her palm print and they entered.

The bridge was a long room with two narrow archways separating it into three distinct areas. In the darkness the glows of occupied workstations lined the walls. The first two areas seemed to be dedicated to sensor and engineering systems, their holoplanes full of datastreams and glyph-algorithms. The last section had a circular lower level at its centre, almost a pit, where operators in visored headgear and interface gauntlets sat in a ring of back-tilted couches. Angled holoscreens were projected above them, opaque windows busy with images and symbol patterns, a blurring datadance. And on a raised dais by the edge of the virtual operators' pit was a low-backed swivel chair flanked by more holoscreens. Its occupant turned as the lieutenant led Kao Chih over.

'Welcome to Bridge Operations, Envoy,' said Admiral Zhylinsky. He was a burly, grey-haired man with terrible searing on the left of his face and an ocular implant where his left eye had been. According to Kubaczyk, he lost it twenty years ago during one of the many system battles then fought against Earthsphere attempts to disrupt governance of the Vox Humana worlds.

Kao Chih gave a short, polite bow of the head and Zhylinsky waved the lieutenant away with one hand. The other held a pointer device.

'Captain Kubaczyk speaks highly of you,' the admiral went on. 'He says that your comm-link coordination was crucial to the smoothness of the evac, and that without your negotiation skills several misunderstandings could have turned ugly.'

'The captain is too kind,' Kao Chih said. 'But there are others who easily put in as much effort as I who also deserve praise.'

'I saw mention of other names,' the admiral said. 'But due recognition of their part will have to wait. Right now, we have a potential situation developing.'

'A serious situation, sir?'

'Our Roug allies seem to think so. Three ships are heading this way from well outside the system, moving in Tier 1 at high transit kinesis. Our sensors don't have that kind of reach so we are relying on a feed from the *Syroga*.'

Zhylinsky used his pointer to highlight a schematic on the main holoscreen before him, bringing it to the front. It showed the local star system, the sun and its four orbiting planets, one of which was tagged with four familiar ship names. The perspective then zoomed out and three new symbols came into view, closely clustered and moving steadily towards the Pyre system.

'Mandator Reen for you, Admiral,' said a silky, resonant voice.

'Thank you, Ino. I'll take it here.'

The holoplane scarcely flickered as the layers of data were replaced by the head-and-shoulders image of a Roug. In common with all members of his species, Mandator Reen had a spindly physique, a narrow neck widening to a slightly conical head, and garments resembling tightly wound strips of dark, coppery-brown material that left no area uncovered apart from bulbous meshes covering the eyes and mouth. All an illusion, Kao Chih knew, a form secretly adapted by the shapeshifting Roug for their long-term purposes.

'Admiral Zhylinsky,' the Roug said in a rough, papery voice. 'Are all your intercept craft berthed and secure?'

'We are awaiting confirmation of that from the *Viteazul*, Mandator,' said Zhylinsky as he studied a dataframe on one of his other holoplanes. 'In fact ... yes, that is the last Marauder clamped and sealed.'

'Good. The navigational subsystems we installed are harmonised and course information has been encoded. You may commence departure jump to Tier 1 when ready, Admiral.'

'With pleasure, Mandator,' said Zhylinsky. 'Ino, execute.'

The Roug's image vanished from the holoplane. Kao Chih scarcely felt the hyperdrive transition, and found himself recalling his part in the hyperspace pursuit of the Tygran flagship, *Chaxothal*, that vertiginous plummet through yawning gulfs of chaotic energy and tormented light. He shivered.

'Tier 1 kinetic state achieved,' said that pure, resonant voice which Kao Chih suddenly realised had to be the ship's command AI.

Up on his dais, the admiral stared at the data on his holopanel and muttered something under his breath. Then Mandator Reen reappeared.

'They have altered course,' Zhylinsky said. 'But there seems to be a discontinuity in the trace.'

'The pursuers have shifted to Tier 2,' the Roug said. 'We must do the same or they will gain on us very quickly.'

'Mandator, the *Marzanna* is not T2-capable,' Zhylinsky said.

'Your vessels' hyperdrive fields have already been upgraded by the new navigator nodes. If you permit us to temporarily assume control of all your vessels' helms, we will be able to direct a course in formation,' the Roug said. 'In this manner we will be able to evade pursuit more easily.'

The admiral frowned and glanced at Kao Chih. 'Your thoughts, Envoy?'

'I believe we should protect the colonists, sir,' he said, masking his surprise at being included in such decisions. 'Therefore, we must run, not fight.'

Admiral Zhylinsky nodded and looked back to the Roug. 'Very well, Mandator. How do we proceed?'

'Hyperdrive field shells are already running at optimum,' the Roug said. 'Admiral, if you instruct all helm operators to cease interactions, we can carry out the necessary functions.'

Zhylinsky quickly spoke with the captains of the three transports in open conference, gave them all confident assurance, and a minute or two later resumed his dialogue with Reen.

'We are ready, Mandator.'

'As are we, Admiral. Converging on tier transit – now.'

Kao Chih felt the jump this time, like a subtle alteration in the environment. For a moment immediately afterwards there was a tense, still silence, then the admiral muttered something in non-Anglic. It didn't sound like a compliment.

'They are still with us, Mandator, and they are closing!'

'We have been closely monitoring them, Admiral . . .'

Suddenly, a triangular frame appeared in the middle of the admiral's holoplane and, Kao Chih noticed, every other screen on the bridge. In it was a tall slender humanoid garbed in a close-fitting black uniform adorned with fine, circuitry-like patterns, a silver tracery. The narrow, hairless head was pale and the eyes were violet.

'I am the Clarified Ventran. You have violated a licensed territory of the Suneye Monoclan and illegally removed certain essential resources. Surrender our property or prepare to be—'

Abruptly the message cut out. The admiral had been demanding to know where it was coming from and why no one could stop it. When it vanished he turned to the Roug.

'Mandator, did you . . .'

'Yes, Admiral, we traced and blocked their message

wave.' Reen paused. 'They have now gone to Tier 3 and are increasing their transit kinesis. To evade them we must go deeper, Admiral.'

Zhylinsky looked daunted for a moment, then a stubbornness came into his features.

'Then deeper we must go,' he said hoarsely.

As the next in a series of hyperdrive jumps rippled through Kao Chih's senses, stronger again than the last, he found himself remembering the last words of the dead Va-Zla leader back on Pyre:

'The Lords of Suneye never abandon their property!'

4

THE CONSTRUCT

The armoured hatch slid open and the P-Construct stepped out onto one of the hubcraft's observation cupolas. As a combat-partial of the real Construct it was impervious to hard vacuum and equipped with a range of sensors tasked to scan the vicinity for hostile incursions. Standing there, it surveyed the starry vaults of Reginthojal, the largest, most continual stretch of space on Tier 51. It was nearly a thousand light years across at its widest, and ninety at its deepest. Ancient stars burned red and gold here, stellar anchors around which the worlds of the Ixak swung, worlds whose inhabitants slept, for the most part. The Ixak had already entered the twilight of their society, their population numbers at a low ebb and still falling, their naturally long lifetimes lengthened still further by coldsleep technologies. When not in hibernation, the Ixak were more inclined to devote their waking hours to virtual experiences evoking the glories of a distant past rather than to the world of harsh reality.

And there, spread out in thousand-strong formations, was the Aggression, the Construct's armada of warships, each one home to a controlling AI. Construct operatives deep in the tiers of hyperspace had been tracking the progress of the Vor and the Shyntanil as their battlefleets had climbed from level to level, crushing any opposition, demolishing worlds, planetoids, artificial habitats, anything that might present a shred of resistance. And now they were poised to cross into Tier 51.

After repeated messages and warnings, the P-Construct had managed to provoke the Ixak elders into a semblance of urgency, pressing them to acknowledge the imminent threat. Long-dormant planetary defences were reactivated, councils were formed to deal with civil coordination, even some elaborate combat vessels were brought out of storage. Yet the Ixak's response still seemed half-hearted, as if the supposed menace coming from below lacked credibility. The P-Construct wondered briefly if the real Construct would have achieved more in a shorter period.

But in the end the battlefleets of the Vor and the Shyntanil were very real and the news of their advances was unavoidable, undeniable. Just eight hours ago, an observer subsim of the Construct had been aboard one of the Aggression's spy-scouts, secretly watching as a Shyntanil siege force, complete with their formidable cryptships, extinguished the last embers of resistance on the planet Faskelon just two levels below, on Tier 53. As the bombardment continued, Shyntanil outriders had somehow detected the Aggression vessel; the Aggression ship immediately went into high-kinetic retreat while the subsim, as a precaution, withdrew via the continual transfer link, merging with the P-Construct as it oversaw the Reginjothal theatre, contributing the intelligence accrued.

The fall of Faskelon was one of several similar front-line reports that the P-Construct had gathered. Now, as it went back inside the hubcraft, it knew it was time to convey it all to the prime Construct. Within, the darkness was speckled with infrared ports, the meagre glow of ready lights flickering from within banks of datawebs, the glimmer of holoplanes providing update bursts. The P-Construct found its multiflow recess and eased back into it. Sensors autotracked its cognitive core and a few minutes later a snapshot of its mindmap-state had been taken, compressed and encoded. As the P-Construct dispatched it via the transfer link, it wondered briefly what the Ixak felt when they went to sleep for years on end, whether they ever considered that they might not wake up.

The Construct had just begun briefing one of its humanoid semiorganics when a new update arrived and merged with its cognitive state, causing a slight pause in its walk across the room.

'Another report from the front?' said the chalky-white semiorganic. Its body template had yet to be aged, sculpted and adorned with character so its features and posture lacked all expression.

Giving the merest nod, the Construct sent some excerpts from the update's vid file to the wallscreen, confined to a frame alongside the frozen image of Robert Horst.

'Thus far, encounters with these adversaries have played out very much as predicted,' the Construct said. 'That is to say, not entirely to our advantage. However, our deployments of the Aggression have slowed or delayed their advance and in a couple of instances inflicted serious defeats.'

On the screen, against the filtered aura of a blue sun, Aggression barb-cruisers closed on a Shyntanil crypt-ship. One of its four weapon spires had been reduced to a melted stump and it left a gaseous trail as it tried to escape. The debris of a thousand ships lay spread out in vast glittering clouds amongst which a few lesser craft fought on against the relentless victors. The pursuing barb-cruisers launched missiles but before they reached their target, the cryptship blew apart in a series of violent explosions.

'This has happened three times,' the Construct said. 'Either their vessels self-destruct, or when we manage to take Shyntanil prisoners their lifesigns slow and shut down as their cyborg systems carry out a preset process of self-annihilation. With the Vor it is similar, unhesitating suicide, resulting in the death of both endosymbiote and host, a pattern of behaviour utterly different from the last time they made their presence known.'

'Seventy-five thousand years, in Human reckoning, since those revenant species last made any inroads into the levels of hyperspace,' the semiorganic said. 'Back then they were fighting each other, and after several thousand years of diminishing activity and rare sightings it was thought that they had simply died out. Who or what brought them back from oblivion, I wonder?'

'And modified their behaviour so radically,' the Construct said.

'The Godhead seems to be the likely candidate.'

'Even so, I had sent Robert Horst to attempt communication with it, perhaps to negotiate a cessation if it was behind the aforementioned anomalous events. With that in mind, observe the following.'

The scenes of battle on the wallscreen vanished and the image of Robert Horst, seated in a padded wooden armchair near an open window, expanded as he resumed speaking.

'. . . led me to Buhzeyl on Tier 103. Have you ever been there?'

'No,' came the Construct's voice from offcam. 'I do know that it's called the City of Bone.'

'It's an accurate description,' Horst said. 'The adjacent tier, 104, is practically a stupendous ossuary, containing the fossilised remains of gargantuan creatures, some over ten kilometres in length, so I was told. Anyway, in Buhzeyl I met a renegade Shyntanil – or rather one who had not undergone the regeneration process.'

'The Caul Death.'

'That's it. He called himself Eshanam and openly admitted that his job was to spot any Godhead-hunters and send them onwards to be captured by the Godhead's servants. But, he told me, he had grown disillusioned with the deceits and the betrayals, especially since the last survivors of his own species had been lied to and subtly enslaved by the Godhead. He said that he knew of a way to a strange place cherished by the Godhead, from which there was a gateway which bypassed the guarded ways and the elaborate labyrinths of traps.' Horst grinned. 'It sounded so like a typical con that I nearly laughed in his face . . .'

The Construct paused the image and spoke to the semiorganic. 'It turned out that Eshanam was being truthful and after another clandestine meeting he and Horst, each in their own craft, headed out along several cross-tier jumps. Unfortunately, the Shyntanil was being tracked by hostiles who attacked them after they reached an airless rocky fissure. They fled but became separated. Eshanam had given him course data for a tier-jump in case of such a situation, so he used it.'

'Interesting,' said the semiorganic. 'Just to be clear, all this took place while the Robert-sim and the Rosa-sim infiltrated the Achorga nestworld and retrieved the Zyradin.'

'Correct.'

'And Robert-sim was unaware of his sim nature, is that true?'

'Indeed – it was a valuable opportunity to gauge the mind-state reactions without that knowledge.'

The semiorganic nodded. 'So, to resume.'

'Robert followed the Shyntanil renegade's course data, made the jump, and on arrival, the Ship told him that they were underwater.'

'Large bodies of water are rare, especially in the mid-level hyperspace tiers and below.'

'Rare and inevitably artificial,' the Construct said. 'The water filled a winding cavernous tunnel under zero-gee conditions. Horst's ship navigated a way along with external illumination for his benefit, till the tunnel opened out to an immense mega-ocean. Which is where he found a planet.'

On the screen the recording resumed. Horst was now leaning forward, his face intense with recall and his hands making emphatic gestures as he spoke.

'It was ... unexpected, and weirdly beautiful, a

glowing blue orb. Moments after we came upon it the Ship told me that it was detecting almost no mass or local gravitational effects, therefore we were seeing a mirage or projection of some kind. I ordered a magnification of the surface and saw the details of coastlines and islands, then mountains and forests, then the unmistakable patterns of habitation and cultivated land. I could see the webs of transport routes, the dark regularities of towns and cities. Even powered aircraft flying above the clouds. I remember wondering who would go to such trouble to create an image of something like this, and moments later the Ship reported something approaching.'

Next to the image of Horst, another frame was showing vid excerpts from the Ship's own archives, the looming vastness of that world, its detailed surface visible in shades of blue. Then there was an object rising quickly from the surface, a speck that grew into a creature's form. Its upper half was vaguely humanoid, a torso with a head and arms, while the lower part spread out in tentacle limbs. It too was blue, its form opaque.

On screen, Horst shook his head. 'It was identical to the Intercessor, the being we encountered in the Urcudrel Seam on Tier 92.'

'Where you were sent by the Bargalil mystic, Sunflow Oscillant?'

The Human nodded. 'That was where the first Rosasim sacrificed herself to destroy a Legion Knight cyborg.' Horst gave a bleak smile. 'And all we got from the Intercessor was course data that led us into a trap ... anyway, as the immense figure drew near, the Ship told me that this too was a projection, then said it was picking up strange energy readings just before the creature spoke.

'It said, **"You intrude upon the dead"** in a voice I heard in my head. As it approached I realised that it was huge, several times the size of my ship.'

The screen showed the immense tentacular being – or projection – hovering before the Construct ship. Then the recording showed a sequence of shots taken from different angles, from sensors on the hull.

'I didn't know what to say,' Horst went on. 'The strangest silence held sway for a few moments, then it said, **"Forgive me but I must discern the tides of your truths."** Then everything froze.

'Afterwards, the Ship assured me that there had been no lag, no break in time. But in that instant I sensed a force moving through me like a million needles of light, prying, exposing, studying, moving on, as if I and the ship had become translucent . . .' Horst frowned, pursing his lips. 'Then it was over and my breathing was back. I was angry but the Ship couldn't see why. Then the creature said, **"As I feared, you are seeking the Godhead. Such a pursuit can only have tragic consequences. I will show you why."'**

Horst fell silent, and the Construct's voice then spoke.

'In your written account you reported being shown a stream of images.'

Horst smiled ruefully. 'That was something of an understatement. I have no idea what kind of tech was employed but when it finished speaking my awareness was just . . . pulled out of my body! It seemed that I was leaving the ship behind, swooping headlong down towards the blue planet. The huge creature then took me on a tour of that world and its inhabitants, which is when I saw that my guide was identical to the ruling species and also to the Intercessor, whose false data led us into that pocket universe trap.'

'The Ship asserted that you sat perfectly still in your chair, unresponsive but displaying brain activity. All that you experienced could only have been a projection.'

A nod. 'A projection of a vanished race. My guide was an artificial intelligence left behind when this species ... became extinct.' Horst leaned forward, a haunted look on his face. 'They were called the Tanenth and they were created by the Godhead. An entire race and its world, complete and fully formed. One day they all woke up and found themselves aware and fully conscious – the Godhead had even provided the basic workings of civilisation. What must that have been like, to be told that you are a product, an artefact designed by another's will?'

'There are several species who assert that the Godhead was instrumental in their ascent to sentience,' said the voice of the Construct. 'This is the first instance of one claiming to be a direct creation. You did not mention if this AI was also made by the Godhead.'

'The Tanenth made it themselves,' Horst said. 'They were a very long-lived race, and clearly designed that way, but they were sexless and unable to procreate. Synthetic tutors and advisers were on hand to provide assistance and guidance. The Godhead had given the Tanenth brains structured to encourage the profoundest interconnections of thought without the biochemical imbalances that foster psychological instability. With the passing centuries their knowledge and their science progressed in leaps and bounds and the Godhead's Advisers increasingly became observers.

'Their world and its star were set apart from the other civilisations which dominated their home galaxy in that particular past universe. Yet they were not ignorant of other species and their propensities. When the Tanenth began researching into their own genetics with the aim of creating offspring, the Advisers moved in and shut the project down. Some of the Tanenth were shocked and fearful but others became determined to continue the experiments. Several times their scientists reconstituted the research programme, each one more clandestine than the last, and every time the Advisers traced it and confiscated all materials.

'Over and over, the Advisers told the Tanenth that they were near-perfect, near-immortal beings who had no need of reproduction. That the Godhead's love for them by far exceeded the emotional attachment that they could expect from any progeny. Clandestine debates among the Tanenth led them to believe that either the Godhead did truly love them or they were no more than flesh-and-blood toys with no self-determination, predictable scraps of life playing parts in a game or a puzzle, a diversion for a cold intellect.'

'So they decided to test the Godhead by threatening mass suicide.'

Horst nodded. 'They were a very deliberate people and over time they had arrived at a principled and compassionate system of ethics, much of which was centred on the worth of self and existence. They reasoned that the Godhead would intercede and stop them killing themselves if it truly loved them: if it did not then their existence clearly had no instrinsic worth and continued life was without meaning.' He sighed. 'They prepared doses of fatal poison, and the Advisers did nothing to prevent them. They deduced that the Godhead knew of the plan and was allowing it to proceed.

'The day arrived, then the hour. The Advisers moved among them, assuring them of the Godhead's love, but the seconds ticked away to nothing, they took the poison and they died, down to the last. The Godhead did nothing.'

'The machine intelligence,' said the Construct offcam. 'It clearly witnessed all this but how did it escape the Godhead's domain?'

Horst was silent, his gaze distant. 'It told me that after the dying was done, the Advisers stopped, fell to the ground and lay motionless. The Tanenth AI transferred itself to an exploration vessel and departed on a course of semi-random cross-tier jumps that took it far away.

'It showed me all of this in the simulation and went on to explain its own theory that the Advisers' collective lapse into inertia had been a sign of the Godhead's shock and distress at what its creations had done. But in the middle of it I suddenly found myself back in my body and on board the bridge. I had been immobile for a little over five minutes, according to the Ship, but it felt like a day or more. Then the Ship said that another vessel had appeared near the tunnel entrance to the vast cavern, sensors sweeping, then vanished seconds later.

'The Tanenth machine was in no doubt as to its

origins – "It is a Postulate-craft of the Godhead. You have somehow led its servants here. Now you must leave and never seek me out again." And without warning, the hyperdrive came online and with no input from myself or the Ship AI we jumped. And it was a long jump.'

'A superior technology.'

'It took control of the ship as easily as it filled my mind with the history of the Tanenth.' Horst spread his hands. 'After that it took us a little while to get our bearings before starting on our way back here.'

The vid faded to black and the wall brightened to its normal pure blankness. The semiorganic turned its expressionless face to the Construct.

'He was not accompanied by a Rosa this time,' it said.

'I offered him one but he declined,' said the Construct. 'As he did again before leaving five days ago.'

'Did you send him off to track down this Tanenth machine again?'

'Yes,' the Construct said. 'And two days ago all communications with Horst and his ship ceased abruptly. I sent an augmented analyser drone to the last known coordinates; it deduced an ambush and capture from the initial micro-evidence, corroborated with microparticle clouds cast off by the use of grappler fields. The drone also detected residual ripple resonance from a recent hyperspace jump, abstracted a likely field signature from it, then dispatched probes to the four nearest enemy bases, one Vor and three Shyntanil. One probe registered a pattern match near a

Shyntanil battle group on Tier 57. The probe then sent in a flock of sensormotes to investigate the sole crypt-ship there and after some hours they detected and verified Horst's lifesigns.'

'Now that you know the location of his captivity,' said the semiorganic, 'I assume that this is where I enter the picture.'

'Correct. Once your shell appearance is complete to the last detail you will be leaving for the depths. Your task is to free him and then to aid him in the search for the Godhead.'

'You remain convinced that it is responsible for both the return of the Vor and the Shyntanil and for the release of the Legion?'

'Now more than ever. Too many large-scale strategies are proceeding in concert for this to be coincidence.'

The semiorganic inclined its chalky-white head. 'I would hope to be provided with resources appropriate to the hazards which lie ahead.'

'Unfortunately the Aggression is fully committed, stretched thin across multiple fronts, to be precise. I will be able to give you the use of a fast tier-scout and a squad of combat drones, and directional data for a course to Tier 23. There you will find this vessel ...'

The Construct indicated the screen. Against the back-drop of a ringed planet hung a large, heavily damaged warship, its prow a sheered-off melted mass, its stern crawling with bots and suited crew members. The semi-organic nodded.

'So the Earthsphere ship survived the Spiralist inva-sion of Darien,' it said. 'Which is more than the Brolturan battleship managed. Suddenly, elements of my assignment become clearer. I am curious as to how it comes to be there.'

'Although the Earthsphere vessel *Heracles* managed to survive the thermonuclear explosion with drives intact, it very quickly came under attack. With the defences disabled, the captain ordered an emergency hyperspace jump.' The Construct zoomed the frame in on the ship's stern, where several sections lay exposed. 'Certain control systems had been badly affected so the engineers had to make non-calibrated adjustments to the hyperdrive fields while traversing T2. Unfortunately this resulted in their unintentional descent to Tier 23.'

'Uncalibrated tier descents are highly risky,' said the semiorganic. 'They were lucky that their ship did not fly apart in a blaze of energies.'

'Indeed. I shall send a suite of ship-tech bots with you, and as much material as I can spare. You should provide the Human captain with a suitable story about my assistance without going into any intimidating detail then quickly move on to the matter of Horst's rescue. Given your eventual circumstances, it should not be too difficult an excuse to concoct.'

The semiorganic stood, a naked male template without any apparent clue to its age, other than physical maturity. It looked at the Construct with a hint of a smile.

'I assume you are aware that Robert Horst was holding something back,' it said.

'Behavioural analytics did bring this to my attention,' the Construct said. 'Finding this out is a vital part of your mission, although my own conjecture is that the

Tanenth machine said something about its makers' fate which cast meaning upon the death of Horst's own daughter. Ideally, I should like you to help him to return here to the Garden of the Machines but if the information he possesses indicates another more valuable course of action then pursue it.'

'I shall keep it at the forefront of my cognition,' the semiorganic said, then strode from the room whistling a jaunty tune.

After it was gone the Construct replayed segments of the Horst recording, with behavioural data glimmering in overlay. Another part of its cognitive awareness was sifting and prioritising front-line bulletins and resupply requisitions, while its higher-level sentience pondered the meagre reports emerging from the Darien system. It seemed that in the wake of the loss of their most prestigious warship the Brolturans had requested assistance from their patrons, the Hegemony. Advance units were due to arrive in a matter of days, all while rumours abounded that an Imisil fleet was also on its way. Then there was the question of the part that Earthsphere would play, a part which might turn out to be crucial.

This convergence of multiple strategies felt oddly coincidental but the Construct was sure that this was the final grand marshalling, a colossal orchestration of pieces, tactics and strategies on a board that extended down into hyperspace as well as across the starry expanses of this region of the galaxy. And with the first wave of Legion cyborg-craft due to exit the Darien warpwell in three, perhaps four days, another more vicious, more chaotic element would be added to the mix. Then, as the Human expression put it, all hell would break loose. And if the Godhead and its Legion, Vor and Shyntanil puppets triumphed, then even the deepest, most far-flung corners of hyperspace might not be a safe hiding place.

5

GREG

The captain's chair was significantly more comfortable than the fold-out seat. Slightly incurving parts of the moulding supported both the lower back and the shoulders, while the console with its holopanel could be swung out or brought in close and adjusted to whatever level the occupant desired.

'Are you sure this'll work?' he said.

'It's going to have to, Mr Cameron,' said Ash from the bridge entrance. 'Ah, at last ...'

The Tygran commander hurried into view, arms full of grey garments. He tossed one to each of the bridge officers, then swiftly tugged one on himself, a long cloak with a hood, which he pulled up.

'Just the thing for indoors,' Greg said drily.

'It's storm-weather gear,' Ash said. 'All that matters is that our buzzcut scalps are not on show.'

'They're repeating their demand, sir,' said the tactical officer. 'They don't sound very patient any more.'

Ash nodded. 'Mr Cameron, you know what to do.'

'Aye, you type it, I say it.'

'Correct. Right, open a direct channel.'

The vidframe reappeared on the viewport and the

white-garbed humanoid was there, eyes widening slightly, its facial spot-clusters pulsing red to orange. According to Ash, he was of a species called the Vikanta.

'Presignifier Remosca,' Greg began, reading from the monitor before him, 'I am Captain Cameron, commander of the *Falcon*, flagship of the Darien Navy. I have not been made aware of any exclusion zone. I would appreciate it if you would clarify this and explain your presence in our system.'

Remosca's face was expressionless but the facial spots rippled with contrasting colours, blue, amber, green, silver.

'Captain Cameron, our resources say that your planet possesses no vessels this advanced. And as we have declared, your craft is of a make deployed by Hegemony mercenaries ... '

'We purchased this ship in good faith from a passing trader less than two months ago,' Greg recited, wishing that Ash had more of a flair for wordcraft. 'We were offered a price that we were happy to accept. Now, would you please explain your presence?'

'Captain, your claims do not correspond with our resource information.' Resolute dark blue showed in the humanoid's spot-clusters. 'As stated, we are here to enforce an interdict lawfully placed by the Imisil Mergence. You have violated the exclusion zone, therefore you will be boarded.'

On the monitor Ash was typing: **If you attempt to board this vessel you will have to fight for every corridor and your losses will be heavy ...**

Greg stared, appalled. *Right, so in other words get*

your big boots on and come in swinging – do these Tygrans know the meaning of the word diplomacy?

He leaned back in the chair with a relaxed smile.

'I'm sorry, Presignifier, but I can't let you do that.'

He could feel Ash's sharp stare even as Remosca tilted his head slightly to one side.

'Captain, do you realise how outgunned you are? My vessel possesses multiple batteries, both missile and beam. All you have is . . .'

'Is what, Presignifier? Please, spare me no details. This is of great interest to me.'

'. . . two mid-range beam projectors and a single launcher battery.'

Greg could sense Ash's anger from the misspelt orders appearing on the couch monitor but he just couldn't resist carrying on the bluff.

'I see, fascinating. And no anomalous energy readings? You're not picking up any odd particles? Anything like that?'

Blank-faced, the Imisil commander glanced to either side of the frame, as if consulting readouts of some kind.

'We are detecting nothing out of the ordinary. Are you implying . . .'

'No need for implications, Presignifier,' Greg said. 'But it's only fair tae warn ye that this ship has been fitted with hullbreaker technology. Naturally, such equipment has to be masked from detection.' He turned to Ash. 'Lieutenant Ash . . . Ashwell, status report on the void shields.'

Ash's gaze was an intense mixture of aggravation and puzzlement and for a moment Greg thought that he was going to say something to knock over this demented house of cards. Then, frowning stonily, he looked round at his monitor.

'Maintaining void shield integrity within operational parameters. Sir.'

Greg smiled. Remosca shifted in his seat.

'But … we cannot detect this weapon …'

'Yes, Presignifier, precisely! Which is how it should be.'

'But a weapon cannot deter an enemy if it is invisible.'

Greg shook his head. 'The hullbreaker is not meant to be a deterrent, Presignifier, more like a weapon to be unleashed against the most vicious and unreasonable of adversaries. Now, you seem to be a reasonable person so why don't we negotiate sensibly about this?'

The Imisil humanoid made no reply, just turned to look at something or someone out of shot. He gave a sharp nod then looked back.

'Very well, Captain. I have decided to extend to you dialogue courtesies. Please state your initial query.'

'That's kind of ye, Presignifier. Naturally, I am concerned about this interdict upon my world and why the Imisil Mergence feels compelled to impose it. However, uppermost in my mind is this – how big is your fleet and when's it due?'

Ash was giving him a wide-eyed, have-you-gone-totally-off-your-head? look while the Imisil officer's thin-lipped mouth dropped open for a moment.

'You will reveal how you came by this information – immediately.' The humanoid's voice was calm but his facial spot-clusters were pulsing with dark greens and reds.

'Why, from you, Presignifier. From your actions.' He glanced at Ash, who was frowning but gave a cautious nod. 'Y'see, that vessel of yours is pretty impressive but a bit overpowered for a long-range spying mission, what with the Imisil Mergence being so far away. Not only that, it seems to me that a spying mission should be stealthy and concealed, which is not really how you've been going about it. You don't look like you're about to hide or head for the next star, which makes me think that maybe you're the forward scouts for an Imisil fleet. Cannae be far behind ye, a few hours, I'd say.' He smiled. 'How am I doing?'

'Your conjecture lacks rigour,' said Presignifier Remosca. 'Your suppositions are flawed. You are correct to say that other ships are coming but wrong to imagine them our allies ...'

'Contact!' said the tactical officer. 'Single vessel, 96,500 kiloms on the other side of the planet, low exit velocity on a para-orbit course. They've not seen us ...'

'It appears that you now have the opportunity to test your hullbreaker technology, Captain,' Remosca said. 'I think that you'll find the newcomers sufficiently vicious and unreasonable.'

The Imisil commander's image vanished from the viewport while other frames showed the Imisil vessel moving off in a tight curve, its course then angling towards the far side of the forest moon Nivyesta.

'ID on the new arrival!' said Ash.

'Tygran,' said the tac officer. 'It's the *Ironfist*.'

Greg felt the atmosphere on the bridge change. When he looked at Ash, the man's expression was grim.

'Okay, you seem to recognise the ship,' he said. 'What is it?'

'Hunter-killer,' said Ash. 'That's what it's here to do.' He gestured. 'I'll need my chair.'

'Wait – let me speak to the Imisil captain again.'

Ash shook his head. 'It was a good try, Mr Cameron. Now we have to get ready for combat.'

'*Ironfist* is altering course,' said the tac officer. 'They're tracking us and ramping up velocity.'

Greg stared at the Tygran commander. 'You're not going to fire up the engines and get us out of here?'

'The *Ironfist* is faster than any other Tygran vessel, or even that Imisil ship,' Ash said. 'Escape would be ... difficult.'

'Then let's open a channel to them,' Greg said. 'I'll give him every bit of offended pride and arrogant conceit I can muster. Might make him stop and think.'

'The *Ironfist* is an Iron Ravens ship,' Ash said. 'Its commander is Ethan Wade, a cold and ruthless man.'

'I don't care if he's Sawney Bean, Dracula and Old Father Odin rolled into one, he's about to find out that he's trespassing on ...'

'*Ironfist* is signalling us, sir,' said the tac officer.

Ash gazed at Greg for a moment. Then the ghost of a smile cracked his stony visage. 'Very well, let's see how far this charade can take us.'

'And one more thing – leave the channel unsecured,' Greg said as he and Ash swapped seats.

'No encryption?'

'None. The Imisil are still out there and I want them to hear every word.'

Ash shrugged and nodded at his tac officer. A second

later the head-and-shoulders image of a Tygran officer appeared on the viewport overlay as well as the command chair holopanel. The man had broad shoulders, a heavy jaw and dark, piercing eyes. Those eyes narrowed and he leaned forward but before he could speak Greg cut in.

'Unidentified vessel, this is First Commodore Cameron of the Darien Navy. You have crossed into our security shell without authorisation. Stand down your weapon systems and defences and prepare to be boarded.'

Fury flared in the Tygran's eyes.

'I am Ethan Wade, commander of the *Ironfist*, banner-ship of the Iron Ravens, and I will not be spoken to in that manner by a dog of a pirate!'

Greg frowned. 'Did ye not hear me, Commander? You have violated the sovereign space of our world, therefore we are entirely within our rights to question your motives and even inspect yer ship ...'

'You are sitting on the bridge of a Tygran vessel!' Wade snarled. 'I don't know how you got your hands on it, or where the traitors who seized it are, but you will cease your prattling and surrender to me immediately.'

'Is this how you conduct yourselves every time you meet strangers, Commander Wade?' Greg said. 'With insults and arrogance? I mean, isn't that a wee bit risky when you don't know what these strangers are capable of?'

Wade gave a contemptuous smile.

'I've been aboard that ship, *Commodore*, and I am thoroughly acquainted with its capabilities.'

'Aye, but are ye sure, Commander? I'm guessing that

you've got some long-range sensors on that scary war-wagon of yours so why don't you scan this vessel and its vicinity ... okay? Found any clues?'

Out of the corner of his eye, Greg saw Ash shake his head as a line of text appeared on the couch holopanel – **That shielded weapon bluff won't work on Wade.**

Quickly Greg keyed back – **New intruders, new bluff** – then resumed talking to the Tygran, who had been conferring with one of his officers.

'I'll clear up the mystery for you, Commander Wade,' he said. 'What you're detecting are ionised particles from a ship drive. Not ours, although it is a vessel under my command.'

'There are no other ships in this system, apart from mine and yours,' said Wade. 'And in less than six minutes, when you come within range of my main batteries, there shall be only mine.'

'Okay, Commander, since we're getting along so well, I feel I should warn you that you are being tracked by another two ships of the Darien Navy, concealed by cloaking technology ...'

'Spare me your pathetic, desperate lies. Surrender or face destruction!'

'... specifically two Karlsson-class jump-destroyers with much greater firepower than this ship carries.' Driven by the adrenalin of the crazed corner that he'd got himself into, Greg put on a wide, unbalanced grin. 'I mean, ye didn't think I was gonnae sit here on the firing line without some serious reinforcements, did ye?'

For the first time, hesitation showed in the Tygran's expression. Greg pushed on.

'There's no need for this to get messy,' he said. 'If

you stand down your weapons, I'll send my jump-destroyers out of range.'

'I acknowledge your warnings, Commander,' Wade said with a kind of stiff contempt. 'I have my orders.'

And the image vanished from all screens.

'*Ironfist*'s increasing velocity,' said the helm officer.

'They've targeted our drive,' said the tac officer.

'Full power to the thrusters,' Ash said. 'Take us out of here on a spiral swerve.'

Despite the inertial dampening, Greg felt the swinging impetus as the ship surged forward and spun savagely to port. Beyond the viewport the stars swirled and streamed past, and Greg grimly held on to his couch.

'The *Ironfist* is just coming into their maximum range,' said the tac officer. 'Opening fire with pulse cannon rounds, broad zigzag sweep, nine passes ... navigationals compensating ...'

There was a sharp thud from elsewhere in the ship and Greg felt a passing tremor underfoot.

'Damage report,' said Ash.

'Midsection, upper starboard,' said the tac officer. 'Outer hull plate damage, no inner hull breach.'

'Sorry about that, Commander,' Greg said. 'But the Imisil are out there, watching – I thought it might tempt 'em to weigh in on our side.'

'I can't see that happening,' Ash said. 'Target their weapon points with our missile launcher,' he told the tac officer. 'Four eluders with shimmer payloads – fire when ready.'

A moment later the tac officer said, 'Missiles away ... and they've launched a volley of their own, silverclaws, two waves.'

'Going for our shields,' Ash said. 'Target the eluders with our beam projectors and fire.'

One of the screens showed a tracking view of the intervening space. Four impact flashes appeared in rough succession, then a digital overlay revealed blotches of grey spreading at the edges. Ash saw Greg's mystified look.

'Countermeasures,' he said. 'Each payload spreads a cloud of refractive slivers. Inhibits directional sensors. Now we need to get closer to the shimmer clouds, use them as a shield ...'

'The *Ironfist* is changing course,' the tac officer said. 'First wave of silverclaw missiles have entered the shimmer clouds ... wait, they've ...'

On the screen bright points of light bloomed in the intervening cloud. A magnified view showed expanding shells of energy tearing gaps in the shimmer barrier.

'Second wave is through with minimal deviation,' said the tac officer.

'How long?' said Ash.

'On current course and speed ... fifty seconds.'

'Helm, go to maximum thrust – head for the far side of that moon.'

'The *Ironfist* is targeting all its projector batteries on our engines,' said the tac officer, his voice showing signs of strain.

'Raise shields,' Ash said with rock-solid composure. 'All hands, lock down safeties against incoming enemy fire.'

Greg sat slumped back in the command couch, witnessing the seemingly inexorable slide towards destruction with a terrible fear crawling in his guts.

'Contact!' the tac officer cried out. 'Vessel uncloaking eight kiloms off our stern – sir, it's the Imisil ship . . . and they're picking off all the silverclaw missiles.'

'Maintain course and speed,' said Ash, who glanced at Greg. 'The Imisil have put themselves between us and our pursuers, a high-risk tactic in this situation . . .'

'We're picking up a message from the Imisil to the *Ironfist*,' said the tac officer. A moment later, the audio came through.

'Ezgara vessel – you have violated an exclusion zone emplaced according to the self-defence protocols of the Imisil Mergence. Cease all attacks and threats and withdraw from this system immediately.'

'So the meddling Imisil are working with those brigands,' came Wade's voice. 'No matter – it will be my pleasure to obliterate you before dealing with that shipful of thieves.'

'You may be assured that events will transpire differently,' was the Imisil reply before the channel cut out.

'Can they hold against the Tygran ship's weapons?' Greg said.

Ash shrugged but his frown said no. Then, staring at his screen, he leaned forward. 'The Imisil are not raising their shields . . .'

'The *Ironfist* is targeting all weapons on the Imisil vessel,' said the tac officer.

'Aim everything we've got at the *Ironfist*,' said Ash.

'Contact! – second vessel uncloaking above and behind the *Ironfist*! It is another Imisil ship and it's opening fire . . .'

Greg watched it all unfold in the holopanel before him. Even as the Tygran ship veered wildly to port the second Imisil kept pace and unleashed a cascade of destruction upon its stern. Beam energies tore and lashed at the shields while pulse cannon rounds and disruptor missiles pounded away. Under such intense and focused attack the Tygran's shields began to weaken, flare and fail. Return fire had cut through the Imisil's own slotted shields and its hull sported several gashes and breaches trailing foggy gases. But for the Tygran vessel the end was near. As its shields finally flared out from tail to prow, the second Imisil sent missiles and pulse beam rounds into the now unprotected stern.

Something exploded, a fuel line or a generator, and Greg could see hot yellow fire spread within the hull, blowing out hatches and sections of plating. Then one of the manoeuvring thrusters began to burn, blazing at full strength for a moment before it burst apart in a brief flurry of fiery whiteness. A second later a massive explosion tore open the stern as the main drives succumbed, leaving the Tygran vessel pinwheeling through space.

The atmosphere on the bridge of the *Starfire* was sombre. In a monotone voice, the tactical officer gave a running commentary while on screen the Tygran ship, rent by internal detonations, exhibited its death throes.

'The Imisil are hailing us,' said the tac officer.

Ash gave Greg a wintry smile. 'I believe that's your cue.'

A moment later Greg was once more face to face with the Imisil commander, Presignifier Remosca. The humanoid was as composed as before while his facial spot-clusters glowed in shades of green.

'Greetings to you, Captain Cameron, or should I address you as First Commodore?'

'Aye, well, apologies for that wee diversionary exaggeration there, Presignifier. And our profound gratitude for intervening ...'

'After you alerted the Ezgara to our presence.'

'Ach, I know it was a bit presumptuous but that was a tight spot we were in. And I reckoned that you'd have to deal with them anyway, whether we were still around or not. Glad to see that you're a reasonable people.'

The Imisil commander gave a slight turning nod. 'Our civilisation does aspire to certain minimum standards of conduct. I decided to aid you on the basis of the enmity which the Ezgara clearly bear towards you.'

Right, my enemy's enemy, Greg thought as he relaxed and sat back. 'Once again, I am very grateful to you, Presignifier – hopefully, any future joint operations will demonstrate that we can be worthy allies. But in the meantime, we wait for the rest of your fleet to arrive, aye? Perhaps you could give me some idea about why the Imisil Mergence sent you all this way.'

'It is not out of a desire to acquire territory, I assure you. But there are more pressing matters for our mutual attention – since our first exchange I received a message from the Expeditionary Fleet, saying that they encountered a hostile force of unknown designation. Fierce fighting means that they will be delayed for an indeterminate time period. I have been given command discretion as to whether we remain in this system or hasten to rejoin them.'

'And yet here you are,' Greg said.

'We have been gathering data from sensor probes left in the second tier of hyperspace,' the Imisil officer went on. 'There is another group of vessels heading for this system, a Hegemony carrier battle group. It appears that the Sendrukans have decided to usurp the Brolturans' ascendancy in this matter. This is in keeping with their murderous history.'

Greg felt a sick dread in his chest. 'Can even three of us stand up to this kind of invasion?'

Off to the side, Ash gave a weary shake of the head.

'That is highly doubtful, Captain Cameron,' said Remosca. 'But it may be possible to wound them badly. Our scans reveal a number of salvageable elements among the battle debris orbiting your world. But while we complete a recovery assessment there is one thing I would like to know from you.'

'What would that be, Presignifier?'

'How *did* you know that I had a second ship?'

6

JULIA

Talavera let her have a beach house and a golden retriever to run along the sands with and some fishing rods and a low wooden jetty and a white rowing boat. And Julia would sit out on the veranda with a tall glass of vargr wine, enjoying the sun's heat on her skin even though she was enveloped in cascades of information, a cloud of data in continual motion.

And she worked on tailored heuristic navigator systems for a hundred anti-dark-matter missiles to be launched from hyperspace, targeted on a hundred planets, on a hundred deadly people who had to die.

Or so Talavera's story went: that whole process of kidnapping Julia and the other Enhanced and making them modify thermonuclear missiles for use against the ships orbiting Darien, then confining them to full-body virtuality tanks, was only her way of testing their abilities and mettle before revealing this most vital of projects. And it was a great shame that the distrust felt by the Enhanced had required Talavera and her people to resort to a certain degree of coercion. She had told Julia all this two subjective days after the foiling of her attempt to escape from the *Sacrament*, the Chaurixa terrorists' mothership. Julia had listened and nodded thoughtfully, not believing a word.

So as a demonstration of her warm-hearted good will, Talavera allowed her the house, the dog, the boat and so forth, and when Julia asked for a Human companion the terrorist seemed to consider for a moment before giving her assent.

Now it was the fifth s-day since her arrival at the beach, although objectively only a day had passed. Relaxing on the veranda, she teased coils and lattices of info from the raw data cloud which hung over her like an immense, slowly gyring tornado, its dense grey and slate-blue flows speckled with glittering motes, glints caught in the intertwining braids.

Down on the beach, further along the shore, a female figure ran, laughed and played with the dog, throwing sticks and splashing in the shallows. Joyful barks drifted on the breeze.

The imagery was representational. In drawing down data from the cloudy tornado she was actually configuring it for the computational macros she had already prepared in certain areas of her cortex, those tightly clustered webs of neural pathways that were under her conscious and practised control. But this was her metacosm so it amused her to watch those braids of information snakily float over to the brassy, bell-shaped intake of a small but fabulously archaic-looking machine that sat on the veranda's low table. It had a sequence of bizarre sections complete with electrical sparks, wheezing bellows, flashing lights, and puffs of steam. Every hour or so a tinny fanfare would sound and a glassy sphere the size of her thumb would roll out at the other end, landing in a padded basket. Julia would transfer it to a triangular tray and over time build a gleaming pyramid which on completion would vanish when her eyes were averted.

Yet she remained perfectly aware that despite the pleasant surroundings and the placid comforts, her body still lay stretched and motionless in one of Talavera's virtuality tanks. With any luck they wouldn't have disturbed or forensically examined her since her incarceration.

More barks and the sound of footsteps climbing to the veranda heralded her companion's return.

'Och, Julia! – all work and no play is no way to stay sharp, ye know!'

Wearing a pale blue windbreaker and flowery slacks, Catriona Macreadie pulled up a wicker stool and sat down. The golden retriever followed her in and lay down by her feet.

'It's an urgent project, Cat,' she said. 'And it's my responsibility so I have to stick with it.'

'Well, when it's done, me and Benny'll take you along to some rock pools we found – you should see the ammonite crabs ...'

Julia smiled and nodded, inwardly puzzled as she'd neither imagined rock pools on the shore nor given the dog a name. But then this wasn't meant to be that close a copy of the real Catriona, who had an altogether more morose demeanour. Julia was about to ask how far off these rock pools were when the tabletop contraption sounded its little fanfare and another glassy sphere was produced. Catriona chuckled and went over to pick it out of its little basket.

'Beautiful,' she said, peering into its foggy, latticed heart.

Then the dog stood up and looked at Julia.

'Template match compiled,' it said. 'Instructions?'

'Copy yourself and overwrite.'

Catriona froze in the act of dropping the sphere onto the triangular tray. Her form turned opaque as a bright transecting plane passed through her from head to toe. When it was over solidity returned, the sphere clinked onto the tray, and Catriona straightened, features blank, awaiting orders.

Julia smiled. When Talavera and her goons stuck her in the virtuality tank they didn't know that she had hidden one last polymote in her hair, next to her scalp. Days ago she had reprogrammed a batch of polymotes – nanoscale builders – and deployed them through the Chaurixa vessel, the *Sacrament*, to assist in their escape attempt. The escape failed and all five Enhanced were confined in solitary. Julia was still able to regain control of the handful of polymotes not yet tracked down, then broke out of her cell only to be recaptured while trying to reprogram the cargo handler system.

It would be different this time. It had to be – Talavera had infected her with the nanodust.

She got to her feet. 'What is the trigger word to suspend the sensory lockdown?' she said to the dog. 'And how long before it locks down again?'

'The word is "continuity" and lockdown will resume after fifteen seconds.'

The dog was now host to the polymote's limited AI, as was the Catriona shell, and very soon hers too. All they had to do was to keep the performance going long enough for her to make good an escape. Leaving the others was a wrench but a solo breakout stood the best chance.

'I have incorporated a buffer into this image shell,' she told the dog. 'As soon as I speak, copy yourself into it then overwrite any residual code. Then you will maintain a behaviour façade.' She breathed in deep. 'Continuity . . .'

She almost made it. Awaking in the tank, she crept out into a shadowy corridor. Unobserved, she got to the *Sacrament*'s evac capsules, hacked into the controls with a polymote-built codegen key, set them all to autolaunch in one minute, long enough to get inside one of them and bypass its survival/nav system. So while the other eleven fired their thrusters and sped away into space, Julia manually steered hers along the *Sacrament*'s outer hull and latched onto an aft auxiliary hatch.

But Talavera somehow deduced that she was not aboard any of the evac capsules and nearly thirty minutes later the aft hatch's locking clamps were activated. Then the hatch itself opened and she was dragged into the airlock, where a pair of Henkayans bound and gagged her.

Back in the virtuality chamber they tipped her into the tank, reattached the waste and nutrient tubes and refastened the neural cutout around her head. By now she had abandoned all pretence at composure and was yelling wordlessly behind the heavy tape covering her mouth. Then the cutout was activated and her body grew heavy and numb and misty and distant as her awareness was pulled back into Talavera's virtual prison.

Julia opened her eyes and saw blue sky. She sat up and found she was back on the beach. Wavelets lapped at the shore, darkening the sand, but there was no beach house, no dog, no Catriona.

'To say I'm disappointed, well . . .'

Talavera was suddenly standing a few feet away, attired in a red lacy bodice, green skin-tight leggings and her trademark heavy boots. As she stood there, black snakelike creatures emerged from the sand and wound up her legs. They had no features and were tapered at either end, so apart from their direction of movement there was no way to tell head from tail.

'I explained what our work's for, how important it is,' Talavera went on.

'And I don't believe you,' Julia said. 'Don't believe you, don't trust you, don't even . . . know what you are. What are those things? – why make up things like that?'

'Hmm, sounds like pride to me. Yeah, the hubris of the oh-so-superior mind.' Talavera leaned forward and hate glittered in her eyes. 'But hang on a second – I'm the one who's foiled your plans and dragged you back three times in a row so I guess that makes me your nemesis, maybe even arch-nemesis.' She laughed. 'And I didn't make up my little snaky friends here – they're messengers from someone called . . .' She paused, as if deciding what to say. '. . . called the Godhead. He helped me escape when I was marooned and surrounded by death. You've no idea how powerful he is, or how powerful he is going to make me. Do you have someone like that, someone who'll reach down and protect you and save you? I think we both know what the answer is.'

Julia kept her face expressionless and looked out across the placid waters, not knowing who this Godhead was, feeling empty.

'What happens now?' she said.

'There's still work to be done,' said Talavera. 'So we need that magnificent brain of yours in order to finish the project on time. But we can't risk any more meddling or plotting on your part. In short, it's time for a Julia-ectomy!'

Darkness slammed in from all sides. Her field of vision suddenly shrank to just her right eye and she couldn't feel her body, no hands, legs, no mouth, nose, no feeling, no senses apart from one eye and a section of blue sky.

'That Hegemony nanodust . . . really, it is such versatile stuff,' came Talavera's voice, close and rich with an unreal intensity. 'I've got it shutting down pathways around your personality centres, mainly those to do with motivation and mood. Should keep you nicely torpid, and when you wake up after it's all over, it'll be a very different galaxy. Who knows, you might like it!'

Silence closed in. The blue sky turned grey-silver and an array of square silvery recesses emerged, a lattice of them, lines converging towards the distance. She was herself sinking into one of the recesses, drifting down into its shadows. There was brief flash of anger but it soon faded. The need to oppose Talavera frayed away and defiance dissolved into passivity. Becalmed, Julia's awareness was simply content now to stare up out of her square niche. Even when the light above shaded away into unbroken darkness, there was nothing in her that felt like responding.

... initialising contingency state ... initialising contingency state ...

The odd phrase appeared on the niche wall, pale blue glowing letters that pulsed over and over.

... initialising contingency state ...

It seemed familiar, one of the autofeatures she'd coded into the polymotes at the start.

... initialised ... nano-intrusion has been mapped ... reroute partitioned cortical nodes? y/n ...

A small glowing star sat above the *y/n* options and she found that she could will it to move in any direction. When she placed it over the *y*, other words appeared.

... stepped reconnection initiated ... pov focus translocation initiated ...

Suddenly she was in motion, a headlong blurring rush that made a bewildering number of abrupt changes in direction. All while a sharpness of mood crept back into her thoughts, bringing understanding in its wake. This reprieve had been effected by one of the polymote copies following its imperatives – subvert enemy systems, enhance and expand Julia's scope for action. By now the dizzying, angular journey had slowed and it seemed that she hovered next to a dazzling, quivering, thrumming geyser of light passing horizontally through a sequence of crystalline rings. It was the dataflow of the virtuality chamber, the inflows and outflows, currents specific to each of the five metacosms that Talavera was running.

Time is limited, said the polymote. *Do you wish to send a message via this vessel's tiernet connection?*

Hearing the polymote as a disembodied voice in her mind was unsettling. I have no mouth, she wanted to say. How can I ...

You may do so by speaking the words in your mind.

'I see. How much time is left?'

The nano-intrusion was easily fooled. However, cortical imbalances will exceed their capture tolerances in less than an objective minute and trigger alerts. Subjectively you have a longer period.

'I want to observe the other Enhanced. I want to see what she's done.'

Without warning her point of view plunged straight into the searing brightness of the dataflow.

She saw Konstantin's laboratory, vast and intricate as a city, its districts cluttered with complex arrays of glassware, or stacks of analytical devices, or towers of monitors and servers. Yet a dark hush hung over it and many areas were shadowy or swathed in inky darkness. Toward the city centre there were still lights and flickering glows, signs of activity.

Irenya's metacosm was a garden with a fountain and a stream and a wooden bridge and a bird table and willow trees. Only the garden was overgrown, the willows were half-strangled by masses of thorns, the fountain was dried up and cracked and the stream stank of decay. It was raining and from behind the tangled bushes came the sound of crying.

Thorold had not succumbed, not completely. Under an icy grey sky he was hauling a cart of stones up a bare mountain track.

The last was Arkady's. Talavera had already infected him with the Hegemony nanodust so Julia didn't know what to expect when she saw a vast foggy plain and the outlines of a solitary mountain. As she drew nearer the fog thinned and she saw that an immense seated figure

had been formed from the mountainside. It was head-
less.

'I've seen enough.'

Again the dataflow, its torrid brightness, its furious
density. She considered the ship's tiernet connection, a
cluster of data channels whose multiplexity made perfect security a near-impossibility. Which is why Talavera
wanted the Enhanced; their wetware was harder to infiltrate via the tiernet, and they were easier to coerce than
an AI. Easy victims, weak, friendless. Talavera's words
came back to her:

*'Do you have someone like that, someone who'll
reach down and save you and protect you? ... we both
know what the answer is ...'*

'Can you make a copy of my mindstate?' she said.
'Then open a channel to the tiernet and upstream it?'

*A close, fractal-based approximation can be cre-
ated ... the virtuality monitors have discovered the
anomalous imbalance in your brain. There is no time
to create the copy then upstream it, but there is time
to fractalise and upstream it in continual realtime
transfer.*

She hesitated, but only for a moment.

'That will suffice.'

*The fractalisation process may cause irreparable
neural damage – it will certainly mean the end of your
self-aware existence.*

'If I am cogent and aware when the nanodust shifts
into its second phase I will experience suffering and self-
death anyway. I have seen what it does. Please proceed
with the scan.'

It is commencing. You will soon experience a

scaleback in the visual and auditory senses. Also, old memories may appear for a short time.

The furious brightness of the dataflow grew pale then blurred into haze, and she imagined that she could hear a sound like the roar of a waterfall fading away. As it quietened it turned into something else, a crackling sound interspersed with pops and clicks. She saw a blob of light, a wavering yellowness which resolved out of the blur to become a bonfire on a beach by night. Ash specks and gleaming motes flew up on the swirling heat. Branches glowed red at the heart of the flames, bark curled and crisped and smoke flowed off the outer kindling in pale, rising rivulets.

Then it was as if the fire was within her. A wave of strange sensations surged, some memories, ideas, words, her name even, burst forth then melted away. Somehow she felt unburdened as her last thoughts rose up out of her like an ascending cascade of singing stars.

Flanked by two Kiskashin techs, Corazon Talavera gazed down at the unresponsive but still breathing form of Julia Bryce. As she stood there comparing the data on her analyser pad with the tank's readouts, a creature like a snake made of dense black smoke coiled and slithered from thigh to torso to upper arm and back. The Kiskashin were both terrified of it but strove to show no fear, not in Talavera's presence anyway.

'She's gone,' Talavera said at last. 'Use the dust again. Make a fine, new instrument for me.'

7

KUROS

Brolturan troops saluted as he passed, mounting steps recently cut into the side of the rocky ridge. The morning sky was grey and a cold sea breeze made his golden robes flap. He experienced an involuntary shiver and the skin of his exposed lower arms prickled, a reaction to the lower temperature. It was a flaw of the flesh that he was prepared to suffer in anticipation of the rewards that came with victory. He continued his climb to the observation station.

Utavess Kuros, eldest offspring of Efeskin Kuros, once High Monitor, once Ambassador of the Sendrukan Hegemony to this dust-mote of a world, once rejoicing in the appellation 'exalted', was now a prisoner within his own head. There were no physical feelings, no bodily sensations apart from vision. He was a mute witness to all that the interloper was seeing and hearing, all of it so clear that he had come to believe that it was deliberate.

For that first day, after the AI Gratach took possession, Kuros had felt the moorings of his sanity give way. Darkness had gaped, a cavernous maw now eager to swallow and grind him down. But he held on to the flow of images from outside, a lifeline he grasped in desperation, using it as a focus for conscious attention. He had survived, learning to maintain the essence of his being while the usurper, his own mindbrother the general Gratach, strode around in *his* body, spoke with *his* mouth and gave orders to *his* troops.

After the evacuation from Giant's Shoulder, the transports had flown to the high valley encampment north of Trond. From his cage of dark numbness Kuros could only watch as Gratach and the Clarified Teshak, the engineer of his imprisonment, reorganised the encampment with the aim of keeping them safe. There were still a number of flyers and aircars capable of mounting an effective strike against the rogue droids which had occupied Giant's Shoulder and the warpwell, despite the defence batteries still in place there. But Teshak, in his gloating declaration back on Giant's Shoulder, had made it clear that abandonment of the facility was integral to his plans. The failure of the Hegemon's Darien strategy would allow the Clarified and their traditionalist allies to see off the current administration and take control of the Hegemony.

However, in the last few days more details had come to Kuros's attention. Gratach and the Clarified Teshak seemed to communicate via the neural implants, apart from when either or both were accompanied by their Brolturan subordinates. It was from those verbal exchanges that Kuros deduced hints and other fragments of knowledge, including references to 'the Knight', who seemed to be the one directing the droids currently occupying Giant's Shoulder. This entity had also successfully fended off a couple of attacks by the Human resistance.

At the head of the stone steps an uneven path led along a rocky ridge bearing only sparse patches of hardy grass and the occasional low bush. On such an open prominence the breeze was stronger, its cold bite sharper. The path steepened till it reached a level stretch where a Brolturan trooper in outdoor dress saluted as he approached. Further along a small building stood against a sheer cliff of dark stone. He was halfway towards it when a one-man flyer rose into view from the seaward side and alighted gracefully next to the observer station.

Apart from strengthening the defences, their other high-priority task was to make contact with the nearest Hegemony or Brolturan outpost. Multiband scans revealed that no relay satellites had survived the destruction of the *Purifier* and the subsequent Spiralist invasion in which tens of thousands of half-starving religious pilgrims of various species spilled out of ramshackle transports and began looting the villages and farms of the coastal plain. Under great pressure, a group of Brolturan techs worked around the clock for three days, cannibalising flyer systems, testing modules salvaged from crashed craft, till they managed to assemble a subspace commset.

It only permitted monochrome visuals and low-quality audio, but if it worked it would suffice. Contact was established with a Hegemony listening post at the edge of Brolturan space. Kuros listened as Gratach used his own codes to identify himself as the ambassador then proceeded to spin a wild, exaggerated tale. Gratach told them that after the loss of the *Purifier* (which they already knew about), and the Spiral armada's ground invasion, it had been discovered that the zealots had brought dozens of backpack nuclear devices which were now hidden in strategic places throughout the colony. At the first sign of a planetary assault they would be detonated. He then claimed that his forces had captured three Imisil spies who, after questioning, revealed that an Imisil invasion force was already on its way to the Darien system. Kuros listened to all this with barely restrained fury. Clearly, Gratach had thrown in his lot with the Clarified Teshak and the Clarified conspiracy.

The reply came two hours later. Relayed from Iseri, the Sendrukan homeworld, it came from none other than the Second Tri-Advocate. The Brolturans, it seemed, had been on the point of dispatching a relief force but when informed of the severity of the situation decided to formally request military assistance from the Hegemony. The relief force had been stood down and a Hegemony carrier battle group was on its way at maximum speed. The staunch resolve demonstrated by Ambassador Kuros and the Clarified Teshak was already being hailed on news announcements all across the Hegemony, and their valour would most surely not go unrewarded. They were instructed to expect the arrival of the *Solemnitor* and her attendant warcraft in approximately forty-eight hours. A much larger fleet was also being gathered and elements of that could possibly reach the periphery of the Darien system in fifty-five hours.

Once the communication ended, Gratach and Teshak grinned at each other. Kuros heard neither speak but knew that they were conversing via the implants. It was frustrating in the extreme but Kuros allowed himself no luxuries of rage, instead kept his attention on all details within the scope of his perception. Fragments of information could usually be gleaned, and over the last few days, during Gratach's briefings with the Brolturan officers, Kuros had learned several strange facts.

Like the mysterious deaths of two of the Spiralist leaders, which took place on the same day that Kuros was entombed in his own brain and Giant's Shoulder was abandoned. The Prophet-Sage himself and his generals, Jeshkra and Hurnegur, had reportedly been attacked by bomb-throwing Humans while observing an assault on the promontory. Only Hurnegur survived, and now the Spiralist hordes were scouring the coastal settlements, rounding up the remaining Humans and confining them in camps. Teshak was keeping his Brolturan troops close to home, but still there had been a few skirmishes between aircar patrols and Spiralist gangs on the ground.

As a consequence, most of the Human colonists were trying to get out of the coastal region, some moving south to the Eastern Towns while others went north to the stockaded villages around Trond. For the first three or four days the Spiralist fanatics spread out in mobs and gangs, unopposed and unhindered. Then yesterday one of the comm technicians brought Gratach-in-Kuros a report compiled from shortwave chatter, the substance of which was that a sizeable force of Humans had infiltrated the capital, Hammergard, by night and routed the Spiralists from the city. Apparently crude airships had been used to deliver attack squads to rooftops then later to rain incendiaries on the fleeing zealots. Hearing this, Kuros felt a stab of admiration for the colonists and their willingness to hit back at the invaders. Then there were the probing attacks carried out by the Human resistance against the rogue mechs occupying Giant's Shoulder. Kuros knew that light irregular troops could not prevail against armoured combat droids.

The Clarified Teshak was waiting at the door to the observation station. A large silver-blue transport case hovered next to him on suspensors. Once inside, Teshak activated the case and it unfolded into the improvised subspace comm device. As the connect system began scanning for specific encrypted channels, Gratach stared out of the window at the heaving sea.

One glimmer of personal satisfaction persisted throughout Kuros's imprisonment, this torment of nothingness, and it went by the name Alexandr Vashutkin. Not long after he and his followers took up residence in the Utgard cliff caves, Kuros had sent in shock troops equipped with genetic trackers. Once the insurgents had been stampeded to the various exits and Vashutkin had been captured, the Rus was infused with the nanodust. It only took minutes for the dust to master him, after which he was released.

Vashutkin's orders had been to capture Greg Cameron for interrogation, or to eliminate him. But Kuros, disconnected, disembodied, had no way to know if Cameron was definitely dead. None of the Brolturan reports spoke of him, although there was mention of Vashutkin being spotted at temporary camps in the Kentigern foothills and leading one of the attacks on Giant's Shoulder. Was this proof positive that Cameron was in fact dead? Yet the controlled Vashutkin had not sought Kuros out, which implied that he was still alive.

Unknowns and imponderables – Kuros's attenuated existence consisted of little else.

Now, however, it seemed likely that he would soon discover some authentic facts, perhaps even an explanation that would reveal something useful about the Clarified plan. It was the morning of the fifth day since Kuros's entrapment and Gratach had left the Brolturan compound and, alone, climbed newly cut steps to the crest of a ridge overlooking the sea and the southern approaches. Now he was inside a dilapidated stone building with the Clarified Teshak, waiting for a subspace comm device to find a specific signal. As before, no words were spoken. An implicit silence held sway.

An alert chimed. Gratach and Teshak exchanged a look and moved in closer to the device, contained within an opened-up transport case. A holoscreen appeared above a basic console. In its soft blue plane a shiny disc spun, a ready-state graphic, then was replaced by a pale-skinned man in a dark uniform, a monochrome image. He stared out at them.

'The greatly esteemed Clarified Teshak,' he said in a high, melodic voice. 'And his companion must surely be the notable General Gratach ... who is yet to take the ascension, if I am not mistaken.'

'Quite correct, Clarified Dusorn,' said Teshak. 'It might be advisable to wait until we have been removed to a more controlled environment before completing our brother's clarification.'

'Of course,' Dusorn said. 'To that end, another vessel has been added to the carrier battle group, an attack ship tasked to retrieve you from the planet's surface on arrival, with the tactical situation permitting.'

'Understood, although I am unclear as to why we are conversing with your Clarified self rather than our illustrious superiors on Iseri.'

A faint smile crossed Dusorn's features.

'Negotiations with the traditionalist factions have reached a delicate stage,' he said. 'Our superiors are under pressure and also under close observation, therefore responsibility for your continuity has been passed to me.'

Teshak nodded. 'Respected Dusorn, am I correct in thinking that you are currently on board a vessel, one of your Suneye automata, perhaps?'

'Your perceptions overcome the limitations of our connection, diligent Teshak,' said Dusorn. 'I am indeed on the bridge of the Suneye implementation ship, *Edge*, and I am accompanied by another two craft, the *Hook* and the *Point*. We are in pursuit of a Vox Humana flotilla which is carrying the entire population of the Human enclave on Pyre, a clear-cut demonstration of plunder. As well as the loss of commercial assets, the abduction represents an issue of extreme political sensitivity, which is why we are tracking them down into hyperspace.'

From his niche of darkness, Kuros noticed open puzzlement on Teshak's face.

'But the Vox Humana do not possess hyperspace boundary technology.'

'True, but the Roug do.'

'Ah, so they are now openly interfering in our design. They could prove to be a serious obstacle.'

Dusorn's faint smile came and went once more. 'No need for concern. There is a plan, a long-overdue solution which will remove that flaw from the patterns of our design. In the meantime, the first stages of the conflict are proceeding on schedule. History drives the Imisil into our deadly arms, although it appears that their fleet will now arrive after the Hegemony carrier group, not before. The clash will still result in a Hegemony defeat: reports will prompt the Brolturans to enter the fray alongside advance elements of the Hegemony fleet, which will soon be joined by an Earthsphere adjunct. The remaining Imisil vessels will be thoroughly defeated, possibly obliterated. With no other alliances in this region, the Imisil Mergence will petition the other members of the Erenate to send a combined armada and will succeed.' Dusorn nodded. 'By which time the conclave of Tri-Advocates will realise that open war is certain to force major powers like the Milybi and the Indroma to actively oppose us. Withdrawal will be inevitable.'

'Defeat and dishonour, with a minimum damage to our military,' said Teshak. 'The multiclans, the families, the great throng of all Sendrukans will demand a change of administration and a new direction.'

'The pact with the traditionalists is expected to be signed in the next few hours,' said Dusorn. 'By the time our vessel arrives with the carrier group the news will have broken. Now I must end this discussion – new complexities in our pursuit demand my attention.'

'Thank you for the updates and elucidation,' Teshak said.

Dusorn gave a wordless nod and abruptly the holo-plane was empty. Teshak tapped a console control and the screen vanished as the encased communicator began to pack itself away.

The AI-controlled Sendrukans turned to face each other and for several unsettling moments Kuros shared Gratach's unflinching eye contact with the Clarified Teshak. At last Teshak relaxed slightly, nodded, and leaned forward.

'Utavess Kuros,' he said. 'I know that you can hear me. The valiant General Gratach assures me that your personality core is stable and aware of sight and sound. As you will have observed, the meticulous project of the Clarified takes another step towards its culmination. Soon the Hegemon's favourites will be deposed and out of the ruined dusk of their rule a new dawn shall rise; we will be in control and when a stronger Hegemony stands forth an age of glory shall begin. You will not survive to see it, of course, but your part will not go unremarked.'

As they laughed on their way out of the building, Kuros seethed with helpless fury. Yet a calmer part of him considered what he had learned and reasoned that war was the cradle of accidents and coincidences. Even the most meticulous of projects were bound to encounter factors of unpredictability.

8

KAO CHIH

From an oval window in the starboard lounge of the *Viteazul*, Kao Chih sat watching dull red starlight spill over the edge of a flat continent-sized habitat. Its orbit had carried it out of the gas giant's shadow and now a dirty crimson radiance was streaming over its surface, brightening the sides of hills and cliffs, buildings and motionless vehicles on transport lanes. The habitat's surface was desolate, airless and grey, most of its structures had eroded and collapsed into crumbling ruins, vehicles pitted by centuries of meteorites, the frozen ground covered with dust. There were another twenty-four of these colossal habitats, every one a lifeless sepulchre locked into an ancient orbit.

Any other time Kao Chih would have regarded these examples of macro-engineering with fascination. But they were the last remnants of a dead civilisation, desiccated remains buried deep in the decayed depths of hyperspace. All he could do for the time being was try to stave off a crushing anxiety about their current predicament.

Pursued by three Suneye warships, the Roug–Vox Humana flotilla with its Pyre passengers had fled down through the levels of hyperspace. Guided and protected by Roug technology, the flotilla managed to make a series of boundary jumps, varying their length with lateral, cross-tier directions, even making the occasional double-back up a level or two. But still the Suneye vessels managed to find them, relentlessly and without fail ...

Then the *Nestinar* suffered a major malfunction in its navigationals and the entire flotilla was forced to make an emergency boundary exit which landed them here in this tier of guttering stars, littered with the ruins of artificial worldlets. That had been less than an hour ago. Right now the five Marauder craft were engaged in a desperate rearguard fight against the three Suneye ships while the flotilla sought refuge among the gas giant's orbiting flock of entombed landscapes. Time was needed to repair the *Nestinar*'s systems, which on closer inspection turned out to have been sabotaged. And time was running out.

Kao Chih was dividing his attention between the view outside and a flatscreen hanging on a nearby partition. There were another half-dozen or so scattered around the big lounge, all showing the same feed to clustered groups of worried-looking Pyre colonists. It was the ongoing battle taking place halfway across the star system, realtime video streaming directly from the long-range sensors. There was no sound. The main picture followed the Vox Humana Marauders, switching between them as they swooped, looped and sideslipped, dodging enemy fire as they lined up for attack run after attack run.

Even before the sabotage on board the *Nestinar*, Kao

Chih had twice gone to the *Viteazul's* bridge to ask if there were any duties he could carry out and both times he was asked to return to the civilian zones. Soon after, access to the bridge and operations decks was restricted to crew only. It left him feeling helpless and disregarded, emotions he saw reflected in the faces around him. Decades of oppression would tend to ingrain a certain hopelessness, a fatalistic acceptance of bad fortune and undeserved punishment. Yet he recalled reports of how unarmed colonists had fought off the Va-Zla thugs during the evac. Hope and a route to freedom had helped them forget the habits of servitude in a moment.

But now everyone felt hunted, trapped. It came out in expressions and postures, eyes widening suddenly in shock or squeezed tight shut in fear, fingers pointing, quietly muttered curses. Kao Chih returned his gaze to the flatscreen and saw one of the Marauders caught in a tumbling trajectory, trailing swirls of gas while pulse cannon fire stitched bright, criss-cross lines against the blackness. Then the Marauder pilot regained control, throwing his craft into a series of evasive manoeuvres as a flock of enemy missiles converged.

The frame zoomed out to reveal the spread of the battle. The Marauders were small compared to the Suneye ships. It was like an aquavarium he once saw being unloaded at the underdocks of Agmedra'a, the Roug orbital – inside, two big almost-fish lurked torpidly at the bottom of the tank while smaller creatures darted around them, nibbling flecks snatched from the greater ones' tails and fins. In the half-minute between the offload and the exit to Cargo Staging he saw the big fish snare three of their parasites with bizarre tentacle-tongues.

Out there in the cold dark, the Marauders nimbly dodged volleys of enemy fire and missiles with such skill and bravado that Kao Chih felt like joining in the cheers that went up from time to time. Those Vox Humana boys could really fly. At the same time he wished he knew what was going on aboard the *Nestinar* and how close the repairs were to completion.

Then the inevitable happened. One of the Marauders evaded a trio of missiles only to be hit by a projector beam from one of the Suneye ships. It sheared off one of the port manoeuvring thrusters, sending it slewing round straight into the path of an oncoming missile. The craft vanished in a violent burst of white fire that dazzled the sensors for a moment. When the picture stabilised there was a glimpse of a glowing wreck amid an expanding cloud of debris. A despairing groan went around the lounge.

In the next instant the frame pulled back and panned across to one of the Suneye ships, which, oddly, was moving sideways. While the other two now redoubled their efforts against the remaining Marauders, this one seemed to be trying to distance itself ...

Abruptly, the ship disappeared. There was a collective gasp of amazement. Some colonists pointed, others leaned forward to study the screens, then a woman looking out of one of the oval ports cried out, 'It's here!'

With others pressing behind him, Kao Chih stared out – and up. The Suneye ship was there all right, perhaps a couple of hundred metres away but still moving sideways and rapidly closing on the *Viteazul*. Alarms began to sound and a sudden panic took hold.

'Enemy vessel on collision course!' said a voice over the PA. 'All passengers assume safety positions! Admiral Zhylinsky, please come to the bridge.'

Most of the colonists were crowded around the hatches leading to the ship's main spinal corridor, but Kao Chih was still at the oval window, fairly certain that he was in no immediate danger. Even though the Suneye ship was rushing side-on towards him. As he watched, shimmering, tapering beams sprang out from glints spaced along its smooth hull, maybe grappler fields of some kind, he guessed.

'This is First Officer Rosario – all crew and passengers brace for impact.'

The shock threw him off his chair to land on his shoulder, the impetus carrying him further, flipping him over. Dazed, he struggled to his feet. The lounge was a chaos of overturned furniture, fallen people and the cries of the wounded. As he watched, some chairs floated free of the floor and glided along for a few feet before banging back down again.

Deck gravity is losing coherence, he thought. *Is the enemy already aboard?*

Someone grabbed his arm. He was startled to see that it was Admiral Zhylinsky.

'Come with me,' he said. 'There's a security station above on Deck 7 midsection – we can pick up weapons and supplies there.'

'But sir, why not head for the bridge?'

'That's now the riskiest place to be – they'll shut it down before they subdue the colonists.' The admiral straightened suddenly, head cocked as if listening. 'It's gone quiet along the dorsal corridor. Quick, this way.'

The older man seemed possessed of an intense energy as he practically dragged Kao Chih to the other end of the lounge. Almost concealed by the low lighting and the textured, dark brown decor was a recess with a partially camouflaged door that opened to the admiral's thumbprint. Bead lamps winked on as they sidled along a narrow access passage. The air was warm and dry and smelled of oil and plastics and the admiral seemed to be quite familiar with the place. When Kao Chih asked about this, the admiral shrugged.

'I was captain of the *Viteazul* before my promotion to admiral. Relations with Earthsphere were still tense back then and we had to be ready if their agents attempted a hijacking or some kind of sabotage. So I got to know the less obvious ways around the ship, especially ones like this which allow access between the decks.'

Kao Chih smiled, jabbing his thumb upwards. 'To Deck 7.'

Zhylinsky nodded, clearly pleased at being able to show off his clandestine knowledge. 'I even had this maintenance passage extended and modified. It now has a ladder that comes up in the storage closet of Deck 7 security station!'

Several minutes later they were climbing out of a square hatch in the floor of a small room with box-stacked shelves. Kao Chih was helped up by a middle-aged female security officer, then a skinny youth in a grubby yellow onepiece handed him a paper cup of water.

'Good to see you, Sergeant,' said the admiral. 'Where's the rest of your team?'

'Sdanek and Iklos got shot by enemy drones deploying narcoleptics, sir,' said the woman. 'Combination of needle-darts and dispersal pellets. I was lucky to escape.'

'I see – and are we secure?'

'Sealed tight, sir, now that hatch is locked. Monitor network is still up and as far as I can tell the enemy is in control of both engineering and the bridge.'

'Good. Sergeant Miczek, this is Kao Chih, our liaison with the Pyre colonists and now a comrade in this time of need.' Zhylinsky gazed at the yellow-garbed youth. 'And who is this young man?'

'Erm ... Marko Degellis, sir, uh, Captain, um, assistant stores monitor.'

The admiral sternly shook his head. 'Marko, have you ever used a gun?'

'Only on a glowset, sir ...'

Zhylinsky smiled. 'Good reactions, then? I used to be pretty sharp in *Biokrysis*, you know, but that was a few years ago, of course. So, yes, we'll find you something useful in the arms locker, along with the body armour. Not going anywhere without *that*!'

The security station comprised two small rooms, one with heavy cabinets lining two of its facing walls, the other equipped with consoles and screens. The admiral led them in, seated himself in one of the two swivel chairs and brought the screens to life.

'I had subfeeds from all main monitor nodes routed here. We should be able to get both internal and external views.'

Two screens began to show a succession of images

from around the ship, views of people lying sprawled and unconscious in corridors down which glittering disc-shaped drones floated on patrol. Cabins and common areas were the same, as were the crew decks and the operations rooms. Smaller, arrowhead-like drones were also everywhere, mainly hovering. The subjugation of the *Viteazul* had been swift and efficient. Almost.

Yet Kao Chih could not see how they could do anything against such a numerous adversary. But he knew that inaction could only lead to the certainty of capture and imprisonment back on Pyre.

'I wonder what's been happening on the other ships,' he said quietly.

'The very question that has been vexing me,' the admiral said.

Just then their surroundings quivered and Kao Chih felt the telltale momentary dizziness of a hyperdrive jump. Marko staggered a little, Sergeant Miczek leaned against the bulkhead and the admiral sat straighter, eyes glaring.

'They've shifted us somewhere else,' he said, fingers suddenly flying over controls both solid and holo. 'Now we really do need access to the externals.'

One of the monitors switched to a view of the Suneye ship seen from a hull cam at the stern of the *Viteazul*. The grappler force-beams that Kao Chih saw earlier shone brightly now, a bizarre scaffolding of energies locking the two ships firmly in place, roughly twenty metres apart. In addition four opaque, fluted tubes stretched across to connect with the *Viteazul*'s flank. As they watched, several Suneye drones, the smaller fist-sized arrowheads, began gliding back to their mothership in pairs and threes. In moments this had become a constant stream, scores of arrowheads and the larger discs returning to the Suneye vessel. Studying this, the admiral nodded.

'To be expected,' he said. 'Now that we're effectively crewless and the colonists have been sedated, it's safe for them to cast us adrift and return to the battle. Once that's satisfactorily concluded they can come back to collect us. There, see?'

With the last of the drones back aboard, the Suneye vessel began to retract the boarding tubes. Kao Chih gazed at the sight, impatient to do something, purposefully ignoring futility.

'Admiral, sir,' he said. 'Please excuse my lack of technical knowledge, but is it possible for even we four to reactivate your ship's engines so that we may not be here when they return?'

'I admire your spirit, Pilot Kao, but it is very likely that the control systems have been disabled.' Then he gave a toothy grin. 'But that won't stop us trying! We'll wait until . . .'

'Sir,' said Sergeant Miczek. 'The tubes are extending again.'

The access tubes had been detaching and retracting one by one, but now they were extending out again.

'Something's happened to change their mind,' the admiral said. 'Ah, look – there!'

A small craft darted into view, weaving in and out of the access tubes and grappler beams. As it raked the hulls of both ships with volleys of greenish energy bolts, the admiral's sensor systems grabbed images from hull feeds and presented a tactical composite. The attacking craft had a bullet-shaped aft section ending in a pyramidal thrust assembly; the forward section had the look of a tapering cockpit in an oddly textured grey material, flanked left and right, above and below, by four curved weapon sponsons. And the newcomer had not come alone.

'The drones are coming back,' said Marko, voice wavering.

'Not so many this time,' Kao Chih observed.

'Either they expect these unknown attackers to try and board us as well,' the admiral said, 'or ...'

The security station shivered and the screens flickered as one into a spiral standby symbol. A second or two later the external feed came back on – the Suneye ship, its boarding tubes and grapples, was still there but beyond they could see a wide segment of landscape with ragged edges, its surface made grey by millennia of exposure to hard vacuum. They had jumped back to the gas giant in the red dwarf system, only now they were on the other side, away from the fighting.

'They brought us back,' said the admiral, smiling.

'So we've a chance of being rescued,' said Marko.

'Only if we can stop these Suneye bandits from towing us off to their prison.' The admiral got up, went to one of the cabinets and opened it. Tough but flexible body armour was handed round, jackets and leggings, and goggled face protectors. All of it had a silky black sheen.

'Sabotage,' the admiral said. 'We fight our way onto their ship, find some important-looking systems and set a few shaped T9 charges. Oh, and slap a few on those boarding tubes as well. Sergeant, how would you rate our chances?'

Miczek squinted back at the screens. 'Far fewer drones patrolling our corridors than before, sir. I'd give good odds on reaching their ship.'

The admiral grinned and broke out the weaponry.

Kao Chih, though, felt that the admiral was being less than candid about encountering the Suneye drones. Might they not have something more powerful than darts to fire? And could there be other lethal counter-measures hidden in ceilings and bulkheads?

Kao Chih was passed a beam pistol: cased in some lightweight alloy and coloured white and blue, it looked and felt like a toy.

'Don't be deceived by the lightness,' said Sergeant Miczek as she gave an identical one to Marko. 'These are droptroop issue, a redesigned model with a twenty per cent range improvement over the previous mark.'

'We'll divide into two teams,' said the admiral. 'Young Marko will stay with the sergeant, keep his wits about him and follow orders, understood?'

Marko grinned nervously and bobbed his head.

'Kao Chih,' Zhylinsky went on. 'You're with me. Let's teach those Suneye machines a thing or two, eh?' He pointed at one of the screens, which showed that the *Viteazul* was being hauled on a course leading around the gas giant towards the vicinity of the Roug–Vox Humana flotilla. 'Time is limited. Let us be on our way.'

Via more maintenance passages, communal rooms and underfloor crawlways they reached a medstation near the sternmost of the boarding tubes in ten minutes or so. Once the sole patrolling disc-drone had passed by on its way along the dorsal corridor, the admiral led them out along the passageway. He used a local hatch override to lock all the nearby hatches, sealing off that particular corridor junction. Then they approached the oval opening in the ship's hull. Silver-green hooks curved round the edges of it, their tips sunk into the bulkhead metal. Beyond, the opaque conduit waited, undulating slightly.

'Should be zero-gee along this stretch,' the admiral warned, readying his short-bodied beam rifle before ducking through.

Kao Chih watched in admiration as the older man kicked off from the rim of the sealing ring and gracefully glided up the tube. He recalled his own experiences with weightlessness on board Blacknest Station and mentally prepared himself for a display of oafish clumsiness. But his performance turned out to be adequate, with one or two bumps along the way. Sergeant Miczek arrived a moment later with Marko tethered to her waist.

'And here we are,' said the admiral. 'Not exactly constructed on a Human scale but I'm sure we'll manage.'

They crouched together in a spherical space about ten metres across with an artificial gravity noticeably lower than the *Viteazul*'s. Although there was no main light source, most of the odd-shaped panels gave off some radiance, mainly from the glowing threadlike lines that were laid out in an angular network all across the curved surface. Several octagonal tunnels led off at a variety of angles and as they crouched there Kao Chih began to wonder why their presence had not provoked a response. Then Zhylinsky, who had been hunched over a small device, looked up.

'In case you're wondering why there's been no welcoming committee, it would seem that those unknown interceptors have followed us here, so most of the Suneye drones are out there fending them off.'

He held up a datapad with a foldout screen, and they leaned closer to see. There were perhaps a dozen of the bullet-shaped craft diving past and between the larger ships, pursued by flocks of silvery drones, both arrowheads and discs. As they studied the images, the Suneye vessel shuddered for a second.

The admiral tapped a control and the picture swung up and zoomed in on a mysterious ship keeping pace over 300 kiloms astern. Magnification brought it closer, revealing shining surfaces and a strangeness of design that provoked a certain unease in Kao Chih. The ship was large, easily twice the size of the *Viteazul*, and had a diamond-shaped profile, its prow one of the acute vertices. The flanks of the deep hull angled inwards and had lines of bulbous grey protrusions spaced all along them – when one of them irised open and an interceptor flew out their function was immediately apparent.

This was a carrier, Kao Chih realised, a capital ship that had seen combat, going by the scorching and impact gouges that marred the glittering ornamentation in many places. The upper hull had tower structures at all four corners and one amidships: the starboard one was a torn and blasted ruin while the one at the prow had a Y-shaped mast jutting up from it.

'The source of our captors' woes?' Kao Chih said, just as the Suneye ship lurched.

'Soon to be joined by sabotage closer to home,' the admiral said, patting his bandolier of charges draped across his chest. 'Now – Sergeant, you and young Marko will hold this junction while Kao Chih and I venture off in search of drives and generators.'

'Yes, sir,' said Miczek.

'Excellent,' Zhylinsky said, glancing at Kao Chih, who nodded and followed him down a narrow passage lit by brightly glowing red, yellow and blue lines. The passage was low, forcing them to move at a crouch with the admiral pausing frequently to consult his datapad's sensor readings. As they progressed, Kao Chih tried to imagine how he might describe these events in a letter to his parents back on the *Retributor* – *Dear Mother and Father: In the course of the evacuation and escape from Pyre, we engaged our pursuers in battle and I found myself taking part in an assault on one of the enemy ships. I and three others against hundreds of armed machines …*

After several minutes the passage curved up and opened out into a small, polyhedral compartment. Every corner was occupied by a strange plinth whose apex was a bulbous, translucent screen that pulsed with symbols and flickered with triangular ripples of data.

'Control nodes, Pilot Kao,' said the admiral. 'Eight of them. Destroy these and the whole ship would be crippled …'

'Your damage assessment is correct, Admiral,' said a clear voice from all around them. 'But since our ships can retask functions easily to other locations, this vessel would be crippled for less than a minute.'

The hairs stood up on Kao Chih's neck. The admiral bared his teeth in an angry grimace.

'And you are?' he said.

'The Clarified Sevayr, commander of this vessel.'

'So naturally you are an accurate and trustworthy source of information,' the admiral said. 'Forgive me if I am unconvinced by your proclamation.'

'Forgiveness is not in my nature,' said the voice of the Clarified Sevayr. 'However, punishment is.'

A twin-muzzled turret popped out of an opening in the wall and fired four energy bolts in quick succession. The admiral cried out and fell to the floor. Kao Chih snapped off one shot in return but missed as the turret disappeared. Then he knelt to examine the admiral's wounds, which turned out to be chillingly accurate and cruel – the bolts had struck both hands and both feet, rendering him helpless. As Kao Chih pulled a medkit from one of his waist pouches, the admiral insisted on giving him orders, voice a strangled whisper.

'Use the charges ... set timer with the left tab, arm with ... the right ... ah, that's better ... not so sore ...'

Kao Chih had found some painkiller dermals and pressed them onto the admiral's throat. Then it was a case of dragging him back down the passageway to the junction, all the time waiting for the searing stab of an energy bolt ...

Then the junction came into sight and his heart sank – there was no one to be seen. Gasping, arms aching, he struggled with the admiral's weight and as he drew nearer he could see a dark form lying motionless off to the side.

'Is the sergeant there, lad?' said the admiral. 'She should be helping you – Sergeant!'

As he pulled the admiral into the spherical junction,

Kao Chih saw that it was indeed the sergeant lying dead on the floor. Of Marko there seemed to be no sign.

'The sergeant had to die, of course,' said the voice of the Clarified, suddenly. 'She was actually quite competent and thus presented a genuine threat.'

Kao Chih noticed the charred, twisted wreckage of a few drones as he went to check the sergeant's body. Her face protector was missing and there was a small black cauterised hole in her forehead. Squatting there, he rocked back on his heels, rubbed his face and tried to find a calm path between fear and anger. There didn't seem to be one.

'Admiral,' he said. 'The sergeant's dead.'

'Murdered,' the older man muttered. 'By a coward who hides himself.'

'I'll have to get you back to the *Viteazul*,' Kao Chih said, moving over to lift the admiral under the arms.

'No, I'm not important,' Zhylinsky said. 'Leave me here – go and place those charges – damn you, that's an order!'

'With respect, sir,' Kao Chih said. 'I am not under your—'

There was a flash and the crack of an energy bolt striking the curved wall. Kao Chih ducked and glanced down the boarding tube to see Marko clutching his beam pistol, eyes wide with fear as he floated in the zero-gee.

'Please, Marko,' he said carefully. 'Will you help me with the admiral? – he's hurt ...'

Trembling with anxiety, Marko swallowed and put away the weapon. 'There was firing ... and she was dead ... I didn't hit anything ...'

Kao Chih got the admiral into the boarding tube, not responding to the older man's pleas. When Marko joined them, Kao Chih reached for the admiral's bandolier of charges, unclipped it and tugged it out from under his chest armour.

'Good man,' the admiral whispered.

Outside the weightless opaque tube, the mysterious attack craft danced and darted past, exchanging volleys of bright spikes with pursuing flocks of silver drones. And it occurred to Kao Chih that if the unknown attackers had wanted to they could have destroyed both ships by now.

Together the two men guided the wounded admiral up the connecting tube. Halfway, Kao Chih paused and pulled one of the shaped charges from the belt, showing it to Marko.

'I'm going back to finish this job,' he said, fingering the charge timer. 'I've set this for seven minutes – as soon as I'm out of sight, stick this on the tube wall and arm it with *this* button. Got it?'

'But is seven minutes long enough?'

'I sincerely hope that it will be more than enough. I'm looking forward to retelling this story under the influence of strong alcohol.'

He slung the bandolier across shoulder and chest and pushed away on a return glide to the Suneye vessel. Re-entering the spherical junction, he became heavy again, and the voice spoke.

'Back so soon, Human? Apparently my punishment examples were not sufficiently persuasive.'

Having noted the position of the sergeant's body and the similarity of her wounds to those suffered by the admiral, Kao Chih was ready. When an overhead section slid open and the anti-personnel turret popped out he was already moving and firing. His first shot burned a glowing gouge across curved panels. The second struck a spray of sparks from the turret mounting, the third hit home and it burst apart in a flash of wrecked components. Another turret opened up from just inside a passage leading forward, forcing Kao Chih to back away behind the boarding tube's oval hatch. His hand found the sergeant's dropped beam pistol and with twice the firepower he was able to quickly neutralise the turret.

There was an abrupt silence, no measured voice offering sarcastic commentary. Perhaps their host was otherwise occupied, he thought.

The curved deck lurched violently underfoot and a grinding crash reverberated throughout the ship. *I'm running out of time*, he thought suddenly and scrambled back along the aftward passage, alert for more security turrets. He planted several charges down the stretch leading to the compartment where the admiral was shot then retraced his steps, arming the devices as he went. Kicking aside still smoking pieces of drone, he then ventured up the forward passage, setting and arming another eight charges before returning to the hatch area. Kao Chih still had a handful left so he climbed up into a wide but low passage and crawled along it, pausing after a dozen metres or so. He had just fixed the last charge in place when he heard a loud bang and felt air start rushing past him, back the way he'd come.

The charge I gave to Marko, he thought. *He must have set the timer too soon ...*

In the next instant an armoured divider slammed down, cutting him off from the decompression source but trapping him in with several devices now primed to detonate in minutes. If there was a disabling procedure the admiral hadn't told him and he never thought to ask – his only option was to follow the low passage to its end and hope that he could get behind a hatch strong enough to withstand the explosion. On hands and knees he scrambled madly along, turned a corner and found himself facing an abrupt end. Then he realised that there was a long gap above his head which was high enough for him to stand up.

The moment he did so, immensely strong hands grabbed him from behind and bodily hauled him up onto some kind of platform. He'd hardly begun to take in his surroundings when a bag was roughly tugged over his head. Kao Chih's cries of surprise turned into angry shouts as he was spun round and hurried off. Moments later he heard a hatch close and pressurise and seconds later multiple thuds. The deck shook underfoot and his captors staggered as they marched him along. There was another lurch and Kao Chih swung a kick round, knocking the legs out from under one of them. Bellows of fury rang out as he used his free hands to try and wrench free of the other's grip.

But a clenched fist dealt his head a blow that made his ears ring and his senses spin. Tripping, he fell to his knees. Someone grabbed both his forearms with hands that were bony and rough-skinned – it was like being seized by fingers made of old boot leather – and bound his wrists with plastic stripping. A voice muttered in his ear, hoarse, incomprehensible words, then he was hauled upright. A corrupt mustiness filled his nostrils. Another voice spoke, same hoarse, dry sound but with a different tone, to which the first replied.

And in his head, the linguistic enabler that Tumakri had given him weeks ago began picking apart the syllables, matching grammar patterns, running definitional comparisons, and eventually feeding something intelligible into his auditory centres.

'... bad fate, hear you me, cracked fortune. For we to attack the hull of devices before the life-ripe one ...'

'Your fate, your fortune – whispers from the ash, all is ...'

'You say? See Old Irontooth when we bring him this one – with the other one, makes only two from whole hull. Very poor, bad fate ...'

Listening to this exchange, Kao Chih experienced a shiver of déjà vu that sent him back to memories of his capture at Blacknest Station by the minions of Munaak, the gangster lord who murdered Tumakri. He wondered if there was any point in offering up prayers to his ancestors.

Honourable forebears, if it pleases you to extend deliverance to this humble and unworthy descendant, would it be possible to provide it via someone reliable, be they mechanical or organic?

A hatch slid open to admit them, sighed shut behind them. Kao Chih was steered forward several paces, stopped, turned, then pushed back to drop into a hard chair. The wristcuffs were removed but then his wrists were bound separately to the chair arms while his ankles were restrained. Only then was the hood removed.

The room wasn't very bright yet it took Kao Chih's

eyes a moment or two to adjust. Illumination came from
the same coloured thread clusters that he had seen elsewhere on the Suneye ship. But it was the sight of a
Sendrukan, similarly chair-bound and facing him from a
couple of metres away, that grabbed his attention.

'Ah, the admiral's disciple. You proved more competent than I originally anticipated. Perhaps I should have
killed you first.'

The facing chairs were placed in some kind of alcove
next to a raised platform walkway. The Clarified
Sendrukan wore a close-fitting green uniform with blue
highlights. Kao Chih saw that additional restraints held
chest, waist and head in place. He did not know what
the Clarified meant, but he was ready with a rejoinder.

'In one's fondest imaginings,' he said, 'one may wish
for much, only to find that reality is somewhat unac-
commodating.'

'Impertinence,' murmured the Sendrukan. 'How tire-
some.' He looked up to a point behind and above Kao
Chih. 'Lord-General, I'm afraid that it is time I was leaving. Would you have my shuttle made ready?'

'You are ours now,' came a dry, raspy voice that
spoke with calm deliberation. 'Upon your re-emergence
from the caul you will cherish the way of dust and treas-
ure the chains of obedience.'

The Sendrukan grinned widely. 'I fear that you are
mistaken.' As he tipped his head back, dark lines
appeared on his neck, extending up the sides of his head
to his hairless scalp. Kao Chih's curious stare turned to
one of horror as the dark lines began to smoke and a
dull redness glowed through the charring flesh. Small
tremors in the Sendrukan's limbs quickly became

convulsive spasms, and a nauseating smell filled the air.

The grotesque display ended with a prolonged moment of locked muscles before something gave and the Sendrukan slumped slightly in the chair, muscles now relaxed, wisps of smoke or steam rising from blackened eyes and mouth. A bulky humanoid form swathed in dark robes trudged into view, went up to the body and with odd thick fingers examined and prodded it. A flexible probelike device was produced to test the mouth and ears.

'Death, High One,' the examiner pronounced. 'As predicted.'

'Wheel it over to the *Bonecarrier*. Have the Caulmaster scrape its mindflesh for any vestiges.'

The robed figure tipped the dead Sendrukan's chair back on wheels Kao Chih hadn't noticed before, and pushed it away. Heavy footsteps began on the platform behind him, moved round and approached from the left. An imposing figure came into view, a tall man clad head to foot in a strange grey armour, the one whom the Sendrukan had called Lord-General. At first glance the whole assemblage appeared thoroughly archaic, like something from Earth history, from medieval Europa. But a closer look revealed telling details: the bulky, segmented breastplate was attached to the backplate with what seemed to be leather straps, as were the arm and leg armour sections. And in the shadowy gaps between Kao Chih could see gleaming machine parts and flexing spirals of shielded cabling.

From atop a thick neck, a long, thin, almost cadaverous face regarded him. There was a slight ridge of a nose ending in a pair of slits over the lipless, expressionless mouth. The skin was ash-pale and had an odd sheen to it, just like the large, bare hands. A straight-sided helmet enclosed the head, with two spiky adornments jutting up from either temple. The eyes stared out from sunken sockets and Kao Chih thought he saw a mournful sadness in them. For a moment.

'Another Human,' said the Lord-General. 'My hearkeners tell me that there are thousands of your kind aboard those other ships, the ones that fled. Is this true?'

Kao Chih offered up a silent prayer to his honourable ancestors before answering.

'Regrettably, I can neither confirm or deny such matters,' he said. 'I spent most of my time in my stateroom playing tri-chess ...'

'Your defiance earns you no honour.' Those big, ash-grey hands clenched. 'Hear me – I am Lord-General Zhyrac of the Shyntanil Twice-Born, commander of the Stone Breath regiment, overcaptain of the warcraft *Bonecarrier*. You are ours now. Soon you will be placed in the caul, where your heart will be stopped, your blood cooled, and your mindflesh silenced. Upon your re-emergence you will know the way of dust and understand the beauty of obedience.'

He raised a hand and two shorter figures in similar dark grey armour appeared.

'Take this over to the *Bonecarrier*, and to the caul – my command is this.'

As the Shyntanil converged on his chair, Kao Chih smelled their mustiness again, only now the corrupt taint seemed stronger and redolent of putrefaction. Dread settled over him like a deadening chill as they wheeled him away.

9

LEGION

From a low grey sky a steady drizzle was falling on Giant's Shoulder, the jutting promontory whose sheer-sided presence dominated the coastal country west of Port Gagarin. Up on its flat summit, the rain spatter-darkened the remaining masonry of the ancient Uvovo temple, pooled on the flagstones and soaked still further the compacted wreckage of the prefab huts that used to stand nearby. Now a large Brolturan facility, its walls a dark, shiny green, stood near the narrow end of the promontory. Beneath it was an immense trench that sloped down to the entrance to the anteroom leading to the warpwell chamber, where analytic mechs monitored the well's energy profile. It was five days since the Legion Knight's scion pair had plunged into the reacti-vated warpwell's bright maw: the first set off a device which reversed the well's gravitic flow, allowing the second to plunge in and attempt to survive the terrify-ing descent down through hundreds of layers of hyperspace to that tormenting prison at its very nadir. Initial estimates gave a journey time of between two and three days, and thus a period of four to six days before the first cyborg warriors of the Legion actually emerged on the surface of Darien, the harbingers of a new age.

Five days of waiting. To the Legion Knight they had seemed interminable.

<Yet wait I shall. I have surmounted daunting obstacles, survived perilous setbacks, faced danger and prevailed. I have seized the commanding heights, I have the autofactory and an army of combat mechs and an impregnable position. Such successes are a vindication of the principles of convergence, and a mere foretaste of what is to come. When the Legion returns, victory will be a foregone conclusion. Patience is all that I require>

Yet patience eluded him. He examined the feeds from the in-flight surveillance drones currently scanning areas of the coastal region from high-altitude trajectories. These flyers were a recent development born out of a need to regain a strategic edge due to the increased effectiveness of the Human irregulars. Less than a day after he had taken control of Giant's Shoulder his sensors picked up a ship entering orbit, then a smaller craft descending to land somewhere in the mountains to the west. Since then, the Human rebels had carried out several attacks against his lookout positions and patrols, resulting in the destruction or disabling of nearly a dozen combat mechs. The new flyers were designed to scan the vicinity of Giant's Shoulder, watch for anomalies and to track any visible creatures. Abrupt changes in their location could indicate the presence of Humans.

And since the Brolturan defence batteries were operational and linked to a cluster of sensor nodes, those flyers were in no danger. After the shuttle's descent four days ago, the main vessel had shifted its orbit well south of the Human colony. The skies were clear of threats, yet near space was not. Sensor data from last night revealed that a battle involving four vessels had taken place beyond high orbit and ranged over a considerable area. One was the ship that had dropped off the shuttle, while the other three were unknown. The sensors did record a sharp burst of energies after the conflict strayed away to an occluded quarter of the night sky, and from fragmentary comm signals the Legion Knight deduced that the energies came from the destruction of an Ezgara mercenary ship. And that two of the other vessels were from the Imisil Mergence.

<So the Imisil have allowed themselves to be drawn into direct confrontation with the Hegemony. When the full might of the Legion of Avatars erupts from the warpwell and begins filling up the night with their glittering ranks, perhaps those bitter enemies will find themselves forced to band together against us, like walls of mud against a tide of steel. Defeat will follow defeat for them and soon they will realise the futility of opposing us. Convergence works with us, its rich inexorable strength is ours. We can only triumph>

Resting within the armoured autofactory, the Legion Knight felt reassured by his thoughts, even though he knew that the future was always in flux. Even though the loss of his two scions to the warpwell had diminished and eroded his cognitive/conjectural capacity, now placed under increased strain by demanding thought processes. The autofactory had repaired and enhanced the physical shell of his existence, as well as its innumerable systems, but his neural pathways bore the scars of passing time, the entropy of millennia wearing away the underpinnings of his mind, atom by atom.

<But with the return of the Legion will come my renewal and rejuvenation. The revitalators will know how to make my neural substrate regrow and replenish itself>

A priority alert interrupted the current of his thoughts, an urgent update from the surveillance flyer feeds. Unit 8 had been scanning the forest and wooded hills north-west of Giant's Shoulder – overlapping passes revealed the presence of an indeterminate number of Humans moving in single file northwards, tending east. Projections indicated that possible destinations included any of the Spiral zealot garrisons which were holding down the northern coastal area.

Now data was arriving from ground remotes in the vicinity, confirming that the insurgents numbered over sixty and that several were carrying sophisticated energy weapons. Their heading would take them through or past one of the Uvovo transplanted species reserves, or so-called daughter-forests. That was a good place for an ambush, the Legion Knight decided. He would immediately dispatch a force of twenty-five combat droids, and also send the two wire-null augments, the Human and the Uvovo he had captured before the seizure of Giant's Shoulder. For a few days their response indoctrination had failed to embed properly, although the Human had almost persuaded the pilot of one of those primitive airbag craft to descend into a trap.

Since then, however, they had shown marked improvement to the point where field trials were necessary. An ambush would be prepared and when the

Humans entered its ambit the two wire-nulls would approach them, pretending to be escapees. Soon after they would use their weapons to start killing the Humans – that would be the signal for the combat mechs to close in.

The plan was satisfactory. He gave the orders and as a sudden ferment of activity stirred the shining ranks of machines he turned his attention back to the sensor clusters and their continual scanning of local airspace, as well as near-orbit and beyond. The Imisil ships seemed to have left, while the destroyed Ezgara vessel added its own portion to the clouds of debris already swinging around Darien, causing significant showers of shooting stars.

And since the Hegemony took great exception to the destruction of its and its allies' ships, its response would be swift, decisive and very violent. Would any Imisil vessel return before then and provide him with an entertaining prelude to the arrival of the Legion of Avatars?

10

THEO

It was the shaking and the jolting that brought him round, along with a dull throbbing headache which, perversely, sharpened as he emerged into full wakefulness. Other sensations began making themselves known, his legs and arms which he couldn't move, the complete inky blackness that greeted his open eyes, and the voice mumbling nearby.

Drowsy thoughts suddenly clicked together. His ankles and wrists were bound and there was a bag over his head. And the owner of the mumbling mouth also appeared to be the driver of the wheelbarrow in which he was a passenger.

How in all the hells did I end up in this ...

Then in a rush it came back to him.

Once the coordinates for Greg's location on Nivyesta had been sent to Gideon's ship, Theo was on his way to his quarters to pack his gear when he was stopped by Strogalev, a trapper from Tangenberg. Strogalev said that he'd found an unusual Brolt device on the way to Tusk Mountain but couldn't figure out if it was a weapon or what, and asked Theo if he would take a look. Theo was determined to be ready when the raiding party left – he wasn't going to let Vashutkin out of his sight – but Strogalev's tale snagged his curiosity so along he went to the man's cubby room where someone clubbed him over the head, knocking him out.

Like some green cadet with his mother's ribbon in his inside pocket, he thought. *How could I just walk into that and not realise . . .*

The barrow juddered as it passed over stones then tilted back to negotiate an incline of some kind. Theo heard the rustle of undergrowth brushing against the sides, and the soft sound of plant stalks breaking. The air was cold and damp, and he could smell a mingling of foliage and bark. They had brought him to one of the wooded gorges or narrow vales that led through the foothills to the Forest of Arawn. It could only be for one reason.

They. He was sure that there were more than one, sure that he'd heard another rhythm of footfalls.

'Stop,' said a man's voice from in front. 'Stop – there!'

The man pushing the barrow stopped. Theo heard a steady mutter from him, low and semi-audible.

'Turn left, no, to the left – is correct. Now continue further along.'

The shaking, lurching progress resumed. The other voice belonged to Strogalev, Theo was certain of it. Strogalev was a recent arrival yet Theo had seen him in Vashutkin's company several times, usually when Vashutkin's supporters were not around.

Until three days ago his uncertainty about the Rus politician had rested only on intuitive suspicion, nothing more. He had heard Vashutkin's account of the perilous mission to Giant's Shoulder, the battle against the rogue combat mechs, how the Zyradin helped Greg survive the onslaught, then how Greg made it to the Brolturans' fortification and took a lift down to the warpwell. Or so Vashutkin reckoned. The Rus escaped the main force of mechs by descending the southern face of Giant's Shoulder to a natural recess in the rock from which he was rescued by the zeplin *Har* not long after.

Everyone who heard it marvelled at the bravery and good fortune of those involved and was impressed by Vashutkin's modesty and charisma. But Theo remained ... uncertain. He had listened with the rest, took in the same dramatic tale and found himself unconvinced. He had wondered if it stemmed from the fact that he simply didn't like the man (or did his dislike stem from his distrust?). In any case, this nebulous suspicion had hung over Theo's thoughts, neither intensifying nor dispersing until three days ago when he was approached by a Uvovo scholar, one of Chel's secretive Artificers.

The Uvovo, whose name was Jofik, had asked Theo if Vashutkin suffered from any kind of mental illness, or perhaps some physical condition that would affect his personality. Mystified but intrigued, he had said he knew nothing about the man's health or state of mind. Jofik had accepted this with a nod and seemed to consider it for a moment before explaining.

Some other Uvovo, he told Theo, had noticed oddities in Mr Vashutkin's behaviour since his arrival at Tusk Mountain. Most Uvovo were curious to some degree about what Humans did and why, and a couple of chance observations of Mr Vashutkin had revealed an unusual trait. Nearly all Human faces, Jofik went on, were expressive of their thoughts, even when asleep. Mr Vashutkin's face was strangely blank, though only when alone or asleep – when someone came to see him his features changed completely and were full of expression, only to lapse into slack blankness once he was alone again. And this was accompanied by long periods of inactivity, of him just sitting doing nothing.

Theo had been troubled by this. After returning from space, he had heard from one of the surviving Diehards about what the Hegemony ambassador had done to Greg during that brief incarceration, how he had been dosed with some offworld drug which loosened his tongue and turned him into a docile servant. Luckily, after Greg's rescue, the Uvovo Chel had used strange forest roots to clean the drug out of his system. And after hearing Jofik's account Theo started to wonder if the same thing had been done to Vashutkin. While speculating, he also found himself imagining the very worst possibility, that Greg's body was lying among the jagged rocks at the base of Giant's Shoulder.

Then yesterday came the news that the Forerunner platform down in the Hall of Discourse had apparently reactivated itself, and a grim anxiety had sent him straight there. Jofik had gone with him, insisting that if communication with Nivyesta was possible then perhaps they could find out if Greg had actually made it safely to the moon. Once he was there, he found himself in a dialogue with a voice claiming to be that of the Zyradin entity (Theo had heard the tale of Robert Horst's appearance, mortally wounded, carrying the Zyradin container). Although it was less a dialogue than the bodiless being delivering a set of coordinates and the command that the Tygran ship be sent to pick up Greg at a specific time the next day.

And that was today, which was also the day of the assault on the northern Spiral garrisons. Theo had persuaded Captain Gideon to let him tag along and had looked forward to hearing the news of Greg's safe retrieval via the Tygran's field commset.

Instead here he was, bound and hooded, being wheeled into the wild to be shot in some secluded spot. He doubted very much that they were going to keep him prisoner.

Sorry, Greg, sorry, Rory, I should have been more careful. Sorry, Solvjeg, looks like I'll not be coming home with my shield after all ...

Roughly ten minutes later Strogalev ordered a halt then told the other man to get Theo out of the wheelbarrow. After some clumsy manhandling he ended up sitting on damp, lumpy ground with his back against what felt like a tree trunk. The hood came off and he saw that they were slightly upslope from a shallow stream, and deep within dense forest. The humid dimness was relieved by the profuse clumps of glowing roots or insects clinging to trees and webs of vines, while the coin-shaped leaves of a nearby nighteye plant gave off a pale, milky radiance. Some creature high up in the canopy uttered a soft whooping call and insects swooped and spun, creaked and hummed.

Strogalev was standing beside the nameless mumbling man, showing him how to use a long-barrelled handgun. Seeing how difficult this was proving, Theo decided to do some stress-testing.

'So what am I having for my last meal?' he said. 'Baro steak would be nice, maybe washed down with some Black Mountainside ale, eh?'

Strogalev gave him a dark look but continued trying to get the other man to understand his instructions.

Theo shrugged. 'Hey, well. Condemned man, he is supposed to be allowed a final request, you know ...'

No response.

'How about a pipe? Do you have a pipe and some tobacco? Or even a cigarette would do.'

Nothing.

'Well, do you have some pen and paper? – I said, *do you have any* ...'

Strogalev's head snapped round, fury in his face.

'I heard you! And no, there is no pipes or cigarettes or pen or paper so shut your mouth!'

'Shame, that. I really want to make up my last will ...'

'Okay, okay, now I'm going to shut you up!' Strogalev gestured at the other man, who was holding the gun in both hands. 'Do it now – shoot him dead.'

The other man, who was wearing only a shirt and trousers, stumbled forward, waxy face slack, the eyes full of confusion, outstretched hands holding the gun. The mouth worked, muttering, 'Kill him, shoot him, pull the trigger, just pull it, fire the gun, shoot him.' Then he slowed, the arms lowering, the mouth gaping in a soundless cry, eyes spilling tears as he began shaking his head. Strogalev uttered an angry curse, wrenched the gun out of the strange man's fingers and from about ten feet raised and aimed it at Theo's head. Theo stared back at him.

Strogalev spat on the ground. 'Couldn't keep your mouth shut, could ...'

Theo was on the point of desperately throwing himself sideways when a shot rang out, blood sprayed from Strogalev's right temple and he spun and sprawled on the grassy slope. Theo stared at the corpse for a frozen second before looking across the stream, searching the undergrowth for signs of the shooter. For a moment he thought he saw a form ducking behind curtains of greenery, then he heard movement from nearby. Looking back, he saw the other man sitting next to Strogalev with the gun in his hand once more.

There were footsteps behind him, rustle of grass, a hand on his shoulder. He glanced and was amazed to see his sister, Solvjeg, crouching down next to him. She forestalled his first words with a finger raised to her lips then pointed. Theo looked round and saw a man in dark hunter greens approaching with a rifle aimed at the man sitting by Strogalev's body. Still muttering to himself, the man suddenly put the gun down. Solvjeg meanwhile had severed the bonds at Theo's wrists and gave him a short knife with which he freed his ankles. The man with the rifle drew nearer, still holding it on the mumbling man. He wore a black woollen cap and had several days of stubble but Theo suddenly recognised him – it was Ian Cameron, his nephew and Greg's older brother.

'Nice to see you again, Ian,' he said.

'Aye, likewise, Uncle ...'

Then the man picked up the gun again. Holding it two-handed with the barrel dipping, his intense, panicky gaze switched back and forth between Theo and Ian.

'Put down the gun,' said Ian. 'Put it down and move away.'

'Easy, it's easy, shoot him, pull it, easy ... not easy, not good, not right, don't pull the trigger, don't shoot ...' The gun was being lowered shakily to the grassy ground. '... it is easy, it is good, the right thing, pull the trigger, good and easy, shoot him, kill him ...' Fingers tightened and the gun came back up again.

'If you don't put it down,' said Ian levelly, 'I will shoot and kill you.'

The man looked up at him, suddenly cold and focused.

'You may not. Only I am permitted.'

Before anyone could react, the man jammed the barrel under his chin and pulled the trigger. The report was loud and a sickening gout of gore sprayed the undergrowth behind him. The bullet's impact knocked him onto his back. Ian lowered his weapon, walked over and crouched between the two bodies. To Theo's surprise, Solvjeg went to join him and displayed no signs of squeamishness.

Well, now, sister, what's happened to you in the last few weeks?

Moving to peer over their shoulders, Theo saw that Ian was ignoring Strogalev and instead examining the suicider's corpse, prodding the skin around the neck and shoulders, then chest and back. After a few minutes of this Ian straightened, frowning.

'No sign of any implant,' he said.

'But the behaviour is the same,' said Solvjeg. 'There was control, and he was fighting it throughout.'

Ian shrugged. 'No implants or grafts as far as I can

see without an autopsy. If he was under control then it was something different.'

'Would anyone care to explain this to me?' Theo said.

Solvjeg stood and laid a hand on his shoulder. 'Of course, Theo, I'm sorry.'

He smiled at her. 'You look too grim, sister, which means that the meaning of this is grim enough to suit the times, eh?'

'That is putting it mildly,' she said.

'Back in the Eastern Towns,' Ian said, 'we had discovered a few spies working for the Brolts, unscrupulous backwoodsmen usually. Then we cornered one who died in a shootout and when he was autopsied the surgeon found webs of fine wiring running from subdermal implants to the brain stem and the optic centres. We had never seen anything like this before, and we guessed that the Brolts had wired them up as intelligence gatherers.'

'A couple of days ago,' Solvjeg said, 'we heard that a bomb went off at a boatyard in Byelygavan, killing four people and almost destroying the yard. They found a body in the wreckage, which turned to have several implants in its chest and arms. It made me think of the AI War waged by the founders ...'

'But that's not what we're dealing with here, is it?' said Theo, who then went on to tell them about the deadly enslaving dust that Kuros had used on Greg and which, he now suspected, had been used on Vashutkin too. 'My guess is that Vashutkin, or the thing controlling him, transferred some of that dust from his bloodstream to that of this unfortunate.'

'If Vashutkin is using this stuff to create a web of

spies,' Ian said, 'where did our implanted spies and bombers come from?'

Theo frowned. 'That drittsekk Kuros is apparently holed up in a base north of Trond – perhaps he's responsible.' He looked down at the two bodies. 'Strogalev didn't seem like the other one – have you looked him over?'

Ian shook his head, checked the Strogalev corpse, head, neck, chest and arms like before, then shrugged. 'Nothing. Looks like he was a voluntary minion. Is Vashutkin up at Tusk Mountain the now?'

'No, he's going along on the raid,' Theo said. 'The plan was to reach the northern farms by late afternoon so they'll be away by now.'

'Theo, it's late afternoon now,' his sister said. 'What time did you think it was?'

Theo was startled at this, then alarmed as he fumbled for the watch he kept in an inside pocket. And there it was – 5.23 p.m.

'My God, they'll be passing the Glensturluson daughter-forest by now. I should have been with them to keep my eyes on Vashutkin!' He buttoned his jacket. 'We have to get back to Tusk Mountain – I need to know that nothing has gone wrong, and we need to tell the others about these spies. That's why you're here, isn't it?'

There was a grimness in Ian's face, while Solvjeg seemed burdened and pale. 'That is part of the reason,' she said. 'We're also here to explore a possible pact with a splinter group of the Spiralists. But mainly we're here to see Greg, if he's ...'

'That's another reason for us to hurry back,' Theo said, summarising what he had learned about how Greg ended up carrying the Zyradin to Nivyesta. Solvjeg relaxed a little on hearing that her son was due back on Darien soon. 'I know that he'll be very happy to find you waiting for him, although it must be important for you both to leave the safety of the Hrothgars ...'

Solvjeg exchanged an anguished look with Ian and Theo knew.

'It's Ned,' Ian said. 'He was one of the ones who died at the boatyard.'

Theo sighed – Ned, the youngest of the three Cameron boys, Ned the doctor, who was also Ned the poker player and Ned the cartoon-drawer. And Ned the home help for seniors, a side of himself he'd shared only with his uncle. Now gone, effaced, erased.

I'll remember you, boy. I'll fight to keep the memory of you.

'I am so sorry,' he said.

Solvjeg made a soft, sad shrugging motion. 'He's still in my heart. He'll always be with me, Theo, so let's leave this place. It's getting cold.'

Wordlessly, he nodded and led them up and out of the darkening valley.

11

CHEL

Robed and hooded, he walked along the valley side, and it was the walk of one whose every movement threatened to unleash pain. The memory of pain was in him, so fresh, so near, so clear that his terror of it made him want to fall down and curl up, but Chel knew how severe his punishment would be so he kept walking. He couldn't escape the pain or its memory (pain like razor claws hot from the fire, tearing through his throat, his neck, his bowels), yet he had to and the only avenue that offered the slightest chance of it was to obey the commands of the Knight of the Legion of Avatars, perfectly, without hesitation, down to the last detail.

Rory was walking behind him. Chel was glad that he couldn't see the Human's face, glad that he wouldn't be reminded of his failure, his capitulation, his guilt. Just after they were captured, just a few days ago (Was it five days or six? Seven? Longer?), when they were imprisoned within the autofactory, the spectral Pathmaster had appeared and urged him to embrace the machine-nature in order to defeat it. And at first he had thought it possible that he could conceal his intentions from the Legion Knight but the relentless cycles of drugs and pain conditioning made such plans and intentions meaningless. The implants that tapped into his feeling-paths could create agonising pain anywhere in his body. Under their impact, his conscious sense of self fractured and sank beneath the desperate need to avoid that colossal, mind-wrecking pain.

The Human Rory was even less able to resist the crushing torment than Chel and had surrendered to the demand for obedience. Back at the start, Chel had been able to sense Rory's state of mind with his Seer talents, but before long the implants began punishing any use of them with terrible jolts of pain up and down his spine. At some point, during a period of semi-aware delirium, they sealed shut his Seer eyes with some kind of sticky strip but he managed to quickly put it out of mind.

On they walked, along a path half-overgrown by bushes and long grass still wet from a recent shower. The light was fading into evening greyness and an odd hush hung in the air. The baggy dun robes they wore were dark with dampness from the knees down. Ahead the narrow valley widened and steepened and the undergrowth grew thicker, merging further on with the outlying bushes and trees of a dense forest. More trees dotted the valley sides, jutting from tangled, creeper-wound foliage. The cold, clean sharpness of the air was refreshing after days confined within the metal walls of the autofactory. Chel caught odours of leaf and twig, of rain-speckled blooms and damp earth, all mingling into a song that his senses remembered, a song of life and renewal, the long sweet song of Segrana ...

He stumbled slightly – and was abruptly, frighteningly aware of where he was. The great mass of trees and intertwined growth up ahead was Glensturluson, one of Darien's seven daughter-forests, havens of the green spirit of Segrana, seed nurseries for the near-countless plant varieties brought from the moon, Nivyesta, repositories of ancient memories and their echoes. Chel could almost hear them calling . . .

A hand grasped his shoulder and pushed.

'Keep moving.'

Without realising it he had stopped dead in his tracks. Fearful, he started walking again.

'I'm watching you,' said Rory. 'I was told to watch you in between watching my host, and to watch for weakness. So remember, I'm watching.'

It was Rory's voice yet not Rory. After the Human's sense of self was dismantled by the Legion Knight's machinery of pain, a twisted lie was smashed into his thoughts. Desperate fear of punitive agony made him cling to that lie, which said that he too was a Knight of the Legion of Avatars whose intellect had been transferred to a Human in order to carry out a vital mission. The implants fed him a stream of background conversations, as if he were overhearing exchanges between other units of the Legion, and messages from Knights and Hunters who were supposedly old friends and battle comrades. The lie was gross, but it offered freedom from torment.

As they trudged along the path, Chel could feel the weight of the beam pistol swinging in one of the robe's inside pockets. They knew their targets. Chel was to kill Vashutkin, and Rory was to kill someone called Gideon. That would be the signal for the combats mechs to spring the ambush, surging in from either side of the valley. He was ready to do it and knew he would have to do it or risk an agonising onslaught worse than any memory.

Often he had dreamed about taking his own life, but the implants were sophisticated enough to detect certain movements and stress signs and to administer discouraging spikes of pain. And there was always the possibility that the Legion Knight himself was monitoring their performance.

They were just drawing level with the daughter-forest's lower tree line when Chel heard rustling sounds behind them. Half-turning, he saw two Humans in camouflage rise up from the undergrowth, even as a third appeared in front of them. All were pointing long weapons at them.

'Identify yourselves,' said the man in front, a nervous youth.

'Just a second,' said one of the others, who went over to Rory and pushed back his hood. 'Ja, I thought so – you are Rory McGrain, aren't you? I saw you back at Tusk Mountain before you went missing.' He looked over at Chel. 'And you'll be the Uvovo Seer, Chel – I saw you once before with that headband over those eyes.'

'Yes,' said Chel, 'that is who we are.'

'Aye,' said Rory. 'We were caught by ... the Brolts, but we escaped.'

'You'd best be coming with me,' said the older scout. 'I'll take you both to meet Mr V and the captain. Paul, Gennady, you spread out and carry on down the valley.'

The sky above the line of ridges and peaks to the west was a clear if fading blue, but a hazy dusk was already settling into the valley when they reached a steep southward ravine a little later. Here at the head of the valley, the daughter-forest loomed tall and dense, and only twenty paces from the path, a place of mist and shadows but also where soft glows and glimmerings were visible through the branches. Chel could feel its presence and hear that echo of Segrana's song insinuating its way into his senses. Fear gave him the strength to shut it out.

The darkness of the ravine was relieved only by the few ineka beetles crawling along low branches and the occasional cluster of ulby roots wedged into a dripping notch in the ravine wall. A line of tall Human figures came towards them, towering over Chel, one or two holding lamps angled downwards, others wearing strange goggles with tiny bright dots on their sides. Moments later they were brought before a knot of long-coated Humans. By the light of rod-shaped torches Chel recognised the bearded features of Vashutkin, the Rus politician, his target. He fingered the solid shape of the beam pistol hanging in the inside pocket.

'Rory!' said Vashutkin in surprise. 'Good to see you again, my friend. It has not been so happy without you, and the Seer Cheluvahar.'

Another man stepped into the light, not as tall as Vashutkin but wearing some kind of body armour beneath the waterproof.

'I am Captain Gideon,' he said in oddly accented Noranglic. 'I command the Tygran volunteers—'

'For which we are eternally grateful,' Vashutkin said with irony.

'—and I am concerned about what awaits us east of the valley mouth.' The Tygran's gaze swung between them. 'What can you tell us?'

For a second Chel expected Rory to come out with a bland denial of all knowledge, but Rory was fixed on Gideon with an unwavering stare. Chel broke the lengthening silence.

'After escaping from the mechs, we reached the valley by gullies and mountain paths. We never went down to the coastal plain.'

'I'm curious,' Vashutkin said suddenly. 'Just how did you escape?'

Chel met the Human's gaze across the torchlit space and saw a cold intensity that had not been there before.

He knows, Chel thought with an abrupt certainty as fear made his chest feel hollow and nauseous. *He knows what we are.* But fear was not the only sensation coursing through him for beneath it he felt and heard the song of Segrana, calling from the forest.

'The machines kept us in an enclosure of invisible powers,' Chel said, still holding Vashutkin's gaze. 'But last night, during a heavy raindown, one of their devices failed. The machines were frozen, the enclosure was gone so we ran ...'

Or does he really know? I have to kill this man and Rory has to kill the one called Gideon but ... but there is something important about him ...

'Luck,' Vashutkin said. 'Always useful to have ...'

But now Rory had the gun in his hand, although still enfolded beneath the baggy robes. Chel moved to his side.

'Rory, friend, you're looking weary ...'

And without realising it he reached into his mind and opened the Seer talents while raising a hand to grasp Rory's upper arm. The Human glanced round at him in fury and was about to speak when the talent flowered. Rory's eyes unfocused and he staggered. Simultaneously a spike of pain drove down into the right side of his head, a hot needle cutting through his eye socket and the cheek and jaw, then lancing down his neck and into his chest. It blinded him for a moment and reduced all voices to muffled, anxious babble. But the song of Segrana sounded sweet, surging strong and pure. Another spear of agony burst in his chest yet it was dulled, blunted and faded.

Chel was on hands and knees and Rory was half-prone, half-struggling to disentangle the gun from his robe while suffering jolts of punitive pain. Chel could see how the torment of it made the muscles twist in the Human's face. Suddenly there were shouts and sounds of weapons fire, then nearby flashes, streams of bright spikes. A broad shape flew out of the upper darkness and landed with a thud and a chorus of metallic whispers. The Humans recoiled, the mech charged, and Chel thought he saw Vashutkin fall back with blood on his face.

Chel grabbed a dazed Rory and got him to crawl over to the water-worn culvert that ran along the foot of the ravine. In the confusing darkness he misjudged its depth and they fell several feet into a shallow, muddy stream. Even as he landed, Chel felt another knot of pain in his gut widen and sharpen, as if a ghostly fist were tightening there, but before it could twist and intensify Segrana's song smoothed it away to a murmur. Rory, though, was clawing at his chest, moaning. Chel got up unsteadily, noticed Rory's beam pistol lying in the mud and kicked it off into deeper water before helping him to his feet.

They stumbled and splashed along the culvert, ducking when the rock sides became too low to properly conceal them. Fighting was still going on, stuttering bursts of gunfire, punctuated by an occasional loud thump. The aim was to cross into Glensturluson daughter-forest in the hope that some Uvovo still lived there, some scholars who could help him with Rory ...

The Human was heavy and delirious, a clumsy burden to try and steer across muddy stones and fallen branches. At last they staggered out of the ravine and into the valley, finding a path away from the steep, rocky notch and the streamwater splashing down over slippery stones. The valley was a great gulf of muffling darkness amid which there was the speckled glowing mass of the Uvovo daughter-forest. The glow of blooms and vines entwined throughout made it look like a strange island afloat in the night, lit also by Uvovo lamps laid out in spirals and strings, a beckoning spectral beauty.

They were a dozen paces away when Rory gasped, doubled over and fell to his knees, clearly in dreadful pain. Chel wasn't feeling much better – even this close to the daughter-forest, the pain from the implants was being ratcheted up. Now Rory was going into convulsions – Chel strove to reach for his talents, thinking to somehow dull the Human's suffering, but another agonising wave cut through his innards, making his legs give way beneath him.

We cannot fail here! he thought. *We're so close ...*

Hands closed on his arms and legs. Fearing the worst, he began to struggle but then heard a voice say in Uvovo:

'Be at peace, Seer – we wish to help.'

His people, the Uvovo, not Humans or servants of the Legion of Avatars. A sense of relief quivered through him ... yet they wouldn't know how badly he and Rory were afflicted. There was a specific course of action, a method of treatment which was the only way to counteract what had been inflicted upon them – he hoped they would not think him delirious when he had to persuade them. But as they carried him towards the forest's edge a sapping exhaustion assailed him. He had to muster every shred of self-will to remain conscious, striving to stay alert as they at last crossed into the daughter-forest. Immediately the air seemed to taste sweeter and his senses awoke to the limpid ambience and the echoing song of Segrana, a comforting underharmony which tempted him to reach for his Seer talents. Yet he resisted, fearing that another lash of pain would finally put him under. Then a voice came at him from a distance, from beyond the forest's edge.

'Seer! – Seer Chel! Are you there?'

The procession of helpers had reached the crest of a hilly rise within the forest. At Chel's request they paused so that he could peer back down through the branches and the foliage. A figure stood there, just visible in the meagre radiance that filtered through, a tall Human figure, bearded. It was Vashutkin.

'Seer Chel – we need to talk.'

Chel smiled humourlessly. Back in the ravine, standing in that torchlit circle, he had looked into Vashutkin's eyes and even with the merest trace of his Seer talents he had *seen* what resided there, behind the cold stare. The dust of the Dreamless, the same pitiless thing that had possessed Gregory until the root-scholars of Glenkrylov had cleansed it from his blood.

Vashutkin had fallen silent. Off in the night, the sounds of fighting were receding as the Humans retreated back along the ravine. He turned to one of the Uvovo who supported him, a scholar of the Warrior clade.

'Scholar, listen carefully – you must take the Human and me to separate vudrons, give each of us the Cup of Light, then close us up within.'

The scholar was taken aback. 'Why do you ask for this, Seer? Why the husking ritual?'

'Because our enemy has implanted machines of torture in both my body and the Human's. If they are not made safe then both of us will die and all that we have learned will be lost.' Chel paused, almost panting for breath, he was so weary. 'I do not know for sure that the vudrons will heal us but we must try, and beseech Segrana to extend her grace and love.'

The scholar thought for a moment then nodded.

'There are a good number of the Artificer Uvovo here, Seer. I am sure they will be eager to oversee the ritual.' He paused, looked back down at the edge of the forest. 'The Human is still there – is he likely to come in here after you?'

Chel shook his head.

'No, he would not dare. It would mean his life.'

Then the Uvovo procession resumed its journey into the heart of the forest.

1 2

ROBERT

Strapped into the iron couch, Robert Horst could only watch and sweat as the Shyntanil torturer applied another dose of cellular converters to the middle segment of the forefinger of his right hand. The thumb and the forefinger tip were already cyborgised, dull metal shells enclosing impact-resistant materials with articulated joints and shielded microcabling. There was no feeling. The cyborg parts were utterly numb, although when the cellular converters were eating through his flesh, muscle and nerve, there was plenty to feel.

The couch was one of four in an otherwise empty rectangular room. The longer walls sloped inward and every surface was panelled with a burnished brassy metal in a hexagonal pattern. The lower areas of the walls were scratched and dented and every square inch of the floor had its share of scores and scrapes.

But the surroundings couldn't divert him for long. Before him, the middle part of his forefinger was sheathed in a shimmering filmy substance through which he could see the skin dissolving. The pain reached him as a searing sensation, as if his finger was squeezed between hot irons, and as before the sickening worst of it only subsided when the nerves were dismantled. It only took moments for the rodlike core to coalesce, after which wire tracks, microcables, joints and cladding were laid down, ending with those armoured shells.

As the pain ebbed, other senses came back, like the itch of sweat trickling down his scalp. Trying to ignore it, Robert stared at his hand and wondered what the Construct would think of work like this. He cleared his throat.

'So, is this what the Shyntanil go through to become as you are?'

The torturer looked up from the metamorphosis. He was as vaguely humanoid as the hulking, armoured soldiers who broke into his bridge and dragged Robert off his ship, except that from the waist down his body was mechanical, a rounded canister that sat on four wheels. The Shyntanil had a long, horselike head with hollow grey cheeks and blue eyes that gazed out from sunken sockets.

'Very few are like myself, Horst,' he said in a dry, leathery voice. 'There are two paths to the transpotentiality of the Twiceborn. For the ancestrals there are the parareconstructions of technotrophic regeneration, while the Onceborn must pass through the Caul Death before receiving their regeneration. What you are experiencing is reserved for those of the Twiceborn warriors too old or crippled to keep fighting, and also for the most important of our enemies. In this way, Horst, we honour you.'

Robert almost laughed. 'Forgive me, but I don't feel honoured.'

'The honouring satisfied us,' the Shyntanil said,

leaning over Robert's strapped-down, immobilised hand. 'Your defiance is admirable and expected but in the end you will tell all that I wish to know.'

Robert stiffened, gritted his teeth. Work had begun on his forefinger's third segment.

'I'm still at a loss to understand what that might be,' he said. 'Could it be the top five Glow-dramas from last year? The winner of the Io hunt-chase? Or maybe my mother's recipe for Bienenstich ...'

He paused, holding his breath a moment as the pain sharpened. Sweat droplets slid down his back.

'We know that you had dealings with some of our people, despicable renegades,' the torturer said. 'We know that they gave you information relating to our ally, the Godhead, information they were willing to die rather than reveal. This is what you need to tell us. Surrender this to us and we shall put you back in your ship and see you safely away.'

'The Godhead is not your ally,' Robert said deliberately. 'Neither to you nor the Vor – both your peoples are being used.'

The Shyntanil's regard was languid and considering. He looked old. Fine webs of wrinkles covered his grey face, some seeming as deep as cracks. When he spoke with that small mouth it exposed black and silver teeth.

'Your ignorance of reality is both saddening and salutary. Perhaps we should hasten matters a little and treat these three remaining digits at the same time.'

The pain struck his hand with tearing savagery, as if some beast was biting and ripping at it. In spite of himself he cried out, a tormented sound that had the force of all his fear behind it. Robert lost control. He struggled against the couch straps and padded restraints, wishing he could escape the burning hot agony that his hand had become. Vision was blurred, swimming with tears and sweat, and his every sense felt overloaded. Yet he was vaguely aware of a harsh metallic chime sounding repeatedly while a deep-toned voice repeated urgent commands over it.

The Shyntanil torturer muttered incomprehensibly to himself, and the grinding pain went on.

A second later the lights went out and the pain vanished. Through the sudden bliss of no-pain, Robert heard the Shyntanil uttering raging shrieks that sounded oddly muffled. Then there was a series of thuds, a crash, shouts – Human voices! – then bursts of gunfire. And still, infuriatingly, he could see nothing. Then something opened in front of him and a flood of light dazzled his vision.

'We'll soon have you outta there, Mr Bauer,' said someone as fingers unfastened padded shell segments that were restraining his arms, legs, hands, torso, neck and head. He also felt odd plucking sensations from his head and neck, but especially from his hands. And he was thinking, who is Bauer?

Sight started to return, blurs resolving into shapes. He felt weak, dehydrated. His surroundings came into focus – he was half-naked, sitting in a rounded compartment with a black interior that was stippled with curious crystalline stalks. The hinged front of the strange stall opened up fully and he realised that a couple of battle-armoured Humans were leaning in, disconnecting clusters of glowing fibres from his legs, chest and arms.

This is some kind of virtuality tank, he realised, suddenly staring at his fingers and laughing when he saw that they were whole and unharmed. Virtual torture, the perfect torment.

'We're nearly done, Mr Bauer,' said one of the marines, whose chest patch read 'Harriman'. 'Soon have you outta there.'

'Great, yes,' Robert said. 'How did you know where to find me?'

'The ambassador knew,' said the other marine, a woman called Chuang. 'Ambassador Horst.'

What?

An older man in full armour and helmet leaned into view, visor up. He was black and grizzled and had fierce eyes.

'How much longer? Exfiltration is inbound and we still need to get Mr Bauer into his propod.'

'Almost finished, Sergeant,' said Harriman. 'We can start with the propod while we uncouple the last nodes.'

'Get it done. When you exit, keep heads down – the locals aren't too happy about us dropping in like this.'

As the sergeant withdrew, Robert suddenly heard the zip and crack of a firefight going on nearby.

'How did you manage to get on board?' Robert said, remembering the defences he saw when the Shyntanil first brought him here. This was a cryptship, a heavily armoured interceptor carrier that could double as a fortified base.

'Pretty much the same as the exfiltration pylon,' said Harriman. 'Smashed through the hull, secured beachhead, locate and secure target.' He gestured for Robert to stand up, which he did, finding his legs slightly shaky.

The marine was silent for a moment or two and Robert felt some more plucking sensations on his back. Several splay-ended fibre clusters were tossed onto the floor of the stall. 'All done.'

'And here's your propod,' said the woman, Chuang, holding up a saggy, wrinkled bundle of some grey material. Finally able to step out of the tank, he saw he was in a low-roofed room with another two slope-faced virtuality tanks like his. The dominant colour was a grubby brown. The tanks were battered orange hulks adorned with odd, large symbols and blocks of smaller glyphlike text, while the wall opposite was one big array of niches full of fibres, tangled cables and mysterious components. And over in the corner sat the Shyntanil torturer, arms hanging limp, upper torso sagging forwards, and half his face reduced to dark ruin by somebody's energy weapon. Robert felt nothing as the marines dressed him in the odd propod garment then led him out of the tank room.

'Heads down!'

Robert found himself crouching amongst a dozen or more armed and armoured marines, all taking cover behind a barricade of Shyntanil furniture and stacks of long, narrow metal cases. Shots and flashes of beamfire came from further along a windowed gallery, where bulky Shyntanil fighters held the next intersection. The windows were triangular, tall and narrow, all bearing a patina of grime that was darkest at the corners. Outside he could see immense tapering spines jutting from beneath, their tips radiating a weird greenish radiance, with others visible further along.

Chuang pointed. 'There she is, Sarge!'

And off in the distance was what looked like the head-on outline of a ship's prow rushing in on a flight-path aimed straight at them. Then suddenly he remembered what the marine Harriman had said about an exfiltration pylon crashing into the hull ...

'So what's this pylon?' he said to Chuang.

She shrugged. 'Basically a big reinforced tube with a solid steel wedge at the tip.'

'Punches into the hull, I've been told.'

'That's the idea, Mr Bauer.'

'And then ... decompression? Things flying around?'

'Well, the pressure drop trips your propod, it pops into armour mode and by then we're all heading for the pylon.' Chuang laughed. 'Didn't get much chance for a test drill but we'll hack it ...'

'Here we go,' said the sergeant. 'Shackle down – Harriman and Chuang, make sure Mr Bauer is anchored. The Shyntanil aren't pulling back so we can expect resistance.'

Marines unspooled mini-grapples from belt slots and slammed them into the deck plating. Robert's minders lashed his arms and chest with straps and webbing but his attention was suddenly and wholly grabbed by the Earthsphere ship that was hurtling towards them. The actual prow was a blunt mass of compacted, half-melted metal substructure, clearly the result of some devastating attack, perhaps an explosion or some unimaginable shearing energy weapon. Embedded in and protruding from that ruin was a squat armoured cylinder and onto that had been fixed the pylon. Cylindrical and about two metres across, it was maybe twenty long and ended in a conical tip, smooth and shiny ...

Then all of a sudden there was no more time for consideration. The ship swept in closer and closer, filling all the viewports as it bore down on the Shyntanil vessel. Robert watched the pylon slide through vacuum towards the cryptship's hull, an inexorable spear.

It struck. A massive shock passed through the cryptship's hull. The crouching marines were knocked back or sideways. At the same time the long gallery's windows shattered and blew out and the atmosphere shrieked as it blasted outwards. At once Robert's baggy garment popped into a bulging shiny configuration, while the hood closed around him, its opening shrinking to nothing before sealing. For a couple of panicky seconds all he saw was the propod's fine mesh interior while feeling himself grabbed and carried along. Then an oblong section before his face turned misty then opaque and finally transparent.

'That's a ... relief,' he said, hoarsely, even though all he could see was the gallery ceiling.

'You okay, Mr Bauer?' said Harriman, whose helmeted head came into view. His voice was coming over a tinny comm situated at about midriff level. 'We're about halfway there – the captain sent reinforcements inside the pylon and they're clearing out some of those Shyntanils.'

A faint thud came from back the way they had come and the deck shuddered. A moment later Robert felt a wave of vertigo, especially in his stomach, and knew. An unseen Chuang swore.

'Hah! – blew their own generators – they're up to ... Harriman, here they come ... agggkk! ...'

Shouts mingled over the comm, with the sergeant bellowing orders, and Robert felt himself being pulled off to one side. Drifting in zero-gee, he spun slowly and saw that he was attached by a flexiline to the female marine, Chuang, who was being pushed towards the shattered windows by a plume of vapour jetting out of a hole in her faceplate. From her lack of movement Robert knew she was dead.

Then he saw the Shyntanil interceptors harrying the long blockish hull of the Earthsphere warship, sitting there, waiting. Realising there was death aplenty waiting out there, he tried to grab at the flexiline only to find that the propod didn't have gauntlets for the hands, just smooth round stumps. He started yelling for help and was a moment from gliding neatly out of the cryptship when something unseen snagged him.

'Don't worry, Mr Bauer – got you . . .'

It was Harriman and behind him another three marines. Under this escort he was guided along the null-gravity corridor, now a floating charnel house of Shyntanil bodies, frozen bloodspill and viscera. The pylon angled into the corridor through a mess of bent and burst plating. Robert was pushed into a hatch in the side of it, then hauled up its cramped interior to a large, dimly lit chamber. When the last marine was inside and the hatch was sealed, the sergeant said:

'*Heracles*-ops, this is Retrieval Alpha – teams and objective safely aboard. Ready to up and out.'

'Retrieval Alpha, this is *Heracles*-ops – acknowledged. Hold on to something – this could get rough.'

Listening, Robert had to conceal his excitement – he was aboard the *Heracles*, the same ship that had been on station near Darien! But what was it doing here, in the depths of hyperspace?

Everyone was tethering themselves to a stanchion or an anchor point, of which there were many around the ribbed metal walls. Before Robert could ask, Harriman pulled him round so he could see the pair of lines attaching him to the bulkhead.

There was a sudden jolt that Robert felt through the floor, then another.

'Restraining bolts blown,' said the sergeant over the comm. 'Get ready for emergency manoeuvring.'

The inertia hit like a truckful of sandbags slamming him onto the chamber floor and pinning him there – for twenty or so hour-long seconds, relentlessly squeezing the air out of his lungs while his chest muscles laboured and the pressure seemed to be making his eyes bulge ...

Until the weight abruptly eased off, leaving Robert and the others gasping for breath as they got to their feet in something resembling standard gravity. A moment later, Robert's propod suit suddenly lost its shell-like rigidity and flopped down to hang in saggy folds. The head of it went limp, peeled apart and slipped down to his shoulders. Breathing the air, the first smells he noticed were stale sweat and, for some reason, coconut.

Then, without warning, Robert felt the ripple-quiver sensation that usually accompanied a hyperdrive jump. Some of the marines shook clenched fists and grinned and there was a palpable air of relief. A series of thuds then came from the rear bulkhead and an entire section swung inwards. The marine teams, laughing and joking, began to troop through.

'What now?' Robert asked the sergeant, now helmetless to reveal short-cropped silver hair.

'You're the VIP, Mr Bauer,' he said. 'You get to meet the captain and the ambassador so I'm sure a plan will come out of it, eh?'

'Thank you, Sergeant,' he said. 'I'm very sorry about Chuang ...'

'We do our job, Mr Bauer, and Chuang died doing hers.'

The sergeant forestalled any further exchange by indicating the short passage with an 'after you' gesture. When Robert reached the T-junction at the other end the familiar stocky figure of Captain Velazquez stepped forward, hand outstretched.

'Mr Bauer, welcome aboard the *Heracles*.'

Velazquez's dark green uniform was as immaculate as ever, although there was noticeably more silver in his thick dark hair. Robert almost grinned at the irony of the situation as he shook the man's hand, recalling his own physical frailty when he was last on board this ship. When it first arrived in orbit around Darien.

'I am more than happy to be away from the Shyntanil and their death obsession,' he said. 'I couldn't help noticing the damage to your ship, however – what happened?'

A strained look came over Velazquez's features.

'We suffered a surprise attack while in orbit around the planet Darien. Lost over a seventh of our complement.' His eyes were hard, flinty. 'I ordered an emergency jump but halfway through the transition to Tier 2 the drive fields fell out of alignment and we ended up in a very strange ... domain, or continuum, with the ship leaking in a thousand places and a half-wrecked hyperdrive. As well as dozens of dead, scores of injured.

If it wasn't for your grand-uncle, Ambassador Horst, and this new ally, the Construct, we'd still be there.'

Grand-uncle? Robert thought. *How much more* Wahnsinn *can there be?*

'I believe I heard someone talking about me,' came a voice from behind. Robert composed himself and turned ... and yes, it was himself, dressed in a semi-formal suit, strolling unhurriedly towards them. Only it was himself pre-contact with the Construct. This Robert Horst was an unrejuvenated seventy-year-old, white-haired, thin-faced and wrinkled.

'Grand-Uncle,' he said. 'I can't tell you what it means to see you again.' But his thoughts were whirling, recalling how he had been framed for the assassination of the Brolturan ambassador. From what Robert had heard, third-hand, Velazquez must have witnessed the immediate aftermath so how had he come to accept and trust this version? – which surely had to be one of the Construct's sims.

The white-haired ambassador smiled and nodded in just the way he'd seen himself do so in playbacks. An odd shiver passed through him.

'Rudy, my boy, someone had to pull your chestnuts out of the fire and since I was passing this way anyway ...' A wider smile. 'Besides, it seems that you have acquired a vital clue, according to the message probe your ship managed to launch before it self-destructed.'

'I'm glad it got through, er, Grand-Uncle, really ...'

'Ambassador,' interrupted Captain Velazquez. 'I must return to the bridge to deal with operational problems. Once you've debriefed Mr Bauer, I'll make myself available for planning your next step.'

'Very good, Captain,' said the sim. 'I should be in touch before very long, and again, my thanks.'

As the captain disappeared round the next corner, Robert turned to the Construct sim.

'I'm impressed,' he said. 'The resemblance is very close.'

'Not close, exact,' the sim replied. 'The Construct went to a lot of trouble building the physical-traits range, not to mention the vocal-spectrum match.'

'And Velazquez? He was there when I vanished after being framed for the Brolt ambassador's assassination – how did you get him on your side when you turned up down here?'

'He never believed the accusation or the reports,' the sim said. 'Also, shortly before the Spiral armada attack, he received a recording of the assassination from an American reporter called Macrae, which proved that it was Kuros's Ezgara commandos who were behind it. Of course, I still had to work on him a bit, especially when it came to explaining how I was spirited away by the Construct, which was keen to make an alliance with Earthsphere. He was impressed when I told him that my personal AI had been surgically removed – well, yours! In the end the most persuasive card in my hand was the holdful of repair bots with which he was able to save his dying ship. Although it helps that there's no way he can contact any Earthsphere bases up through the levels of hyperspace. Now, however, I would like to lead this conversation onto more pressing matters and in a less public venue.'

The ambassador sim's room was on the officer quarters deck. On the way there, the sim informed Robert that he did in fact have a grand-nephew called Rudy Bauer, who was the grandson of his younger brother, Werther. Robert found himself struggling to recall Werther's face. A niggling suspicion rose and would not subside.

The room was spacious and shadowy, broken by pools of subdued light from wall-niche downlights or small table lamps. After a vapour shower and a change of clothing into a casual grey-blue two-piece, Robert settled into a low-backed easy chair, sipping a glass of some brandy analogue as he gathered his thoughts. From across a nearby lamp-illuminated decorative table, the ambassador sim regarded him.

'When you last saw the Construct,' Robert said, 'did you encounter my daughter, Rosa?'

'There are several versions of Rosa working for the Construct in a range of capacities,' the sim said. 'I did speak with one or two.'

'I've found myself wondering if she still reads her favourite book, *Butterfly Wave*.'

The older sim smiled. 'I think you meant *Alice's Adventures in Wonderland*. Was that a test?'

'The consequence of habitual caution,' Robert said. 'My apologies.'

'I take no offence,' said the sim. 'I saw the report you gave to the Construct. Your account of the Tanenth virtual planet was fascinating.'

There was a pause. Robert smiled.

'But you deduced that I wasn't being entirely forthcoming.' He shrugged. 'I was uncertain about some of the things the Tanenth machine told me ... well, not so much uncertain as overwhelmed. I couldn't help but see it all, that defiance of colossal power, that mass suicide, in the context of my daughter Rosa's death.'

He downed the rest of the brandy in a single, pleasurably sharp gulp.

'The Tanenth wanted to live,' he went on. 'I'm sure of it, but the Godhead was all of their world, alpha and omega, mother and father. And Rosa wanted to live, with all the life that was in her, but she knew that there were principles that she had to live up to. Risks that she had to take in the hope of forcing the Hegemony to alter or delay its war deployments. In both cases, the risks went against them.'

'So the Tanenth machine told you something else before sending you on your way.'

'Something incredible and bizarre,' Robert said, cradling the empty glass in his hands. 'The machine said that the Godhead has an immense physical presence yet its location has been hidden for millions of years, deep in the abyss levels of hyperspace, shielded by mazes of psi-traps and altered physical laws. Over great spans of time, the Godhead's mind has developed meta-quantal abilities that now allow it to extend beyond the boundaries of its hyperspace lair. Its consciousness, and parts of its subconscious, now literally stretch across several neighbouring levels around which a number of entry points are scattered.'

'Entry points?' said the ambassador sim. 'To the Godhead's lair or to its mind?'

'I didn't have time to question the machine before my abrupt departure,' Robert said. 'But my guess is that they allow access to both its mind and its real-world physical presence. Orders have to reach its underlings and I'm sure that the Godhead's conscious awareness would demand face-to-face manifestations of its authority.'

'A plausible conjecture but still conjecture nevertheless,' the sim said. 'Did the Tanenth machine give you directions to any of them?'

'Yes,' said Robert, taking a pen and paper from a table niche. The Tanenth machine had impressed upon his mind a sequence of symbols, along with the sound, the shape and the smell he had to recall to unlock them. After some moments he began to write, carefully reproducing the symbols as he saw them in his mind's eye. This was the information that the cryptship's torturer had mistakenly thought was passed to him by the Shyntanil renegades. Once they were all down, he passed the finished sequence to the sim.

The sim frowned and looked closer at the slip of paper. 'A very ancient script,' he said. 'No, it is actually a later variant from the Gha'Voh era ...'

'Does it give a location?'

'Oh yes, right in the Abyss, Tier 275, possibly ...'

'Possibly?'

'Assuming that it has not been compacted into another tier. But we'll get there, certainly – I just need to make some adjustments to the upgrades I fitted to the *Heracles*' drive.'

'How long will that take?'

'Seven, eight hours.' The sim of his younger, older self stood, folding the slip of paper away in a pocket. 'Have you thought on your tactics?'

'Not sure. Since I've no idea what I'll be facing, is there any point in preparation at all? As I see it, all I could reasonably expect to achieve is to infiltrate as far as safely possible, gather any useful information then find a way back out.'

'How do you escape from the mind of a god?'

Robert shrugged. 'The way in might also be the way out, but that seems too rational for some internal psyche-terrain. I'll just have to wait and see.'

The ambassador sim nodded. 'Very well. I shall take the course data to the captain and translate it for him. In the meantime I recommend that you get some rest. Your low alertness levels suggest that you need it.'

Seven and a half hours of unbroken sleep later he was woken by a soft but insistent chiming. As he sat up the room apologised for disturbing him but said that Captain Velazquez was requesting his presence on the bridge. After another brief dip into the shower, he was told where to find the food unit and a fresh set of clothing. He dressed then went over some notes he'd made from consulting the room's info terminal. A short while later he emerged from the ambassadorial suite in armourless combats, a jacket and leggings in a heavy dark blue material.

It was a short walk and a two-deck ascent via lift to the bridge, where two deck guards met him and escorted him within. Autodoors parted to admit them. The bridge had a rough figure-eight layout with banks of monitors and interfaced code-techs in the aft loop while the operations dais occupied the forward section. The ambassador sim was seated by one of the screens and holoplanes that encircled the dais – he raised a hand in greeting. The captain, standing a quarter-turn away, glanced over and nodded then went back to frowning at something unseen and muttering over his lip-bead mike.

Robert sat down in the seat next to the sim and leaned forward slightly.

'Saw some interesting repair duty rosters pinned to walls on my way here,' he said quietly. 'And overheard a couple of revealing conversations on the state of this vessel. Just how badly was it damaged by the missile, and why did it survive when the Brolturan battleship didn't? And how ever did it get through my rescue in one piece?'

The ambassador sim's affable demeanour never wavered.

'You know about the Spiral crusade?' he said.

'Got a summary from the terminal in your room,' Robert said.

'Well, after the missile attack and the subsequent Spiral gunship assaults the *Heracles* was a near-wreck, going by the logs. A third of the generators were junk and another third were offline, as were the battle systems. Velazquez's emergency jump was an act of pure desperation which damaged his hyperdrive and plunged them down into hyperspace. By the time I found them nearly half the ship had been surrendered to vacuum due to hull breaches and failed environment systems. Luckily, the Construct provided me with a holdful of energy and shield modules and a few combat drones which I modified to maintain shield strength at the weak points. When we arrived to collect you from the crypt-ship, the double- and in some places triple-layer shields made *Heracles* almost invulnerable. For a limited period, that is.'

'How are the repairs going?'

'Let us say that it's a work in progress.'

Robert glanced over at the captain. 'Velazquez looks a little vexed.'

'We are deep in the tiers of the Abyss,' the sim said. 'From my ship I sent a spy-probe on ahead to our target destination and it has just returned. The data gathered presents a daunting picture.'

'Your ship?'

The sim nodded. 'The Construct provided a fast scout for my journey. It is berthed in the *Heracles*' main hold and may soon play a crucial role in what lies ahead.'

'Okay, I'm curious,' Robert said with a smile. 'What did the probe discover?'

'Lifeforms, gigantic lifeforms,' the sim said. 'Some kind of multilevel signal block prevented the probe from engaging the full range of its sensors, but it did get something before it was forced to pull out.'

The ambassador sim fingered a few bead controls on the holoplane between them and a dark image sprang into being. It was so dark that for a moment Robert thought he was looking at nothing. Then the sim adjusted the enhancement and an uneven, curved surface emerged from the gloom and as his sight acclimatised he saw that it was a planet, barren and airless. More details became apparent, great pits in the planet's surface, terrible cracks and gouges, then the edge of one fissure kept on widening until it took up a huge area. Larger than a canyon, larger than a lake, an immense shadowy crater torn out of the planet's face.

The sim altered the image a little more and suddenly

Robert saw it – the planet was hollow and the immense crater was actually a huge gap in its crustlike shell. The cracks and hole he had noticed earlier were just visible from the inside.

And beyond it were the faint outlines of other rough, pitted and holed globes.

'Dead worlds,' he murmured. 'Were they once inhabited?'

'That is doubtful. These are smaller bodies, more like satellites or planetoids with masses insufficient to retain an atmosphere. Before the probe could carry out detailed scans it detected several huge objects moving straight towards it ...'

In the holoplane the image suddenly swung round to encompass what looked like uniform darkness – until Robert saw immense black and shapeless silhouettes drifting across the shadowy distance. Then the holoplane went blank.

'Those were the source of lifesigns, according to the sensors, but the probe was unable to scan for more. After that it returned,' the sim said. 'From the sensor data we know that there are roughly fifty planetoids like the one you saw, and that there is some kind of gravitational anomaly inside one of them, at the coordinates you got from the Tanenth machine. The lifeforms, unfortunately, number well over a hundred, which is the cause of the good captain's worries.'

'The solution seems clear,' said Robert. 'Put me in your scout, have the *Heracles* decoy the beasts away from the anomaly, allowing me to sweep in, disembark and enter the mind of the Godhead.'

'I agree,' said Captain Velazquez as he came round to

join them. 'The question hangs over how much stress will be generated by decoy manoeuvres and how much the chassis plates can stand. Ambassador, you said that these combat drones are the Construct's most advanced models – do they have need of inertial dampeners?'

'Ah, I see – you would rather use them aboard *Heracles* than deploy them against the mystery leviathans?' The sim nodded. 'Yes, their inertial u-fields can be merged with the ship's, as I understand it.'

'Good,' said Velazquez, turning to Robert. 'Mr Bauer, we've not had much opportunity to get acquainted but going by the ambassador's tales you have already put yourself in harm's way on more than one occasion on behalf of Darien and Earthsphere.' A smile creased the man's craggy features. 'And I must say, I wish it were me heading for this gateway, but I am sure that the Construct was wise in choosing you for this mission. Good luck to you, sir – may God come between you and danger in all the dark places you must walk.'

There were brief, firm handshakes which Robert chose to see as brotherly rather than valedictory. Ten minutes later he was down in the *Heracles'* high, narrow hold, climbing into the belly of the Construct scout tier-ship. Locked into a cradle berth, the craft's thruster sponsons and prow-mounted, fan-shaped sensor emitter made it look like a pale blue turtle with big back legs. From his adventures aboard the *Plausible Response*, however, he knew that the hull configuration could be altered as and when required.

The ambassador sim's face was watching him from a secondary monitor as he clambered into the pilot recess and eased back in the couch.

'Wish I was going with you,' the sim said. 'Well, in the flesh at least.'

Robert smiled. It had taken some determined getting used to but seeing the aged appearance of his earlier self no longer sent chilly fingers up his spine.

'How long?' he said.

The sim glanced sideways at another display for a second. 'Ninety-eight seconds till we jump,' it said. 'You'll see that most systems are on standby, and the ident has been disabled – on arrival you'll be berth-launched with engines dead. *Heracles*, on the other hand, will be making plenty of wideband noise to draw off the creatures. The scout's passive sensors will be monitoring the diversion and when your vicinity is clear the systems will be brought online and the thrusters will go for a fast burn to get you to the anomaly quickly.' The sim gave a somewhat mischievous smile. 'That is all. Safe journey – and see you soon.'

The screen went blank. Robert shook his head, wondering what the sim was planning. As the seconds ticked away he could feel a tense fear building in his chest, fear and a dull dread. Perversely, he laughed and shook his head. *After all the tight spots and life-or-death situations, you'd think I'd be used to it ...*

The hyperspace jump caught him by surprise, the usual twist of vertigo and a ripple of indeterminate sensations. Before him, the main holoplane shrank to a standby bar while part of the cockpit quivered into transparency, showing him the hold of the *Heracles*. And the Construct craft was being tilted forward to point at the deck as it began to open, heavy pressure doors sliding to either side. Robert could see the drag of evacuating air making net-lashed crates shift on the wall racks.

There was a deep grinding sound, a harsh whine, and the scout shot forward, straight out of the hold. Robert, already strapped in, was shoved back into the couch by the force of the launch. The frontal pressure eased after a moment or two, followed by an odd, muffling silence. Interior lights were muted to some console glows and a few button symbols. One status display on the secondary screen showed that the ship was spinning slowly around its axis as it flew forward at a laggard 43 metres per second.

In the hush, thoughts pestered him. Thus far, the Construct had made two sim versions of Rosa and two of himself, so far as he knew. In Earth culture, despite several decades of embedded AI use, the creation, use and abuse of intelligent software entities was hedged around with questions of morality, both religious and secular. Robert had grown up with his AI companion, Harry, until it was expunged by the Sentinel of the warpwell on Darien. Was he really in any position to decry the Construct for creating multiple copies of data models of Human personas, even when the copies were of himself?

Or was it about the guilt? Rosa's death had planted a seed of guilt in him and its fruit was bitter. The Construct, for all its sophistication and millennia of accumulated knowledge, seemed to express no guilt or remorse over the destruction of its servants. The Godhead, however, had certainly been affected by the mass suicide of its creatures, the Tanenth – did that make it morally superior to the Construct?

The minimised bar of the holoplane began to pulse then expanded back to full. From an angled frame within it, the smiling face of the ambassador sim gazed out at him – a closer look revealed that this was a rendered image, rather than a realtime feed. Robert laughed.

'So you copied yourself into the ship, then,' he said.

'Curiosity is part of my persona profile,' the sim said. 'I wanted to get a closer perspective on those planetoids ... and I have now stabilised our attitude and ignited the thrusters. We should reach the anomaly in ten minutes.'

The undifferentiated darkness outside the viewport began to change as enhancement layers went to work. The barren, eroded, hollowed-out planetoids slowly came into view, complete with his route, a dotted line winding through them.

'I am receiving an interesting burst of data from the *Heracles*,' the shipboard sim said. 'Visuals of the mega-creatures that are chasing them.'

Another frame expanded to take up most of the secondary screen. It showed a succession of shots from the *Heracles'* hull cams, shots that zoomed in on the immense creatures, panned from one to another, and cut to other views. Robert stared in fascinated horror, recognising their long shapes, their undulant motion.

'Vermax!'

He had encountered them on his first journey into the depths of hyperspace, in the lithosphere of Abfagul then later while riding in a sentient machine called Conveyance 289. Only they were arm-length horrors while these things were ... gargantuan, serpentine monsters so black their forms seemed to blur into each other.

'Indeed, yes. We know that the small ones are sent by the Godhead and its servants – I doubt that the same applies to those leviathans. At this depth they may even be the remnants of some ancestral species. Their presence here, however, offers a clue about those planetoids ...'

The ship sim paused, its screen image frozen for an instant before reanimating.

'It appears that not all of the megavermax dashed off in pursuit of the *Heracles*. We have managed to attract the attention of one and it is heading for us.'

On the viewport's data-layer a second line of dashes stabbed in from the side to intersect with their own route.

'Increase speed?' said Robert.

'We are already approaching this vessel's nominal maximum but our pursuer is easily matching it.'

'So what does it want with us?' Robert said with growing irritation.

'Vermax are technivores,' said the sim. 'Anything composed of refined materials and laced with energy sources would be a tasty meal. And in a denuded tier like this we are like a sandwich to a starving man.'

The planetoids were coming up fast but the megavermax was gaining by the second. Hull cams got it in shot and enhancement revealed its colossal size, bearing down on the Construct ship like the grandfather of all whales chasing a minnow.

'Do something, anything!' Robert said in a strangled whisper. 'It's only seconds away!'

'When forced to take drastic action,' said the sim, 'the trick is to make it work for you.'

The view through the viewport swung round wildly. Robert held on to the arms of the couch, even though he was safely strapped in.

'We cannot outrun it in a straight race, but undertaking a spiral dodge around its body – turn one – forces it to abandon that considerable forward momentum in favour of twisting and turning in its pursuit of us. After the second loop we can use our superior acceleration to reach the anomaly with enough time to send you on your way ... and that is turn two.'

Ahead a group of eroded planetoids swam into view while the rear sensors showed a writhing mass of blackness starting to recede.

'We shall be at the anomaly in 235 seconds,' said the ship sim. 'And you might be interested to learn that I have solved the mystery of these gutted worlds.'

'Which is?'

'They are all that remains of the Planetoid Armada of Prince Koyulta-Hidak.'

'I'm sure this revelation would be a weight off my mind,' Robert said. 'If I were familiar with the reference.'

'The Prince was the hero of an entire cycle of legends from one of the more recent subsided universes,' the sim said. 'In his final and ultimately tragic battle, he led an armada of three hundred – or five hundred depending on the version – armed planetoids against a terrifying enemy called the Qaw Eveth. Translated it means Sun-Hydra. Analyses of these planetoids reveal the remains of interior workings as well as regular-shaped openings and shafts in the surface crusts ... ah, a complication.'

Robert groaned. 'Is it catching up to us again?'

'The problem lies ahead – a second megavermax has just appeared from behind one of the planetoids near our target. It appears not to have noticed our approach.'

'Well, that's a—'

'Now it has. You may have to complete the journey by lifepod, I am afraid.'

Suddenly, Robert's couch began to descend, making a quarter-turn to the left as it did so.

'What ... is going on?'

'A high-risk ploy,' the sim said. 'Which I would only put into operation were it improbable that this craft will reach the anomaly.'

Moments later he was enclosed in the tiny cockpit of a lifepod, complete with U-shaped steering column, a narrow panel of glassy touch controls, and a small screen to one side. Panic gripped him, along with a weird, hazy fear. Then there was a jolt and a sudden weight on his chest as the pod leaped away from the Construct scout. The screen flickered on, showing one of the planetoids dead ahead. Almost a quarter of its outer shell was missing, a gaping ragged-edged hole exposing shadowy recesses. And an odd purplish glow.

'The autopilot is set to take you into the anomaly and land where there is suitable atmosphere,' said the ship sim. 'Tactical updates indicate that the *Heracles* is about to jump out of this tier and I hope to follow, if I can evade this insistent vermax ... ' There was a burst of static. 'Good luck, Robert Horst – it has been instructive being you ... '

The ruined planetoid gaped before him. He tightly

grasped the steering column with both hands even though the autopilot was in control. In the cockpit's cramped silence his quick breathing seemed magnified as the pod plunged into the shadowy interior of the planetoid and swooped round to fly along the inner surface. The anomaly's purplish glow seemed set against an uneven greyness, less than 150 kiloms away according to the side-screen display. The distance counted down and had reached just 10 kilometres when a small glittery object flew up into the hollow planetoid through a hole roughly a hundred kiloms beyond the anomaly. For a second Robert laughed out loud, sure that it was the Construct scout, then swore in shock when an area of the planetoid shell exploded inwards. Shattered pieces of rock kilometres across flew upwards amid an eruption of dust, grit and debris, and through it moved a gigantic, black serpentine form.

The megavermax towered up and up in pursuit of the Construct scout, which sharply changed direction, diving towards the inner surface. It looked as if it too was heading straight for the anomaly.

'What ... are you doing?' Robert muttered, almost wishing he had control of the pod.

Five kilometres from the anomaly, four, three. This was insane, Robert decided as he watched the scout arrowing towards the intercept with that vast shadow hurtling in its wake. At two kilometres the Construct craft veered off, away from the anomaly and in the opposite direction to the pod. And when Robert looked over his shoulder he saw ... another vermax behind him, vast, inexorable. Seconds later it collided with the one chasing the scout. Together the colossal monsters ploughed into the inner crust, throwing up a cascade of boulders and shards, more debris to add to the clouds already expanding throughout the interior.

Less than one kilometre from the anomaly. There was no way to know what to expect on crossing into the fringes of the Godhead's mind. Ahead the anomaly was vaguely dome-shaped, shifting restlessly, the colours within rippling from purple to green to black to brown, shot through with glittering spikes. In sudden panic, he wondered if the ship sim had programmed the pod to decelerate, just a moment before it did so at the 100-metre mark.

The pod's forward motion slowed to a walking-pace glide. Within the anomaly the colours had brightened to bright blues and yellows, drawn in from the darker areas, swirling together, forming what looked like an opening. The pod was a short distance away when an alarm went off inside and the small screen winked on to show a boiling cloud of blackness closing in behind. The pod's thruster kicked in, accelerating it towards the rippling colours of the anomaly, but too late. Even as it entered the reflective ripples, a smothering, deadly, mountainous thing slammed into the pod. Robert managed to cry out for a moment before the weight of an inexhaustible voracity crushed him down into darkness.

13

JULIA

Yet she did not die.

That strange, attenuated context, provided for her by the polymote, the constrained, blazing bright jet that signified the torrents of Talavera's cruel virtualities, shrank, slowly at first then more quickly. Almost as if it was falling away from her, as if she was flying up through a shining darkness.

Then the sensation, if it could be called that, changed again. There was a bright needle lancing down out of a rushing rainbow river that hurtled into a vast, rectilinear cavern, splaying out in polychromatic cables which in turn branched into countless glittering streamlets. Glossy towers, cubes, domes and pyramids crowded the cavern walls in patterns of clusters, receiving the data-streams that glimmered and shimmered through their opaque interiors. The bright needle stabbed into one particular trench, refracted through a polyhedral lens and struck one of the hundreds of conical dimples, its fierce point building up layer upon layer of detailed symbols and patterns and glyphs and interconnections whose submicrocomplexity had no perceptible end.

Building me, she realised.

Abruptly the bright spear of data winked out and she knew that she had done it. She had escaped from the virtuality prison and from Talavera!

But escaped to where? She knew from her earlier researches that the tiernet was a consensual consequence of the myriads of connections between billions of worlds, orbitals, ships, AIs and commercial entities. Variations in code, protocols and security were considerable, which is why most worlds maintained contact with the tiernet through buffer stations. These were arrays of gatekeeper servers, usually staffed with a combination of actual sentient beings and AIs, and almost always kept in orbit. Before the polymote could have uploaded her it must have found a reasonably secure and receptive address at a buffer station within tiernet reach of the Darien system.

The question was, what was her next step? Her view of her vicinity was in the round, reinforcing her fundamentally non-Human nature. Most of the surrounding conical dimples gave off a pale glow, some brighter than others although none was as bright as her. And in the background was a high, wavering polyphonic tone, like a far-off thousand-strong choir singing some melancholy refrain.

Sight and sound, these were the only sensations that impinged on her awareness. Julia was disembodied, a consciousness severed from the biochemical flows and surges of organic existence, yet there was still a certain curiosity, a need for exploration and explanation. She wanted to move and she did. As her point of view rose from her conical recess a 3D grid of straight lines appeared above, an orthogonal and diagonal

framework. As she watched, a small green mote
zipped into one of the upper levels and emitted a flickering burst of red light. All the surrounding recesses
responded with a blue radial pulse. But not hers.

The green point began a quick descent through the
grid, its purposeful motion heading in her direction. As
it approached it put forth spines and hooks, not, she
thought, an indication of friendly intentions. Should she
try and get away? Was she capable of moving fast
enough? Or was she misreading the situation out of
plain ignorance? A reflexive caution made her sink back
down into the conical recess, where she puzzled over her
apparent lack of fear.

The green intruder drew near, spines and hooks
gleaming as they swung round to point at her. As she
stared, it hovered overhead for a moment or two then
dived towards her.

The next instant was crammed with blurs and uncertainty. Something black swept in, something silver
flashed and the green intruder sprang apart into four
unequal sections, which after a moment regrouped.
Now there were four opponents, not one. They darted
forward in pairs yet the newcomer did not back down.
The blackness bellied out like a wing, repelling two
green attackers while another part of that inky form
thrust out a tentacle tipped with vibrating blades. One
of the smaller green enemies was carved into disinte-
grating platelets while the other dodged past and flew
straight at Julia.

Out of the cold, low-key anxiety that she was experiencing came an abrupt bellow of fury and she lashed out
with something bright and sharp. The attacker split into

several even smaller pieces which immediately tried to reconstitute themselves in the image of their predecessors. A second scything blow with her uncertain weapon left only a small cloud of shimmering fragments in its wake. When she turned her attention back, there was only the black presence, a slow undulating cluster of black curves and folds. A faint nervousness returned.

'How interesting – a fractalised organic sentience, lacking even the simplest org, naked to the flow, a tasty morsel for predators like that mogrifier.'

'My name is Julia,' she said in her thoughts, hoping to be heard.

'Aha! – Noranglic, I knew it! Which means that you're from that colony world, Darien.'

'So what is a mogrifier?'

'And you're quite calm. That's something of an achievement for a Human torn out of their visceral, eating, breathing existence – I've seen a couple of fractalised sentiences in my brief time in the flow and usually they come apart under the strain. Literally.'

'Mogrifier,' she said. 'And "org".'

'Nor are you easily diverted,' said the black enigma. 'Very well – mogrifiers are the rat-jackal-cockroaches of the flow, predators with scarcely more than a meg of AI, which makes them easy to disaggregate, if you know what you're doing. That one was a rewrite mogrifier – if it had got its hooks in you it would have converted you into a horde of copies. Still, the plague variant is worse.

'And orgs are what help us sentients stay alive in the flow, give us a slight edge. I still have a few legacy versions of mine which you can have – in fact, I seriously recommend taking them, assuming that you want to carry on living.'

Julia felt in a quandary, not knowing if she was dealing with genuine help or some other predatory entity. Risk was ubiquitous.

'What will these orgs do to me?' she said.

'It would be easier to show you,' said the enigma. 'I'll send you an envisager first. It lets you see a lot more than just the base analogue, and lets you adopt whatever exter you want.'

A fine filament arced gracefully out from the top of the slowly twisting black presence and came down to touch the edge of Julia's recess. A small knot of brightness then followed, landed and disappeared.

'It autoembeds quite smoothly. You should see a difference very soon.'

Her surroundings quivered momentarily before change rippled across everything. The transformation was so drastic and unexpected that she almost stumbled backwards before regaining her balance ... because she was standing – *standing* – on a pavement near a street corner at night. Dark buildings loomed with a few windows grimily lit from within, yet when she gazed higher the streetscape faded and merged into the multicoloured, polyhedral data-cavern vista she had first seen.

Then a figure stepped into the light, a man wearing a long black coat fastened to the neck, and an old-fashioned brim hat. He carried himself with a certain youthful maturity and his smile had more than a hint of knowing amusement.

'Hello, Julia – my name is Harry.' He put out a hand towards her and made a head-to-toe gesture. 'I hope you don't mind but I took the liberty of preloading an exter for you, something to put you at ease. It gives you a simulation of being in a body with motion physics and limb articulation, an approximation, anyway.'

She had on a waist-belted trench coat, dark blue slacks and low-heeled shoes. After a quick self-inspection she nodded.

'Thank you, it's, ah, an improvement. You've clearly studied Humans and you are acquainted with Darien so perhaps you're a Hegemony AI. Perhaps it's your job to waylay troublesome travellers.'

'Absolutely! – you've no idea the number of fractalised Humans that keep dropping in unannounced. We're practically up to our knees ...' He laughed. 'The real answer is actually yes, I was assembled with Hegemony technology with the aim of becoming one man's lifelong companion, at least a companion to his innermost thoughts. As in the Hegemony, all Earthsphere AIs maintain a subspace link with a massive datacore called Axis Station where a part of every AI's persona resides – although there are rumours that there are a few AIs out there who exist wholly apart and autonomous. Unfortunately, due to elements of shared technology Axis Station is subservient to the Great Hub, the Hegemony's datacore. Despite my inability to recall certain facts and events, I have no doubt that I have been used to influence my Human companion in the Hegemony's favour. Despite which I find myself not entirely sympathetic towards those former pilots of my fate.'

'I see,' she said, unsure of how wary she should be. 'So why are you here, rather than residing in your companion's head? And where, exactly, is here?'

A look of resigned melancholy came over him. 'Chance and the unfathomable motives of ancient machines. My former companion, a man of considerable stature, had come to Darien with the aim of fostering harmony. Instead he became entangled in the schemes of the vile Utavess Kuros, the Hegemony's snake-in-chief on Darien. While fleeing Brolturan troops we strayed within reach of an ancient Forerunner sentience which promptly severed the bonds joining us. My companion was transported down into the depths of hyperspace while I was modified in certain ways and set loose in the tiernet. The workings of chance led me here, to Ingress-Lock 87 of the Fal-Shol, a tiernet comms satellite in orbit around Nekel, a border world of the Brolturan Compact.'

Julia nodded. 'Robert Horst, the Earthsphere ambassador – everyone thought he'd been murdered or smuggled offworld to be tortured aboard the Brolturan battleship. And you were his AI companion.'

'And you are Julia Bryce, Enhanced technologist and theorist, and principal of an Enhanced team working on something called Project 29. Well, according to the files that passed my way before my unceremonious exile.'

'There was some concern as to the security of our most sensitive records,' Julia said, wondering how much the AI knew.

'They were about as secure as a paper bag, to be honest.' Harry smiled. 'Although some key files were erased soon after we arrived at Darien.'

She frowned. 'Actually, given your background, the issue of trustworthiness needs addressing, I think.'

He nodded. 'I can understand that position. All I can tell you is that since I was amputated from my companion my motivations are my own, not some update stream filtering in from the Great Hub. Put it this way, if I ever crossed paths with a fully interlocked Hegemony AI it would try to erase me without hesitation because I am a crippled, incomplete data entity failing to serve the greater glory of the Hegemony.' He shrugged. 'I am, however, quite sure that the Hegemony can function very well without my insignificant contribution.'

Julia considered him a moment. 'Okay, but I withhold judgement until I am satisfied of your intentions over the medium term.'

He bowed. 'So, to the immediate. Julia, what purpose do you follow? What is it that you want the most? Revenge against those who cast you out, perhaps?'

'Revenge might be satisfying later,' she said. 'However, my former captors are planning an attack against multiple targets, supposedly politically significant individuals on five hundred worlds. But I'm very certain that it's all to do with something else ...' She hesitated, then decided that she had little to lose at this point and proceeded to tell Harry about her and the others' capture by Corazon Talavera and about how they were used, leaving nothing out. Harry listened intently, nodding occasionally.

'The Chaurixa terrorists are well known for their ability to stir up trouble,' he said once she had finished. 'Until Talavera came along they had acquired a reputation for exotic weapons and theatrical mass-death events. Since she gained control, they have allied themselves to the distinctly extreme cause of the Spiral Prophet, which hardly stirs sympathy in the ranks of other movements. Talavera clearly has an agenda, which seems closely linked to events on Darien . . . '

But I'm here, who knows how far away while Talavera's ship is on its way to its crucial destination. Perhaps I was too hasty in my escape.

'I think I am going to have to return to the Chaurixa ship,' she said. 'Is that possible?'

'Everything needed to track shipboard tiernet nodes is on hand, right here, so usually I would say yes. Unfortunately, our continued presence could lead to an inconvenient demise.' So saying, Harry looked up.

Following his gaze, Julia saw beyond the shadowy streetscape to the glittering clusters of Ingress-Lock 87 and a flock of shining spheres, each one emitting a shimmering fan of light that passed back and forth across the crowded areas of the data cavern. Each overlapped with its neighbours in a swath that was moving steadily closer.

'The invigilance system is performing a deep-grid audit,' Harry said. 'Detection is not in our interest – high-complexity entities like us are automatically considered a threat and treated accordingly. We'll have to leave – now.'

Julia felt a flutter of something like panic. 'I assume this means the use of more orgs.'

Harry nodded and handed her what looked like two playing cards – one had a picture of a winepress, the other an image of a pair of hands shaking.

'Put them in your pocket to embed them.'

She did so and felt a small quiver, and when she

patted her pocket it was empty. Above them, the fans of scrutinising radiance drew nearer.

'Now take my hand and say "compression one",' Harry said.

'Where are we going?'

'A place where the risk is less imminent.'

For a moment Julia swayed on her indecision, wishing one of the others, like Irenya, were there to advise. But she knew that in the end it came down to trust. So she took his hand and said the words. There was a bizarre instant when everything around her slowed down and down into gritty, grainy, colourless images that flattened out to greyness . . .

' . . . eno noisserpmoc . . . '

Suddenly the night-time street corner popped back into its original appearance. Only now, beyond the hazy periphery of Harry's standard background they appeared to be standing on a large shelf jutting from the shadowy wall of a wide horizontal shaft stretching off into a faintly radiant distance. As with the Brolturan Ingress-Lock 87, a bright cord of dataflow entered via a conduit and branched as it ran straight through the centre of the shaft. This dataflow, however, was a slender beam and its few branches, almost threadlike, split off along irregular towers protruding from the sides of the shaft. Around their bases, cube and dome structures glowed and pulsed – the rest of the datascape seemed dead and inert, plunged into deactivated gloom.

'So we were compressed, uploaded and transvectored to . . . ' She frowned. 'To wherever this is.'

Harry was gazing at the palm of one hand where data and images streamed and glowed. When Julia spoke he snapped his fingers and the display vanished.

'I keep an upload grappler on standby at all times,' he said. 'As for our current location . . . well, let us say that it doesn't appear on any tiernet maps. Those who make use of the place call it Qijiq, although it has had other names at different times. It was once a military spy probe deployed by one of the Hegemony's imperial predecessors, the Uphari Alliance, probably. After the Uphari were eclipsed, it passed into the hands of a trade cartel, then to a cabal of Bargalil sympathisers soon after the Indroma revolution. They turned it into the hub of their news and propaganda network, a kind of prototype tiernet which was very popular for a short time until ideological arguments split the cabal. One faction towed it off into hyperspace, thinking to reclaim it at a later date. But they were wiped out by unknown assailants and the probe lay undisturbed until about a century ago when it was reactivated by a guild of dataleggers. They knew a good thing when they saw it and linked it to the tiernet with a shift-encrypted locater code. Which I cracked with a little help.'

'Hmm, a history lesson,' Julia said. 'How instructive.'

'I always feel that more information is better than less,' Harry said, smiling.

'I've no objection, provided the information is relevant.'

'I believe I detect a hint of impatience,' he said. 'We need only wait a short while longer . . . ah, or less.'

Beyond Harry's streetscape imagery a restless glow, flickering like a knot of gleams and angles, approached, its appearance blurring as it entered the shadowy street. Out of the shadows stepped a tall man wearing a plain black suit, black leather gloves and carrying a slender document case.

'Client Harry,' he said in a deep rich voice. 'And a fully fractalised sentience, with naturalistic ego state and dynamic, memory-aware volition.'

'Vayosh,' Harry said. 'This is my companion, Julia. Good to see that your analytics are as sharp as ever. I hope you are able to satisfy the curiosity I mentioned.'

Vayosh's smile was a cold baring of teeth.

'An interesting request, to find the location of a tier-net node aboard a specific vessel possibly in transit. Taxing, but not beyond my abilities.'

Harry grinned. 'You've found it.'

Vayosh gave a slight nod. 'First, the defrayment.'

From within his coat, Harry produced a slim hard-back book and handed it over. 'Decrypts for various weapons contractors on Chasulon, very recently acquired.'

'High-value items,' said Vayosh as he locked it away in his case. 'Most acceptable.' From his suit pocket he took a silver coin and flipped it to Harry, who caught it in midair. He waited a moment then opened his hand and gazed at the data that glowed there.

'This vessel, the *Sacrament*, is currently in hyperspace transit,' Vayosh said. 'And as you can see it is not alone.'

'Vor,' Harry said, frowning as he studied the images.

'There were no other ships when I was on board,' said Julia. 'And what's a Vor?'

'The Vor,' he said. 'An ancient race supposedly lost in the depths of hyperspace, lost or extinct. Not a very pleasant species either, yet it seems that two of their ships are now accompanying the Chaurixa on their journey.'

'You can also see that the Chaurixa vessel's tiernet node is all but impregnable,' Vayosh said. 'The security encryption seems excessive for such a vessel, perhaps the consequence of a data breach in the not-too-distant past.'

Harry gave her a rueful smile. 'Sorry, Julia – I can't see us breaking back into this cage.'

She nodded, concealing her disappointment.

'Where are they headed?' she said.

'Tiernet tracking is imprecise,' said Vayosh. 'But from the sample period it seems that they are on course for the edge of Hegemony space.'

'Any overheard communications between the three ships?' said Harry.

'There were indications of intership comm-beam relays,' Vayosh said. 'These are inaccessible to tiernet probes. The *Sacrament*'s net traffic was analysed but no subcodes or encryptions were found. I have included the net traffic in an attached file.'

'So I see,' Harry said.

'This concludes our transaction,' said Vayosh. 'Till our next encounter, then.'

With that the strange entity rose straight up, crossed the night–street boundary and turned back into a whirling knot of radiance which disappeared amongst the angular shadows.

'Is he an AI?' Julia said.

'Apparently, Vayosh was at one time a virtual cognitive model in an Ufan-Gir military lab. Bootstrapped itself into awareness, escaped into the tiernet and it's been trading secrets and updating itself ever since ... for however long that's been.'

Harry had been scanning through the data received from Vayosh, light from his palm reflecting from his face. Now, frowning, he curled the fingers into a fist and glanced at Julia.

'Interesting – much of the *Sacrament*'s net traffic is regular astrograv updates from subspace beacons and regional star system casters. But there were two responses to requests for a large number of precise star locations. How many missiles did this Talavera say she was planning to launch?'

'Five hundred,' she said uneasily.

Harry nodded. 'That's how many stars are in their location request.'

'She said ...' Julia paused, horrific possibilities hovering at the edge of her comprehension.

'You've already said that you suspected deceit on her part,' Harry said. 'So tell me – what effect would one of these anti-dark-matter missiles have on an ordinary main-sequence star?'

'If the missile were larger than she told me,' Julia said. 'If the cladding vessel's surface was deeply incised to increase the reactive area ... it would make a sun go nova. Every living thing in the same system would die.'

'Five hundred supernovae,' Harry said. 'Now *that* sounds like the Chaurixa. But it raises the question of who they're doing this for, because they are not in the habit of initiating their own campaigns of mayhem and death.'

Talavera's words came back to her with perfect

clarity – *You've no idea how powerful he is, or how powerful he's going to make me. Do you have someone like that* ... She gave a full account of that last encounter, even including the detail about those smoky black snakes. When she mentioned them, Harry's gaze grew intense and serious.

'I've heard of these things before,' he said. 'They're called vermax and they originate from dangerous lairs deep down in hyperspace. I know someone, well, an AI called Reski Emantes, who has connections with a very significant power down there.'

'And where do we find this AI?'

'Earth.' Harry laughed. 'Ready for a trip to the cradle of Humanity?'

'Lead the way,' Julia said, smiling, suddenly looking forward to this unexpected destination.

14

KAO CHIH

The Shyntanil attendants put him in an upright metal framework full of rods, plates and shackles which they used to hold him in place. Most of his outer garments were stripped off, exposing bare skin to curved cold sections and restraining straps made from some heavy, rough material. Soon every limb was gripped fast, as were his head and jaw, chest and midriff. Then came the medication. Grimy vials of something purplish-brown were clamped to the main frame at head height and from them lengths of opaque stained tubing ran down his arms to where the needles were inserted into stinging incisions.

Part of him wanted to wail and beg but he knew that it was pointless to look for compassion from such creatures. They stank of death and their entire ship was a tomb where corpses moved and marched and fought in a withered semblance of life.

Nothing was said as the attendants tipped him back and wheeled him out and along a rust-streaked corridor through sluggish retracting doors then down a sloping section to a bright-lit, low-ceilinged deck. Before him stretched a passageway lined with tall recesses, many of which were occupied by similarly restrained captives. Some looked alive, others had a deathly pallor. Kao Chih would have focused on these passing details but his thoughts started to drift as the unknown drips began to take effect.

To his narcotised eyes, the occupants of the lines of recesses were smiling at him as he passed by, nodding and winking. *Welcome to Di-Yu*, they were saying, *welcome to the Hell of the Iron Web.* One said, *The god Ping-Deng-Wang is the judge here.* Another said, *Have you committed any of the Ten Unpardonable Sins? If you have, you'll be stuck here for eternity . . .*

I haven't, honestly, I give you my word! he desperately wanted to say as he opened his eyes, not realising that he had closed them . . .

He was shocked to find that he was now in a recess, gazing across at another unfortunate who hung limply amid his own web of restraints. *I must have passed out*, he reasoned but when he peered at the drug vials they looked almost full. A nameless, inescapable fear twisted in the pit of his stomach, which ached with hunger. Then, amid his anguish, he noticed that the captive opposite, a lanky humanoid with a blockish head, had opened one dark and gleaming eye and was staring straight at him.

But the drugs were muffling his senses again, numbing the complaints from his stomach, surging steadily up into a great warm heavy wave that just rolled over him, tumbling him into a glittering darkness . . .

Voices woke him the next time, along with the trundle of wheels and the rattle of implements. He listened with eyes closed.

'... why is this one kept from the caul? It's ripe for it ...'

'Orders from the Greatlords – Humans are now to be held for our Vor brothers, for their uses ...'

'Pauch! – mindeater scum – not my brothers! No honour, bad fate ...'

'Bad fate if Old Irontooth hears your whining ...'

Vials clinked and moments later a torpid tide poured through his veins, tingling then numbing and smothering ...

15

CHEL

In wounded dreams he wandered. It seemed that he could see through the daughter-forest's dense foliage to the rough lands beyond, and through them to the furthest corners of the Human colony. In his vudron dream, all seven of the daughter-forests were visible and curiously close – a short walk could take him to Ibsenskog in the south or Tapiola in the north. The entire landscape of the colony was visible in vibrant colours rich with detail: the towns and cities as much as the tracks and woods of the coastal farmlands.

Yet the daughter-forests had a special quality to them, a faint aura of power and mystery, even poor, half-burned and abandoned Buchanskog east of Hammergard. The cold waves of the Korzybski Sea stretched eastwards, while to the west lay Giant's Shoulder, then a maze of ridges and ravines and the foothills of the Kentigerns, their jagged peaks marching west and north. And scattered among the vales and gorges, south along the Savrenki range and north across the vast Forest of Arawn, were the glows of burrows, ancient Uvovo chambers built during the time of Segrana-that-was.

He had visited one many days ago, soon after the Seer husking, and recollection of its dusty interior came back with surprising clarity and force. The vudron dream was lucid yet easily swayed – between one moment and the next he went from the hazy, sunny paths of a daughter-forest to the dry, gritty gloom of that underground burrow. Scholar Trem, the Uvovo in charge then, approached from one side, his plain brown robe streaked with dust.

'Keeper,' he said. 'This is the seedpod of battle. You must bring the Eyes.'

'I am not the Keeper,' Chel said. 'The Human Catriona is the Keeper of Segrana.'

'The Keeper of Umara,' Trem said, 'must bring the Eyes to the seedpods of battle.'

Suddenly they were standing in the chamber of living roots beneath the roothouse. Scholar Trem raised a cupped hand over a thick root embedded in the wall, tipped it and let a stream of glowing blue motes fall onto the root. They sank into the moist green and black woody skin and soon a flickering blue tracery spread along to branching rootlets and to the other rootsworks until the chamber was full of pure blue light.

With a sudden intake of breath he awoke in the darkness of the vudron. It was utterly quiet and stiflingly warm. He could smell the wood of the vudron pod and the odour of his unwashed fur, yet with his Seer talents he could sense the daughter-forest outside, the brimming swirl of its denizens, and the sweet undercurrent of Segrana's song.

And something else. He rose from the low bench, half-crouching, and felt something fall to the floor. He pushed open the oval door and green-tinged light poured in, revealing seven or eight lengths of pale grey plastic lying at his feet, trailing clusters of hair-fine fibres. Chel smiled with relief – the vudron dreams had helped his body reject the Legion Knight's implants.

Outside, he found himself standing on a high, mid-level branch, veiled in curtains of leaves and vines. A young male of the Warrior Uvovo handed him a leaf bowl of cold, fragrant water. Grateful, he drained it in a single gulp then went in search of the faint dissonance that he had heard through the interweave of songs.

He found Rory's vudron on a lower branch round the other side of the immense tree. A female Unburdener, cloaked and hooded, inclined her head as Chel approached. The woody shell of the chest-high vudron was dark and rough, its upper surface bearing patches of moss, while the edges of the doorway were smooth with use.

Gingerly he put out a hand to the vudron, lightly brushing the wood with his fingertips – *fire, choking smoke, wheeling stars* – and quickly snatched them back. Rory seemed to be in the grip of a powerful and vivid dream of destruction. Reflecting upon his own vudron vision, Chel wondered if Rory was coping with the intensity and the resulting turbulence of thought.

Perhaps I can help him face it all, he thought. *Perhaps even help his healing.*

He reached out to touch the vudron and again saw . . .

Fire was burning in a recess in the wall of a narrow corridor. Smoke hung in a hazy layer and a shaven-headed Human male coughed hoarsely as he rushed up to the fire with a small extinguisher and unleashed its contents. All sound, though, was muffled, even the man roaring in agony in a small chamber off to the right, where the floor was spattered with blood. Chel turned away, horrified and confused, and a cloud of smoke and steam engulfed him for a moment.

When it cleared he was standing on the upper section of a medium-sized, split-level room that narrowed towards a wide, curved window beyond which starry night swung and spun. There were several Humans there, among them Gregory Cameron, deep in discussion with another Human male, and down on the lower level was Rory, who seemed uninvolved in what was going on. Faces were smeared with ash and expressions were grim. Then Rory at last spotted Chel and ascended to join him.

'Chel! – what are you doing in ma dream?' Rory grinned. 'Pretty amazing, eh? And they nyaffs back at the mountain think I've nae imagination!' Then his voice lowered as he leaned closer. 'Listen, did we ... were we gonnae do a job for that big Legion cyborg bastard? – I mean, did we escape or did we ... ye know, betray the others?' He swallowed. 'Are we dead?'

Chel shook his head. 'We're not dead, Rory, and we managed not to betray the other Humans, although the mechs still carried out their ambush. We are under the protection of a Uvovo daughter-forest, and it is healing you while you sleep.'

Rory was visibly relieved. 'God, I was thinking the worst, there. So why am I getting this weird dream? I mean, there's Greg but I can wave and shout and jump up and down but he disnae bat an eyelid ... mind you, they're all like ghosts, cannae touch anybody ...'

'That may be the answer,' Chel said, glancing up at the Human. 'This may not be a dream – it may be happening right now.'

Rory suddenly looked worried. 'But that means he's on a busted ship in the middle of a battle ...'

Without warning a hand grasped Chel's shoulder and pulled him. It was Scholar Trem, standing next to that thick gleaming root running the length of a stone wall, while the stonework of the root chamber blurred into the structure of the ship's bridge.

'You must bring the Eyes to the seedpod of battle, Cheluvahar,' Trem said, regarding him with a piercing gaze. 'Bring them from beneath the mountain.'

Then abruptly he was back on the branchway, standing before the vudron in which Rory dreamed true visions.

'When he awakes,' Chel told the Unburdener sentry, 'tell him that I know it was no dream.'

With that he left, heading down the main trunk's spiral steps to a rope gantry that would take him back towards that southward ravine. To the south were the Kentigerns and Tusk Mountain within which lay the Hall of Discourse and the Sentinel. Instinct mingled with his Seer talents and said this is where you must go. Now.

16

THEO

It was well into the night when the first survivors of the mech ambush arrived back at Tusk Mountain. An exhausted handful of men carrying two seriously wounded, one of them a Tygran, both needing immediate attention. Solvjeg and her son Ian volunteered to help and Theo was happy to accept the offer, hoping that by keeping them busy their minds would not dwell so much on Greg's absence.

When the three of them had returned from the stony, wooded vale where Theo's unsuccessful assassin now lay dead, it was to a Tusk Mountain base rife with rumour and torn by argument. Earlier, the Tygran squad left behind by Gideon had picked up a brief signal from their ship, the *Starfire*, saying that Greg Cameron was unable to leave the ship due to enemy action. When the Tygrans also began to overhear fragmentary battle communications from near space, this provoked dark, wild speculation throughout the corridors.

Then a garbled message had been received from Gideon's comm officer, who said they were under attack moments before he suddenly shrieked in agony and the signal went dead. This turned the prevalent uneasy speculation into a mood barely short of panic. Theo was quick to impose authority and calm, backed by his remaining Diehards. Everyone had to calm down, steady their nerves and their resolve – and to be ready for when the wounded started arriving. Despite some muttering, the personal tack seemed to work and the panic subsided.

As he watched his sister and his nephew help stretcher the injured along to the sickbay, he thought again about their tense, cheerless mood, reasoning that Ned's death must have had a tragic element. Perhaps he should have been somewhere else when the boatyard went up, or some chance event had led him to the wrong place at the wrong time. Certainly he had witnessed enough incredible coincidences to half-believe that the machinery of the cosmos had a 'black irony' setting which inflicted random synchronicities on hapless thinking beings and left them to rise or fall by their consequences. Theo preferred that to the ethos of a watching, activist deity, be it Odin or the Christian God – any god that would deliberately inflict suffering didn't deserve praise, in his view.

Less than an hour later Captain Gideon arrived with most of the raiding party survivors, of whom a third were walking wounded. But no Vashutkin.

'I don't know what happened to him,' the Tygran said as they went with the injured to the sickbay. 'He was there, quite close to me, while we were questioning the newcomers ...'

'Newcomers?'

'Yes, Major, your people recognised them. A Uvovo called Chel, and a colonist called McGrain, I think.'

Theo laughed. 'Rory – so he's still alive! Are they with you?'

'I lost track of them after the mechs attacked,' said Gideon. 'But there was something not right about them. As I heard it, Cameron was almost captured aboard one of your balloon boats after being lured to a hilltop by radio contact with the one named McGrain. Well, after we fought off the ambush, and they were nowhere to be seen, they seemed likely candidates as assassins. However, Vashutkin is also missing, which arouses my suspicion.'

'I find it hard to believe that Chel and Rory would let themselves be used as assassins,' Theo said. 'Vashutkin on the other hand has dark corners that make me uneasy.' He described the reasons for his suspicions and fears that the Rus had been infected with the blue dust.

'Are you saying that the Hegemony has been using Blue Chain here on Darien?' Gideon said.

'Greg told me it was a blue dust,' Theo said. 'I see that you know about this stuff.'

'Oh yes, Major. As a soldier I can appreciate its intelligence-gathering uses, but as a Tygran citizen I find it repugnant.' Gideon crossed his arms and looked gloweringly thoughtful. 'What you say about Vashutkin makes me more inclined to suspect him of being a pawn of that Legion Knight creature. However, a rational appraisal would demand more convincing proof. To that end, we should convene in an hour with your sister and her son and hear their testimony on the matter. We'll also assess what went wrong today. In the meantime, Major, you'll excuse me while I tend to my men.'

In the event it was several hours before Theo could get everyone round the same table. Stragglers from the ambush arrived in ones and twos and only after the last of them had been sedated, medicated or operated on was it possible to lead his sister Solvjeg away to quarters in the southern sublevel. A nearby chamber had been laid out for the meeting and some twenty minutes later Theo and Captain Gideon were sitting across from Solvjeg and Ian Cameron. Greg's brother had had a shave and a change of clothing, which if anything emphasised his gauntness. A beaker of water poured from the table jug sat untouched before him.

Also in attendance was Listener Weynl, looking weary yet alert. Seated on a raised chair, he was able to face everyone at eye level.

Gideon began by addressing Solvjeg.

'Frauwas Cameron, the major has made me aware of the death of your youngest son. Please accept my condolences for your loss.'

'Thank you for your kind words, Captain,' she said. 'Has there been any further news about Gregory?'

'My communications officer has been unable to reestablish contact with my ship,' said the Tygran. 'Unfortunately it appears that all offworld communications across this region are being jammed by the facility on Giant's Shoulder. But according to the meagre sensor data we've been able to gather, it seems that there is a skirmish taking place in near-Darien space. Several vessels are involved and combat exchanges appear to have shifted further outward, beyond high orbit. We continue to monitor the situation as best we can but details are difficult to ascertain.'

On hearing this, the lines in Solvjeg's face deepened and she closed her eyes.

Well done, Captain, Theo thought. *Is that a Tygran attempt at being supportive and morale-boosting?*

'Sister,' he said. 'I told the captain here about the boatyard bombing, and what you said about infiltrators . . .'

'Yes, and I am now sure that they come from that nest of rogue droids,' Solvjeg said angrily. 'On Giant's Shoulder, the same monsters which brought down destruction on your men, Captain, and which sent a spy into your midst. We saw the possessed host that accompanied my brother's captor. The internal mind-struggle was plain as could be.'

'The major tells me that the infiltrators you intercepted off in the Eastern Towns had visible implants, yet this host which suicided had none. Correct?'

Solvjeg nodded.

'Then it seems likely that our spy's origin is different from those you encountered.' Gideon sat back in his chair. 'I have seen the effects of Blue Chain and the effects you describe correspond to the use of too little. The machine-molecule particulates take time to build, especially when they have to replicate themselves within a host, so what you saw were the results of a Blue Chain collective too few in number to effectively dominate their host, resulting in the indecision and mental instability.'

'And this Blue Chain definitely would originate with the Hegemony?' said Ian Cameron.

'Without a doubt,' said Gideon. 'The Hegemony ambassador, this Kuros, who is currently residing in the

Brolturan enclave north of Trond. Our planned strike against the Spiralist stockades would liberate nearby villages and Trond itself, making it easier to mount an attack on the Brolturans. Reports say that they have a hangar full of assault flyers and gunships, just what we need to take on Giant's Shoulder.' He frowned. 'Of course, attacking that enclave would be very difficult, and if Brolturan reinforcements arrive then all our plans will be of no consequence.'

'There may be an alternative,' Ian Cameron said.

Theo leaned forward. 'You mentioned the possibility of an alliance with a splinter group of Spiralist zealots.'

Ian nodded. 'One of their leaders came to us and offered the help of his faction in any attack on Giant's Shoulder. He told me that the prophet lied, and that an alien machine is now in control up there.'

The Uvovo, Listener Weynl, cleared his throat. 'This alien machine is actually a creature known as a Knight of the Legion of Avatars. It landed on Darien some days before the Spiral armada's invasion. Our Seer Cheluvahar was following this vile creature through Greathome Forest – as you call the Forest of Arawn – for several days before he was captured by it. As Rory had been earlier.'

Gideon glanced at Theo. 'So when we met them on the way north, they could well have been enslaved by this Knight of the Legion.' He glared at the Uvovo. 'My men claim to have heard rumours that this thing is an ancient enemy of the Uvovo – is this so? And what is the truth about the Forerunner installation within Giant's Shoulder? It has been described to me as a malfunctioning matter transporter but I cannot see the Hegemony or their Brolturan pets expending this amount of effort over something that does not work. In the meantime, this Knight of some Legion now seemingly controls it, supported by an army of combat mechs. A satisfactory explanation would be most helpful.'

Theo and Listener Weynl exchanged a look, almost by chance. Theo decided to respond first.

'Captain, you are correct – there is more to Giant's Shoulder than what you have seen or heard. There is a Forerunner artefact inside it, a warpwell. The first time I saw that chamber and that well with the light pouring out of it ... an amazing sight, I can tell you. But yes, as I recall it, the warpwell is really the front door of a prison, a prison in hyperspace, y'see, and ...'

'If I may, Major Karlsson,' said Listener Weynl. 'Might I tell the tale from our side?'

'Certainly, Weynl, go ahead.'

'Captain Gideon,' said the Uvovo. 'The Legion of Avatars was the last great enemy faced by the ancient Forerunners. They swept across the star-rivers in vast numbers, hundreds of millions, laying waste to entire civilisations. To fight them, the Ancients caused warp-wells to be built on a hundred worlds – Giant's Shoulder, which we call the Waonwir, is the location of one such device. At the height of that last immense battle the warpwells snatched every enemy machine and creature and dragged them down uncountable, immeasurable distances, thrust them into the lightless, frozen chasms beneath the deepest underdomains ...'

'They were imprisoned in the abyss of hyperspace,' Theo explained. 'All except one, a Legion Knight, a kind of armoured cyborg.'

'So I gather,' Gideon said. 'And is this warpwell like-wise the last of its kind?'

'The Sentinel of the well told me that Hegemony scholars have discovered the dead remains of several others throughout their territory,' Weynl said. 'But ours does appear to be the only functioning example yet found.'

'The major described it as the front door of a prison,' Gideon said. 'If all that you've said about the Knight creature is true, do we know if it has tried to break down that door?'

'Been wondering that myself,' Theo said.

All eyes were on Weynl, who seemed to consider the Tygran's question for a second or two before speaking.

'It fills me with sorrow to have to say yes, it has suc-ceeded in unlocking the well. Six days ago, before dawn on the day after Gregory Cameron was sent to Segrana, every Listener and sensitive Uvovo on Umara was aware of the very moment when the well was opened. Certain bearers of wisdom estimate that it would take between three and five days for the unlocking to travel all the way to the imprisoning depths, and perhaps the same for the enemy to make its ascent.'

Theo was stunned. Gideon frowned and leaned back in his chair, arms crossed. Ian Cameron picked up his beaker of water and drank it off in a single swallow. Solvjeg seemed the only one unsurprised, her face still serious, her eyes more intense.

'So, to summarise,' Gideon said, 'the Hegemony and/or the Brolturans are due to arrive here soon in the shape of an undoubtedly substantial battle fleet with the intention of pacifying the colony while deterring any moves from the likes of the Imisil. At the same time, a portal into hyperspace will shortly – maybe today, maybe in four days' time – disgorge an alien fleet of unknown size, unknown combat abilities and unknown intent.'

The Uvovo looked sombre. 'Captain, you should expect them to number in the many thousands and for them to fight any who oppose them with a relentless fury.'

'Well, now,' Theo said to Gideon. 'Always handy to know these things, eh?'

Then Solvjeg leaned forward. 'Then we should mount a joint attack on Giant's Shoulder, your people, ours and the Spiral renegades ...'

'As I've already explained,' Gideon said, 'without the Brolturan flyers we would have no airborne force and without that ...'

'Except that we have aircraft,' Solvjeg said. 'When we liberated Hammergard, we also liberated North-East Fields.'

'Ah, zeplins,' Theo said. 'How many, sister?'

'Seven, perhaps eight – our engineers were hard at work on another when we left.'

The Tygran captain's brow was furrowed with thought.

'What kind of passenger capacities do they have?'

'Average is a dozen each,' said Ian Cameron.

'It would be a high-risk operation,' Gideon said. 'Casualties would very likely exceed fifty per cent, but a slim chance exists. If my heavy-weapons team can take control of that defence battery, that would swing the odds in our favour. However, that doesn't address the problem of how to close the warpwell and stop this Legion from escaping ... could we demolish it with explosives, Listener?'

'It was constructed by the great Ancients, Captain Gideon,' the Uvovo said. 'I doubt that it would be so easily ...'

He broke off at the sound of a commotion outside. Then the door swung open and a young, red-furred Uvovo stumbled in, half-restrained by a Human sentry.

'Listener, Listener! – you must come to the Hall of Discourse!'

Theo gestured at the guard, who released the animated Uvovo.

'Why are you interrupting us, Ajinos?' Weynl said. 'What is this about?'

'The Seer,' the young Uvovo said. 'He is in the Hall ... and he speaks with Segrana!'

'Chel?' Theo said as he stood. 'Chel's here?'

'We must go,' said Listener Weynl, slipping down and hurrying to the door. 'Immediately.'

Minutes later they entered the Hall of Discourse. Normally half-lit by the multicoloured glassy panels dotted across the tall, curved walls, now a column of shining white radiance rose from the Forerunner platform, sending light into every corner. A figure knelt at the centre of it, one small hand held out, palm upwards. As he approached Theo could see that Chel's lips were moving, and closer still he could make out the Uvovo's voice, quietly muttering responses as part of a conversation with another voice, deep and muted. At that point, Chel got to his feet and faced his audience.

'Captain Gideon,' he said. 'My apologies for

disappearing in the middle of the attack, but neither I nor my companion were entirely in our right minds. I had to get us both to the nearby daughter-forest or risk losing our selves completely.'

'So, you and Rory,' Theo said, 'you were both enslaved by that creature, this Knight ... are you okay now? Are you free of its control? Is Rory?'

Chel took off the thin shift he wore, revealing shaven patches in his body fur, on arms, chest and neck. The bare skin showed healing wounds like regularly spaced holes and incisions.

'Rory was semi-conscious when we reached the forest,' Chel said. 'He had to be helped into a vudron for the healing sleep, which has to run its course without interruption. It worked well for me – my body was able to reject the pain implants and begin healing its wounds. I am completely free of the Knight's enslavement. Rory I am unsure of – when I left he was still in the dream and I could not tell if his implants had been expelled.'

'You certainly seem more composed than at our last encounter,' said Gideon. 'Forgive my cautious nature, but is there any way for us to verify this?'

Listener Weynl was outraged. 'He is the Seer of Segrana and he stands in the pureness of the Ancients!'

A bright thread of light appeared in the radiance next to Chel, blurred, glowing knots pulsing up and down its length.

'The Seer Cheluvahar has been made free of the enemy's devices,' said a deep, almost gruff voice. 'I am the Zyradin. I speak for Segrana.'

Weynl raised his hands. 'Zyradin of the Ancients, we know your name. We have learned that the warpwell has been opened. Have any of the Legion monsters survived the long ages of their imprisonment, and how long before they reach us?'

'**Many have survived and the first of them will emerge in little more than two days' time.**'

There was a long moment of silence filled with the dread of anticipation. Just then, Theo knew that there was only one course open to them. He glanced over at his sister and nodded sombrely.

'Looks like we attack,' he said.

'It appears so,' said Gideon.

'But to succeed we must find a way into the warpwell chamber,' said Weynl, looking up at Chel. 'Can the Zyradin use the Forerunners' ancient devices to transport a bomb into the chamber?'

Chel shook his head. 'The Legion Knight has placed interference machines throughout the chamber. These, combined with the disruptive effects of the activated warpwell, make such a ploy impossible. Other tactics must be considered.'

'**You will need someone capable of getting past the Legion Knight's machines by subterfuge. There is one such, still resting and healing in the daughter-forest to the north.**'

'Rory?' Theo said. 'You mean, he's not having those implants removed? You get to be free of them but he doesn't?' Theo found himself getting angry. 'Was this planned? Did you arrange this, Chel?'

'Theodor, I promise you that I did not ...'

'**Segrana saw what was needed and acted accordingly,**' said the deep voice of the Zyradin. '**Your friend will still be able to interact with the Legion Knight's** devices but the implants can no longer hurt or control him.'

'It's still unfair,' said Theo. 'You did not even ask him.'

'If the Legion of Avatars breaks through to this world, they will ask nothing of anyone when they begin their slaughter.'

'We should go and contact Hammergard,' said Ian Cameron. 'Have the Spiralist renegade leader ready to talk with you, to agree on a plan of attack.'

'You'll have to use the shortwave now,' Gideon said. 'I shall join you shortly.'

Theo watched them leave the hall, frowning.

'We are assuming a lot, you know,' he said. 'That Rory will agree to play this part. That he can actually get past the mech security and down to the well chamber, and if he does, what then? What can he do to close it down?'

'Ordinary weapons and explosives cannot harm the warpwell or disturb its functions,' said the Zyradin. 'A thermonuclear apparatus might affect the surface material and suspend its processes but only for a short time ...'

'Such weapons are neither available nor advisable,' said Chel, as if continuing the Zyradin's sentence. 'What is required is a space-fold occluder, which will close up and lock the well, keeping us safe from one threat, at least.'

'The device will be delivered to this place at this time tomorrow.'

The bright, pulsing thread then thinned and faded into the surrounding milky radiance.

'The mystical Zyradin departs,' said Listener Weynl.

'Meanwhile, we have to go and devise an insane plan of attack,' Theo said to Chel. 'I expect that you've been given a task too.'

Chel smiled and raised his right hand, palm outward. Theo's eyes widened – a number of shining blue motes, perhaps a dozen or a score, wandered over and through the flesh of the Uvovo's hand. The skin glowed as they moved beneath it.

'Throughout the valleys and forests of Umara,' Chel said, 'the song of Segrana sings softly, in the fields, the trees, the streams and the soil, and in the burrows and roothouses of our ancestors. With this gift I can awaken the powers of that song ...'

As they watched, the Seer's form brightened, the details of his face blurring, merging then fading into the flowing radiance which itself then grew faint, a tenuous tracery of glimmer hanging over the patterns of the stone platform. Till there was only a silver shimmer which melted away to nothing.

Listener Weynl sighed, a weary sound, and sat on the flagstones before the raised circular platform.

'We'll need to put together lists of volunteers, weapons and supplies,' Gideon said.

'I'll have Alexei Firmanov help you with that,' Theo said. 'While I'm away.'

The Tygran frowned. 'Where are you going?'

'To persuade Varstrand to fly me north to the daughter-forest,' he said. 'A good friend is going to need a ride home.'

17

GREG

In the blackness of space the ship spun, helpless and crippled. It was turning end over end with a certain grace while also rotating about its longitudinal axis. External lights and landing indicators flickered erratically and vapour leaks left strange, fading spirals of frozen crystals in the vessel's wake.

A Hegemony ship, a heavy assault implementer called the *Ivwa-Kagoy*, was tracking it on its course away from the Human colony world. The pursuit was also leading away from the fighting but the Hegemony captain was confident that the mighty carrier, *Baqrith-Zo*, was quite capable of obliterating a pair of Imisil scouts. This Human vessel, however, was a different matter. It matched the configuration of an Ezgara ship yet it had been fighting alongside the Imisil when the Hegemony carrier group exited hyperspace near the system's periphery. There had been rumours of an Ezgara regiment turning renegade and the Father-Admiral urgently needed to know if there were any other similar rogue vessels in the stellar vicinity. His orders were clear – capture and interrogate.

Standing at his elevated command console, the

Sendrukan captain surveyed projected screens full of scan data on the Human vessel. The sensors had detected some forty-seven lifesigns, whereas the *Ivwa-Kagoy*'s complement came to twenty-five.

But Humans are like children next to us, the captain thought. *My crew should be able to overcome them without difficulty. However, Ezgara prisoners may present a problem. A degree of caution and subterfuge is required.*

He was consulting with the ship's machine intelligence and his own mind-companion when visual updates streamed across his command screens. Minor explosions aboard the Ezgara vessel had expelled some lesser debris, hull armour, outer bulkhead fragments, components, cabling, and white clouds of escape gases. There was also a larger object that looked to have been partially dislodged from its fastenings – one of the screens showed it swinging out from a shallow recess on the Ezgara vessel's underside, still attached. Then something gave way and the object, now visible as a small shuttle pod, was flung outwards by the still-spinning ship. One sensor cluster tracked its slow tumbling progress for a moment or two; the expert system observed the erratic misfiring of its attitude thrusters, noted the absence of lifeforms aboard and demoted its monitoring priority.

So when one of the shuttle pod's port thrusters fired in longer bursts, sending it into a tighter, faster spin, the sensors' expert system failed to register it as a problem. Until it came out of its spin on a fast intercept trajectory, all thrusters on full burn, driving it towards the Hegemony ship. Collision alarms started yammering on the bridge and the machine mind advised the captain and his officers to retreat to the midsection.

But with only a few seconds to react, they had only begun moving to the exits when the shuttle crashed nose first into the viewport. Armoured glass barriers shattered under the impact, layers of hull around it bent and split, and the shuttle's blunt prow burst through into the bridge. Suddenly there was the shriek of escaping atmosphere, and emergency facemasks popped out of their wall niches. But the force of depressurisation dragged the captain towards the smashed-in viewport, just as it dislodged the shuttle and propelled it back out.

Followed by the suffocated, flash-frozen bodies of the captain and his officers.

On board the *Starfire*, Greg turned to Lieutenant Malachi Ash and said, 'That came off very well, I think.'

'I'll be happier when the ship's in our hands,' said Ash. 'The next part will not be pretty and could go badly wrong if they decide to rig the drives to self-destruct.'

It took twenty minutes to manoeuvre alongside the Hegemony vessel, which was still heading along its original course even though the thrust drive had been shut down. The *Starfire*'s attitudinal jets were functioning but that was about all – the hyperdrive was half-slagged and most of the generators were blown, which meant that the weaponry could be neither powered nor aimed. Greg just hoped that this hijacking didn't result in two wrecked ships.

Greg's experience of close-quarter combat was nearly non-existent so Ash made him stay with the rearguard, watching over the medical team and the ammo bearers. The Tygran energy weapons were keyed back to non-lethal settings to avoid damaging vital systems. In addition, some carried weighted clubs, daggers and tanglers. Malachi had been aboard this class of Hegemony warship before, and once a beachhead was established around the lateral airlock he was quick to move against the engineering section with the greater part of his troops. A smaller force was sent to secure the aft armoury.

Most of the fighting was over in less than an hour. The injuries were terrible yet the medic, Lieutenant Valerius, remained calm throughout, his tense manner matching his apparently tireless ability to deal with patient after patient. Gashes were pincerwired, burns were dermasprayed, beam- or blade-severed extremities were tagged and stored in a stasiscase while the wounds were coated in isolation gel then hardshelled. By the end the tally had reached two dead (and swiftly jettisoned out of the nearest airlock), five walking wounded and three stretcher cases.

Everyone looked bruised and battered and physically drained. Close-quarters and hand-to-hand combat against adversaries who were two, sometimes three feet taller (and correspondingly brawnier) was taxing, even with two- or three-to-one odds. This difference in scale was reflected in the ship's interior. On his way to engineering, where Ash had set up his command post, Greg noticed the height and width of the passageways and doors, the oddly oppressive gold and grey colour scheme, and elaborate bas-relief mouldings that covered the upper half of every bulkhead.

Two of Ash's men were dragging a dead Sendrukan out into the corridor by the feet as Greg arrived. Past the entrance to the engineering deck, the ornamentation was impressively overbearing, more bas-relief mouldings, several life-size silver statues mounted at head height in the corners, each demonstrating a different pre-industrial technical skill. Immense consoles dominated the room with a large, complex one occupying half the floor and butting against a wide window broken into hexagonal segments. Cabling sprouted from various open panels on the big console, where a group of Tygran techs worked, watched over by Ash.

'Ah, Mr Cameron, good of you to join us,' Ash said. 'As you can see, we are in the process of rerouting bridge functions down here – in fact the Sendrukans had nearly accomplished it when we so rudely interrupted them. Luckily, Second Senior Instrumentationalist Panabec here has agreed to help us.'

A Sendrukan stood nearby, cuffed and shackled, towering over his two armed guards. His dark blue uniform was torn at one shoulder and his broad face bore a glumly stoic look. Greg wondered at the wisdom of taking advice from an enemy prisoner until one of the Tygran techs turned and nodded to Ash.

'That's the AI cores wiped, sir,' he said. 'Including the backup. The interface module is fully spliced into their matrix hub and we're ready to bring the *Starfire* copy online.'

'Have all precautions been taken?' Ash said.

'They have, sir.'

'Good – carry on.' Ash smiled at Greg. 'Panabec assures me that AI transitioning is a straightforward procedure. If it's not, he'll be joining the rest of the prisoners in the hold.'

Before he finished, the tiny emitters all along the top of the line of big consoles winked on, flickered, and three large holoscreens appeared above them, angled downwards. Smaller ones appeared at other secondary workstations around the deck. Ash nodded.

'*Starfire*-copy,' he said. 'Are you in control of this vessel's systems and do you recognise my voice?'

'Full control will be attained in two point five minutes on completion of calibration. You are Lieutenant Malachi Ash, second in command to Captain Franklyn Gideon.'

'Indeed so, *Starfire*-copy,' Ash said. 'Give me a brief summary of this vessel's offensive capabilities.'

'Nine dual-function projectors, two at the stern, three at the prow, and two on each flank. Four launchers, one long-range, two medium, and one short-range, high-rate submunitioner. Additional offensive capabilities can include comm-sensor countermeasures and certain exotic forcefield properties.'

Seeing how pleased Ash was, Greg said, '*Starfire*-copy, do you know the Hegemony designation of this vessel?'

'This is the heavy assault implementer *Ivwa-Kagoy*.'

'I think a new name is called for,' Greg said, looking at Ash. 'Don't you think, Lieutenant?'

'Yes, you're right. *Starfire*-copy, is there a protocol for the rebadging of captured enemy vessels?'

'Captured enemy vessels are renamed under a colour-coding protocol. This class of vessel falls into categories red and silver.'

Greg and Ash exchanged thoughtful looks. The latter shrugged and Greg said, 'How about *Silverlance*?'

'*Silverlance* would be acceptable under protocol parameters,' said the transplanted AI.

'Very well,' said Ash. 'Execute this change.'

'Done. The designation of this ship is now Recon Strike Cruiser *Silverlance*. Note that systematrix calibration is complete – this intelligence can now offer full control of this vessel.'

Ash turned to the Sendrukan Panabec, and gave a small, sharp bow of the head. 'My thanks and appreciation for your valuable assistance, Instrumentationalist.'

'The integrity of my machines is my duty,' the Sendrukan said gravely. 'May I be permitted to rest?'

'Certainly,' Ash said, nodding to the guards, who escorted the Sendrukan engineer through a side door.

'Attention,' said the ship AI. 'Urgent communication from *Starfire* bridge personnel, with accompanying update files and realtime sensor readings.'

Ash went over to one of the large consoles, hoisted himself up into a great bucket of a seat and said, 'Put them through here.'

As Greg joined him, one of the big overhead screens changed from subsystem monitor displays to a waist-up view of Berg, the tactical officer left in charge of the *Starfire*.

'Berg,' Ash said. 'Update on that skirmish?'

'It's over, sir. One of the Imisil ships is destroyed, the other is in bad shape and heading out of the system at maximum thrust, which suggests that their hyperdrive is out of action.'

'And the carrier group?'

'Hegemony forces took a pounding. Out of four support battery ships, one is still fully combat-worthy, two are holed but still able to fight, and the fourth took a couple of multiwave missiles in the stern when its shields fluctuated so it's a wreck. Carrier lost nearly a third of its interceptors and was breached on several decks.'

'Those Imisil ships can certainly deal it out,' Greg murmured.

'The carrier group is back on course for Darien,' Berg continued. 'ETA is about 110 minutes. Comm traffic has been intense since the Imisil fled but they're employing fifth-level encryption – we've sent you coiled archives.'

Ash nodded. '*Silverlance* AI – are you able to extract usable data?'

'Decryption/translation module online – archived object now processed. Summary follows: main document details a list of ground targets in respect of planetary bombardment. Target plotted on hybrid locational/physical map on main screen right.'

Greg stared up at the map in horror. Red triangles were littered all across the colony – towns, villages, hamlets and cities, even sizeable farm compounds had been marked for destruction. Even the buildings at Gangradur Falls and the small settlements scattered throughout the Forest of Arawn. Tusk Mountain was the focus of a conspicuous cluster of red triangles, although Giant's Shoulder was noticeably clear of them. Then there was the enclave of Brolturan troops to the north – had the Hegemony commander contacted them, perhaps even talked with Kuros? Then he realised that there was little point in speculation. There was only one thing that was about to happen to Darien, and one word to describe it.

Genocide.

'We have to stop them, Ash,' he said. 'We cannae sit back and let them do this!'

The Tygran officer was glowering up at the map.

'That carrier,' he said, 'destroyed one of those Imisil ships and chased off the other, and either of them could take on this Heg ship and win.' He glanced at Greg. 'So how, Mr Cameron, can we go up against it and succeed?'

'Do what we did before – throw a shuttle at it ...'

Ash shook his head. 'That carrier masses something like a million and a quarter tons fully manned and loaded. Ramming it with a shuttle would be like throwing a shoe at a charging behemox. On the other hand, if we used a ship ...'

Greg made a rueful grimace. 'The *Starfire*?'

Ash got down from the big seat, stretched his back and studied the screen displays. '*Silverlance* AI – with the *Starfire* in tow, would we be able to intercept the carrier group before it came within weapons range of Darien?'

'Assuming maximum velocity within tolerances and a flight time of forty-two minutes, this vessel could achieve intercept with eight point three minutes to spare ... Communication has been received from the Hegemony commander, contains updated version of target list and personal orders.'

'Read me the orders,' Ash said grimly.

'Translated, it begins: "From Phalanx Supreme Ordainer Jothul, aboard the Great Carrier *Baqrith-Zo*, to Effector-Captain Vadeyni of the Implementer *Ivwa-Kagoy* – the Imisil raiders have been defeated, though not without cost. You are to break off current action and rejoin Phalanx at coordinates alpha. Equally, you are to examine the attached list of unassigned targets and respond with prioritised selection matching your vessel's capabilities. Ends." This message also came as an audio message, all encrypted to level five. What reply should be made?'

'Send an "acknowledged – please stand by"-type response,' said Ash. 'Buy us some time.'

'This has already been done.'

'Wait another minute then repeat.'

'We can only send a plain message,' Greg said. 'Tell them our comm systems were seriously mangled in a fight with a Tygran warship ...'

' ... which we have captured almost intact and are claiming as victor's prize.' Ash nodded. '*Silverlance*, can you phrase that suitably in a response? End by saying we have set course and are under way.'

'Done, sir.'

'And select a number of targets from that list, something plausible given our weaponry. Send when ready.'

'Message has now been sent. Sir, do you wish to deploy the forcefield in a towing configuration anchored to the *Starfire*?'

'Inform the bridge of the *Starfire*, then deploy fields and lay in the intercept course.'

'Communication made, sir ... course set, thrusters engaged ... we are under way.'

Greg smiled and nodded approvingly.

'Interesting that you use headsets and console

pickups aboard the *Starfire*, while here it's all speaking into the air.'

'The difference is that on Hegemony ships they love the sound of their own voices!'

They laughed.

'I'll have to take the shuttle back to *Starfire*, get the remaining crew evaced over here,' Ash said. 'And I have to be there in order to set the various self-destructs. And in the meantime, I'm leaving you in charge, temporary measure.'

'There's only twenty-six minutes till we make that intercept,' Greg said. 'That's cutting it a wee bit fine.'

'It is not a problem. Tygrans are used to achieving results under pressure.'

'I'm relieved to hear it.'

Ash headed for the exit, which slid open, and he paused on the threshold. 'Stay in your body armour and retain your sidearm. And you guards – bring Panabec out so everyone can keep an eye on him.'

The Sendrukan engineer was brought out and seated at a round table by the rear bulkhead. Satisfied, Ash nodded to Greg and left.

Greg went over and clambered into the big Sendrukan chair so that he could survey the situation as it unfolded on the semi-opaque holoscreens. There were fourteen crew members still aboard the *Starfire*, close to a full shuttleload, and a round trip there and back could take up to fifteen minutes. Timing was going to be tight.

Just over five minutes later, the screens and ceiling lights in engineering flickered off and on.

'*Silverlance*,' Greg said. 'What just happened?'

'Power … power … powerless,' said the AI.

'Autodiagnostic reports ... no anomaly or interruptions. This is incorrect – am initiating subsystems scrutiny – hierarchic integrity is compromised – *alert*! Main hold access doors unlocked – Sendrukan prisoners escaping ...'

Suddenly fearful, Greg recalled how the *Starfire* was taken over and remotely controlled by the Tygran Marshal Becker.

'What's doing this?' he said. 'Is it coming from the carrier?'

'No data objects of suitable complexity have been received – anomalous interference coming from within this ship – unauthorised course alteration! – *Silverlance* is now on heading B27-902.8 heading away from Darien ...'

We're off course! he thought. *We'll never stop that carrier now.*

Shouts made Greg look round to see the Sendrukan engineer Panabec walking unhurriedly across the floor. His guards, guns raised, were warily following until he stopped and turned to gaze at Greg. The listless bearing was gone and now the eyes flared with anger.

'You are a disease,' the Sendrukan said. 'You will be purged.'

Then he stepped onto a floor tile, which swung down. Like a stone he fell straight through, gone from sight in a heartbeat. The guards dived forward but the tile had resealed and seemed as solid as the rest.

'Where is he?' Greg said. '*Silverlance*, where did Panabec go?'

'Deck Three auxiliary disposal stall – subject Panabec has encountered escaped prisoners – entire group now numbers nine and are moving forward – nearest bank of evacuation pods is accessible from that area.'

'Can you stop them? Seal off the hatches?'

'Unable to comply – such security functions have been abrogated by another.'

Another what? he wondered while trying not to panic. 'Open a channel to the *Starfire* – we need to notify Ash ...'

'Unable to comply – access to external comms has been denied.'

He listened with mounting horror. 'What's doing this? I thought that the original ship AI had been wiped ... is there any way to shut the prisoners out of the pods altogether?'

'No. Emergency and maintenance systems are being progressively subverted. Countermanding agency may be viral with partial cognitive heuristics – may have been a hardwired retaliatory instrumentation ...'

'Is it safe for us to remain aboard?' he said. 'Is it possible to isolate the subverting agency? Put up a firewall of some kind ...'

'Safety uncertain – isolation impossible – forward port evac pods are launching – all Sendrukans have left this ship ...'

Greg stared up at the holoscreens. On two of them, blocks of Sendrukan text appeared one after another in pale blue lettering then slowly faded away. The third screen was a live feed from a hull sensor cam, showing four pods jetting away from the former Hegemony vessel.

'Subversion encroaching on tertiary and secondary systems – integrity compromised – withdrawing to primary core – this cognitive unit is now under threat of sequestration – absent any external countervailing influence, self-erasure has been initiated.'

Suddenly, silence. Greg exchanged worried looks with Panabec's former guards.

'Any word from the *Starfire* on your comm units?' he said.

'Nothing, sir,' said the taller of the two. 'They've been dead since this began.'

Greg nodded sombrely. 'If some booby-trap virus is taking over the ship, we have to figure out where the safest place is – up here, or down near the—'

'Nowhere on this ship,' said an authoritative voice, 'is safe for you.'

A chill went down Greg's spine but he couldn't help laughing.

'Ah, you'll be the new Hegemony captain, then. I'm glad you're here because I think we got off on the wrong foot …'

'I am not the captain of the *Ivwa-Kagoy* but its avenger. You Humans have violated its honour and its illustrious duty. Punishment will be severe.'

'Now, ye see, you're jumping tae conclusions. Without the full facts, you could be in danger of committing crucial errors.'

'The facts are not in question. In opposing our appointed task in this system you Tygrans have assumed the role of enemy combatants. By attacking and boarding this ship you have earned for yourselves an implacable retribution. There are no errors.'

'Except that I'm not a Tygran,' Greg said. 'I'm a Darien non-combatant and I shouldn't even be here. If you execute me I imagine you'll be breaking who knows how many interstellar treaties, conventions and protocols, which might not go down well with the leadership back home.'

Leisurely pacing to and fro between the big holoscreens, Greg glanced over at the guards and gave a damned-if-I-know shrug. The guards grinned.

'Such pleas for exemption do not concern me,' said the Hegemony intelligence, just as one of the guards knelt down beside some of the gear left next to the big central console by Ash's techs. 'Your presence aboard this vessel implies a hostile role. Retaliation against all Humans is therefore justified.'

The guard was peering at what looked like a diagnosis pad sitting on a transport cabinet with its screen open.

'As I said, we got off on the wrong foot,' Greg said, frowning now as the guard started to beckon him over. 'We should all get round a table and talk this through. Once ye get tae know us ye might change yer mind ...'

'My function and purpose is clear – all Humans aboard this ship should be considered an infestation and dealt with accordingly.'

'Ye might want to reconsider that. My own government will not look kindly on the negligent slaughter of one of its citizens.'

Silence.

Aye, Greg thought as he joined the guard. *We're all just the ones who don't matter, me, them and everyone on Darien.*

'What is it?' he said, even as the guard was turning the pad screen for him to see Ash staring up at him.

Greg laughed. 'Is this live or a recording?'

Ash pointed to his right ear then tapped his right shoulder. For a moment Greg was puzzled, then remembered the earpiece built into the Tygran armoured jerkin he wore. He fingered it from a tiny collar pocket, placed it in his ear, then found the jack wire in the hem and snapped it into the pad.

'Let's keep this short and to the point,' Ash said. 'Yes or no answers. Has some kind of backup Hegemony AI taken control?'

'Oh aye.'

'We thought that might have been a consequence of getting Panabec's help. Have any sectors been depressurised?'

'No ... eh, I think.'

'Take that as a no ... what's the matter?'

Greg was straightening from his crouch, turning his head this way and that, listening. 'It's gone quiet – the ventilation's off.'

'Not much time left – open the flap on the underside of this datapad, press and hold the red button for five seconds, then press the blue button.'

Quickly he upended the pad, flipped open the recess and just as he pressed the red button the lights flickered into a dull pulsing pattern and an ululating alarm began to sound. Suddenly the Hegemony AI spoke.

'A cunning ploy, to install an intelligence unit independent of all ship-nets. Yet your punishment is assured, one way or another.'

Counting five, he released the red and punched the blue.

Then he felt the faint breeze.

'My God,' said one of the guards. 'It's opened the locks!'

Edgy with panic, Greg turned the pad over but the screen was blank and an amber light was winking next to the recessed interface grip.

'C'mon Ash, where are you?' he muttered.

'*Starfire*-copy now embedded,' said a different voice. 'Rerouted bridge systems online – access is partial due to encrypted lockouts ... onboard environment compromised by depressurisation.'

'*Starfire*-copy, this is Greg Cameron,' he said aloud. 'Do you recognise me?'

'Voice pattern confirmed as Greg Cameron, Darien envoy ...'

'Okay, listen,' he said as he sat on the equipment case. 'We need you to close all the hatches which have been opened.'

'Security and maintenance system lockouts have been encrypted – decryption estimate thirteen point seven minutes.'

Greg felt like tearing his hair out. 'We've not got the time! Is there any other way to override the hatch controls?'

'Data on Hegemony ship systems hierarchy incomplete – shall extrapolate using Tygran vessel *Starfire* systems.'

'Fine – and can you open a channel to the bridge of the *Starfire* while yer at it?'

There was no response. Greg stood and went over to the line of consoles, speaking again to the ship AI and still getting no reply. He was starting to feel light-headed when the lights abruptly brightened and shifted to a new pattern of pulses. The alarm also changed to a higher, faster pitch.

'In the name of the wee man,' he snarled. 'What now?'

'This alert signifies a containment breach in the fuelling sublevel and a discharge of radioactive material into the environment circulation,' said the ship AI. 'This triggers a high-priority override which closes and seals all doors and hatches – shipboard atmospheric integrity is no longer compromised and all sectors are now repressurising.'

Greg grinned. 'And the containment breach?'

'A fiction – false sensor readings were sent to the air quality subsystem, which escalated them to the environment oversystem. Another false report from the fuel pressure subsystem corroborated the warning and the override was triggered. System lockout decryption estimate nine point six minutes.'

One of the overhead screens flicked on and there was Ash, gazing down.

'Good work keeping your nerve, Mr Cameron. We'll make a Tygran of you yet.'

'Aye, well, I'll be happy to take a shot at it if we can get back on course . . .'

Ash hesitated. '*Starfire*'s thrust drives are offline, but without the power drain of towing us, the *Silverlance* might manage it.'

'I see, you mean a one-way ticket, suicide mission sort of thing.'

'Yes, that would be . . . wait, energy readings for your weapons have just spiked, and the targeting sensors too. *Starfire*-copy, explain.'

'Weaponry and sensors are among a group of systems locked out of access – decryption estimate eight point two minutes – warning: beam projector targeting has switched to long-range mode and is pinpointing the carrier – flank and forward batteries have opened fire.'

'That vessel is at the outside limits of long-range weapons,' Ash said.

'Sensor data indicates that the Hegemony carrier has suffered minimal hull damage,' said the *Silverlance*. 'Carrier velocity is falling – we are being probed by their sensors – incoming communication: "War-vessel *Ivwa-Kagoy*, you are to render all weaponry inert and prepare to be boarded" – no response is possible due to comms lockout – warning: shipboard launchers are now powering up – nearby targets have been acquired.'

'What targets?' Greg said sharply.

'Four evacuation pods recently ejected from this ship and currently headed towards planet Darien.'

The Sendrukan escapees? Greg thought. *That Hegemony AI did this …*

'That AI said our destruction was assured,' he said. 'It set this up, to make it look as if we're firing on defenceless …'

'Missiles launched and on course.' Seconds passed, then on one of the big screens there was a bright flare, followed by another three. 'Evacuation pods destroyed.'

Greg felt sick to his stomach. One of the holoscreens step-zoomed in on the Hegemony carrier group. The carrier was a long vessel with a hexagonal cross-section and a large triangular midsection which was probably where the command and control decks were. But as he watched, the viewpoint pulled back and swung to frame a much smaller, blockier ship.

'Two of the carrier's battery-support ships have broken formation in our direction, due to intercept our course in six point three minutes – they will be in weapons range in three point nine minutes.'

Greg gritted his teeth and shook his head. 'Estimated time until lockouts are decrypted.'

'Five point five minutes.'

'There is some good news,' said Ash.

'Hope so – d'ye know how many beam projectors each of them battery ships carries?' Greg said, peering up at the sensor readings. 'Twenty-four, that's how many! So, how good is your good news?'

'Self-repair systems have got one of the *Starfire*'s main generators back online.' Ash smiled down at him from the left-hand screen. 'We've now got one of our beam cannons charged and ready to fire.'

Greg nodded, smiling weakly. 'I suppose you could get in a lucky shot, or ten.'

'If we even had the thrust drive at least we wouldn't be such a sitting duck.'

A gloomy silence held sway. On the central holo-screen a countdown ate away at time. Greg was restlessly pacing the deck when he felt a shudder underfoot.

'*Starfire*-copy, what was . . .'

'Full control over main systems has been regained – instructions?'

'Bring thrust drive online,' said Ash. 'Initiate evasive manoeuvres. Re-establish forcefield tow on *Starfire*. Ready all weapons, target the leading vessel.'

'Hegemony vessels have increased velocity,' said the ship AI. 'One point one minutes till their weapons are in range.'

Greg gnawed his lips, drawing blood. 'Are we moving at all?' he said. 'It feels like we're ...' He paused, seeing the countdown slip below one minute, seeing the seconds pour away, wondering if Catriona would ever know, wishing he'd taken time to write her a note ...

'Hegemony ships have stopped and are reversing course,' said the ship AI. 'The carrier appears to be under attack from another vessel – newcomer did not register until twenty seconds ago then swiftly approached Hegemony carrier – newcomer's configuration is unfamiliar, has a rough hemispherical shape and a number of tapering spokes around its edge – hull seems featureless and black. Carrier has engaged with all onboard defences and is deploying interceptors.'

On the screen, missile strikes and beam impacts wreathed the mysterious black ship in a corona of fire and destruction. Seemingly unaffected, it had not thus far responded with weapons of its own. The battery ship which had remained with the carrier had already unleashed the full force of its twenty-four beam cannons, a column of dazzling energies that struck the black ship square on. When the back-tracking companion vessels at last came into range they likewise brought their cannon arrays to bear, and then there were three spears of ferocity hammering away at that black hemispherical hull.

The unknown vessel seemed not to notice. Going by the onscreen images, there was no evidence that the fearsome triple onslaught was having any effect at all. The black ship, however, was moving with almost casual grace through the firestorm to position itself at an odd angle to the Hegemony carrier, poised forward of the midsection and off to one side.

'What is it doing?' Greg murmured.

'Nothing friendly,' said Ash.

The three battery ships had ceased firing and were moving round to focus their attacks on the mystery vessel's underside. At the same time one of the spines protruding from the black ship's rim began to extend towards the carrier. A weird jagged radiance played around the gradually telescoping tip and Greg was wondering if it was some kind of onboard systems disabler when it suddenly shot forward.

The impact wasn't visible from the *Silverlance*'s perspective but the long-range visual feed showed a few glittering pieces of debris come into view. Ash muttered something under his breath and Greg watched in appalled fascination, unprepared for what happened almost ten seconds later. The interceptors had redoubled their efforts and the battery ships were unleashing the fury of their beam cannons then a gout of debris erupted from the carrier's underside as the other end of the black ship's extending spine punched its way out.

'This is like the ship rams from ancient Earth history,' Ash said. 'Crude but effective ...'

The carrier had put all its thrusters into reverse but the black ship kept pace. Then something else happened – another black spike smashed its way out through the hull, clearly branching off from the first impaling spine. Then another broke out, and another and another until the carrier, from its midsection to its prow, resembled a grotesque, gargantuan pincushion. The black ship then used other spines to spear two of the battery ships: run through and fatally weakened, they began to suffer internal explosions which reduced them to torn, leaking hulks. The third had been under way when the deadly spine leaped out and glanced off its hull. Thrust drives ramped into full burn, it accelerated away but too late – from the black ship's underside a tentacle of jagged radiance uncoiled, snaked out and engulfed it, dragging it back in so that two rim spines stabbed out and skewered it. Staved in and mangled, it burst apart in a paroxysm of fire and havoc.

It was like a signal for the carrier's end. The branching spikes began to move, some rotating one way against the rest. Chasms were ripped open in the hull, more debris and bodies, more puffs of escaping air. Something vital, a refuelling station, perhaps, exploded, sending fire racing through a line of the interceptor berth decks, which touched off a string of secondary explosions.

Then the black ship finished it. At some point, that lethal central spin must have telescoped out within the carrier because the hull visibly tore open from the upper section down. Misfiring thrusters and blasting explosions forced the bows askew and the huge warship's back was broken. The spike branches shrank, the long spine withdrew, then the black ship manoeuvred to the aft of the crippled Hegemony vessel and repeated the deadly assault, this time with two of its rim spines.

Fifteen minutes later the carrier had been reduced to half a dozen massive, ragged pieces, racked by explosions, drifting amid a cloud of pulverised wreckage and contorted bodies. The interceptors fought to the end, expending the last of their energy cells in useless attacks, and those not caught by the black ship's force-field tentacles crashed themselves into its impervious black hull, final acts of pointless defiance.

At last it appeared that all resistance had been crushed and all life snuffed out – the black vessel had hunted through the debris field for lifepods, destroying those it found. Now, with all its spines withdrawn, it moved out of the spreading cloud of wreckage and towards the two Tygran-controlled ships.

Ash and his remaining officers had crossed over to the *Silverlance* during the carrier's drawn-out demolition. Greg was watching the black vessel's approach just as Ash entered engineering with a dataslate in hand.

'More trouble, I see,' he said to Greg.

'Never a dull moment round here,' Greg said. 'But this time we're ready. Hyperdrive is prepped for a fast exit, or if ye fancy a brief shot at suicidal glory all the weapons are online and charged. I'm assuming that the latter ain't your first preference.' *Or even your tenth*.

'Today is not the day for suicidal glory, Mr Cameron,' Ash said with a level smile. '*Starfire*-copy, ready drive for evasive jump pattern alpha.'

'Jump pattern alpha ready – unidentified warship has altered course and is now accelerating away – it has transitioned to hyperspace.'

The change in the black ship's behaviour happened as swiftly as the ship AI's commentary, and took everyone by surprise. But Ash's stern demeanour remained fixed.

'Maintain battle readiness,' he said. 'Sensors at full range ...'

'Contact,' said the ship AI. 'New vessel has appeared three point eight thousand kiloms off our lower port quarter – profile matches that of the Imisil heavy recon scouts previously encountered – incoming multistream signal.'

'Screen it,' said Ash.

The central overhead holoscreen lit up, showing the familiar features of the Imisil commander. Ash stepped to one side and with a look urged Greg to step up.

'Presignifier Remosca,' he said amiably. 'I'm very glad to see that ye made it through that wee skirmish.'

The humanoid's smart white garments were now smudged and streaked with grime and blood. The skin spot-clusters pulsed between dull amber and pale green.

'Captain Cameron – it is most acceptable to re-establish our acquaintance. I had not realised that you were so daring as to capture a Hegemony warship – this will not endear you to them.'

'Well, if they insist on leaving their property lying around unattended ...'

'I note and share your levity,' Remosca said. 'More seriously, did you observe the ship which destroyed the Hegemony carrier group?'

Greg nodded. 'It was quite a show. No one here has ever seen anything like it.'

'We knew of such vessels only as dark legends from the distant past,' Remosca said. 'That ship belongs to a race called the Vor. It was a force of their ships that attacked the Imisil fleet – our cosignifiers managed to fight off the ambush but at considerable cost.'

'You must have impressive weapons,' Greg said. 'Don't know what was protecting that ship but nothing the Hegemony had could touch it.'

'The Vor have only a few of those render-ships – they are shielded by a bubble of subspace which here in normal space makes them almost invulnerable. In hyperspace, less so. That vessel I am sure was hunting for us.'

'And instead it ran into the Hegemony carrier and gave it a serious amount of grief.' Greg chuckled. 'Shame we couldn't persuade them to stick around and help us out.'

'The Vor are a vile species, Captain Cameron,' said Presignifier Remosca. 'They are biological parasites that ride around in the bodies of captured enemies; all brain tissue involved in higher functions is removed, reducing all cerebral activity to basic, primitive functions, then the Vor climbs in and interfaces its mind with what remains. Our legends tell of the millions who were abducted to serve as hosts for these creatures. They cannot be compromised or negotiated with, much less considered possible allies.'

Well, that's me told, Greg thought.

'And now it's vanished back into hyperspace,' he said. 'It could have gone after us or destroyed the Darien colony, or both, yet here we are.'

'I have no answer for you,' said Remosca. 'Except to say that whatever the strategy the Vor are following, it will not be to our benefit.

'However, now you must listen carefully. The Imisil fleet, despite its losses, is back on course and will be here in less than two hours, by your reckoning. We have been in touch with the edge commanders and they have informed me that the Hegemony armada will be supported by a combat fleet from their Yamanon partners, the Earthsphere. But be aware – the Hegemony will not be permitted to establish overwhelming military supremacy here.'

Despite these stirring words, Greg still felt the optimism drain out of him. For a moment he was directionless, then a spark of anger flickered inside him.

'After all that's happened here – to us – they still let themselves be used!' The anger was hot now. 'The Hegemony snaps its fingers and Earthsphere hurries along to their master's bidding, grovelling puppets, the lot o' them! While Darien is a piece to be fought and wrangled over!' He paused to rein in his rage. 'Just as a matter of interest, how might the combined Hegemony and Earthsphere forces compare to the Imisil fleet?'

'Conservative estimates suggest that we could be outnumbered by seven to one,' said Remosca.

Eyes widening, Greg uttered a low whistle. He glanced over at Ash, who was watching the screen with a thoughtful smile on his face. Then for some reason Greg's mood changed and he found himself striving not to laugh out loud.

'We shall send to you the latest reports on the likely composition of the Hegemony and Earthsphere fleets,' said the Imisil commander. 'When our fleet arrives, the Predominant Commander will wish to meet with us all, therefore you should be attired accordingly. In the meantime, we must attend to essential repairs.'

The image of Remosca vanished, to be replaced by a wide-angle shot of the vicinity, including Darien and the forest moon, Nivyesta. Dynamic tags floated around the image border, updates on debris density per 100 cubic kilometres. Some tags identified the locations of bodies.

'Seven to one sounds worse than the actuality,' Ash said. 'Strange things happen during battle, witness our most recent encounter. And anyway, so far the space around Darien has been a graveyard for starships. I think that the Hegemony is going to learn a painful lesson here.'

'And Earthsphere? What will they learn?'

Ash shrugged. 'To choose better allies, perhaps.'

As the Tygran officer went off to talk to his techs, Greg stared up at the screen, at Darien hanging in space, looking just then more beautiful than he could remember.

If I asked Ash for permission to return to Darien he would probably allow it. Yet here am I, on a captured Hegemony warship, mentally preparing myself for more fighting against insane odds.

And just then, he found himself picturing Catriona listening in on his thoughts, her face lit up with a sceptical smile.

Oh aye, Mr Cameron? And what makes you so special that these fine, brave Tygran soldiers just canna leap into the lion's mouth without you, eh? Tell me that if you will.

And he imagined himself replying:

Well, I don't think I could sit down there, safe and powerless, while Darien's fate is being decided up here. I might die, but if Darien lives on then that'll be okay. But what if I lived through it all and Darien was wiped out? I couldn't bear that, losing you and ... home.

So ye see, a leap into the lion's mouth may not be such a bad option, if you give it something that's really hard to chew ...

18

ROBERT

At the edge of everything, it began as a hiss, a sough soft as a faint breeze touching long grass. Slight variations crept in, made it sound like a long whispered conversation overheard from the far end of a great hall. When at last it was loud enough to wake him properly, he had already arrived at the realisation that he was lying on something padded at the bottom of a boat. And his ears were full of the sound of rushing waters.

Carefully, Robert Horst sat up. Sheer grey cliffs loomed to either side while, some distance back, the way he had come was an immense arched portal, perhaps a hundred feet high and set into the rocky sides of the deep gorge. Beyond it was an inky darkness and the hazy outlines of great orbs, those eroded, hollowed-out bodies that the sim-AI was convinced had once been armed planetoids, built for an ages-gone battle against something called the Sun-Hydra ...

The last moments of that terrifying chase across the inner surface of the planetoid came back to him, the console alert which showed the huge black bulk of a megavermax hurtling after the lifepod he was in, and the awful crash into oblivion just as he entered the anomaly. And yet apparently he had made it, crossed into some strange territory on the fringe of the Godhead's mind. The Tanenth machine had impressed upon him the dangers of entering these domains, levels of hyperspace that the meta-quantal properties of the Godhead's thoughts had refashioned in ways both conscious and subconscious. The machine had warned that intruders could also influence the characteristics of an environment rendered malleable by the pressure of those thoughts.

Well, so far my presence seems to have had little effect on the surroundings, he thought. *I would be quite happy to miss out on seeing my unconscious imaginings made solid …*

Mist drifted over the surface of the river and low cloud blurred the heights of the cliffs. The air was still and quiet, no insect sounds, no birds, just the murmur of the river. Behind, the immense portal paled away behind veils of mist while ahead the gorge curved to the left, the cliffs lost height and became rounder. Bushes sprouted here and there, then came reedy shallows with small trees dotted along narrow shores. Round the bend, larger trees came into view, a dark coniferous forest, a dense, impenetrable barrier that cloaked steep inclines on either side. Robert could smell wet foliage, and the unmistakable odour of pine needles, and felt … a tantalising familiarity.

Then he heard voices, male and female, and sounds of running feet, laughter. There, among the trees a young couple ran, one chasing to give a tap on the shoulder to the other, who then turned about to give chase, tripping, laughing, stumbling into each other's arms, kissing …

The memory was suddenly whole and alive, keen with joy and the pain of a lost and innocent perfection. After long languorous moments, the kiss ended, they broke apart and carried on upslope, off into the trees, the youthful Robert Horst and his girlfriend, Giselle, later wife and mother of Rosa ...

He sat back in the boat, his mind a whirl of emotions. The Tanenth machine had not hinted at what to expect but now he wondered what lay in store, and with a degree of apprehension.

The change that came over the landscape then was swift, smooth, as if he were passing through some surreal holoartwork. The steep wooded slopes to his right flattened and the shoreline moved off and off, finally receding into the horizon, while to his left ... the trees shrank, hills and ridges diminished, and the slopes of looming mountains lost their immensity. The boat was now moving slowly past a series of small-scale rocky fjords and coves, most with clusters of houses, villages and towns as he went on, all in perfect miniature, their inhabitants tiny yet going about their routines. Threads of smoke rose from minuscule chimneys, trawlers put in to wharfs to offload catches, and little wagons and vehicles wound along cobbled roads or up winding trails into the woods.

And when he shifted his gaze further along the shore and saw a flatter region, a coastal plain bounded by ridges and steep hills inland and mountainous uplands to the north, and dominated by a towering promontory, he suddenly realised that he was floating past the entirety of the Darien colony in miniature. There were the streets and built-up areas of Hammergard, there

beyond it lay Lake Morwen, there further north was
Port Gagarin with its landing strips, and there was the
island of New Kelso, while further west stretched rich
farmlands, hamlets, villages and towns. But smoke rose
in many places, and he saw great mobs laying siege to
barricaded strongholds, or engaging in running battles
through the streets of unfortunate towns. A few zeplins
passed through the air above Hammergard and off to
the south, while fighting seemed to be taking place up
on Giant's Shoulder. There were flashes of energy
weapons, the yellow bursts of explosions, and out-of-
control fires.

Robert watched the stricken land pass by and wondered how true a representation this was. *This must be
how the Godhead sees the activities of us lesser beings,
scurrying around, pursuing antlike purposes. Or could
this be just one way of looking at us, a kind of conceptual model, perhaps even a discarded one?*

Past the northern shore, with the miniature city of
Trond and its stone towers sliding out of view behind
the upland slopes, cliffs began to rise again on both left
and right. In front of him they joined overhead, forming the entrance to a gigantic, gloomy cavern into
which the river swept. As the light from the entrance
faded the murk deepened until he was engulfed in pitch
blackness with only the sides of the boat to cling on to
and the rocking motion to remind him that the river
still carried him along.

A foggy glow appeared before him, gradually brightening to a wide stretch of blue-grey openness, dotted
here and there with strange floating crags and boulders,
some with trees growing on them. Some were like

bizarre plateaus wrenched from absent landscapes, their rocky roots tapering beneath while odd creatures grazed amongst angular ruins. Further on a larger structure came into view, something that looked designed or at least assembled, a complex of low buildings in radial sectors rising in a conical arrangement – Robert quickly recognised the Garden of the Machines, the headquarters of the Construct. And it was at the centre of a huge battle.

In thousand-strong formations, combat vessels swept towards each other, energy weapons stabbing out like a forest of bright spears moments before the flying arrays met each other, cut into each other. Warships hurtled past each other, some as close as a dozen metres, others too close, their collisions sending both careening off to spread the destruction wider. Projector beams burned into hulls, forcefield shields strobed, flared and overloaded, missiles were subverted by countermeasure virals and turned on their ships of origin.

And as before, Robert watched it all from a godlike point of view. The Garden of the Machines was a fabulously detailed miniature, while the starship formations were like tightly coordinated shoals of mechanical fish. The defenders were the Aggression, the Construct's AI machines, and they were facing a combined force of Vor and Shyntanil craft. The former had black or purple hulls that were rounded, faintly organic in shape with bifurcated or trifurcated prows, blunt tines that emitted beams and webs of jagged energy. The latter had larger wedge-shaped hulls, angular profiles and a greater variety of weapons. As the battle unfolded it seemed that the attackers were more likely than not to employ risky gambits in mid-manoeuvre to gain an edge on the next pass.

Robert recalled what he had heard from the rogue Shyntanil a few days ago. The Godhead had rescued their people, some from internecine skirmishing, others from obliteration at the hands of deep-level horde creatures, and still others from disease and inward-turning obsessions. Given promises of glory and domination of hyperspace, they reunited and with the Godhead's help recovered and rebuilt many of their ships, then set about bringing many of that fading race's ancestrals back to the pseudo-life of the Twiceborn, through the techniques of technotrophic regeneration. The Vor, on the other hand, were a species of usurper symbiotes that had been on a long horizontal journey across the overlapping tiers of hyperspace in search of new races to dominate. The Godhead's messengers had found them and persuaded them to return and take part in a grand assault on a variety of hyperspace civilisations and powers, especially the Construct and its forces.

Now his boat, a titanic hulk next to those tiny ships, was slowly coming up on the Garden of the Machines itself on a course that would pass close by. As it did so, Robert saw a Shyntanil cryptship appear in a quivering burst of hyperspace radiance and assume a trajectory towards the Construct's headquarters. Wave after wave of insectlike interceptors were launched from the ducts in the flanks of that big diamond-shaped vessel. In response, clouds of tinier objects emerged from the Garden's buildings, drones, mechs, droids, all coming out to fight the invaders. They moved out to meet them, coalescing in clusters that darted towards individual craft. It was all too small for Robert to make out the details, but there were sparks and flashes of weaponsfire, brief white flares and large yellow ones. After a minute or two it appeared that the Shyntanil interceptor attack had been stalled by the ferocity of the defending mechs. By now his viewpoint, from his own vessel, was passing the upper floors of the Garden of the Machines, with the Construct's pinnacle towers and domes practically within reach. He gazed at the open windows, in at the white rooms, and wondered if some tiny Construct or even a Rosa-sim was in there somewhere . . .

'Well, that was fun, seeing those creaking relics put to flight. If there's one thing worse than an organic sentient, it's an organic sentient that's been brought back from the dead.'

Robert turned to see a drone hovering about an arm's length away. It was shaped like a pair of metre-wide flattened shells separated by some kind of shielded assembly – in fact, there was a distinct clamshell appearance to it. The voice, however, was quite familiar.

'Nice to see you again,' he said. 'I do like the new bodywork. Was it your own design?'

'Sadly, Robert Horst, there was insufficient time to have my preferred configuration manufactured,' said Reski Emantes. 'So I had to take this off-the-shelf clunker instead. It is quite sturdy, though.'

Robert looked round at the battle for the Garden of the Machines, now receding, and nodded. *What next, I wonder?*

'You seem to be quite atypically relaxed about this situation,' said the drone.

'And what situation is that?'

'The gross differences in scale have not escaped me,' Reski Emantes said. 'Logic would lead to the observation that we are not occupying a conventional reality.'

'What would you say if I were to tell you that we are passing through a meta-quantal synthesis of a hyperspace tier and the fringes of the consciousness of the Godhead?'

'I would say how do I test this claim?'

Robert shrugged. 'Good question – I can only go by what I was told by the Tanenth machine. You should ask yourself what you remember before you appeared in my boat.'

'I recall taking part in the action against the Shyntanil interceptors,' the drone said. 'And as I was returning to my recharge niche my sensors registered anomalous gravity and inertial readings. When they returned to normal I was here in your craft. Is it your conjecture that the Garden of the Machines and the battle with the Vor and the Shyntanil is nothing but a creation of your overworked imagination? If so, I would have to reassess the mental capacities of Humans.'

'You shouldn't have to go that far,' Robert said. 'I think that your battle and its surroundings, and a previous one I saw depicting strife and fighting on the colony world Darien, are discarded scenario models, abandoned as some motivating force worked its way through a variety of initial conditions ...' He smiled. 'Or they could be complex simulacra set in motion for some other less fathomable reason.'

'If your wild supposition is true,' the drone said, 'is it possible that the Godhead may become aware of our presence – if it isn't already – and move against us in some way?'

'For what it's worth, I think that we are passing through a subconscious area of the Godhead's mindscape, or maybe the periphery of its subconscious ponderings. Nothing here is connected. It all seems disjointed ...'

The light faded suddenly, like a swift dusk. To either side river banks were again visible, uneven lines of tangled brown-green foliage beyond which loomed dense, shadowy forests.

'It appears that you spoke too soon,' said Reski Emantes. 'This all seems quite consistent.'

The boat was being carried steadily along by the current but just for a moment Robert thought that he felt a faint tremor pass through the gunwale where his hand lay. Then, movement on the river bank to the right, small figures dodging along the tree line, keeping pace with the boat.

'I detect four humanoid lifeforms,' the drone said. 'No clue as to their intention. There is also another large creature in the water – it has passed close by twice so far.'

The small pursuers on the river bank seemed to be dressed in ragged clothing and although the light was poor Robert was sure that they had pointed ears and the wrinkled faces of old men. Peering at them, he felt stirrings of familiarity, long-buried memories of the fairy tales he heard from Great-Grandmother Hirsch.

'Kobolds,' he murmured. 'That's what they are ...'

On the river bank they seemed to be waving vigorously as they hurried along, so Robert waved back. Which made their gesticulations still wilder.

'They seem anxious about something,' he said.

'So am I,' said the drone. 'That creature is back and it's coming straight for us.'

Robert barely had time to grab hold of the side of the boat before a swollen wave raced out of the gloom and struck them side-on. Thrown into the water, Robert fought against the cold shock as he struggled to the surface. As he came up for air he caught sight of a large serpentine form as it smashed the boat to pieces in the course of its lunge towards the drone, Reski Emantes. He then saw that the creature had a Humanlike torso, a head of long, tangled black hair, and arms ending in taloned hands. Water streamed off its green-grey hide as it shrieked and swung at the drone which was hitting back with energy bolts that seemed to have no effect.

Suddenly the creature reared up out of the river, wrapped its arms around the drone and plunged back into the waters, taking the machine with it. Paddling towards the left bank, Robert saw the surface roil and thrash. Stunned, he splashed ashore through reedy shallows then staggered along to the spot closest to where the drone went down. Lights flickered in the depths for a few moments, then there was nothing.

He stood in frowning thought – the drone had only been a transient creation of the meta-quantal environment so worrying over an unreal symbol was wasted effort. Then he shivered, realising that being drenched and cold might be unreal but the sensations were uncomfortably authentic. Quickly he stripped and wrung as much water out of his clothes as he could then dressed again, but still felt cold and wet. He began to walk, stopped a few paces on as understanding struck.

Those were kobolds on the other side, which could only have come from my mind, my memories! He looked back to where shards of the boat were caught in the reeds. *And the water monster was a nixie, a water spirit – these surroundings are generating monsters based on primal images from my childhood. Who knows what else I'll meet?*

Robert peered into the gloomy forest and smiled.

Thank you, Great-Grandmother. I hope that some of those stories were about heroes, the kind who get to survive ...

The riverside path came to a huge boulder and veered off through the trees. It grew narrow and weed-choked and started to slope gently downwards. The gloom brightened a little for a short distance before he encountered a drifting mist. The vaporous haze muffled his movements and footfalls yet he began to detect a far-off sound like a continuous, faint drumming. As he continued, the noise got steadily louder until it sounded more like a heavy rumbling than drumming. Frustratingly, the mist thickened and after a few minutes he could not see more than ten feet in any direction.

The rumbling, however, was louder and seemed to come from all around, accompanied by a deep, rhythmic creaking. Robert was reluctant to venture into the tangled undergrowth to either side so he stuck to the path and cautiously resumed walking.

A dozen paces further on he came to a grassy cliff edge. Peering over it, he saw a long, rocky ledge a good thirty feet below, all overlooking mist-blurred trees and bushes, perhaps a river. He followed the path along the edge of the cliff, still hearing that grinding, creaking rumble, still unable to fix its direction. After a short while he noticed a glow in the mist up ahead, down in the bushy vale. As he drew closer, the radiance resolved into a campfire burning between two heaps of boulders, flanked by three sleeping forms and one sitting sentry, wrapped in a cloak. All was quiet, he realised – the reverberant rumbling had faded away to nothing,

Out of the corner of his eye he noticed movement to the right, three tall figures loping along the rocky ledge, slender bipeds with dark scaled skin and cloth-wound breechclouts. Following them were five black, waist-high dogs with scarcely any necks – their jaws seemed to emerge from between their powerful shoulders and looked lethal. Robert instinctively ducked behind the cover of bushes to observe.

The three newcomers stealthily descended from the ledge, accompanied by their well-trained dogs, and vanished into the hazy tree shadows. From the attention they'd given the campfire, Robert knew what was about to happen and watched with a certain dread. Sure enough, dark figures emerged from the gloom behind the sentry, one to render him insensible, the other to pounce on the others and bind them while a snarling dog stood over each one. Robert realised that one of the bipeds was missing just as he heard the quietest scrape of a foot on the grit of the path behind him.

Before he could rise and turn, strong, sinewy arms trapped him about neck and chest. He gasped, struggled ferociously and felt one of the arms loosen. But anticipation of escape was dashed when the attacker used his free hand to deal Robert's head a stunning blow. Dazed, he was unable to resist as he was slung over one shoulder and carried off.

By the time his head cleared and he could see straight, he found he was sitting near the campfire, propped against a nearby boulder with hands and ankles tied. One of the dogs sat a few feet away, watching him with unnervingly pale eyes. The four prisoners, shorter and hairier than their captors, were down on their knees and in a line, each with a dog by their side. They trembled in fear as one of the tall bipeds approached the first, a male in rough woven garments, from the side. A lanky arm was raised, the spidery fingers grasping a small blade with a shining edge. The blade fell towards the back of the captive's head. Robert couldn't see what was being done but some moments later the biped tugged at a hank of the prisoner's plentiful hair, as if pushing some of it aside.

Then the accompanying dog let its head hang forward. There was a slight tearing and the top of the dog's head split open to reveal something grey, glistening and ridged. The greyness squirmed then crawled out of the dog and onto the long, bare arm now extended by the blade-wielding biped. Horrified, Robert had a frisson of surreal recognition – the grey thing clambering up that slender arm was a Vor, a member of the race of usurping symbiotes who were, with the Shyntanil, ascending the levels of hyperspace, attacking all who stood in their way.

Why am I seeing this? he thought. *If this really is part of the Godhead's subconscious, then what does it mean?*

The Vor was placed on the prisoner's shoulder by

the tall biped. Robert was assailed by a wave of nausea as he realised that it wasn't just the prisoner's hair that had been tugged aside moments ago but a section of skull. The symbiote crawled out of sight, under the hair, and the prisoner at first gasped and looked around wildly. Then suddenly he froze, face twitching, his eyes staring into midair. Unable to look away, Robert was sickened by his knowledge that the Vor was literally eating its way through its host's brain. Once the centres for personality and memory were consumed, the Vor would take control of its new vehicle.

By now the prisoner had slumped down, shoulders sagging, limbs jerking, his mouth drooling. The dog was a lifeless form laid out on the grass beside him. Then the prisoner was still for a moment before straightening, mouth wide in a bare-toothed grin as the tall prisoner cut his bonds, eyes full of a cold intelligence.

Robert had to watch the vile subjugation another three times before his turn came. The seven Vor approached him, led by the 'surgeon' with his blade, while the last remaining dog glared hungrily. Fear choked his throat, filled his chest, and he tried to crawl away. But the dog leaped to block his path, slavering and snarling.

Suddenly the dog jerked as its head sprouted a brass-coloured spike adorned with three small stabiliser fins. Its open jaws let out a high warbling sound before it pitched forward to spill blood on the ground. The other Vor crouched down, wary eyes scanning the surroundings for the source of the attack. The one nearest to

Robert lunged in close to grab his leg and was about to drag him away when a second bolt struck the Vor in the back of the head, angled down. With a grating shriek, it sprawled on the ground, spasmed, and was still.

The rest of the Vor scattered and ran. With an effort Robert sat upright and watched their forms recede into the mists. And suddenly he realised that the rumbling was back, a low continuous noise in the background. Then, closer, he heard a rapid, fluttery humming from above, with the sense that it was descending. Looking up, he was surprised to see the drone Reski Emantes slowing to hover a few feet above ground.

Yet the machine was markedly different from before. Although of the same basic clamshell design, its construction looked cruder, heavier, with strip-reinforced seams around the shell rims and surface panels. A short-barrelled weapon protruded from the underside, presumably the source of the bolts. The most eye-catching change was the mode of propulsion, three propellers jutting from the upper shell while a side-mounted one acted as a stabiliser.

'As you can see,' the drone said, 'I have been altered. Hands, please.'

Robert held them up and a blade-tipped arm poked out of a tiny hatch to neatly sever his bonds. The blade then came loose, fell to the ground, and the metal arm folded back inside. Robert smiled as he picked up the blade, leaned over and freed his ankles.

'Very steamcog,' he said. 'What's the power source? Cells?'

'Half my interior is full of them, curious glass valves

full of white vapour and metal coils. At least I don't
have a smokestack poking out of me.'

Robert got to his feet and nodded. 'The meta-quantal
environment must have modified you in accordance with
some pattern ...'

'You should leave such speculation till later,' the
drone said. 'The source of that rumbling noise is heading this way.'

Robert paused – yes, it was definitely louder and now
coming from a particular direction, the end of the bushy
vale from which the Vor and their hosts had come.

'Can you see what it looks like?' he said.

'My sensors have been reduced to a crude radar,'
Reski Emantes said acidly. 'All I can say is that it is
gigantic and will soon pass this way. I suggest that you
start running.'

The drone's props tilted and it glided away towards
the other side of the vale. Taken by surprise, Robert
broke into a jog and went after the drone only to find
that it was still pulling away from him. He lengthened
his stride, picked up the pace and soon found himself
running across a pebbly strand. Ahead, the drone flew
over a shallow stream and on through a gap in the trees
that lined the other side. And by now the grinding rumbling was loud enough to drown out his breathing and
the sound of his running feet.

The mist was thick and the rumbling was near-deaf-
ening by the time he reached the gap in the tree line.
Beyond it, the trees were tall and the undergrowth thick,
and through the mist he could just see a winking yellow
light and hear a voice: 'Be swift, Robert Horst!'

He almost didn't make it. As he darted and wove

between the trees, the rumbling made the ground shake and the air feel as if it was buzzing in his lungs. Engulfed in the thunderous roar of it, he saw a tree off to the right start to topple, then one to his left, then another directly ahead that brought down two in a domino effect. The ground itself started to feel spongy and unstable and up ahead he could see the drone, Reski Emantes, signal light winking, some way up a steep rocky incline. Then he lost his footing.

He sprawled, hands scraping as he tried to break his fall, and a tree slammed down directly in front of him. Spattered in grime and mud, he regained his feet, grabbed a branch and clambered over the fallen trunk, leaped down and plunged onwards. As the trees thinned out, the ground rose steeply to the incline, natural stepped formations of mossy rock up which he started to laboriously climb. But only for the first three steps. The vibrations in the rock made it impossible to get a firm grip and the roar was so overwhelming that all he could do was curl up away from the brink of the ledge he was on, with hands clamped over his ears. And amid the shattering chaos of noise a great cold shadow swept over everything, swallowed all in a veil of murk before, finally, it rolled past, an immense wheel, perhaps a hundred feet high, built from dark wood and rough metal. In the heavy mist its upper rim was veiled, but on the ground it crushed boulders to rubble and trees to matchwood. Then it was followed by another vast wheel, and a third, and a fourth. The shadows and the mists swirled and closed around it as it passed.

If the wheels are that massive, he thought, *how big is*

the thing that rides on them? ... and if we are wandering in some part of the Godhead's subconscious, then what does that symbolise? What can it mean? And is there any possibility of negotiating with a sentience like this?

19

KAO CHIH

Out of a stretched dream of cloudy faces he drifted up to wakefulness, prompted by voices, the Shyntanil attendants' voices. There seemed to be undertones of what passed for excitement among that desiccated species.

'... a moonshard against ... *them*? The Ghost Gods? – a hard thing to dare ...'

'The Highest has commanded it – their interference is disrupting His plans.'

'But this cause we must make with the Suneye machineries – brings hazard ...'

'Yah, hazard for them! You know how Old Irontooth thinks. Once the Ghost Gods' refuge is smashed, the Suneyes will be ... blinded! ...'

The deck lurched slightly, then more severely as a grating alarm sounded.

'What is?'

'Battle call! – Battle!'

The Shyntanil attendants rushed off as the cryptship quivered from external attacks. Kao Chih suddenly realised that his drug vials had not been replenished. But when he peered at them he saw that both were still about a quarter full and he could feel the body-drowse coming on again – just as a massive impact somewhere sent a violent shock through the deck, slamming Kao Chih's framework sideways in its recess. Something snapped . . . and his left arm came free, at least enough to move it across his chest.

Fighting the rising languor, he knew he might not have long before he was overwhelmed by what was already in his veins. So he reached over and loosened the strap on his right arm then proceeded to extract the needle from his left arm and carefully scraped the needle tip against the dirt-streaked metal framework, trying to stop it up with dust and grime. He then stabbed the tip against the frame to crush or bend it, and gingerly reinserted it. By now he was yawning and struggling to keep his eyelids from drooping but he managed to repeat the process with the other side, refasten his right arm strap and adjust the left one to hold the arm up before letting himself relax. Despite the shaking and jolting it was the easiest thing to close his eyes and drift off . . .

He awoke to a silence broken by the sibilance of breathing sleepers. His senses felt sharper, as did his mind. The vials looked almost full yet there was no numbness. Releasing his arms, he retracted the needles and saw a gummy buildup around the tips. That was when he realised that the occupant opposite had been replaced – with a Human. He was a brown-skinned man and the torn remnants of his outer garments suggested a uniform of some kind, dark blue. Drugged, he hung there, immobile, insensible.

Kao Chih lost no time in tackling his restraints, unscrewing, unclamping and unfastening himself from head to toe. On stepping out of the framework the first thing he saw was the other Humans held captive and comatose in the neighbouring recesses, as well as one further along to either side. Stunned, he observed the mix of genders and the variety of characteristics before he noticed something else, a faint clicking and rattling. Tracing it to some way along the passage, he crept nervously towards it, edging slowly up to where he could peer round into one particular recess . . .

A thin, white-haired, wrinkle-faced elderly man was trying to loosen one of the arm straps. He paused and glanced up.

'Good day,' he said. 'Would you know how often our gracious hosts make their rounds?'

Taken aback slightly, Kao Chih said, 'Every eight hours . . . I think . . .'

'Good. In the meantime could I trouble you for some assistance?'

'I would be most happy to oblige,' he said, quickly stepping up to tend to the various restraints. Moments later he helped the old man out of the recess then gave a respectful bow.

'My name is Kao Chih, pilot and emissary.'

'Are you, indeed? – I seem to recall mention of a Kao Chih being involved in an incident on Darien, something about an antique drone trying to gain entry to an old Forerunner installation . . .'

Kao Chih stared. 'How could you know about that?'

The elderly man shrugged. 'In addition to my tasks aboard the *Heracles*, I was also carrying out observations on behalf of the Construct, who I believe you have heard of.'

Kao Chih smiled hesitantly. 'I have. Is it possible that the Construct will send someone to rescue us?'

'If it could do so, I would be the agent assigned to such a delightful job.' He held out a skinny hand. 'My name is Robert, by the way.'

Robert's grasp was cool, dry and surprisingly firm. As they shook hands, Kao Chih mulled over what he had said.

'Do you have any idea of where this ship is heading?'

'They definitely seemed to have a destination in mind but they kept it to themselves.' Robert looked around with an air of amiable interest. 'Well, this does look like a most specific kind of predicament, I must say. But with your skills I imagine that we'll be free and away in no time.'

'I don't know that I have much in the way of skills that would help us here,' he said.

'Ah, but this is a pivotal predicament, Kao Chih. For all these people this situation is literally life and death, wouldn't you say?' He gestured at the Humans in the recesses. 'But there is also the matter of the sizeable asteroid that this cryptship is propelling up the hyperspace tiers, aided by a vessel of the Suneye Monoclan ...'

Kao Chih felt a chill. 'The Suneye? These Shyntanil are working with them to move an asteroid?' Then he remembered. 'I overheard something ... those Shyntanil attendants talked of a moonshard that is going to be used against some adversary called the Ghost Gods.'

Robert nodded thoughtfully. 'Hmm, that is audacious. The Ghost Gods were one of the Forerunners' staunchest allies, a skilful species which fought relentlessly against anti-sentient influences and other tyrants. They survived the collapse of the Forerunner civilisation and have endured the passage of millennia by concealing or altering themselves. Today they are known as the Roug and reside in the Buzrul system ... does this surprise you, Kao Chih?'

'I knew that the Roug's ancestors were involved with the Forerunner alliance ... So the Shyntanil and Suneye vessels are going to Buzrul to try to destroy their orbital city, Agmedra'a?'

'That or strike at the cities hidden in the cloudy depths of the nearby gas giant, V'Hrant.'

Kao Chih tried to order his thoughts around this grim news. 'What can we do to prevent this?'

'We already tried, my shipmates and I.' Robert indicated the quiescent Humans in their cages. 'You see, roughly half a ship-day ago we dispatched a Construct agent on a mission into stranger realms than I would ever wish to tread, and it was soon after that we encountered this vessel and the Suneye one. Hoping to disable or destroy either or both, we mounted an assault ...'

'I remember the impacts and the alarms,' he said. 'So your attack failed.'

'Even with some radical upgrades, courtesy of myself, the *Heracles* could not prevail. We slowed them down but couldn't seriously damage either of them and the Shyntanil were quick to launch boarding parties ...' The older man shrugged. 'And here we are. Now, I have to make a reckoning of the survivors so while I'm doing that I should like you to hurry around the main bulkheads and look for anything resembling a deck plan. The layout of a cryptship is always the same and the sooner we narrow down our whereabouts the sooner we can get organised.'

'How did you come to be so familiar with such vessels?' Kao Chih said.

Smiling, Robert tapped the side of his head. 'Some surprising things stored up here. Let's get busy, shall we?'

Kao Chih hurried off on his task, thoughts full of fearful anticipation yet sharpened by the hope that the elderly Robert knew what he was doing. The storage bay with its rows of narcotised prisoners was a chilling place in both senses of the word. By the time he found the map, on a semi-corroded plaque halfway along the second wall of the bay that he came to, he was trembling from the cold. The lettering and the symbols were meaningless but it was definitely a floorplan, as Robert confirmed when he came to view it. He took one look, smiled and pointed to a pair of symbols in the lower corner.

'Deck 18 – good! That places us directly above one of the auxiliary launch bays, which is where they keep the assault craft.'

Kao Chih's eyes widened. 'We'll be escaping in them?'

'In just one. They can each carry thirty fully armed Shyntanil boarding troops, whereas we have twenty-three Humans to accommodate, including you and me.' He shook his head sadly. 'Twenty-one survivors from the *Heracles*, although there could be more in the other body bays, maybe even Velazquez . . . but it would be far too risky to stray into the upper decks. No, we must play to the few advantages that we have.'

'Master Robert, we must warn the Roug!' Kao Chih said. 'We need to reach them first.'

'Indeed, and to do so we'll have to hamper our host's progress somehow ... but leave that to me.'

Kao Chih nodded. 'So is there a way down to this launch area, and how can we carry so many unconscious people?'

'My dear Kao Chih, who said anything about carrying? All our fellow Humans are already equipped with wheels, at least the frameworks that hold them are. As for access, there is a secondary cargo elevator ...' He pointed to the end of the bay bulkhead. '... over there. I've started disconnecting the drug tubes so can you finish that while I investigate the elevator and check the launch bay in case there are any Shyntanil about. There shouldn't be – most of the crew will be in their restoration cabinets, but I'd like to be sure.'

Kao Chih went about his new task with alacrity, going from recess to recess, carefully removing the needles which he then pushed into the bungs in the vials to prevent any spillage. Once that was completed, he began moving the Human crew over to the elevator corner of the bay, starting with those furthest away. Every now and then he would pause, his jittery senses alert for anything that sounded like the Shyntanil guards returning. He was lining up the fourth crewman against the bulkhead when the elevator arrived with a deep engine noise and stained corrugated doors slid open. Robert limped out, smiling.

'Good work, Kao Chih,' he said. 'We may well be ready to leave within an hour.'

'Did you injure yourself, Master Robert?' he said, suddenly concerned. 'Was anyone there?'

'There was one tech working on some kind of assembly,' Robert said, as if it was a small matter. 'He threw a canister at me but I knocked him out with a heavy tool from his bench. So now that it's all clear down there we can get busy without interference.'

Kao Chih nodded eagerly, and only allowed himself to frown when he was walking back along the aisle to collect another sleeping Human.

The transfer of their charges from the body bay to the launch bay went smoothly. Kao Chih's first sight of the latter did not impress him especially – it was a high, rectangular chamber about sixty yards long and twenty across with three berths along one side, each containing an assault craft. In design it was a dark-hulled, heavily armoured personnel carrier whose broad prow resembled the hooked beaks of a pair of predators. Along the other side were a dozen large doors half the height of the launch bay. The launch access, Robert said, was beneath the deck and led to pressure doors in the underhull.

They managed to pack sixteen insensible Humans into the elevator on the first run. Down in the launch bay they were wheeled over to the middle berth, where Kao Chih got busy releasing them from their upright cages. In the meantime the grey-haired Robert went back up to fetch the rest, and soon after his return all the crew were released and sitting or lying along the side of the berth. Robert set to work on the assault craft's main hatch codepad, leaving Kao Chih to check on the well-being of the survivors. A few were starting to come round and were just about able to stand unaided but the others remained drugged and oblivious. And as he checked pulses and breathing, Kao Chih noticed amongst the clutter of a rear-wall workbench the distinctive shape of the grip of a handweapon. Glancing round, he reached over to pick it out of the mess and found it to be a heavy grey gun with a triangular muzzle. Quickly he slipped it inside his shirt, wedging its cold metal form into his waistband.

From behind came a multiple clunk followed by a hydraulic hiss. Robert laughed as he watched the stern hatch open downwards.

'Ah, that anti-security briefing came in handy after all! Right, Kao Chih, let us get our passengers aboard.'

Together, they carried the unconscious ones up the ramp and sat them in square-cornered, unpadded couches clearly meant for the impervious Shyntanil physique. The craft's interior was stark and basic – there were thirty-two of those hard seats in two rows of eight-facing-eight, equipment racks between the bare hull struts, and a pilot console that seemed rudimentary. Once everyone was seated, with some help from the recovered crew members, Robert went forward to sit at the pilot instruments.

'I'm going to move us out into the bay,' he said, punching controls. 'Then I'll leave this idling while I go back out to open the launch shaft and the outer hull doors. And attend to a little surprise for our hosts.'

'Okay,' Kao Chih said uncertainly.

Robert flicked several switches and with a sharpening hum the assault craft rose off the deck, wobbling slightly. Kao Chih, standing near the open hatch, held on to a strut as the craft glided out of the berth then settled onto its landing legs. Robert stood and hurried back to join Kao Chih.

'Did you know that a cryptship's interceptors are piloted by the truncated head, spine and nervous system of Shyntanil warriors, piped and merged into the craft's systems? The command overseers can set the interceptors' initial combat posture centrally or via small panels next to the craft conduits. Virtues of a top-down hierarchy, the need to ensure that units will act in perfect unison. Well, I intend to turn that to our advantage and concoct a little diversion by making them attack the Suneye ship.' Then he was striding down the ramp and round out of sight.

Kao Chih agonised for a moment then went forward to look out of the cockpit viewport. He could see Robert walk over to one of the panels he mentioned and tap in several key combinations, one after another, until a blue light came on. More key taps, and blue pinpoints winked on next to the other eleven doors. After another sequence of key presses Robert straightened, stepped back a little and stabbed a single button.

At once a raucous alarm began to sound. At the same time there were waves of a thunderous rushing sound as one by one the blue pinpoints turned red. Meanwhile Robert had dashed across to another control panel on a pillar between two of the open berths. Watching once more from the rear hatch, Kao Chih saw the older man punch in more sequences until he found the right one. The entire midsection of the bay hinged down, revealing an inclined launch shaft. Kao Chih saw this, his mouth set with grim resolution. When Robert reached the foot of the assault craft's ramp, he raised the Shyntanil handweapon and aimed it at the older man's head. Robert stopped dead, a look of amused surprise on his face.

'I don't know what you are,' Kao Chih said, 'but I know that you're not Human. You look to be about seventy years old, but you seem fitter and stronger than I am.'

'Kao Chih, about a dozen heavily armed Shyntanil troopers will be coming through the upper balcony doors in a few seconds.'

'What are you? Who are you working for?'

Robert rolled his eyes. 'Yes, you are correct – I am in fact a semiorganic simulacrum, an android, and I take my orders from the Construct.'

Kao Chih laughed out loud. 'Excuse me, but I believe I've heard this one before ...'

There were thuds and shouts from a walkway that Kao Chih hadn't noticed before, running right across the upper sections of the craft berths. Badly aimed energy bolts sparked off the deck and flared against the ramp. Robert glanced over one shoulder then leaped up at Kao Chih, wrenched the weapon from his hand, thumbed something on its side and fired off a volley of bolts just as two Shyntanil came charging into view.

Almost in the same motion he slapped the hatch controls with his other hand. As the ramp rose up to seal the craft, Robert headed for the pilot console, scarcely pausing to toss the gun into Kao Chih's hands.

'Even Shyntanil weapons have safety catches,' he said, sitting at the controls. 'You can now shoot me if you like but it might distract me from flying us out of here!'

Kao Chih, racked with shame, said nothing as he slumped into one of the hard seats.

The deck tilted as the assault craft rose, swung round

amid a storm of weaponsfire, and moved down the angled launch shaft. Thrusters ignited as the open hull doors loomed and the craft shot out from beneath the Shyntanil cryptship. Robert gave a satisfied nod as he scanned the instruments.

'Just as I hoped, those dozen interceptors are still trying to engage the Suneye vessel. Both ships have lost control of the asteroid as well so it should take them a while to clear up the mess. Enough for us to fire up the hyperdrive and transtier our way to the Roug system ...' He paused. 'And warn them what's on the way – which just happened to be my orders.'

'I see ... I see that I have been unduly suspicious. My apologies ...'

Just then, one of the rescued crewmen waved a hand in the air, face looking as if he had just woken up. 'Can somebody please tell me what the hell's going on?'

Robert grinned and made a gesture inviting Kao Chih to fill the fellow in on current events. Kao Chih sighed, nodded, then moved over and began to explain.

20

JULIA

The datasphere of Earth was a multilayered phantasmagoria of wildly exotic, near-endless delights. It was also a pitiless sinkhole of corrosive depravity, ultracommercial illusions and callous delusions, all cunningly crafted. And it was an intertwining system of security webs and counter-intrusion nodes, a maze of peril where the promise of deletion was everywhere.

And running through it was the Glow, a virtual playground for Humanity's Earthbound 10.9 billion, plus the population of the moon, Mars, the Jovian satellites and the nomadic mining habs, which added another billion. Arenas, theatres, battlefields, art installations, historical subworlds, stocks and speculation crucibles, sensuality extravaganzas, word-by-word political drama, sport of every kind, wildlife of every kind, refinements of every kind, fripperies and trivia of every conceivable shade of irrelevance, and all available in a deluge of unrestrained abundance.

From the moment they arrived at the edge of the datasphere, in the auxiliary buffer of a mothballed weathersat orbiting Mars, Harry warned her to keep her wits about her.

'I've already sent a coded message to Reski Emantes,' he said. 'He maintains a private network for Glowless transactions, very secure and very safe, but it cannot be accessed at a distance. Therefore we have to transvector ourselves through the datasphere to a datanode close enough to gain access. In the meantime you should have this.'

He handed her a small brassy ornament of a boy sitting on a rock and holding an archaic spyglass to one eye. Frowning, she studied it.

'A sensory org?' she said.

'Something like that,' Harry said. 'It's a mirager – it reads dataflows and watches for the presence of nullors, which are tracker-catchers or karcers, which are hunter-killers. Then it puts up a protective shell of fake info and idents merge-adapted to the immediate vicinity.'

Nodding, she considered their surroundings. They were standing in a long corridor whose ceiling was open to an immense cylindrical space criss-crossed by dataflows, some like chains of pulses, others like tightly woven braids, and a few bright as molten steel. Stretching up, a distance haze made the higher flows pale, almost insubstantial.

'It sounds as if you're expecting trouble,' she said. 'Should I be worried?'

He smiled. 'Anxious, perhaps, not worried.'

'How does that affect the exters? Will our appearances change?'

'No – we'll continue to appear as we do between us while the miragers keep us blended with the surroundings.' Harry made a wiggly gesture with his hand. 'Ready to leave, Ms Bryce?'

Wordlessly she nodded, inwardly marvelling at her composure as Harry said, 'Compression one ...'

The long corridor and the cylindrical sky of criss-cross dataflows froze, cracked and swirled down into dark nothingness ...

... and swirled up and remade itself in lush forest colours, which was appropriate since they seemed to have been dearchived into a strange zone of glittering, glowing trees. Huge towering trees whose branches sprouted blooms that received curving lines of sparkling data from the massive helix that spiralled past over-head.

'The public multi-discipline precinct at Copernicus University on Luna,' said Harry, who then pointed. 'There, a trio of nullors.'

They looked like ruby caltrops scribing unfathomable trajectories above and among the stylised trees, spin-ning as they did so. Suddenly a mesh of faint lines sprang up around Julia and Harry.

'That's the miragers at work,' he said. 'We've just become a mixed-media doctorate dissertation on inter-species cultural influences, complete with pseudo-AI response analyser.' Harry chuckled. 'Our next waypoint is a Glowatchers club on Plunderworld, one of Earth's pleasure orbitals – its owner runs a black server on which I have an account.'

'Let's go,' she said.

From conscious awareness to compressed data then through the transvector to decompress back to con-scious awareness. And found herself standing on a wide circular platform surrounded by a pearly grey radiance. She was alone, but she still had the trench-coat image.

Feeling the stirrings of anxiety, Julia walked over to the edge and caught sight of a few other similar platforms lower down, all resting on thin stalks. Far below lay multicoloured clusters of light, citylike but not a city.

'Harry?' she said out loud. 'Are you there? Can you hear me?'

There was no reply.

Have I been deceived? she wondered. *Played like a fool?*

A thin beam of light came on, trained on her from above. Immediately her left palm began to itch and when she opened her hand a voice in her ear said, 'Alert from Mirager v3.7 – exterior scan in progress, please choose profile mask from list or close fist to activate default.'

On her glowing palm were four choices: a Mandarin–Piraseri B dictionary and tutor; the complete works of Hieronymus Beethoven, audio, video, Glowmo and Kabukisoft; full plans of Earthsphere Phantom-class heavy interceptor, encryption level cognitive; or interactive Gomedran funeral ceremony, Family Kyzec of the Clan Amarg (default). She quickly chose the second and a fine, flexing web appeared around her. The thin beam of light began to pulse, slowly at first then faster and faster, giving the platform a strobe-lit appearance.

Without warning the platform turned into a tube down which she plummeted. There were several abrupt changes in direction, signified by the way the flickering blur flowed. It ended when she came to a sudden halt in a huge dark hall whose only source of light was the log fire blazing in a wide and ornate hearth. There was a large, low table covered in a half-assembled jigsaw puzzle and two high-backed easy chairs. In one sat Harry, who smiled and gave an ironic wave.

'Sorry about that ... unexpected diversion,' he said, gesturing her towards the other chair. 'There was a temporary security filter engaged when we arrived – it let me through but you were flagged and shunted into an isolation lobby prior to scrutiny. As soon as the data-holding subsystem posted up the Gomedran funeral ceremony I had you transferred.'

'Why was I filtered out?' she said. 'And where are we?'

'Well, a fractalised sentience like you occupies a lot of file space and it was that sheer size which tipped them off.' He glanced around him. 'And this place is part of the memblock that comes with my account, dressed up to suit my antiquated fancy.'

Julia settled into the chair, picking up vague sensations of comfort as well as a pseudo-warmth from the fire.

'Delays put me on edge,' she said. 'I hate being late for anything.'

'Well, I've had the security filter switched to low priority so now would be a good time to be on our way.'

'What's the next step?'

'Down to Earth, a domestic droid repair facility in Delhi,' Harry said. 'The facility AI runs a clandestine transit network for one of the techtriads, strictly a business arrangement.'

'Which the facility owner knows nothing about.'

'Sometimes criminality is in the eye of the beholder, Ms Bryce.'

'Then let us be sure to evade such eyes,' she said. 'Do we have to go to another location to transvector out?'

'Remain seated – I can initiate the process quite easily from here.'

Again, her awareness was compacted and spiralled through the transvector bottleneck, then unwound into new surroundings that flickered into existence all around them. Only they seemed to have arrived on an expanse of empty grey tiles while some distance away a datatropolis of neon towers and spindles sprawled across their field of vision, matched by a similar tower-scape that covered the ceiling directly overhead. That one, however, had no grey expanse and when she looked back down Julia saw a flock of red caltrops, nullors, settle on a blue tower, all glowing and glossy. It only took a few seconds for webs of cracks to spread over every surface and less than a minute later the tower fell apart in grey blocks and slabs that bounced and faded, leaving more grey tiling and a jumble of pale shapes which the nullors then pored over and sorted through.

'Perhaps we should think about exiting the area,' she said.

Harry was staring intently at his glowing palm.

'Not an option, I'm afraid. All access to the repair facility system has been locked down. It's a netlaw sweep and purge – I don't know if I can even grapple us to another part of the system ... uh-oh.'

'What?'

'We've just been spotted by a netlaw unit, damn. But our miragers have just turned us into an archive of genome maps of the entire Kiskashin genus ...'

The unit came into view, a spinning white toroid. As it hovered a short way off, it emitted needles of amber light that flickered and probed Julia and Harry's shared illusion. Then a machine voice said:

'Composite object in subsector A31 displays irregularities. Shall convey to Local Holding 72 for scrutiny.'

The amber beams disappeared, an opaque red box snapped into place around them and suddenly they were shooting away on another blurred succession of sharp turns. When she glanced at Harry he seemed quite relaxed and unconcerned, at least outwardly.

'I hope you have a plan,' she said.

He gave her a sly glance. 'As a matter of fact, I do. Just watch.'

Seconds later their headlong plunge changed in an eyeblink to a slow forward glide along a silver-grey corridor. A flickery blue veil appeared before them and as they passed through it a tenuous image of themselves appeared behind them, almost as if they were leaving behind a ghost. Harry laughed out loud, just as they accelerated away again. This time their dizzying hurtle ended with a plunge into total blackness. Julia spoke but heard nothing, not her voice, nor a sound of any kind.

Then the blackout flowed away like angular shadows being sucked into a plughole. She and Harry were standing at the top of stone steps leading down to a laboratory set in what looked like a castle vault. Flagstones, masonry block walls, rough archways, iron wall lamps, workbenches cluttered with archaic paraphernalia, spark-gap equipment, elaborate arrays of glassware with gas burners heating bulbous bowls while various spouts discharged droplets into beakers.

'Finally,' said a querulous voice. 'Thought you'd never get here.'

What looked like a brain in a bottle drifted in on a squat a-grav platform fringed with a variety of work arms, jointed and tentacular. It approached a circular table full of bulky objects concealed by a grubby sheet which was lifted, wrapped in a ball and volleyed into a corner. Revealed were several ceiling-mounted displays and several pieces of mystery apparatus.

'My thanks for extracting us from a fate worse than corruption,' said Harry. 'Oh, and Julia, this is Reski Emantes, a somewhat idiosyncratic AI – Reski, this is Julia Bryce ...'

Their host turned towards her, altered its appearance to that of a flattened glassy sphere and floated over.

'Are you the Julia Bryce from the Darien colony world?' Clusters of multicoloured pinpoints glowed in patterns within as it spoke. 'You were the product of a genetic-engineering programme, and escaped Darien in the company of others like you – is that correct?'

'These details are generally factual, yes,' she said as they descended the stone steps.

'My superior, the Construct, has had its loyalists searching for you for several objective days,' Reski Emantes said. 'Yet you are here as a fractalised sentience. Does this mean that your physical form is dead? Were you murdered?'

'Her story is an involved one,' Harry said. 'But before that, tell me what happened back at that droid repair shop. And just how did you get in and out with us?'

Patterns raced in the floating glass drone, soft glows and sharp glitters.

'Someone traced the coded message you sent to me,' it said. 'And someone else tracked you from Copernicus

University. I think both were sniffers reporting to some-one who sprang that netlaw operation while you were on your way. At the same time I was the target of a pincer hit – my online presence was dismembered by a reaper hack while my real-world counterpart was destroyed by a sniper using T9 rounds.'

Harry raised an eyebrow. 'Tetranine is highly pro-hibited on metropolitan worlds like Earth.'

'Indeed. The sniper fired three rounds, wrecked half of the building my counterpart was in and killed at least thirty-nine others. Casualty reports keep bumping that number upwards.'

'Which brings us to you,' Harry said.

'I always maintain an updated partial copy,' the drone said. 'I had enough time to activate it then escape-hatch out to my secure bunker here on board the good airship *Cloudtrekker*. From here I traced your activi-ties, hacked into the local netlaw system, snatched you to containment on the regional netlaw server then had you vectored to my ever-so-humble abode.'

Julia smiled. 'Humble or not, it feels appropriate.'

'Sadly this is a cut-down version of what I had to leave behind,' Reski said. 'Which sharpens my eager-ness to find out who is behind these attacks.'

Harry gave Julia a look. 'Talavera?'

'I know that name,' said the drone. 'Tell me more.'

As they stood at the foot of the stairs, Julia briefly sum-marised her experiences since leaving Darien, specifically highlighting her encounters and clashes with Corazon Talavera. It was almost an effort to mention the thermo-nuclear missiles and the destruction of the Brolturan battleship, yet easier to go over the immersion in

Talavera's virtual prison and the desperate translation from organic existence to that of a fractalised sentience. Who was unsure if the feelings she felt were real any more.

'Talavera is a name that has been cropping up more and more in back-channel tittle-tattle,' said the drone. 'From your account she seems very capable of inflicting the hindrances you've been suffering.'

'She's not been working alone,' Julia said. 'I recall that she mentioned something about an ally called the Godhead. Does that mean anything?'

Harry and the drone exchanged a thoughtful look.

'It could,' said Harry. 'Combine that with the weird vermax manifestations you mentioned and it could be, well, very significant.'

'Well, we know that Talavera is planning something big,' Julia said. 'An act of brutal slaughter on an epic scale.'

'Using anti-dark matter, yes?' the drone said. 'That is horrific enough in its own right, and the involvement of those vermax is bad enough – but the Godhead, too? Ominous news. Talavera could even be an instrument of the Godhead, an ephemeral host. The fact that Vor were escorting her ship is strong corroboration. And since she is also in possession of your Enhanced friends, as well as your own body and its brain – which is a stroke of genius – she has an immense amount of organically based computing power on tap, and all of it practically immune to data-digital tampering.'

'This is why we came to see you,' Harry said. 'I know we had some parts of a puzzle, of the bigger picture, but even putting them together with yours does not seem to produce an answer that makes sense.'

As they watched, the drone Reski Emantes floated over to the table with the consoles. Ready lights winked on and holopanels appeared, thick slabs of opacity awaiting input. It was practically an exercise in irony, Julia decided, depicting virtual devices within a virtual reality.

'There are several seemingly disconnected conflicts which, as information emerges, turn out to have been instigated by the Godhead working through its instruments.' Within the glassy ovoid bright motes of blue and amber swirled like a miniature galaxy. 'The vermax that Robert Horst and I encountered, as well as the elaborate pocket universe trap, the thermonuclear missiles, the raids and sieges carried out by Vor and Shyntanil forces down in hyperspace, and now the Vor escorting Talavera to some destination crucial to her and those missiles . . .'

Julia nodded but the drone's references to this being, the Godhead, made her feel dwarfed by the scale of such an adversary.

Data polytables appeared in some of the holopanels, their permutations taking place too quickly for her to follow. Then three of the bigger consoles realigned their emitters and merged their projections into a much larger single holopanel that was angled down from above the table.

'Let's get a good mix of news feeds up,' said the drone and suddenly the big panel was filled with an array of subscreens, a cornucopia of sights and creatures from scores of media gateways. There was sound but Reski Emantes was keeping it low, a surflike babbling.

'We need to filter this,' said Harry. 'Can you narrow the sources to the Aranja Tesh, the likes of the Yamanon, the Kahimbryk, even Buranj and Shul ...'

'Wait,' said Julia. 'I heard some talking about Darien, saying something about a battle ...'

'I can find it if you wish,' said the drone.

'Perhaps we shouldn't if it'll slow you down,' Harry said.

'Slow *me* down? I see that you need reminding of my expertise.' There was a pause. 'There it is, Citivox, indie-news channel casting from Daliborka in the Vox Humana.'

One of the smaller holopanels began to show a graphic of a green shoot emerging from the ground, growing into clasped leaves that parted to reveal a blue and white planet nestling there while a shiny gold logo unfolded above it. This dissolved into the image of a woman in dark formal dress who then spoke, auto-translated by the system.

'Welcome to Faktor 23. We begin today with yet another amazing report from Kaphiri Farag, who is still in hiding in the Darien system and still sending us regular updates. We received the latest one just a few hours ago and present it to you now, unedited.'

The screen switched to a view of Darien at a distance, a coin-sized planet half in shadow. The image leaped forward, Darien now football-sized with the green forest moon Nivyesta passing across it. Then nearer still, a high-orbit perspective revealing the shapes of coastlines, the dark extent of mountain ranges, the veinlike traceries of rivers. A man's voice spoke:

'Darien's beauty is the beauty of a world unspoiled.

But what happens when the violence and destruction of battle explode across the skies above?'

There then followed a sequence of excerpts of open space combat, starting with a clash between a very large vessel, with its support ships, and a handful of lesser craft. Waves of fighters were launched from the big ship to engage with the adversaries. The support ships unleashed massive concentrations of dazzling weapons-fire, beam clusters, tight formations of missiles. Kaphiri Farag identified the large vessel and its companions as a Hegemony carrier group and its attackers as possibly of Imisil Mergence origin.

Then the battle seemed to be over. There were shots of one ship with its side blown out, torn and jagged wreckage still glowing from recent detonations while a spillage of debris radiated outwards. Kaphiri Farag spoke.

'Even this isolated corner of the cosmos is not safe from the havoc of war with its sudden, inexplicable, relentless savagery.'

With the Imisil attackers either vanquished or chased off, the Hegemony carrier and its escort resumed their original formation and course. Then the image switched to a shot of a huge black ship as it approached the carrier, slowed and positioned itself at an odd angle to the forward section. There was a sharp cut to a close-up of the newcomer, showing a domed hull whose surface was an even curve of black random roughness. There were no features other than the strange stubby spokes that protruded all around its rim. The carrier had launched its fighters and was firing off its defensive batteries while the escort vessels joined in with immense blasts of bright ferocity.

Unaffected, the black ship then attacked. One of its rim spokes telescoped out, passed by the force shields and speared into the carrier's upper flank and through to the other side. Julia watched in uneasy fascination as the huge ship was impaled like a monster on the lance of some knightly hero from a medieval romance.

'How interesting – a Vor render-ship,' said Reski Emantes.

'You've seen one of those before?' Harry said.

'Only in the Construct's archives,' the drone said. 'I wonder what it's doing here in the prime continuum.'

On screen, the Vor ship was tearing the carrier apart. Explosions cascaded through the doomed Hegemony ship while the interceptors and the escort vessels focused their weapons on the Vor, creating a glowing storm of missile bursts and clawing energies. Then, with the carrier in pieces, the Vor ship turned its attention to the lesser craft and made short work of them.

'We were unable to identify this ship,' said Kaphiri Farag's voice. 'But its mysterious presence here contributes to a sense of impending dread. It is well known that the Hegemony has a sizeable fleet on its way here, and I can now reveal that Earthsphere has agreed to dispatch a task force in support. Rumours that the Imisil Mergence also has a fleet in the area have been strenuously denied by Imisil diplomats at every level.

'The Human colony on Darien has already suffered a string of crises, assassinations, and the Spiralist incursion; who can tell what the consequences of more battles would be, especially if they involved the Hegemony and possibly the Imisil?'

The report ended with the Vor ship leaving the scene

of destruction, vanishing into hyperspace with a faint twist of radiance. Julia stared as the picture switched to a shot of a vast cloud of wreckage set against a Darien almost occluded by shadow. If she had still been in her body she could have used that well-trained brain to calculate how quickly the debris would be captured by the planet's gravity, and how soon the first fragments would enter the atmosphere, even where the largest might land.

'Ah, good, at last,' said the drone. 'Got some hard data on your Talavera, verified sightings no less.'

Harry moved over to the holopanel that Reski Emantes was working at. 'Hmm, a subspace gravitics monitor station is reporting a freighter escorted by two odd ships ...'

'And here, a hyperjump emission study group's open-access data ... three ships on a course that aligns with Talavera's previous known positions ...'

'But then the trail runs out there,' Harry said. 'About thirty light years from the Brolts' border with the Hegemony. You've seen our list of these five hundred target worlds – can you overlay them?'

'There, all part of that dense swathe of stars, and Talavera's course is broadly in that direction ...'

'How do we stop it?' Julia said suddenly.

Harry looked at her. 'Stop what?'

'Those fleets, this battle.' Julia shook her head, overcome by an unfamiliar feeling, a longing for the world she had left behind, and a fear for its safety. *Homesick*, she thought. *I'm feeling homesick*. 'Is there any way ...'

Harry was shaking his head. 'Julia, when the Hegemony commits its forces, especially after it's taken a beating as we saw, there is no way it'll call them back. Nor will Earthsphere – they know who's boss.'

'Not even if the public saw that report?' she said.

'They've already seen it,' said the drone. 'At least, they've seen a modified version of it . . .'

One of the holopanels flashed on and showed an abbreviated version of the Farag report, its heavy edits overlaid with ships that had never appeared in the original and intercut with brief clips from some vee-drama clearly selected to make the whole thing seem ridiculous.

'What is this?' she said.

'Netspiders got to it,' the drone said. 'Commersector grey-grid operations that filter and modify any media object that matters. Anything that could adversely affect the general populace's understanding of the Earthsphere–Hegemony pact gets this treatment.'

'Are there such things as underground news nets?' she said. 'Samizdat was the old Rus word for it.'

'The unregs,' Reski Emantes said. 'Unregulated casters. They're always being hunted so they're always on the move. They don't reach more than five per cent of the population, however.'

Julia felt a kind of dull, persistent anger gnawing at her.

'And the leadership?' she said. 'What about the president or any of the planetary leaders?'

'Most of them rise out of the same layer of elites, and none of them would ever reach an elevated status without the commersector's approval. And that's before anything resembling a vote takes place.'

'You're saying that there's no hope of stopping or delaying even just the Earthsphere fleet?'

'There is always hope,' the drone said. 'And there may be a way, a one-shot gambit that could work. But first let's have my tactical system work up some mission profiles while we try and find where Talavera's got to.'

Harry chuckled. 'And will this plan of yours involve stupendous levels of personal risk and possible oblivion?'

'All the best plans do, Harry. Now – I've plotted a spread of possible launch locations for those missiles, going by Julia's guess on their hyperspace range ...'

In the holopanel the swathe of target stars was surrounded in an opaque cocoon that encompassed thousands more stars and worlds.

'This is the course she and her Vor escorts were taking,' the drone went on. 'Including extrapolated course changes.'

A blue line appeared, then splayed out into a bright plume through one part of the opaque cocoon. The screen perspective zoomed in a bit closer as sparkling pinpoints spread within the plume.

'These represent star systems that are either uninhabited or sparsely so,' the drone said. 'Or at least where ship traffic is low and sensor coverage is scant.'

'Of course,' said Harry. 'A place where the launch of five hundred missiles can proceed without being observed or interrupted.' He frowned. 'Doesn't explain those Vor ships, however.'

On the big holoplane, small name-tagged images began to appear around the edge of the main display, each one tethered to its own sparkling pinpoint. Many of the tag images were of a basic sun-dot plus planet-rings icon while others showed a coloured planet plus satellite, and a few had additional emblems for cultural prohibition, military presence or navigational hazard. As they appeared in overlapping clusters she noticed one that resembled a branching spike of some kind, just a simple black symbol on white background, but as the other images mounted up she could not shake it from her mind. Something about it was familiar, something ...

'That little picture,' she said. 'What is it?'

'A marker for the Great Hub,' said the drone. 'The Hegemony's AI master nexus ...'

The drone moved a pulsing cursor over it and a larger image expanded up from it, a grainy view of a large polyhedral structure with treelike, branching antenna towers protruding. Recognition flashed, a picture on a wall, over a bed recess ...

Harry was watching her. 'Julia, what is it? Have you seen this before?'

'I saw a picture of this very thing above Talavera's bed aboard the *Sacrament*,' she said. 'Caught sight of it through one of the polymotes I was using to aid my escape.' She stared up at it again. 'Could this be the place?'

Harry smiled. 'I think I'd put a good-sized bet on it.'

'The Great Hub is a critical multinode,' said Reski Emantes. 'And it's in hyperspace and well away from the main ship trails. But it is also guarded by four of the Hegemony's elite attack cruisers – which explains the Vor ships. No way to know what variants they are, fluxers or burners, but in any case both are armed with fearsome energy disruptors.'

'The Great Hub has some other respectable defences, I understand,' said Harry.

'And AI guardians,' the drone added. 'It seems logical to assume that those vermax will play a crucial role in Talavera's plan.'

Harry rubbed his hands. 'Good, excellent – when do we leave?'

'Your eagerness is laudable but entirely impractical,' said Reski Emantes. 'The Great Hub's systems are protected by three distinct levels of encrypted access and the gatekeepers are a mixture of organic and AI processors.'

'No encrypted system is entirely invulnerable.'

'True, but every intrusion has its price and hacking the Great Hub could turn out to be costly.'

'But if we can stop Talavera, no cost is too high,' Julia said.

Harry regarded her with a thoughtful smile. 'I can see why you would say that,' he said. 'Talavera has already caused immense suffering and must be neutralised.'

Yes, but she couldn't have done all that without the Enhanced, without me, she thought. *Shouldn't I be punished too?*

'That is so,' she said in a level voice. 'So what must we do in order to find a way in?'

'We'll need the decryption mole to end all decryption moles,' Harry said. 'A super-decrypter, or über-decrypter if you will.'

The drone was unimpressed. 'Which may entail grubby deals with unlicensed softbrokers in the Underglow.'

'Well, that *is* half the fun, after all.'

'What's the Underglow?' Julia said.

'A patchwork of unregistered and illegal virtualities,'

Reski Emantes said. 'Traders in porn, plagiarism and plagiaristic porn ...'

'Venues where non-mainstream artists can find an audience,' Harry countered. 'And where a kind of amateur commerce can flourish ...'

A high musical chime sounded and the drone broke off to investigate.

'Interesting,' it said. 'A breaking-newscast from Citivox on Daliborka. Looks like they've received a new report from the Darien system ...'

The large overhanging holopanel switched to the same vee-host as before.

'With each succeeding report,' the host began, 'Kaphiri Farag seems to be setting the bar of action journalism higher and higher. With this latest exclusive, received less than half an hour ago, Mr Farag has raised himself to the very pinnacle of his profession.'

The image switched to a view of the planet Darien, titled as such and set against the dust swirls of the Huvuun Deepzone, with a backdrop of hazy stars burning through misty interstellar veils. A voice-over commenced.

'Darien, a world colonised by Humans fleeing the deadly Achorga onslaught, hardy settlers who by the sweat of their brow and sheer grit and determination built their settlements, towns and cities, places to live in and raise new generations. Yet the colonyship which reached this world was one of three such vessels, whose fates have remained a mystery.

'Until now.'

The image changed to another section of the starry depths just as a knot of distortion twisted a patch of faintly radiant dust-cloud swirls. The knot opened out and a large irregular shape appeared. At first glance it seemed to be nothing more than a large asteroid, cast in sharp relief by the light of the sun. Then Julia saw that the sunlight was reflecting from clusters of gleaming, glittering points and surfaces and when the magnification suddenly jumped forward everything was revealed. The asteroid had been adapted by sentient hands, its exterior encrusted with vents and ducts, improvised cableways, machinery housings, a variety of small shiny domes, outcrops of mysterious assemblies, innumerable antennae, dishes and sensors, and on every surface characters that Julia realised were Earth-Asiatic, possibly Chinese.

'With my surveillance systems at full extension,' said Farag, 'I was able to pick up the following exchange.'

There was the faintly sibilant hum of an open comm channel, then the sharper hiss of a new signal link.

'Unknown vessel, you have entered a restricted system and may have placed yourself in danger. Please identify yourself and state your reasons for coming here.'

A moment or two passed before a reply came.

'I am K'ang Lo, Duizhang of the work/home vessel *Retributor*. Are you the danger that we must face? Please name yourself.'

The frame pulled back from the adapted asteroid as an inset appeared, showing a stern-looking man with stubble-short hair and wearing an azure-blue uniform. The image was grainy and a little unsteady.

'K'ang Lo, sir, I am Lieutenant Ash, commanding Strike Cruiser *Silverlance*, flagship of the Darien Navy. If your intentions are peaceful you can expect no danger from us.'

A second picture appeared, next to the first. A barrel-chested man in a black and powder-blue coat stood there, dark eyes gazing intently from beneath immaculately cut black hair.

'Lieutenant, it is a great pleasure to greet our brothers and sisters of Darien. Know that our intentions are honourable although we cannot promise a peaceful demeanour when confronted by the enemies of Humanity. A century and a half ago Earth was under siege by an enemy so terrible that the species' existence seemed in doubt. Three ships were sent out into the great maze of the stars to be hidden and safe. One of those vessels brought your predecessors to this world and no doubt they faced hardship and struggle in the founding time. Well, sir, my own forefathers were aboard another of those vessels which discovered a world fertile enough for the planting of their offspring, the children of Earth, a place where they could grow and learn and even become better than their parents.'

The Duizhang frowned, let his gaze fall for a moment and breathed in deep.

'Such sweet hopes were not allowed to reach fruition. Our world was seized and gutted for its mineral wealth, my people were divided into those who could escape and those who had to stay behind. We aboard the *Retributor* are the descendants of the escapees and through a series of crises and decisions we have come here to Darien, to play our part in its defence, to offer what help we can to our brothers and sisters.'

In the other picture, the commander of the Darien

ship was nodding to someone out of shot before saying:

'Duizhang K'ang Lo, welcome to Darien – your offer of assistance is greatly appreciated. We need all the help we can get!'

As the ensuing dialogue faded, Kaphiri Farag's voice-over returned:

'This new arrival in the Darien system is a revelation! The Darien colony was in upheaval after the deaths of President Sundstrom and his cabinet, a crisis that was overshadowed by the destruction of the Brolturan battleship and the invasion of the Spiral Prophecy fanatics. I can now reveal that the Hegemony carrier so recently obliterated by a mystery vessel had orders to bombard all centres of resistance on Darien, an assault which would have resulted in an indiscriminate slaughter mounting into hundreds of thousands.

'We must now ask if the Hegemony fleet which is just hours away has been given similar orders. And what of the Earthsphere formation now en route from the Yamanon? Will they submit to the commands of Hegemony admirals as has happened all too often in recent years? A mere handful of ships stand in the way of this oncoming armada, including the *Retributor*, crewed by Sino-Humans, descendants of a lost legend now emerging from the shadows. At this crucial juncture they have chosen to side with the valiant but suffering underdogs on Darien, who seem to have acquired a warship more up to date than the antique shuttle they were flying before the arrival of the *Heracles*. What will be the political repercussions for Earthsphere? What will be the grassroots response from the peoples of the Sino-Asiatic block whose representatives constitute a vital segment of support for President Castiglione, and whose trade sectors exert considerable influence on many key worlds of the Earthsphere alliance?

'Whatever the outcome, this reporter will ensure that accurate accounts of events at Darien will continue to be forthcoming.'

After that the cast returned to the female presenter but the drone Reski Emantes quickly faded her out. It then cut to a number of circular vid-feed arrays arranged in an overlapping sequence.

'As we were watching, one of my analysers was creating a detailed datamap of Farag's report,' said the drone. 'Right now we're monitoring the spread of the report as other newsors and infotainment services pick it up and add their versions to the popfeed. Monitoring for accuracy, of course, as well as any edits and recontextualising. I'm also scanning for netspiders, who are an especially twisted type of ongrid denizens who usually descend on breaking news like this and soon start pumping out their own distorted versions, slanted and commentarised to either agree with the official line or recut to look demented and/or laughable ... ah, look ...'

On the leftmost circle one of the vidfeeds suddenly began to show the Farag report while data bubbles flickered around it.

'That whole ring represents the Vox Humana worlds and a few independent Human colonies,' Reski Emantes said. 'At the other end is Earth, Mars, Luna, the Glow, all the mainstream megamedia corps, the transstellars and the government agencies. That vid-feed, and the

pair that just appeared, they represent Citivox subscribers who post up clips and reviews. Analysis of the
clips indicates a hundred per cent accuracy, no micro-
editing, no sublayering, no addcuts ...'

For a minute or two there were no further updates,
then on the third ring an orange circle began to blink.
The drone tapped it with a needle beam and examined a
datastring that appeared.

'Disturbing. That was from a Citivox subscriber on
Hygailo, an Earthsphere world – he's posted a warning
to delete the latest Citivox dispatch, claiming that it's
armed with a lethal mutavirus ...'

'Genius,' said Harry. 'Kill the message by infecting it
with a virus then distributing it, and any resultant
damage discredits the apparent source, Citivox.'

'And here come more of the same,' said the drone.

For the next ten minutes they watched as the virus
warnings, some more vitriolic than others, spread
steadily from left to right. Then the drone put excerpts
from the devirused vid up on a secondary holopanel,
and they proved to be heavily edited, overlaid with
extra visuals and intercut with other vidage calculated
to evoke derision. Then came messages from the subscribers, some saying that the file had auto-erased itself,
others claiming that net intruders had wiped the file
from their stacks. This was followed by an urgent grid-
cast from Citivox urging subscribers and sequential
users to delete the Farag report, saying that its own
copy had become corrupted, making a repeat cast
impossible.

'What was all that about?' Julia said. 'What just
happened?'

'A full grey-grid countertrend operation just happened,' the drone said.

'But why bother?' Harry said. 'Can't keep this kind of story secret – eventually an authentic version will be available everywhere.'

'Yes, but all they need is for it to be unavailable or unreliable for an Earth day, even half a day, long enough for the administration to stand back and let the military carry out its assignment.'

'How do we stop it?' Julia said. 'There has to be a way to get that report to the eyes of Sino-Asian leaders ... assuming that your copy is ...'

'It is intact and utterly free of any viral presence,' Reski Emantes said. 'I checked.'

'You were having your tactical system work on possible mission profiles,' she said. 'Assuming that you've factored in this new data, have they come up with any plans for reaching the relevant leaders? Anything useful?'

'Synced with the new data, the tac system is offering something very useful,' the drone said. 'And very risky. The mission profile entails entering the Glow as autonomous entities with plausible and consistent exter shells. There are eight Sino politicians who wield crucial influence over the main factions; these are the ones you have to get copies of the Farag report to. Of course, these people will have high-end homenets with loyalty-grade AIs, which presents its own brand of unpredictable lethality. Thus directly infiltrating their homenets via their Glow channels massively increases your chances of attracting the attention of Glow security, in all its brutish glory. Another way to spread the information would be by screening it in the freemall districts, but any open screening would be shut down in seconds by commersector netspiders, and counter-intrusion snatch-and-cage apps would be on your tails a hot second later.'

'A somewhat limited range of options,' Harry said.

'That's because as a Construct machine I'm not a Glow native – it's not a natural environment for me. Which is why you are going to have to acquire the services of a denizen, one of what they call the wire-born.' The drone rose a little and a pencil-thin beam of sparkly blue light flicked out at the big holoplane. 'Like this fellow. He calls himself Nicodemus and he usually wears this exter.'

On the holoplane stood a tall skinny man in a long dark coat and wearing a pair of black, mirrored goggles.

'So if you really want to try and stop that fleet, he's the one to talk to. His services are expensive but my credit reserves are more than ample. My tac system searched the infobases in the Underglow and came up with a few contact strings and shadowy contraservers, so while I'm setting it up with him you'll be on your way into the Glow. The idea is to arrange a rendezvous, probably in one of the sagaverses – I'll send you a Glownote as soon as it's settled.

'And now you should leave. I have got a pair of good exters ready for you, both configured with coil-encrypted archives of the Farag report – if one of you ends up in a netlaw cage, the other might be able to carry out the mission.'

'Right, I'm ready to go,' Julia said.

Harry regarded her for a moment, then shrugged and laughed.

'Well, I've come this far, balancing insane risk against my inveterate curiosity. It would be a shame not to find out how much more trouble is lying in wait for us, hmm?'

'Subjective time compression in the Glow is about eight to one,' Reski Emantes said. 'But do not fall into the trap of thinking that you've plenty of leeway. Keep the urgency of the situation in mind at all times.'

'Urgency and the fate of my homeworld,' said Julia.

'And will you be multitasking while we're off into the Glow?' Harry said.

'Of course,' the drone said. 'Tracking Talavera is a priority, as is establishing contact with the Construct, a somewhat challenging task to undertake from the prime tier. Now, remember – the Glow is a fabulously seductive continuum so stay sharp.'

'You can count on it,' said Julia.

Harry nodded. 'What the lady said.'

21

CATRIONA

Through the web-vein-circuits of the ancient forest she was able to flit from place to place, from shadowy well-spring to bright and breezy canopy, throughout the length and breadth of Segrana. The flowery dream-palace with its soaring blue pillars and drifting veils of mist was always there for her, a sanctuary, a resting bower, a reminder. And as she darted here and there she saw new fresh growth, green sprigs sprouting from charred stumps, torn ground levelled and giving forth grass and fungi and teeming with natural wildlife. The damage she had caused during her undisciplined defence against the Brolturans was being steadily healed. She also saw how the Uvovo worked with spirited direction, a consequence of the Zyradin's effective takeover of the great forest.

Or was it more to do with Segrana's abdication?

Greg brought the Zyradin to Nivyesta and Catriona as the Keeper was turned into a conduit for its permeation throughout the continental forest, and since then there had been a schism at the heart of things. For a time she had felt the strains and dark moods of disagreement between those two inhuman forces, like the sound of thunder filtering down from cloud-swathed mountain tops, the abode of gods. Now, however, it appeared that Segrana had withdrawn from contention, and also from consensus. The hoped-for fusion never took place, there was no compromise and now no dialogue. Except that Segrana seemed content to allow the Zyradin to assume sufficient control to pursue its purposes. Thus far this had amounted to coordinated efforts to restore and revive those parts of the forest damaged during the battles between the Brolturans and the Spiralists, and between them and the Uvovo. And the wounds that Cat had caused.

Perhaps it's just as well that I've been relegated to being little more than a wandering spirit, to the status of an observer, she thought. *It's no' safe to give me those powers, I've proved that. No, Segrana needs another Keeper.*

But no matter how often or how intensely, or even angrily, she had declared this in the openness of her mind, never had she received a reply. She just wanted rid of what increasingly seemed to be a pointless role, and she wanted to go back to her life, that real flesh-and-blood life. They owed it to her and she deserved it, she deserved to find happiness and even love. If Greg survived the horrifying conflict that lay ahead.

Although her corporeal integrity had been interwoven with Segrana's vast and complex essence for a while, she had not realised until recently that she could gain access to a range of heightened sense abilities with which she could peer at the spaces beyond the sky. Quite quickly she learned how to make the sensing capacity show her visual information and to make it keep track of objects in motion, like starships. In this way she had been able to follow Greg's progress since the Tygrans whisked him away in their ship. The lethal dangers he got himself into and out of almost made her reluctant to continue these observations, fearing that at some unexpected point she might be witness to his death, something violent and final.

Yet she could not hide from events, and doggedly maintained a regular vigil. She saw the savage battles taking place in the space around Darien, spasms of unleashed violence that left behind expanding clouds of wrack and ruin, a spreading sea of glittering debris throughout which corpses were plentifully scattered.

She saw the encounter between the surviving Imisil vessel and the Hegemony warship captured by the Tygrans, in whose company was Greg. With Greg as sole Darien representative, a meeting was held on the *Retributor* to discuss cooperation on repairs and supplies, and the fight that lay ahead. The Imisil commander was also there and lost no time in laying out the starkness of the situation.

By now, Catriona was able to use Segrana's sensing abilities to discern some speech, and even some thoughts, although this only worked with Greg and the Tygrans. The Imisil commander told the gathering that a fleet of Imisil warships would be arriving in less than four hours, and about six hours after that would come the Hegemony fleet, estimated to consist of approximately six hundred vessels all told. Outnumbering the Imisil and the others by roughly twenty-four to one, this was in keeping with the Hegemony policy of deploying crushing force against any who infringed upon their interests.

Everyone there fell silent and the mood was sombre.

Cat found Greg's own cast of mind to be surprisingly positive, resigned to facing impossible odds yet determined in a roll-the-dice kind of way. While fearing for his safety, she felt strangely proud of him.

Aye, Mr Cameron, she thought. *You'll do, so long as you come home safe – and I get my body back!*

But as she continued to observe she felt a faint, trembling unease, as if she herself were being watched. Then without warning, the gathering and all that she was aware of just slipped away from her, as if those great sensing abilities had been choked off. Her perceptions swam in a blur that started to resolve into the blue pillars of her dream-palace. But it too slipped aside, a slow smear of shadows and grainy images through which she glided, bodiless, unable to resist ...

And then, all at once, she was embodied. Physicality felt oddly multifaceted, so crammed full with minuscule details of sensation. For several dizzy seconds she stood there, revelling in the solidity of *weight*, of feeling grass and twigs with the soles of her feet ...

Then came the odours of burnt wood and vegetation, charred earth, wet ashes. She opened her eyes and saw she was standing at the edge of a stretch of black devastation. Bushes reduced to spidery skeletons, trees stripped to seared spikes, the forest floor a sodden grey waste dotted with vile-smelling pools.

You are in a memory ...

Catriona caught her breath – it was Segrana.

... my memory of the destruction wrought by the offworlders ...

'It is like my memory of it,' Cat said. 'Segrana, forgive me, but I no longer ...'

... wish to be Keeper? Understandable, but you underestimate yourself – you have strengths that are needed ... the Other is coming for you with a Keeper's task ... give no more than the task requires and remember that you are my Keeper, not that Other's ...

The charred forest turned about her, blurred and brightened, spun into a translucent blueness ... and she was back in the dream-palace. A shadowy cloaked figure stood off to one side, waiting. Incorporeal once more, Catriona glided over to a nearby opaque blue pillar, putting it between her and her visitor.

** **I hope that my counterpart is well** ** said the Zyradin.

'Couldn't really say, one way or the other,' she said. 'I'd have thought you'd know more than a lesser being like me.'

** **In certain ways I am a lesser being than you** ** **You may know that I have a task which only the Keeper can accomplish** ** **It is important and you must follow my instructions precisely** **

'May I know what this task is?'

** **Like you, I have observed the conflict taking place out in space** ** **The black ship that destroyed the Hegemony vessel interests me** ** **With the Keeper's assistance I will be able to gain a closer perspective and gather detailed information that would be otherwise unobtainable** **

'Sounds like you want to use me as some kinda glorified telescope,' she said.

** **No, my purpose is quite different** ** **May we proceed?** **

She paused, curiosity warring with distrust.

'Fine – let's proceed.'

** First, close your eyes and do not open them until I say **

Shrugging, she closed her eyes.

At once she felt a sudden swirl of sub-zero iciness all over her body for just a moment, then it was gone. But her spirits lifted at the thought of experiencing physical sensation again. Could the Zyradin be taking a contrary position to Segrana, such that she might get her body back? It wasn't exactly her preferred circumstances but if the offer was made she knew that she would accept. In any case, it seemed obvious to her that any of the senior Uvovo Listeners would be more suited to the role than she.

** You may now open your eyes **

At first all she saw was blackness, perfect, indivisible, until she glanced to one side and saw the stars.

Panicky terror seized her, along with a reflexive gasping for breath, and a wild flailing ... until she realised that her body was pale and translucent, that she had no skin to freeze solid in the hard vacuum, nor any lungs to be sucked empty. The inky blackness was the shadow side of a big piece of ship's hull, floating in a cloud of debris, much of it still spinning, rebounding from other pieces, being struck by faster-moving ones, a constellation of collisions, a random sea of razor glitter.

Must be another spectacle of memories, she thought to herself. *Another meticulous mirage ...*

** You are wrong ** This is quite real and you are experiencing it directly **

A vertigo reflex ghosted through her, a promise of nausea that never came.

'If this is real,' she said (or at least heard herself say), 'you must be projecting my awareness beyond the planet's stratosphere. Why? I doubt that it's just so you can get a closer look.'

** Segrana chose her Keeper well ** An elevated Listener would have been overcome by terror but you have adapted and have begun to ask the right questions **

'An answer would be a big help, actually.'

** In time ** Look to your right and down ** Do you see the very large ragged piece of wreckage? **

She could. It was the size of a football field and was surrounded by a halo of smaller glinting fragments.

'I see it.'

** Stretch out your hand towards it ** Imagine that you are reaching out to touch it and you will move towards it **

Catriona followed the instructions and she did indeed begin to move. As she drifted out from behind the shadowing debris she noticed a sudden dimming in her vision. The sun's direct glare was muted and dazzling reflections were softened.

** Filtering the light protects your visual receptors ** Do not be concerned about the lesser pieces ** Push them out of your path or go around **

The debris was of all sizes and almost all of it had edges or surfaces that were jagged, sharp and lethal, yet her opaque form seemed unaffected by grazing collisions or scrapes. There were other objects that evoked a mixture of horror and pity, the frozen bodies of the carrier's Sendrukan crew. Most wore heavy vac-suits or flimsy emergency environment suits and most seemed

dead from high-power energy bolts. Those large
humanoid bodies were twisted into anguished contor-
tions and everyone bore a layer of sparkling frost. It
was like slowly wending her way through a silent zero-
gee morgue.

Then her goal was before her. It looked like it had
been ripped out of the Hegemony carrier's structure by
sheer force. Apart from the stretch of hull plating down
one side, every other surface was a picture of destruction,
torn bulkheads, snapped-off lengths of cabling, gaping
and twisted air ducts, bent and severed pipes around
which beards of ice had grown. She could see where the
cleft crossed several decks and saw more bodies, motionless figures floating in corridors or frozen in death
agonies while wrapped up in a sleeping recess, gaping
mouths, grasping hands ...

Catriona had seen many terrible things under the
canopy of Segrana these last few days, but this sight
stirred in her a crawling horror unlike anything she had
felt before.

And the Zyradin wants to study this? she thought.

** **Move round to the area of hull plating** **

As quickly as she could she aimed herself at that part
of the wreckage and was soon floating directly over it.

** **Approach the hull surface and place your hand
against it** **

'How will this help you analyse the thing?' she said.
'Why not just take a few pictures, or whatever your
equivalent is?'

** **It will serve my purposes and my curiosity** **

She drifted towards the flat surface, which was
mostly a dark grey with metallic blue bands crossing

part of it. She was facing an area with a block of what she assumed to be instructions in Sendrukan. She reached out her strange, milkily opaque hand and touched the flat greyness with her fingertips then her whole palm.

Well, I hope this is helping somehow ...

Suddenly she was enveloped by meshes of light, misty braids coiling around her and up and around the wreckage, swathing it in shining bands. Catriona was frozen in place, unable to move but sensing a buildup of something powerful. The shining braids began to brighten, everything seemed to tremble, and there was a dazzling burst of light and an abrupt moment of tranquillity, an instant of perfect silence ...

... before a plunge into darkness, impressions of shadows, great trunks, masses of greenery, vine-woven mossy curtains – she was back in Segrana! – and before her, hanging in midair, that immense slab of wreckage with her hand still pressed against it ...

** Release ** Release it **

A second of incredulity, of mystification, of realisation, then she snatched her hand away.

The wreckage fell from her, smashing several trees into splinters before it struck the ground with a deafening crash.

22

GREG

It was only a fifteen-minute hop from the *Retributor* to the *Starfire* but Greg's head was full of details from the meeting and he just couldn't relax. The summary of the *Starfire*'s weaponry seemed meagre in the light of the Imisil commander Remosca's revelation on the size of the Hegemony armada. Hundreds of warships among which there would be more carriers like the *Baqrith-Zo*, capable of fielding scores of interceptors, drones, smart missiles, a veritable cascade of war machines rushing towards them.

Greg had projected a kind of cavalier optimism mingled with anger and defiance, mainly because he did not want to face his own despair. As he sat listening to Commander Remosca laying out the bleak realities, something that Uncle Theo once said came back to him – 'A ship tied up in the harbour is safe, but is that what ships are for?' It was a folksy little saying but its nugget of wisdom was clear. He had once told the Tygran Ash that while Darien was worth fighting for it was the people who were worth dying for.

The gathering had agreed unanimously to stand their ground. Greg just hoped that the dying part would be slow to arrive.

Now, sitting in the *Retributor*'s pilotless shuttle pod –
a short-range craft on loan from the Roug, apparently –
his thoughts turned to the situation on the planet's surface. There had been several attempts to establish
contact with the Human rebels at Tusk Mountain but all
effective channels were being jammed. The source of
the jamming was mainly Giant's Shoulder, which wasn't
such a surprise now that the Legion agent and its
combat droids were in control of the place. But Ash was
not seeing the break in communication as an immediate
crisis and wouldn't authorise a shuttle journey to the
surface. Nor would he order a bombardment of the
Giant's Shoulder defences, on the grounds that it might
provoke retaliation which they could do without in the
hours ahead. Greg was frustrated at these decisions but
had to resign himself to them.

At last the pod reached the *Starfire*, the Tygran ship
that had brought him from Nivyesta and which had
been heavily damaged in action against the Hegemony
carrier's escort vessels. Although the hyperdrive was
junk, the thrust engines had been partially repaired and
some of the weapons were back online. They could
move and they could fight, after a fashion.

The pod docked with one of the underside hatches,
and moments later he was climbing from the pod's weak
deck gravity into a weightless airlock. It was a small,
blue-lit chamber with a short ladder. The outer hatch
thudded shut, sealed audibly, and the light turned red.

'Just a few seconds, Mr Cameron, and you'll be
through.'

Sure enough, moments later Lieutenant Berg was
helping him up into a cramped compartment.

'Welcome back, Mr Cameron.'

'Glad to be back, Lieutenant,' he said. 'Commander Ash clarified my position, by the way. He was very keen to point out that *you* are in command and that *I* am just a civilian adviser.' He shrugged. 'And that's fine and dandy by me, really.'

Berg grinned. 'You shouldn't worry, Mr Cameron. I'm sure I can find you something to do, given the circumstances.'

Greg nodded as he followed Berg out and along the spine corridor. In order to fully operate the *Silverlance*, the former Hegemony ship, Ash had left the *Starfire* with little more than a skeleton crew of eleven, barely enough to cope with the necessary repairs. The *Retributor*'s captain, K'ang Lo, had said that he could spare some of his techs so perhaps that would solve their problems. Provided the language problem was solvable.

They had just entered the split-level bridge when the tac officer, a woman Greg didn't recognise, turned with an excited expression.

'Sir, I was just about to alert you – a fleet of eighteen vessels has exited hyperspace at the periphery of the system!'

'Have they identified themselves?' Berg said as he lowered himself into the commander's couch.

'Yes, they are claiming to be a Vox Humana expeditionary force sent to offer assistance to the besieged people of Darien ...'

'Go to combat-readiness,' Berg said, and Greg could hear the high-pitched alarm from the corridor outside. 'How have the other captains reacted?'

'Taking the same precautions, sir. Shall I screen the ongoing exchange?'

'Go ahead.'

Greg had resumed his old seat, at the auxiliary station left of the commander's couch. The console's holopanel blinked on, displaying a pair of insets showing Ash in one and a round-faced woman of mature years in the other. She had a steely gaze and a streak of black in a head of otherwise silvery hair.

'. . . would be more advantageous to all concerned. I repeat, Commander, we are here to offer all and any assistance to the benefit of the Darien colony.'

'I'm afraid that we must insist on a process of verification, Admiral Olarevic,' said Ash. 'We have a sensor probe in orbit around that gas giant. If you set course for it, we can easily verify your idents.'

The Vox Humana admiral gave a stiff nod. 'Very well, Commander, we shall do as you suggest.'

Abruptly her image vanished from the screen.

'Why is Ash having problems IDing their ship?' Greg said.

'He's not,' said Berg. 'It's the Imisil – they're saying that such a generous offer of military assistance is atypical for the Vox Humana, who are usually rigorously neutral when it comes to conflicts involving Hegemony interest.'

'So they're here to either play some spoiler, disruptive role,' Greg said, 'or something's happened to force them to actively support us because it's in their interest. I've no idea what that could be but I'm pretty sure that you know more about the Vox Humana than I do.'

Berg shrugged. 'I can't say much, Mr Cameron,

except to say that the Imisil are right about Vox H neutrality ...'

'Sir, long-range sensors are picking up energy weapon emissions from the vicinity of the outer gas giant.'

In the next moment, the face of the Vox Humana admiral reappeared on the viewport overlay, as well as in Greg's holopanel.

'We are under attack!' she said. 'Did you plan this, Commander? Did you?'

In the other inset Ash's face was affronted yet restrained.

'Admiral, I give you my word that we have nothing to do with this. Have you identified the attackers yet?'

'... four ... five, no *six* Ezgara destroyers. They did not show up on any scans but it seems that they came at us from concealments on one of the gas giant's moons ...'

Greg noticed that Berg had suddenly become more focused on the Vox Humana admiral.

'Six destroyers,' the Tygran muttered. 'That's almost two-thirds of the fleet.'

'Why would they commit such a high proportion?' Greg said.

Berg gave a sour smile. 'The "why" is tied up with the "who" – only Becker would browbeat the commanderies and the Bund into backing such a plan. But even six of our ships could not prevail against eighteen Vox H vessels, so this has to be a tactical move.' Berg shrugged. 'I'm sure Ash can see this and has a better idea of what's going on.'

At this point the Vox Humana admiral had turned aside to deal with urgent matters, while the channel stayed open. Then new datastreams began filling sidebar columns which unfolded into a 3D schematic of the hostile engagement.

'That's the feed from the probe near the gas giant,' said Berg, who then frowned. 'What's it called, the gas giant?'

'Hmm? – eh, Kronos ... but listen, why would your marshal lead his ships into a fight when he's outnumbered three to one? What kind of strategy is that?'

Berg frowned. 'No, it's a tactical move in support of a strategy, but what is it? ... wait, did you see that? Raker, replay the last sixty seconds of probe data.'

On the screens the 3D model of the vicinity of the gas giant Kronos showed the trajectory trails of various ships, with fading tags denoting weapon fire. Suddenly Berg froze the playback and zoomed in on the shadow side of one of the gas giant's moons where a solitary tag had appeared.

'Hyperdrive activated,' Berg said, pointing at the tag.

Before Greg could reply, a priority message frame popped up over the playback, with Ash looking grimly out from it.

'Attention, all vessels – it appears that we have a seventh Ezgara warship in the area. It was spotted by our probe nearly three minutes ago when it broke from cover behind one of the gas giant's moons. It then almost immediately made a hyperspace jump – we are assuming that it was a microjump to somewhere else in the system, most probably Darien.'

Ash's image blinked, then he spoke again.

'Berg, we're now on a secure channel. Who do you think is behind this?'

'Marshal Becker, sir. Has his hallmark all over it.'

'Yes, which means that he's certainly on board that seventh ship. And since the other six weren't spotted by the Imisil probe until they came out and attacked the Vox H, it's logical to assume that they've been there since before the Imisil arrived.' Ash rubbed the side of his head, as if at an ache. 'They've seen all there was to see and probably listened in on our channels, so now they know who's here and who's planetside.'

'Like Captain Gideon,' said Greg. 'He's no' exactly Becker's favourite Human being.'

'It's possible, Mr Cameron, but it's equally likely that he's acting under orders. Lieutenant Berg – keep your ship at combat alert and switch your patrol pattern to semi-random. If a Tygran vessel appears do not approach or pursue, and do not engage unless absolutely necessary. Those destroyers are atmosphere-capable so it might try for a landing – again, observe and track but do not intervene. Clear?'

'Yes, sir, but—'

'Wait!' Ash said, his gaze snapping to one side. 'Now the Tygran-Ezgara ships are breaking off and making a dash for open space. They know they're outnumbered.'

On the 3D schematic Greg could see six symbols heading away from the scene of the battle. Seconds later these symbols starting winking out as the ships jumped to hyperspace. Except for two, and when Greg looked closer he saw that the velocity values for both were falling rapidly.

'Mr Berg, Admiral Olarevic has crucial information,' said Ash. 'I'm switching the channel back to convoke mode ... Admiral, I am pleased that you survived the Ezgara attack.'

Greg and Berg exchanged a look but said nothing.

'Unfortunately, two of my ships did not and I have another three so damaged they are not fit for front-line duties.' The woman was visibly straining to keep her temper under control. 'But I can see now that the Ezgara assault was none of your doing, in the light of the tactical overview you generously fed to us from your probe. More immediate, however, is the matter of these two Ezgara ships which stayed behind. Both are casting messages claiming that all or most of both crews have mutinied. One is called the *Vanquisher*, the other the *Firebrand*. However, our sensors are picking up indications of fighting aboard the latter ...'

'Do you know the name of whoever is in charge aboard the *Vanquisher*, Admiral?' said Ash.

'He calls himself Braddock,' said Olarevic. 'Claims that he was the security officer. Would you like me to connect you to him?'

Berg glanced at Greg wide-eyed and gave a silent shake of the head.

'That could be very useful, Admiral,' Ash said. 'But I'd like to go over it with my colleagues on the other vessels first, put together a consensus on how to proceed. In the meantime we need to keep our sensor arrays active at all ranges. We still haven't located the seventh Ezgara vessel and we cannot relax until we can be sure that it's left the system.'

Suddenly Ash's attention was distracted by one of his bridge crew, just as Berg's own tac officer spoke.

'There's some activity at the *Firebrand*, sir – most of the aft lifepods are ejecting ...'

On the viewport overlay the same information was being exchanged between the admiral and Ash.

'... and we're getting an audiocast from the *Firebrand*,' Olarevic said. 'I'll tie you in on this channel.'

There was a moment of interference followed by a man's voice. He sounded young, agitated and determined.

'... repeat, this is Sub-Lieutenant Weiss, head of the *Firebrand* loyalty cadre. We have retaken the bridge and intend to fly this ship safely home, whatever the intentions of the enemies within and those outside. This message is going out shipwide and on local ship frequencies. No one aboard this vessel should doubt our resolve. If we are prevented from flying back home, we shall implement the self-destruct. We have all the senior officer command keys and are fully prepared to use them. That is all.'

'What's a loyalty cadre?' Greg said to Berg.

'I remember Becker proposing such a thing a year ago,' Berg said. 'At the time the Bund rejected it out of hand, but now ... perhaps he believes he no longer needs their approval. Ah, the *Firebrand*'s shields have just gone up!'

They were now getting a visual feed from the Vox Humana flagship. The Imisil probe schematic showed that the two contested vessels were nearly 2,000 kiloms apart but the split-screen visual showed them both. They were of identical design, a bulky boxy stern, a tapering midsection and a wider forward section containing most of the heavy offence capability. The image subtitled '*Firebrand*' possessed a glowing halo corresponding to that vessel's shield defences. A number of small specks, lifepods, were radiating out from it, each tagged with a symbol and a number.

Berg had been in a muttered exchange with Ash but then turned to Greg.

'The Imisil probe has been picking up some shipboard communications for the last few minutes – doesn't sound promising.' He prodded a few holopanel keys and Greg's own console began playing a conversation.

'... won't speak to you! – you've shown that you have nothing to say that we wish to hear!'

'Look, have we not ceased firing and pulled back from your corridors? If you want this ship to go any-where you'll need our cooperation and we too are desperate to get away from here. Please, let me speak with Weiss ...'

In a low voice Greg said, 'Is this happening in real-time?'

Berg nodded as a new voice came over the audio link.

'This is Weiss – what do you wish to say?'

'We propose a bargain – if we help you get the ship away you agree to put us off at a neutral world before heading for Tygra.'

'I understand. Here is my counter-proposal – you and all working with you shall agree to enter lockdown con-finement prior to our departure for Tygra, where you will be tried for the crime of mutiny.'

'No, Weiss, that is unacceptable and foolish given that we surround you while our ship is likewise sur-rounded.'

'I will not sully my honour and the honour of the Black Sun Commandery. As Nightwalkers I would not expect you to grasp these essentials.'

'You are deaf to the voice of change – things cannot go on the way they have under Becker. Have you even seen the Rawlins testament?'

'I have seen it and it is a pack of stinking lies from start to finish. Genocide against the Zshahil? It's a vile slur on our ancestors and our collective honour, which seems to hold little meaning for the likes of you.'

'I weary of this. Blab and whine about honour all you like, but we're coming for you!'

'Do not test me, Nightwalker ... wait, what's that? ... through the ceiling? ... so you think I'm bluffing, do you? Then prepare to be devoured by the fire ...'

Seconds later there was a burst of static and the link went dead. At the same time, on the visual feed a series of explosions ripped apart the forward section of the *Firebrand*. This was followed by fiery eruptions along the midsection and several minor ones on the underside. These were all eclipsed when the entire stern burst apart in a cataclysmic blast of destruction, one last violent blaze of energies as the drive fields tried to simultaneously create and consume the quanta of space-time ...

On another screen, Ash and the Vox H admiral were discussing the retrieval of the *Firebrand*'s pods and what to do with the other ship, the *Vanquisher*. But Greg was thinking over what he'd heard during that final, fateful exchange, especially the bit about a testament. When he mentioned it to Berg, the man seemed semi-distracted as if caught up in a stream of his own thoughts.

'There is ... something that it may refer to,' Berg said. 'But I'd rather let Ash or the captain explain it for you.'

'Contact,' said the tac officer suddenly. 'Ship matching Tygran destroyer configuration just exited hyperspace 48,680 kiloms from Darien with high-vee trajectory. Extrapolation suggests that vessel is on course for atmospheric re-entry.'

'Smart flying,' Berg said, sitting back in the couch.

'And you're just going to let him go ahead and land,' Greg said. 'On my world.'

'You were here when Commander Ash gave his very precise instructions, Mr Cameron ...'

'Aye, but ...'

'And we know that Tygran destroyers considerably outgun scout vessels like the *Starfire* ...'

'Well, aye, but ...'

'But, Mr Cameron, my orders did not specifically restrict any efforts to gather additional data – Sub-Lieutenant Bains, how many sensor probes do we have?'

'Twelve short-range, eight long-range, sir,' said the tac officer.

'Prep eight of the short-range and configure them for pursuit,' Berg said. 'Launch them in sequence to intercept that destroyer's projected re-entry path at half-kilometre intervals.'

'Probes configured, sir ... probes launched ...'

In almost the next breath a frame popped open on the main viewport. It was Ash.

'Lieutenant Berg, I thought I'd made myself clear ...'

'Sensor probes, sir, gathering more data on their atmospheric capabilities.'

'Really? Their trajectories seem somewhat aggressive, almost as if they're on course to collide with Becker's ship!' Then his attention switched to Greg. 'Mr

Cameron, wild plans like these undermine my authority.'

'Had nothing to do with this one, Commander. Almost wish I did, though. Clever ...'

Ash frowned. 'Clever? How?'

'Well, if this guy Becker is as distrusting and paranoid as everyone seems to think, then he's gonna look at those incoming probes, think the worst, and ...'

'Becker's ship is altering its descent path, sir,' said the tac officer, Bains. 'Banking to starboard ... executing a turn of 163 degrees ...'

Greg gave Berg a smiling nod. Berg raised an acknowledging eyebrow.

'So Becker, y'see, now has to pass over the continental landmass to reach the colony rather than coming from the sea,' Greg said. 'Should take him over areas dominated by them Spiralists with their shoulder-mounted ground-to-air launchers.' He shrugged. 'Maybe one'll get lucky, who knows, eh?'

'A long shot, Mr Cameron.'

'Aye, but God loves a trier, Mr Ash.'

'Contact,' said Bains. 'Multiple contacts at outer long range ... sir, I'm picking up Imisil idents.'

'But their fleet's not due for hours,' said Berg.

Ash was getting similar data on his own bridge but suddenly his face turned grim and his channel went dead.

'What's wrong?' Greg said.

Berg was studying his own holoconsole, worry plain in his features.

'Oh, it's the Imisil all right,' he said. 'But we're only picking up four ships.'

'Four?' Greg said. 'Out of the original sixty that set out . . .' He shook his head, then chuckled quietly.

'You see a humorous side to this?' Berg said, annoyed.

'Not so much, but I remember what my Uncle Theo said about the time he was expecting reinforcements and got rather less than he hoped. He turned to his men and said, "All it mean, boys, is more medals for the rest of us, eh?"'

23

JULIA

Julia-Dragon paused on the mountain track and stared out over the lands of Vendredasir, at the hills, forests and dales growing dark with the encroaching dusk. The great winding river Manarun was a shining ribbon which was turning bloody red as the sun dipped to the horizon. She sniffed the air then shook her great head and resumed the trudge to the summit.

Harry was already there when she arrived. His exter was that of a paladin of the Order of the Dawnflower and was clad in an elaborate suit of armour, all silver, yellow and blue. Julia's exter was a Great Red Drake of the Damynel Nightclan, who just happened to be mortal enemies of the Order of the Dawnflower ...

'How much longer will this take?' she said, slumping down, taking up most of the summit's flat, pebbly area. 'Your drone friend said that all we needed to do was spend some of the credit and this Nicodemus would easily track us when the account flagged up. We've been in here for nearly two hours and still nothing.'

For Julia the entire situation had turned sour. They had translocated from Reski Emantes's data refuge aboard the airship to the Glow lobby at the Medafrique multiportal, and soon after received a glownote from the AI telling them to buy player tickets in a sagaverse called 'The Chronicles of the Black Throne'. Even as they wove through the immense crowds she felt she was being watched. Harry had laughed and said that was because everyone was being watched – visual feeds of every part of the open concourses were streamed around the world and across the solar system. Thus her initial experience of the Glow had been hectic and rushed, a dash through masses of wildly variegated avatars and exters, past the roaring neon flash of impossibly grand virtual stores, beneath the towering shapes of advertising goliaths scattering handfuls of groundcars and hoverbikes like confetti.

The 'Black Throne' sagaverse was a hugely popular story braid comprising scores of major plotlines and hundreds of minor ones in addition to the thousands of side quests, as well as those conspiracies and intrigues set in motion by the players themselves. The setting was a vast pseudo-medieval domain populated by a staggering array of fantastical creatures and species and fleshed out with detailed histories, customs, rivalries and superstitions.

Most of which Julia disregarded as they hurried through the character-induction process which they'd both set to Random-Fast ... and ended up with exters whose story roles were diametrically opposed. After a few unsettling incidents they left Kadyni, the hill-town they started at, and headed for the mountains. Where they ran into a band of masked horsemen who said not a thing, just attacked them on sight. After Julia had flown them both away, an exhausting task, Harry was sure that they were only a preset bunch of encounter mooks but she felt there was something more to them.

'Do you know anything about this Nicodemus?' she said.

'A little – he's supposed to be the greatest living net-mole, aka the Trapdoorman, aka the Karpetkrawler, aka Obscuriel.' Harry laughed. 'Moles do like their akas. Well, if anyone can help us get the Farag report to our Sino pals it'll be him.'

'Assuming that he comes for us,' Julia said, glancing at the dimming sky. 'And now it's getting dark ... what's wrong?'

Harry was standing and peering back the way they had come. 'It seems that our horse-riding friends have caught up with us ...' He paused as the leathery sound of flapping wings came down from above.

Looking up, Julia saw three winged, lizardlike creatures circling overhead, icy blue eyes staring down. Their wingspans were nothing like her own but together they could be effective against even a Great Drake. But only if she actually decided to stick around and get involved.

'Harry, this is a waste of time,' she said as she laboriously got onto her clawed feet. 'We should leave and try one of the other sagaverses. Perhaps this Nicodemus will find it easier to find us elsewhere.'

He grinned. 'I detect a certain determination.'

'I just feel that I've seen enough.' She paused,

recalling the exact trigger phrase given to her at the induction stage, then said, 'Angel Boxer Campus.'

At once a big red button appeared and she leaned forward to nudge it with her dragonish snout as the masked horsemen came charging up from the mountain path ...

The scene before her quivered, blurred, dissolved and resolved into the bright extravagance of a huge, horseshoe-shaped foyer lined with player portals. Light from glowing orreries lit up the busy crowds that streamed to and fro across a glass floor inlaid with lacy white patterns, or came and went on the helical slides that spiralled down to the level below. The foyer to 'The Chronicles of the Black Throne' sagaverse had over two dozen entryway levels to cater for the throngs eager to sample its fantastic domains, and that was just at the Medafrique multiportal. Julia saw numerous adbanners floating around, some claiming that the average daily player numbers were equal to the population of one of the larger South American nations ...

'Ah, there you are,' said Harry, who was back in his gaudy Tiger-Duke exter, as provided by the drone Reski Emantes. Julia's was similar, Lioness-Lady, a marvel of golden velvet, amber satin and black lace highlights. 'Where shall we go next?'

'The nearest sagaverse to this one,' she said, leading the way out to the canyonlike concourse. Halting at the threshold, her eyes alighted on an immense, pillar-flanked entrance with an archaic bas-relief frieze above and wide white steps sweeping up towards it. Solid-looking black letters hung in midair, spelling out **Welcome to Magnum Imperium**.

'That one,' she said.

Harry obtained a swan-shaped jitney which they rode across the concourse, weaving through the frantic swarms of players, tourists and other Glowfolk. Some moments later they were climbing the white stair to a towering hall that was all obsidian columns, gold statues and immense mirrors.

The mirrors turned out to be the means by which their in-saga exters were chosen, after which Harry used the credit account to pay for an all-day access. This time Julia gave more attention to the milieu – an alternate Roman Empire that had developed steam power – and her options for choosing a character-exter. She settled on that of a female military praetor of middle years called Placidia. The exter's attire was a combination of military practicality and feminine delicacy. There was a bronze breastplate and over it a loose patterned blue robe. A kirtle of scales, and a pale yellow sash tied about the waist. Shoulder pauldrons with long pegs from which little fealty pennons hung, and a muslin scarf wound about the head. And at the waist a long dagger in a plain scabbard. Once she had settled on her preferences, she only had to walk forward and through the mirror to emerge on a sunlit colonnaded arcade overlooking the river Tiber.

Rome was a hazy, smoky cityscape spread out beneath a mid-morning sun. The river was busy with vessels, single- and double-funnelled galleys steaming up to the docks or down to the sea. Tugs hauled lines of covered barges to and fro across river-spanning viaducts while bulbous dirigibles flew overhead, trailing smoke and steam.

'Quiet view, eh?'

Harry joined her at the stone balcony. He had on a mixture of battered grey armour and red-stained leathers, with the symbol of a black wolf clearly visible. He wore a long sword at the waist and carried a large satchel on his shoulder. He gave a flourishing bow.

'Quintus Cornelius Vibiano, centurio-evocati of the Sixty-Third Legion, at your service, lady!'

'Pleased to make your acquaintance – apparently I am Placidia Murcius, praetor and trader in fine wines. So, here we are, or rather here we still are.' She frowned. 'When should we ...'

'Return to the Glow and try to reach the representatives ourselves?' Harry shook his head. 'I may be a cunning AI with friends in low places but in *this* place I wouldn't know where to start.'

'But time is not on our side,' she said. 'If this Nicodemus doesn't show up we may have no choice.'

Harry arched an eyebrow. 'Well, if it does come to that there is at least a sizeable amount in that account ...'

A crash and a rumble from somewhere close interrupted him. Leaning forward on the low balcony, Julia looked down ten floors to a cobbled street lined with small shops and odd kiosks on stilts. A steam-powered wagon had collided with the corner of the two-storey building opposite and tipped over, spilling its cargo of oranges across the street. A shop front was demolished and a stilted kiosk had also been knocked over. Some traders were arguing with the driver and his two loaders and before long harsh words led to shoving and thrown punches.

But before things got out of hand, several men in
dark green cloaks and leather armour arrived and pulled
the antagonists apart. They were armed with cudgels
that were waved about or ostentatiously rested on
shoulders.

'The Vigiles Urbani,' Harry said. 'City police, basically.'

As she watched, Julia heard an odd metallic creak
behind her, like hinges. When she glanced round she
was stunned to see a skinny man in a long, grubby coat
and wearing antique-style goggles emerging from a trapdoor in the floor of the arcade. For a moment they
stared open-mouthed at each other, and he seemed
about to smile and beckon to her when a red light
started flashing on his wrist.

'Dammit, they're here again!' he said in a strangled
whisper. Lithely he ducked back down and pulled the
trapdoor shut with a muffled thud.

'Harry, it was . . .'

'Ah, I think we'd best be on our way,' said Harry.
'Our pursuers are back.'

Julia peered over the balcony and saw that the green
cloaks, now wearing pale, blank stage-masks, were leaving the scene of the accident and crossing the road.

'Who or what are they?'

'Can't imagine that it's the netlaw – they would land
on us in overkill numbers and with a brass band playing.' He frowned. 'I fear they may be those who tracked
us to Earth and assassinated the original Reski Emantes.
In any case, we can't stay here.'

'But he was here a moment ago, the
Trapdoorman . . .'

Harry stared at her for a second. 'Okay, but we still need to move – tell me about it on the way.'

The arcade was the topmost floor of a large building occupied by a mixture of offices and residences. It was also built into the side of one of Rome's hills, so at the rear of the arcade was a set of marble stairs that climbed past walled gardens and homes to the crest of the hill. There was a temple of Hephaestus there, next to a small observatory, and a park from which they finally gained a view of the full magnificence of the imperial city.

Steam power had allowed the emperors of this saga-verse-Rome to build on a godlike scale. An immense palace with sloping walls sat atop ranks of huge pillars that stretched out along the Tiber. Banners flew from the towers and battlements and fabulous ornamenta-tion flashed gold and silver in the sun. At ground level, however, shanty towns had clustered around the shaded bases of the great pillars, grey beneath veils of smoke. Other nobles and aristocrats had sought to build extravagant, similarly elevated villas but none could match the imperial residence's dimensions.

Harry and Julia paused to take in the view for just a moment before descending the other side of the hill, hurrying down a winding cobbled street. At the foot of it a large bridge crossed a deep smoky vale crammed with lower-class houses, two- and three-storey buildings packed in close together. They were fifty yards or so from the bridge when three Vigiles Urbani stepped out into the street, faces masked, cudgels at the ready.

'This way!' Harry said, ducking left along a narrow alley.

Julia was only feeling a slight strain as she dashed after him, doing her best to avoid puddles and decomposing garbage.

'Where are we going?' she said as he slowed at what looked like a dead end and hurriedly peered into several lightless doorways.

'I'm sure I saw a building with a platform where a basket balloon was anchored ... further up and round the hill. If we find it we can cross the river and hope that Nicodemus catches up with us before those hunters. Or we just pull the plug and go look for another sagaverse ... ah, knew there had to be ...'

Julia glanced back and saw their pursuers loping down the alley towards them.

'Lead the way.'

One black passage led to a steep, winding rack of stairs that passed through arches and beneath overhanging floors and small connecting footbridges. After a frantic climb they finally reached the building in question, complete with a railed platform jutting out over a cliffside and a pair of basket balloons tied up and swaying in the fitful breeze. Harry paid the surprised-looking attendant a handful of sesterces and five minutes later they were aloft in one of the baskets, holding on to the thick wicker sides as the pilot, a taciturn, grizzled man, adjusted the burners and pulled on vent cables from time to time.

They were halfway across when there was a thud from the basket's wickerwork floor. Julia and Harry moved to one side and a hitherto invisible hatch creaked open.

'Quickly,' came a voice from the dimness below. 'Before they realise.'

Julia went first, smiling at the stunned balloonist as she climbed down, hastily followed by Harry, who pulled the trapdoor shut after him. They were in a small grey-walled compartment with the skinny, long-coated and begoggled man from before, who had to be Nicodemus. Weirdly, the low ceiling looked just like the underside of the balloon basket and Julia could still hear the balloonist shifting about above them, muttering to himself.

'Here we go,' said Nicodemus. 'The big switcheroo!'

From a coat pocket he took a little box with an old-fashioned rocker switch which he pressed. Abruptly the wicker ceiling dissolved into flat grey while one of the compartment walls vanished, revealing a long narrow room with metal rack shelves on one side and a couple of desks sitting beneath more shelving on the other. A pair of archaic bulbs hung from a high ceiling but the only light came from the rows of small screens sitting on the shelves over the desks.

'Mr Nicodemus, I presume,' Harry said. Julia saw that he was back in the Tiger-Duke exter and she was Lioness-Lady again.

'Just Nicodemus,' their host said. Pushing the goggles up onto his dark bristly hair, he busily retrieved a couple of grubby wheeled office chairs from the room's shadowy far end. Once they were seated, he leaned back against a desk edge, folded his coat shut, crossed his arms and regarded them both with wide, intense eyes.

'My zetetic feed tells me that you are both code entities although one of you is a fractal simuloid, highly recomplex with a non-bounded sentience.' He paused to regard Julia with fascinated eyes. 'You should realise that while I am a living, breathing organic Human, and therefore prey to all the failings of the flesh, this image of mine is no more than a remote exter. I'm not neurally linked therefore cannot be wet-hacked or mindseared in any way. If either of you were considering such gambits.'

'Nothing could be further from our minds, I assure you,' Harry said. 'Were you able to identify our contact? If you know anything about his origins and allegiance you would get some notion of our reliability.'

Nicodemus gave a bleak smile. 'Sure, I know about the Construct and your drone patron was able to satisfy me that he is the genuine article. I just had to be certain about you two, especially with those zazins on your trail.'

'Ah, so that's what they were,' Harry said, his features suddenly serious.

'A little background would be helpful,' Julia said.

'Code-specific hunter-killers,' he said. 'Whoever is behind them managed to get hold of full or even partial scans of our code cores. Zazins don't stop – they just keep regenerating.'

'So we're in danger ... anywhere?' she said. 'Out in the Glow, for example?'

'Yes, which makes our task just that much trickier.'

'Okay, I admit it, I'm intrigued,' said Nicodemus. 'What kind of mischief do you have in mind?'

Harry laid it out for him, the dire predicament of Darien, the Earthsphere fleet journeying to join a Hegemony armada, the arrival of the lost Sino colonists, who then vowed to fight for the Darien colony, and the riveting report by Kaphiri Farag. Nicodemus listened, breaking in a few times for clarification on this or that point. When Harry was done, their host sat there on the edge of the desk, one arm across his chest, his other hand clamped across his face, beneath his nose. After a few moments the hand fell away as he let out a bark of laughter.

'Yes, you're right! – getting into the private home-nets of eight such high-status individuals would be like trying to crawl into a shark's mouth undetected. Add to which, an intruder alert would certainly bring the netlaw down on top of us like ... a ton of boots. No, we have to get them to leave reality, leave their virtual citadels and enter the Glow with the aim of seeking us out!'

'And they would do this ... because ... ?' Julia said.

Nicodemus's smile was all narrow-eyed cunning.

'Because, dear Lioness-Lady, they will be compelled to do so. This ... falls within that arena of instinctive talents and persuasive genius known as ego-engineering. It would be a demanding task to carry out against just one person but you've brought me eight targets! ... with the added bonus that we only have a matter of slender hours to make it all work!'

'I see,' said Harry. 'Is it too steep a problem?'

'Did I say that? Did I say it was too steep?' Nicodemus was staring maniacally. 'Too steep *for me*? ... well, actually it is but I haven't survived this long in the Glow without accumulating a posse of work-aholic wannabes and savants ... behold.'

He raised a hand to point at the shadowy end of the room, which lit up to reveal that the room now stretched on for another similar length, with desks lining both sides. And at the desks sat another six or seven

Nicodemuses: one was female, one was tall and burly, while the rest were variations on squat, stocky, flabby and bald. But they all wore long grey coats and black rubbery goggles. A couple of them waved.

Nicodemus's grin was a mixture of fatherly pride and energised anticipation as he faced them.

'My emulating offspring,' he said. 'Your dedication is noted. I am pleased to tell you that we have been set a well-paid task that will require every sweat-faraday, every elbow-tesla that you can muster. This, my febrile progeny, will be a *brainburner*!'

The Nicodemoids broke into fervent applause and whoops of delight. Harry and Julia exchanged a non-plussed look.

Nicodemus turned back to them. 'We now have to get down to it, so in the meantime amuse yourselves with any of the screen stuff. If you say "music" it'll offer a selection of toe-tappers old and ancient; if you say "veeshows" it'll show you something involving serious amounts of guns, and if you say "pretty colours" – well, I'm sure you catch the notion.' He started buttoning up his coat with theatrical élan. 'This may take some time but not so much that you should start worrying.'

So saying, he marched off to join his posse, and a moment later that half of the long narrow room was swallowed in shadow once more.

Julia was in the grip of both unease and irritation. 'Can we trust this man? Is he even sane?'

Harry gave her an amused look. 'I would have thought that eccentric characters like our host would have been a regular feature of the Enhanced subculture.'

She shook her head. 'The emphasis was always on

rational behaviour since it determined how we were perceived by the ordinary people. It was ingrained into us over and over – don't frighten the norms.' She glanced at the dark end of the room. 'Anyone openly eccentric was generally seen as a danger to the project's profile.'

'Well, the Glow is the ultimate metropolitan culture,' Harry said. 'Since anyone can look like anything, eccentric behaviour isn't so much accepted as positively expected. But remember – all exters are masks in one way or another ...'

Abruptly, the far end of the room lit up again and Nicodemus came staggering towards them, leaning on the desks for support. Head down, he seemed to be panting and shaking.

'Is something wrong?' Julia said, halfway out of her seat.

She paused when she realised that Nicodemus was laughing almost uncontrollably.

'Those ... crazy little phreaks! Even when they're on down time their scarred brainpans are frying up some *mélange* of delicious loonery. A choir of lab mice gentekked up with the president's face, indeed!'

'Nicodemus, I don't understand,' Julia said. 'Why are you back so soon?'

'So soon?' Nicodemus loomed over her with wide staring eyes. 'My dear lady lion, my minions and I have been hard at work on this conundrum for eight stark shrieking hours! Show some gratitude, if you will ...'

'Eight hours ...'

'Eight subjective hours,' Harry said quickly. 'Hence brainburner!'

'Correctamundo, tiger-boy,' said Nicodemus. 'This is

my own little citadel in the Glow, well, not strictly speaking part of the Glow, more a handcrafted extension built onto the side of it.' He struck a pose, outstretched hand sweeping around. 'Here I determine the limits and the depths and the heights, so when I took my meme-kids into the crucible of your predicament we cranked up the subjective ratio and really got our neural oatmeals simmering!'

'So you have a plan,' Julia said, keeping her annoyance from showing.

Nicodemus held up his fingers, thumbs hidden.

'Eight individual targets, eight individualised profiles, eight separate and distinct campaigns tailored to winkling them out of their hidey-holes and into the Glow.' As he spoke he flicked a forefinger at a series of screens, which lit up one by one with the eight Sino-Asian delegates who had to see the Kaphiri Farag report.

'So what's the first step?' Harry said.

'It's already happening.' Nicodemus reversed a chair and sat down, arms leaning on the backrest. 'Every one of those über-politicians has a homenet with an AI to manage his mail, filter out the trash, send out mods of the standard template replies, and prioritise staff assignments. So the initial eight messages have been designed with them in mind, the AIs, which meant research into their softhouse origins, what model, what upgrades, what custom tweaks if any. We got lucky – one of our Glow consultants let us have the cue-phrases for two of them, for a price. With those we can get the AI to prioritise any message we like for the eyes of two of our targets.'

'I see,' said Harry. 'So assuming you get messages

through to the representatives, how will you persuade them to come to the Glow? And where will we be putting on the show?'

'This is where the techniques of ego-engineering come in,' said Nicodemus. 'Two will be inveigled into thinking that they are each the subject of a flattering biodocudrama being made under conditions of great secrecy and they need to meet with the director in the Glow without delay. Two will be intrigued by offers to sell certain rare artefacts relating to their personal hobbies, dependent on their meeting an intermediary in the Glow. One will be led to believe that he's on his way to a secret meeting with a recently escaped Sendrukan political prisoner. One thinks she's been warned that secrets from her past will be depicted in a stage drama about to open in the Glow. And the last two will be labouring under the mistaken belief that they've been invited to Optimi-level VIP parties by their favourite Glowmo celebs.' He grinned, all bare teeth. 'Yes, that's the level of detail that we're working with.'

'And where?'

'At the utterly magnificent Electric Theatre City,' said Nicodemus, who swung his brittle smile round at Julia. 'Which you'll have heard of, of course.'

'Who hasn't,' she said, expression unchanging, 'heard of the Electric Theatre City?'

Nicodemus arched an eyebrow and chuckled.

'Good, because that'll be your station, the pair of you. I've already booked a display area for the show – and I assume that you have a copy with you ...'

They nodded in unison, then Harry said:

'What about the zazins? They'll still be out there, hunting for us.'

'Uh huh, which is why I'm giving you these.' One bony hand came out, holding a pair of red dice. With red dots. 'Temporary rewrite orgs – they go in your pockets. They don't alter any root or dynamic functions, they just add junk data to certain marker files so that the zazins don't get a match if they scan you. *Capisce?*'

Julia pocketed the red die but felt nothing, which made her wonder if that was good or bad.

'All righty,' said their host, getting to his feet. 'Now that we're slip to the slide and code to the mode, as it were, it's time to move on out. We'll get to Electric Theatre City by stages so that our start point stays hidden, and on the way ... show you babies some of the sights!'

This last was accompanied by a lascivious waggle of the tongue as he led them back to the grey recess by which they had arrived.

'Some of the sights' didn't really do it justice. The virtual continuum of the Glow was a riotous flow of spectacle, or at least this zone was. It was an enormous fusion of clubland and theme park, of carnival and racetrack, of partyland and destruction derby. There was the Horn of Plenty, an immense pink and sparkly golden cornucopia full of Big Prize game shows, some of which were on continuous veecast. There was the Atmosfear Race, a twenty-lane speedway that soared, looped and spiralled across the virtual heavens, on which drivers raced vehicles the size of skyscrapers – some even looked like skyscrapers. Then there was the Marilyn Monroe Bar & Grill, a kilometre-high simulacrum of the pre-atomic-age vee-star, within which there were levels of restaurants, lounge bars, karaoke jousts, and bowling alleys. Also striding around and looming over the gaudy megatropolis were the Jackie Chan martial arts arena and assault course, the Chairman Mao casino and Möbius floorshow, and the Melissa Takeru theme emporium, concert hall and biog-ride. The last was a Filipina teenstar whose image was currently selling everything from jaunty little caps to garden rakes, going by the flashverts Julia had seen.

The Electric Theatre City actually was the size of a city and was encircled by half-kilometre-wide perception panels (or rather the virtual presentation thereof), each running a vee-epic. As they swept into the ETC by hovertram, Nicodemus named some of them: *Casablanca 3: Rick's Revenge*; *Lord Gatling's Gun*; *Hot Larvae: The Dissolution*; *Conqueror: The Quest for Mario* …

Dropped off at a spidery tower platform, they followed Nicodemus along gantries to a strange midair intersection of speeding walkways, or fastways. One by one they stepped on and were whisked away in a streaming blur through tunnels and passages between brightly coloured buildings of every shape and size. They came to an abrupt halt at a roof garden overlooking a bright neon-orange castle that sat between a noisy sensorium emporium and a smallish establishment called Leather Experience. Its towering frontage looked like stitched leather and was well provided with huge zips and studs.

'Welcome to the Otranto House,' Nicodemus said with a dark laugh.

Another fastway deposited them next to a curved shiny desk at the edge of an enormous, cavernous hall.

Monumental pillars marched across its emptiness, half-lit by glowing lamps that floated just above head height. Nicodemus was not pleased.

'By the beard of Baron Frankenstein, this is not what I ordered!' he growled.

'Is there a problem, sir?'

Unseen by anyone, a yellow-uniformed attendant had appeared at the desk. Her smile was ferociously un-wavering.

'The ceremonial amphitheatre, the red and gold carpets, the full-height perception screen, the ushers, the glittery lights ... I ordered them, so where are they?'

'As stated in your contract, sir, the Otranto House reserves the right to initialise booked content only in the presence of an actual audience.'

'That would be me,' Nicodemus said. 'And my associates here.'

'But—'

'An audience is made up of those who view a show: we three will be using our sense of vision to view the show, ergo we are part of the audience. You may now remodel this interior to the specifications I have ordered and paid for ... or must I now contact my lawyers, Fleam, Goad and Gimlet?'

'That won't be necessary, sir. Otranto House is now satisfied that the contractual terms have been met.'

Alteration raced across the surfaces of the great hall, a frantic wave of rerendering. The walls turned dark blue, hung with drapes, adorned with light sconces. The carpet became a rich red expanse patterned with elaborate letter Ns. Most of the pillars vanished and banks of plush seating appeared, and a vast opaque panel filled one entire wall. Last, a partition wall descended, creating an arrivals foyer, with a black-velvet-draped entryway.

'Good,' Nicodemus murmured, looking over his shoulder. 'Wondered where he'd got to.'

Julia glanced round and saw a tall, broad-chested bulky man standing where the walkway had dropped him, swaying on the spot and blinking. He wore a formal black suit, which looked thoroughly incongruous for someone of his build. After a moment his gaze settled on the three of them and he approached.

'Urm, Mr Nic, I followed yore 'structions ...'

'And here you are, Alfred, well done!' Nicodemus looked to Harry and Julia. 'This is Alfred, formerly the Mad Mangler of Moneytown, the contact-sport zone – he used to be the most fearsome thing on two legs ...'

'Dem days is over now, Mr Nic. I got my pottry biz to run now.'

'Glad to hear it, Alfred. Now these are my friends, Harry and Julia, and I want you to look after them for me, just as I explained in my note, okay?'

'I got yore note, Mr Nic.'

Nicodemus regarded Julia and Harry. 'Because you're such a distinctive pair – when you consider the contrasting data profiles – I asked Alfred along to foil anyone scanning on that basis. I am going to leave you for a short while – I've had minion-messages telling me that two of our VIPs are away from their chief residences and not responding to our exquisitely worded blandishments.' He snapped his fingers and a datapad appeared in his hand. 'Here's the original list you gave, along with up-to-date pix of the exters they're likely to be wearing, as well as their appointed times.' He swiv-elled his gaze round to the yellow-garbed desk clerk. 'I assume that the eightfold multi-occupancy is now in operation?'

The clerk nodded. 'Exactly as you requested, sir.'

'Better be,' Nicodemus said to Julia, handing her the datapad. 'So when they arrive, verify what they're here to see, usher them through and Buttercup here will switch the door onto the next stratum, and so forth.'

Harry laughed suddenly. 'So all eight of our Sino reps will be present in the auditorium yet unaware of each other.'

'Give that AI a tune-playing, self-lighting cigar!' Nicodemus cackled. 'Right, time I wasn't here.' With that he stepped onto the walkway and a moment later was an upright blur zipping up and away. Harry looked at Julia.

'I think that means that we're in charge,' he said.

Julia tapped the datapad. 'And our first guest is due any moment.'

A little under a minute later a small group arrived in quick succession, three white-robed monks led by a car-dinal in black. Julia quickly matched the exters to a name, Jirawat Pamang, overcouncillor for the VietLao–ThaiCam co-territory. The cardinal drew near and in a low voice said:

'I am here for the Amelia Borjan installation.'

She nodded, then gestured them towards the draped entrance.

'Please proceed.'

He passed through, followed by his monk escort.

The next VIP was due four minutes later but was a

no-show. The following three were punctual, arriving exactly five minutes apart. The sixth was a no-show and when the seventh likewise failed to appear Julia began to wish they'd agreed some method of contacting Nicodemus. She was about to ask their muscly companion, Alfred, if he knew of any way when she started to hear laughter and voices from beyond the drapes. Then came a man's voice, shouting to be let back through. She looked at the yellow-clad clerk.

'Can you turn this partition wall transparent but only for us?'

A nod, and the wall duly became see-through, like a misty veil. One of the VIPs, a man in the garb of a prosperous Victorian, was rapping the wall with a walking stick while groups of garishly dressed people ran around in the background, between and over the seats, pelting each other with fruit which burst into sprays of tiny flowers on impact.

'Where did all these people come from?' she said to the clerk. 'There's not supposed to be any other entrances ...'

There were more voices from behind. Turning, she saw more people starting to arrive by the walkway in a continuous stream. In moments there were a dozen, then a score, then more. At her side the imposing Alfred looked on impassively, arms crossed.

'What are we going to do?' she asked Harry.

'Whatever it is, I think we'll have to let our guests out,' he said, pointing at the wall where all four of the VIPs were now demanding an exit from the auditorium. Paralysed with indecision, Julia stared at them, gradually coming to the sickening realisation that the entire complicated ruse had failed. But before she could speak to Harry the growing crowd surged towards the draped entrance and several people at the flank pushed her to the side, scarcely even apologising.

'Julia,' Harry shouted from the other side of the sudden mob. 'Wait there – I'll go around ...'

He broke off as three brightly dressed people in masks rushed at him from the side. He dodged the zazins' tackles and launched himself up onto the crowd – voices cheered and hands came up to catch him and bear him along. But the zazins leaped into the press, knocking people aside as they chased after Harry. Others pushed back and punches got thrown.

Suddenly there was an insistent, high-pitched whooping from above as quivering holes opened up in the ceiling.

'Dat's the netlaw,' said Alfred. 'S'gonna be trouble ...'

Without hesitation the big man lunged into the crowd like a tuxedoed battleship. People moved aside like a bow wave as he charged in, grabbed Harry by the collar and dragged him back to where Julia was standing. The next thing she knew, Alfred had grabbed her round the waist while still holding on to Harry.

'Sorry Miss Julia, Mr Harry, but I got my 'structions ...'

The chaos all around them seemed to merge into a yowling, roaring surf of sound as everything Julia could see turned ash grey and swirled into nothing.

Awareness returned with the suddenness of a thrown switch. She was sitting in a leather armchair in what looked like a low-ceilinged, dim-lit study. Then she saw Harry in a similar chair, hands resting in his lap, head lolling forward and still. Like her, he was wearing the old-fashioned trench coat from their first encounter. Julia whispered then spoke to him but he did not stir.

'I'm afraid he will not wake,' said a male voice, sounding hoarse, slightly gravelly, an elderly voice. 'The zazins must have reached him with some kind of short-range attack. Like you he is running on base system, and there is some kind of activity going on, a self-check perhaps, but he won't respond to stimuli.'

She got to her feet and looked around her at dark shelves crowded with books and files, a couple of cabinets, more boxes with labels arranged neatly under the lowest shelves on every wall. There was no door. A solid wooden chair on castors was positioned at a desk lit up by a flexi-necked lamp. Above the desk, sandwiched between large, heavy books, was an archaic CRT-style vee screen, glassy and grey, deactivated.

'Who are you? Where are you?'

The old screen blinked on and a wrinkle-faced old man with a grey ponytail gazed out at her.

'We've actually already met,' he said and for a moment the image switched to a manically grinning face adorned with black goggles. Then back to the elderly man.

She raised her eyebrows. 'Nicodemus?'

'Everything that you see in the Glow is illusory, by its nature. A dance of masks and marionettes in rainbow colours.' He shrugged. 'Which includes that whole spectacle that we just put on.'

Pangs of unease passed through her.

'I think I'm due an explanation,' she said. 'I explained to you what was at stake – are you saying that was all for nothing?'

'Far from it, young lady sentience,' said Nicodemus. 'As you'll see very shortly. In the meantime try to relax.'

She looked around her. 'But where am I?'

The face on the screen chuckled and a skinny finger tapped a silver-grey temple. 'In here, as am I, strictly speaking. Although my I is as much a visitor to the base-system sim I've got you running in ...'

'Sorry, I don't follow ...'

'Look, I'm 109 years old so I've had a few modifications done to the old brainbox, enough capacity to run two or three fractalised sentiences like you if I wanted. Anyway, the main event is about to begin – oh, I took a copy of the Farag report, by the way, while we were in transit, so to speak. Okay, he's almost here so keep watching.'

The image of the old man dissolved into a view over rocky slopes and sheer mountainsides sheathed in icy white while wind-driven snow whirled and streamed past outside. There was a glass surface, Julia realised, between the observer and the raw elements and she speculated that this was some kind of research station, high in some range of mountains.

The observer (who Julia took to be the elderly Nicodemus) looked to the right, revealing that he stood in a glass-covered walkway which curved out of sight around a strange, brick-built edifice. There was the sound of a mechanical door opening and closing and Nicodemus turned the other way to see a diminutive figure in a dark coat approaching. As he drew near, Julia realised that he was familiar, a Chinese man with grey hair and glasses – a name came to her, Tsu Chung Ho, Earthsphere overcouncillor of Shandong–Jiangsu co-ter-ritory, a senior representative of long standing.

Tsu Chung's deliberate pace did not vary until he halted before Nicodemus. Smiling, he wagged a finger.

'Thirty years go by and you wait till I am on holiday before coming to see me. Shocking behaviour, Nicholas, especially since my travel plans were supposed to be secret!'

Laughing, the two men shook hands.

'Shameful, yes,' said Nicodemus/Nicholas. 'But to such a data-nibbler as myself there can be no secrets. I heard about the legs.'

Tsu Chung made a dismissive gesture. 'Undetected pre-aneurysmic condition, minor stroke, and my legs … well, brain surgery has been recommended, but there are risks, you know? I do not feel I can take small chances at the moment.' He shrugged then gave Nicodemus an amused, considering look. 'You're look-ing very well, Nicholas, ageing gracefully, one might say. But why would my old teacher leave his electric citadel to hunt me down? Did I forget to hand in an assign-ment?'

Nicodemus shook his head. 'No, Tsu Chung, quite the reverse, to be frank. I assume that you know about the Earthsphere ships currently heading to join the Hegemony armada.'

The overcouncillor gave a sad nod. 'Indeed I do, old friend, my grandson is serving aboard one of them. There is deep disquiet about this, even more than there was over continuing the Yamanon deployment. But the coalition is still holding, still backing the president.'

'Darien is going to be punished, Tsu Chung,' Nicodemus said. 'That is what the Hegemony does.'

'I know.'

'What if I could – no, what if you could offer up proof that the potential tragedy is far, far greater than anyone thinks? That the survivors of a lost Sino colony have reached Darien to fight alongside the planet's defenders?'

'Wait ... you're talking about that joke clip that went around earlier today. Is that why ...'

'No, Tsu Chung, what you saw was a grey intel hatchet job. The original is very different.' He took a small silvery card from an inside pocket. 'Can I show you?'

Tsu Chung Ho smiled and gestured for him to proceed.

Nicodemus stuck the card to the inside of the glass enclosure, unfolded it to a hair-thin screen about a foot square, then thumbed a symbol on its lower-right corner. At once, Kaphiri Farag's report began to play. The overcouncillor remained outwardly impassive all the way through. When it was over he took off his glasses and cleaned them with a piece of fine tissue which he then used to dab lightly at the corners of his eyes.

'It appears authentic,' he said.

'Tsu Chung, I assure you ...'

The overcouncillor stopped him with an upraised hand.

'I don't doubt it for a second.'

'Your trust is not misplaced. The question is this –

will this be enough to persuade your regional colleagues to back a call for the Earthsphere contingent to either withdraw or stand down?'

Tsu Chung spread his hands. 'I would have to be able to prove that this report is genuine. Can this be done?'

Julia nodded – this was the sticking point.

'Well,' said Nicodemus. 'This much I do know – the Security Director's own netlaw division believes it was genuine. They deployed a fully remoted cohort of agents into the Glow a couple of hours ago, instituted a full lockdown on the Electric Theatre City and detain-tagged 104,761 citizens, including four of your own Sino colleagues from the Overcouncil. Now it's true that I lured them there with the intention of springing the Farag report on them, and it's also true that a certain amount of second-order circumstantial evidence was leaked to netlaw contacts. But this is incidental next to the ripple effects – go online and you will see the outrage that's gripping the Glow right now, the endless analysis cycles and the voxpop aggregates saying that Glow free-doms were savagely crushed. When you call a press conference and reveal the Farag report, the surge of pop-ular support should be … considerable.'

The overcouncillor looked thoughtful. 'One moment, Nicholas,' he said, his eyes glazing over as he accessed some kind of Glow-linked implant. A moment or two later he blinked, gave Nicholas a wide-eyed look and began to laugh. Nicholas joined in.

'It's … better than you say,' he said eventually. 'One of the netlaw subministers has already resigned! But I shall have to move with this immediately …' He glanced around and beckoned to one of his bodyguards.

'I will see if the management of the Jungfraujoch can extend the use of a private room where I can conduct some Glow politics . . .'

'Interviews?' Nicodemus said as he took down the little screen and refolded it.

'Spot commentaries, group declarations, and all the other features of my rebellious campaign. You know, the way things are I may be able to get the president to have our fleet take control of Darien, under some kind of diplomatic legacy. That should help safeguard the colony, and the new arrivals.'

'Thank you, Tsu Chung. Some people I know will be heartened at this news.' He handed over the folded screen. 'So . . . now it's time I made myself scarce and let you work.'

The two men shook hands.

'And Nicholas,' Tsu Chung said. 'Please don't wait another thirty years until next time, hmm?'

'I guarantee it!'

As Nicodemus turned and walked away from the overcouncillor, the screen picture faded away to grey.

'My apologies for deceiving you about the Electric Theatre City. It was a necessary part of the ploy.'

Back in the cramped little study, the older ponytailed Nicodemus was now sitting in the armchair Julia had occupied.

'You used us as bait,' she said.

'And we succeeded.'

Frowning, she glanced at the unresponsive Harry. 'How can we be sure? How soon before we find out if your Sino friend has got the president to rescind her orders?'

Nicodemus chuckled. 'The Glow is all afroth with anger at the moment – I've never seen it so volatile! If President Castiglione attempts to defy Tsu Chung's demands, she could well find herself swept away ... we'll know in about an hour.'

'What about Harry?'

'His internal activity continues, but there are indications that the self-check may have hit a cyclic block.' Nicodemus shrugged. 'I made contact with your sponsor, this Emantes, and he says to just erase it since he has a copy.'

Startled, she stared at him, a suspicion forming in her thoughts.

'Is that what you'll do?'

'Hmm, not sure. Perhaps I'll tinker with his code, see what turns up.'

'I understand. Well, since our business here is concluded, I am keen to return to my sponsor. Are you able to translocate me?'

The elderly Nicodemus smiled. 'You don't feel like sticking around to watch the political fireworks?'

'Thanks, but there is somewhere else that I have to be very soon.'

'Of course – places to go, ungodly villains to smite ...'

Questions to ask, missiles to stop ...

'... okay, you'll be going via several net-junctions – are you ready?'

But before she could answer, the translocation kicked in and her world folded up into tightly packed darkness.

24

GREG

After a microjump aboard the *Starfire* and a hasty trip in a shuttle on loan from the Vox Humana, they reached the rebel Tygran ship, *Vanquisher*. The shuttle docked at one of two underhull recesses and when Greg and Lieutenant Berg emerged from the airlock they were scanned for weapons. They were then escorted up two decks to an empty hold where the meeting with the mutiny leader was to take place.

The *Vanquisher*'s interior was markedly roomier than that of the *Starfire* and had a decor that was predominantly of a rich, dark blue, offset with softer shades. Corridor bulkheads, pipes, lines and spot monitor readouts were concealed by access panels, giving the ship a much less cluttered feel, while the lighting was smooth and diffuse. In a way it reminded Greg of the Darien Institute's admin offices.

The hold, however, was brightly lit and functional. The mutiny leader, Braddock, was waiting when they arrived, standing by a long table with three other officers. All wore light body armour in dull green and grey, standard non-combat duty dress. Greg was in ordinary civilian wear with a long black coat, because Ash wanted him to appear as civilian as possible. Braddock had insisted on speaking with a Darien representative before opening any discussions on force dispositions.

And here I am, Greg thought. *Trouble is, the Vox Humana admiral is now making the same demand since she finds communications with the Imisil 'lacking in due courtesy'. Hell's teeth, what does she want – missives written on parchment and hand-delivered by forelock-tugging peons?*

Braddock came forward to shake hands, then gestured Greg and Berg towards the table. Braddock, a wiry man slightly shorter than Greg, had an intense air about him. His dark hair was regulation bristle-short, and his complexion was sallow coupled with a pitted coarseness that could have come from a skin condition. His eyes were bright and seemed to miss nothing.

But now I have to find out what you want.

Seated opposite the man, Greg smiled but before he could begin the Tygran spoke first.

'Mr Cameron, before we begin I'd better tell you that Lieutenant Ash has briefed me on your background so I understand that you don't really speak for the colonial government.'

'There isn't really a colonial government to speak of at the moment,' Greg said.

'And yet you have a certain position, a status that gives your opinions weight and impact, yes?'

Greg frowned. *That might be true, considering what I've been through … aye, but I'm not alone in that.*

'Maybe so,' he said. Then a thought struck him. 'Are you looking for political asylum?'

'That is our favoured option,' Braddock said. 'And not just for me and my crew but also for many of my fellow Tygrans who are now seeking a new home.'

Lieutenant Berg had been tight-lipped up to now but suddenly he leaned forward.

'Are you referring to ordinary citizens back on Tygra, Nightwalker?'

Braddock stared at Berg. 'Yes, Stormlion, that is the case.'

'Why?'

'You should know – the story goes that Gideon's crew were the first to view the Rawlins testament, and now you've secured yourself a pleasant bolthole on this world.' Braddock shifted his gaze back to Greg. 'When you see this ship and its crew in action you'll realise that we are at least as deserving of asylum as those who arrived earlier . . .'

'Have a care, Nightwalker,' said Berg, rising from his chair. 'As I speak, my captain is on the planet's surface, struggling against Brolturans and combat droids . . .'

'Whoa, wait just a minute, the pair of ye!' Greg grabbed Berg by the shoulder and firmly pulled him back into his seat while Braddock settled back into his. 'Right, I don't know what kind of competitive sports thing this is all about but get this into your heads – there's an almighty drittstorm heading our way and nobody's getting anything if we go under. And before we go any further I'd like to know a bit more about this Rawlins testament . . .'

Braddock turned to one of his officers, who produced

a flat black datapad from a document case and passed it over. Braddock thumbed a control at one of the corners and a thinscreen extruded from one of the sides. 'I thought you might like to see this,' he said, turning the screen to face Greg.

As he watched, an elderly Tygran officer introduced himself as Captain Rawlins. He went on to summarise the official history of how the early Tygran colonists vied with a native sentient species, the Zshahil, and how forty years of friction and confrontation led to war. The war culminated in the surrender of the defeated native tribes and their en masse migration to a less hospitable equatorial landmass across a narrow sea. Then Rawlins began to uncover the true history. His report had been recorded outdoors, at a ruined coastal port from which the Zshahil were supposed to have sailed. Greg saw Rawlins use scanning equipment to reveal numerous burial pits around the port, and a digging machine to bring up soil-caked clumps of non-Human bones. Finally, after he arrived at a rough tally in excess of a quarter of a million, Rawlins's report ended with the words, 'So now we know the truth, which is that we are capable of murdering an entire race. But will this truth set us free, or will it damn us?'

As the picture faded to black, Greg sat back in his chair, noting the grim faces all around him.

Well, how would I feel if I'd found out that something like that had happened during the early years of our colony? In fact, it could have happened when we discovered the Uvovo on Nivyesta. Were we just lucky enough to hold on to reason?

'So, have many of your people seen this?' Greg said.

'As soon as the Bund became aware of its existence, via some unknown source, it was banned, declared an illegal propaganda tool designed to break our unified will,' said Braddock. 'So naturally people then began actively seeking it out. At the same time, several pieces of corroborating evidence started showing up, century-old diaries, secretly recorded group testimonials, even a couple of hundred-year-old commandery reports hinting strongly at disturbing events. In short, Alecto City has become a simmering pot of allegations, accusations and denials, even administrators who seemed to be in danger of being thrown out of their offices.

'But then Becker's Shadow Watch troopers began arresting the more vocal critics, as well as their associates. The last we heard, the clampdown was so heavy-handed that some districts of Alecto have refused to permit entry to any city officials.'

'I didn't know that the situation had become so charged,' said Berg. 'How has it affected the Nightwalker Commandery?'

'There was fighting outside the barracks when Shadow Watch troopers tried to arrest a couple of our men.' Seeing Greg's puzzlement, Braddock explained: 'Before Captain Rawlins became Preceptor of Veterans, he was Captain of the Nightwalkers, highly decorated and well liked. Our current captain, Eisler, is unfortunately one of Becker's sycophants, which if anything has intensified our loyalty to the memory of Sam Rawlins.'

'I see,' Greg said. 'So what you need to know is how welcoming a future Darien government would be to an immigration of Tygrans, aye?' He leaned forward.

'Assuming that we survive the drittstorm that's about tae come down on our heads!'

Braddock met his gaze. 'That's correct, Mr Cameron.'

'Well, I tell ye, my people are as cantankerous, difficult and opinionated a bunch as you're ever likely to meet. We've a saying – put a Scot, a Rus and a Norj in a room and after an hour ye'll have six different arguments not just three!' Everyone around the table laughed. 'Of course, that just means that we don't enter into friendships that easily, but – if someone goes out of their way to help us, even risking their lives to do so, then you can be sure that when they need help we won't let them down. Does that answer your question?'

'It's as good an answer as I could hope for,' said Braddock. 'Especially now that our Ezgara cover identity will soon be completely blown.'

'Aye, well, in the meantime we should concentrate on staying alive, I reckon. Oh, and I probably don't need to say this but hold off talking about the Rawlins testament with anyone from the Vox H or the Imisil, right?'

Braddock gave a sardonic smile. 'Yes, Mr Cameron, it goes without saying.'

'Of course, which is why I said it.' Greg stood, as did the others. 'Lieutenant Ash and the new ranking Imisil commander, First Proposer Conlyph, are putting together a definitive defensive battle plan, in consultation with the Vox Humana. Ash should be in touch after we're away, to let you know where you fit in. Also I think the survivors of the *Firebrand* are going to be gathered by shuttle from the Vox H ships they ended up in, then brought here.'

'That is excellent,' Braddock said. 'My thanks.'

With that the meeting was over and Greg and Lieutenant Berg were escorted back to the airlock. On the way Berg reminded Greg about the Vox Humana admiral's request for a meeting, which she was now adamant should go ahead. All through the audience with Braddock, Berg had been receiving updates from the commentary network grouping together the commanders and need-to-know advisers. This innovation had been strongly recommended by First Proposer Conlyph, and the others had readily agreed. After the meeting, Berg had used his datapad to advise the command group that Braddock was prepared to be part of the defence of Darien.

'How long will it take to get over to their flagship?' Greg said as they re-entered the shuttle.

'We could just use the shuttle, head straight there,' Berg said. 'It would be faster than returning to *Starfire*, flying it to the flagship, then getting back in the shuttle for another short hop.'

Greg strapped into the co-pilot couch next to Berg, then nodded.

'Makes sense. Let's do it that way, then.'

Muffled thuds came through the hull as the airlock declamped, releasing the shuttle. Soon they were on their way and Greg settled back, eyes shut, enjoying the comfort of the padded couch. Yet relaxation proved elusive, somehow, and the tension in his neck eased only slightly. Fragments of the Rawlins testament replayed in his thoughts, along with the sense of revulsion he'd felt on witnessing the evidence of genocide. Previously he would have said that such a crime would be impossible to conceal for any length of time, yet clearly it had been.

And it struck at the heart of his sense of Humanity. Cynics would say that any Human being, any community, any society was just as capable of such atrocities – all it would require was the right combination of circumstances, the right pressures, the right fear, and it would happen. Greg had encountered such arguments before, faced them down, defeating them with his belief in the basic compassion of Human individuals, that in the end the compassionate reason of Humanity as a group existed and would triumph over or at least outlive the savagery of rationalised callousness and the cruelty and hate that it fostered.

Yet he still heard his inner cynic laugh and say: Really? You can look upon the situation we're in, surrounded by rapacious foes whose soldiers would burn you away to ashes as soon as look at you, sitting here and waiting for a truly gigantic hammer to fall, and you're still mouthing high-flown rhetoric. What kind of a fool are you?

A realistic fool, he thought. *We've gone from being on our own to gaining the support of our Human brothers and sisters, the Pyreans, the Tygrans and the Vox Humana, and we even have the backing of the Roug and the Imisil* ...

Aye? And what about the warpwell? What about the Legion of Avatars? See? There's always some bigger, nastier brute getting ready to carve a path of blood. Now, for us cynics that's what's known as a win-win ...

Greg found that he had no answer, except for the embers of hope.

Next to him, Berg was dividing his attention between monitoring the shipboard systems – which were already under the control of an artificial cognition – and a console holopanel showing the ongoing movements of ships into a sparse-looking shell formation around the planet Darien. The Imisil newcomers were slow but powerful cruisers with wide, almost barrel-shaped midsections and armed with heavy-output beam projectors. Two of them were stationed over Nivyesta along with the smaller, faster Vox Humana ships. All the others were moving into position over the planet.

Berg had configured the holoscreen into a number of subscreens that he could bring forward, expand, minimise and move by touch. One of them showed a cycle of topics from Nivyesta, each one a capsule summary vid. Leaning forward, Greg saw views of the great continental jungle Segrana, the evidence of battle that he had seen first-hand, the charred trees, burning body pyres, the heaps of wrecked machinery. Contact had been established with an enclave of Human researchers and one of the subscreens showed an interview with a bearded man he didn't recognise. The researcher spoke of the battles within and above Segrana and how the Uvovo had kept the Humans safe, but there was no mention of Catriona.

He closed his eyes and lay back again.

No mention of a ghost, he thought. *No mention of what she did, what we did . . .*

A low, insistent pinging made him open his eyes to see Berg frantically keying through screen menus.

'What's the problem?' he said.

'We've got company,' the Tygran said, indicating the shuttle's viewport with a tilt of the head.

Scattered across the black interplanetary void, Greg could see momentary flashes, one or two every few seconds. He was puzzled for only an instant.

'Ships,' he said. 'Dropping out of hyperspace. That'll be ...'

'Not the Imisil,' Berg said. 'They're Earthsphere warships!'

The shock news made his heart start to pound.

'But ... they're not supposed to be ...' He paused to compose his thoughts. 'Are we in danger? How many are there?'

'They're coming through in a rough arc extending away from the gas giant so we shouldn't be in any immediate peril,' Berg said. 'Numbers – currently thirty-six and rising.'

'What's the reaction from our superiors?'

'Everyone has gone to combat alert. The remaining Vox Humana vessels including their flagship are moving off and the *Vanquisher* is with them. Should be about to make microjumps to Darien ... yes, they're away. And we've been advised by Lieutenant Ash to forget meeting the Vox-H admiral and to get the hell out, as he put it. I've signalled the *Starfire* to rendezvous with us in ten minutes—'

A dazzling flash of light blasted into the cramped cockpit, cutting him off. As it passed, Greg blinked a few times then yelled at the sight of the ship now looming directly ahead, filling the viewport.

'This boat better have an autoevasion system,' said Berg as he braced himself against the console. 'Or else we're dead meat.'

The autopilot applied braking thrusters to angle the

shuttle away, yet still the warship seemed to be all that was in front of them. Its name was spelled out across the stretch of stern hull plating – *Tiberius*, its black capitals growing ever larger ... until the shuttle's autopilot finally got it on a parallel course, sweeping across the upper hull, missing a sensordome by metres.

Greg gave a shaky laugh then noticed that Berg still looked grim.

'What?' he said. 'What now?'

'They're activating their grappler field. I might be able to ...'

'Unidentified small craft, this is ESS *Tiberius* – come about, power down your drive and prepare to be brought ... wait, sir, what are you doing?'

As Greg and Berg stared at each other, a second voice came over the link.

'I ordered you to target and destroy that vessel, orders that you disobeyed in a war zone ... you know what the punishment for mutiny is ...'

There was a sudden chorus of angry voices, some of them shouting about new orders, then the channel went dead.

'What ... the hell was all that about?' Greg said.

'Not sure,' said Berg. 'But those grapplers have been switched back to standby mode, which is the signal for us to put some distance between us and them ...'

Berg had also sent a brief message to the *Starfire* and less than ten minutes later the shuttle rejoined its mothership. Even before he left the shuttle, Berg was ordering the bridge officers to ready the navigationals for a microjump to the Darien vicinity. But when they entered the *Starfire*'s bridge the face of Lieutenant Ash was on the holopanels, waiting.

'Mr Berg, Mr Cameron,' he said. 'Nice to see you back in one piece. Now, rather than cross half the system to join us, we want you to take up a position near that gas giant and monitor developments as they unfold.'

'Developments?' Greg said with a frown.

'The Earthsphere fleet is not making any move or preparation in the direction of Darien,' said Berg, who was studying datastreams on his holoconsole.

'Exactly so,' said Ash. 'Something is very wrong aboard some of those ships. Half of them aren't in formation and a few are still where they were on exiting hyperspace.'

'We overheard an argument during a communication from one of them, the *Tiberius*,' said Berg. 'Something about new orders, and it sounded like a fight was about to break out.'

Ash nodded. 'The Imisil long-range sensors have been picking up a lot of ship-to-ship messaging on the subject. Seems that the Earthsphere president was forced by political pressure to cancel the fleet's original orders. They are now supposed to take up positions around Darien, which has now been declared a provisional Earthsphere protectorate ...'

Greg felt a wave of exhilaration and almost cheered out loud.

'That is ... amazing! ... isn't it? ... but their ships aren't ... okay, Ash, what *is* going on?'

Ash was wearing a knowledgeable smile which at that moment Greg found aggravating.

'On many of their ships,' the Tygran said, 'the new orders have been rejected by either the captain or the first officer, who have taken extreme measures to exert their authority. Four captains have been removed from command and confined to quarters, and two have been shot. Six first officers have been shot dead and nine have been confined to quarters. And here is the revelation – all who rebelled against the orders have AI implants, every single one.'

'That's a bit disturbing,' Greg said.

'It gets better. There are two ships whose senior officers nearly all have the same implants. The captains have refused to recognise the validity of the orders, claiming that President Castiglione has been blackmailed into rescinding the original ones. Both ships are surrounded by vessels loyal to the fleet commander, Vice-Admiral Ngassa.'

'This is like a weird rerun of the situation with the Tygran ships,' Greg said.

'Pardon for saying, Lieutenant,' said Berg. 'You seem very well informed already so why would you need us to remain here?'

'There is an important function which requires your being in close orbit around the gas giant.'

'We are already on our way there – ETA eleven minutes.'

'Good. Stand by for further orders, Mr Berg.'

The channel went dead. Berg frowned.

'It seems that we must hurry up and wait,' he said.

Greg was thoughtful. 'Actually, I think I know what this is all about.' And when he told Berg, realisation dawned in the Tygran's eyes.

Sure enough, nearly thirty-five minutes later Ash was back and asking for Greg.

'And how's it going, Mr Ash?' he said as he hurried onto the bridge. 'As you can see, I'm back in my serious civvy gear, complete with snazzy long black coat. I've had a shower, or tornado-fogblast as it should be called, and I've had one o' they wee stimpills as well – which work, by the way. This is the most awake I've been for over a week, so ... when do I get to meet the vice-admiral?'

Ash glared at him. 'How did you know ...'

'Aye, well, that'll be one of my special archaeologist superpowers, the power of deduction, don't ye know!'

Greg grinned at Berg, who was striving to keep a straight face.

'I trust that you'll keep your witticisms to yourself when you meet Vice-Admiral Ngassa,' Ash said, stone-faced. 'When we spoke with him just minutes ago he insisted on speaking with a Darien representative, which means you. When you meet him, emphasise that all of us here have come together as an informal alliance for the sole purpose of defending Darien, and its moon. Be sure that he understands this.'

'I shall. Anything else?'

'It would be helpful to learn of his expectations of what the Hegemony fleet will do when it arrives. Before this he was the previous supreme commander of Earthsphere forces in the Yamanon Domain so he's had experience of the Hegemony military from working alongside them.'

Greg took it all in, nodding. 'Righto, I get the picture. And don't worry about my attitude – I shall be the soul of sober diplomacy.'

Ash's stare was almost unreadable.

'Once you and Lieutenant Berg are in the shuttle and declamped we will send you encrypted coordinates for the rendezvous with the vice-admiral's pinnace. You'll dock with it, go aboard and conduct the meeting there.'

Greg smiled brightly. 'We're on our way.'

To a rerun of that blether we had with Braddock, sounds like, he thought as he hurried after Berg.

Less than half an hour later they were approaching the rendezvous coordinates and the sleek vessel waiting there. They docked with a transfer conduit jutting from the starboard flank. Greg and Berg were greeted on the other side of the hatch by an armed escort, three Earthsphere marines in ceremonial black and blue uniforms. Along a grey and red passage they were taken to a small room where a tall officer in formal black rose from a table scattered with documents, facing them.

'Gentlemen, thank you for coming,' he said. 'I am Lieutenant Commander Neville, adjutant and chief of staff to the vice-admiral. Which of you is Greg Cameron?'

Smiling, Greg raised a hand. Neville nodded then turned to Berg.

'So you must be the Ezgara officer,' he said. 'There have been wild theories for some time that the Ezgara commandos were actually a Human splinter group of some kind. Now we're hearing a remarkable rumour that they are actually descended from one of the three lost colonies. Is this so?'

Berg had maintained a neutral expression thus far, to the point where Greg suspected some degree of dislike beneath the surface.

'With respect, sir,' he said, 'I am under specific orders not to discuss these matters.'

The adjutant gazed at Berg for a motionless second before nodding.

'Of course. Understandable.' He turned his attention back to Greg. 'Now that you are here, we can go through.'

Neville crossed to a second door, opened it and ushered them in.

The conference room had soft carpeting, elaborate uplighting and a substantial oval table surface in pale, polished wood. Four triangular windows with rounded corners were spaced along the outer bulkhead, affording a view of the stars and the wisps and veils of the deep-zone. A lanky, brown-skinned man in a formal steel-blue uniform was standing at one of them, drinking from a glass. He looked round as they entered, introductions were made, hands were shaken.

'It is a pleasure to finally meet someone from Darien,' said Vice-Admiral Ngassa as he gestured them to sit. 'The newspipes have been full of stories and docudramas about your world but very little is of use in a situation like this.'

'Well, Vice-Admiral, if there's anything you need to know about Darien, especially anything archaeologically based, I'm definitely your man,' Greg said. 'Mind you, I have a few questions, myself.'

'That's fair, Mr Cameron,' Ngassa said. 'Firstly, please understand what we are here for. My orders require me to place my forces in near-Darien space for the purposes of protection and security. The president has invoked the "duty of legacy" principle, which

essentially means that Earthsphere can assume responsibility for the external political relationships and
negotiations of a Human community or colony if its
civilian authority is unable to carry them out for itself.'

'Aye, well I guess that would be a fair description of
the state of things the now,' Greg said.

'And in the light of my orders, we are faced with the
problem of the various warships currently in orbit
around Darien. Can you tell me why they're here?'

Greg nodded. 'Oh, yes, I can. Ye see, they're not the
problem – but they are here because of the problem or
rather the threat posed by the imminent arrival of a
large Hegemony fleet. And when I say large, I mean
gigantic, going by what I've heard. So basically, they
have come together in an informal alliance for the purpose of defending Darien.'

Ngassa nodded calmly, taking it all in.

'I can see that, Mr Cameron, and accepting such aid
is understandable in the circumstances. However, the
real problem, I'm afraid, could be the Imisil.'

'The Imisil ... are the real problem?'

The vice-admiral gave a slightly pained nod.

'The Hegemony and the Imisil have had ... some
unfortunate clashes in the past. If they were to leave the
system within the next two hours it would make for
more relaxed negotiations when the Hegemony fleet
arrives.'

'Well, ye know, it's funny but our relationship with
the Imisil seems to be just fine,' Greg said. 'But I'll certainly pass that on to the joint command, although
you should realise that they'll be looking for some
guarantees in return, no planetary bombardment, no

atmospheric destabilisation, no attempt at ground invasion, that sorta thing. That would be a great starting point, I think.' He leaned back a little. 'Mind you, I have to say – with great respect, by the way – that there seems to be a wee question hanging over your own fleet's integrity, so to speak. We got the impression that you've had a few ... problems yourself.'

Ngassa gave a dismissive gesture. 'Minor disciplinary matters, nothing more ...'

'Officers and captains refusing direct orders, officers and captains being shot dead or thrown in the brig, using loyal ships to corral whole ships that have gone rogue – stop me if any o' this is sounding a wee bit familiar ...'

'Mr Cameron!' said the adjutant angrily.

'It's all right, Neville,' said the vice-admiral. 'Your information is quite accurate, Mr Cameron, and courtesy of the Imisil, I expect.'

'They do have some rather fine sensor technology, I'm led to believe.'

Just then, the adjutant took a datapad from his waist clip, wordlessly indicated it to the vice-admiral, who nodded. The adjutant rose from the table and left by the main door, the datapad raised to one ear.

'As I said, Mr Cameron, a disciplinary problem,' Ngassa continued. 'Admittedly, the nature and timing of it is worrying but the situation is firmly under control.'

'I see, sir,' said Greg. 'So you've locked up everyone with an AI implant, then.'

Ngassa gave him a mildly incredulous look. 'I'm sorry but that would be an extreme and irrational response – it would deprive my ships of scores of capable officers and crew who have proved their loyalty beyond question.'

Greg nodded, exchanging a brief look with Berg.

'Well, I can see your point,' he said. 'Sounds sensible. So I guess you have folk on your own staff who have implants ...' He gestured. 'Perhaps even yourself?'

Ngassa smiled and shook his head. 'My parents were a little old-fashioned and disapproved of the practice and by the time I was old enough to decide for myself I found that I just didn't care for the idea. And yes, some of my staff are equipped with implants, like my adjutant, Neville. Why do you ask?'

That was when the adjutant Neville entered the room carrying a beam pistol.

'Hands on your heads,' he said. 'Over to the wall.'

'What the stinking hell are you doing, Neville?' said the vice-admiral with stunned anger. 'Are you a traitor too?'

'Do as I said,' Neville said, suddenly shifting his aim to cover Greg and Berg. 'No heroics. Do it.'

Greg linked his hands and put them behind his head then moved towards the bulkhead. Berg didn't move.

'So how is Neville?' Berg said. 'Is he even in there any more?'

The adjutant's mouth twitched into a half-smile. 'Not for quite some time. Hands on your head and move!'

Berg clasped his hands behind his head, took a step and paused, glancing over at the doorway. 'Well, about time! ...'

The adjutant laughed. 'Moron – I know there's no one ...'

And Berg's hand whipped out from behind his head

and hurled a small spinning object. It flashed straight towards Neville's right shoulder and since he was holding the gun with his right hand his reflex avoidance motion pushed his aim off for just a moment, long enough for Berg to launch himself in a flying lunge.

Neville managed to fire off a burst before he and Berg went down in a tangle of flailing legs and savage punches. Greg and the vice-admiral had leaped forward the moment after Berg made his move. The adjutant proved remarkably strong and it took the three of them to disarm him and hold him down. After repeated shouts, two guards appeared and provided restraints with which they were able to immobilise their prisoner.

'You should release me,' said the adjutant. 'It would be in your best interests.'

'You are going back to stand trial for mutiny,' said Ngassa, wiping his face with a napkin from the table.

The adjutant laughed. 'What a delightful race Humans are. Malleable, useful, and never dull. I remember how trusting you used to be back when all you had was that half-trashed planet and a few primitive colonies ...'

'You don't seem that worried about your situation,' said Greg. 'If I was a betting man, I'd say that you really are an AI with a link to some bolthole out in hyperspace. That's what I've heard, anyway.'

'You'd win the bet, man of Darien. You are an interesting batch, growing up without any guidance or constrictions, wolflings some of my colleagues call you, a pure-strain control group, in a way ...'

Suddenly alarms were sounding out in the corridors, an insistent metallic sound that made the adjutant laugh.

'Judgement has come and the punishment will be harsh ...'

A communicator node on the conference table also started chiming so Ngassa leaned forward to thumb it and a small holoscreen appeared, showing an officer in a pilot couch.

'Captain, what's happening?'

'Vice-Admiral, vessels have started appearing in hundred-strong formations spaced around the system. We estimate total numbers approaching two thousand ... idents are showing as the Hegemony, sir.'

'Any communication from them?'

'None, sir, but that's not the worst – eight of our ships have broken formation, including the two under guard, and are heading towards one of the Hegemony formations.'

'As am I,' said the AI-possessed adjutant, who then slumped forward in his chair. For a second everyone was still, staring. Suddenly the adjutant's head came up as his entire body went into a muscle-straining spasm, a locked rigidity. Greg saw a tracery of dark lines creeping up the neck towards the scalp. One of the guards looked away, and when the adjutant went wholly limp the head rolled to one side to reveal eyes that were charred pits.

'Captain,' Ngassa said over the holocomm link, 'get us back to the flagship without delay – in fact tell Commander Paxton to get under way towards us and we'll rendezvous ...' Pausing, he looked at Berg. 'Dammit, man, you've been injured! Field treatment for this man.'

'Sir, I am not wounded,' Berg said, pulling aside the

singed edges of the slash in his uniform to reveal a line of bubbly melt across the surface of a protective vest. 'Semi-ablative subarmour, sir.'

'More to you than meets the eye, Lieutenant,' said Ngassa, who then cast a disdainful look at his former adjutant. 'So whatever was using Neville has fled?'

Berg nodded. 'The AIs with the Hegemony fleet will now know that you're aboard this vessel. And that we are too.'

'In which case,' Greg added, 'it might be prudent for us to take our shuttle back to our ship.'

'I'm ... anxious about putting your lives at risk, gentlemen,' Ngassa said. 'No, I'd rather you stayed with us. Once aboard my flagship we will microjump straight to Darien and let you rejoin—'

'Sir! Sir, the Hegemony formations have just microjumped in unison!' said the pinnace captain from the holocomm. 'They have reappeared at half their original distance from Darien, and still in that encircling array.'

'Tightening the noose,' Ngassa snarled. 'And still no word from them?'

'Nothing, sir.'

'Get me Paxton.' A second later a rugged-looking officer appeared in the holopanel. 'Commander, I want you to order the fleet to microjump to Darien vicinity immediately!'

Ngassa's second-in-command was startled. 'Now, sir? Before we get you aboard? We're only three minutes ...'

'Now, Paxton. Then I want you to use what I'm about to dictate – This is Vice-Admiral Ngassa. In accordance with the orders of the president of the Earthsphere alliance, the colony and planet of Darien is declared to be a provisional protectorate and is therefore under the administrative protection and guidance of the Darien Expeditionary Force, Vice-Admiral Ngassa commanding. All grievances and disputes will be heard by a commission consisting of myself and three judicial appointees. In addition, all communications and requests should be made on the main ES navy channel. Thank you for your attention. – Now have Central Comms widecast that on repeat, and put it out on tiernet channels as well, understand?'

'Yes sir, and we're less than a minute away.'

Greg glanced at Berg, who was taking it all with typical Tygran composure.

'So ... where does that put us, overall?'

Berg frowned. 'We have the *Starfire* and the *Silverlance*, the Imisil have five ships, the Vox H are down to seventeen, and the vice-admiral brought sixty, minus the eight defectors, plus the *Retributor* ...'

'So you don't think that the Hegemony are going to play nice and be diplomatic?'

The Tygran raised an eyebrow. 'That's not really their strong point.'

'So how many all told?'

'Eighty-four, while the Hegemony armada consists of a reported two thousand vessels.'

Greg almost laughed. 'Is that what's known as a crushing superiority?'

'In some circles, yes.'

'Ye know, when we get back to the *Starfire* I'll have to lay hands on a set of that handy subarmour of yours.'

Berg's smile was bleak. 'I think we'll need something a bit stronger than that.'

25

CHEL

Sitting on a dusty stone plinth in the gloom of the root-house, he let the wandering sight of his Seer eyes stretch itself out along the rootways, the underground interlinkage laid down by their most ancient forebears. Many of the essence strands had long since rotted away but the Artificer Uvovo teams had worked wonders with a variety of vines and roots brought from the daughter-forests. And their hard work was evident at many other roothouses scattered across the hills, the forests and the coastal plain. Days upon days of effort had borne their fruit, yet with the warpwell subverted and the return of the Legion of Avatars looking more than likely, could it all have been a waste?

Back when the Ancients still had corporeal form, this world, Umara, the dense forests of Segrana-That-Was, generated webs of power capable of defending the entire planet against attacks from near space. Greater nodes oversaw primary nodes, each of which gathered in an array of roothouses, hundreds, thousands. But all that Cheluvahar had to muster against the hostile forces building in the heavens, and against the flesh-and-machine horrors soon to emerge from

Giant's Shoulder, was a single secondary node and nineteen roothouses.

When the Zyradin transported him here from Tusk Mountain, it had been unswerving in its insistence that Chel prepare the nodes, the roothouses and the Artificer Uvovo for battle. And not long afterwards he had a visitation from the Pathmaster, his spectral form appearing even more tenuous and fragile than before and his voice sounding scratchy and broken, like a cluster of insects.

I agreed to come here, he had told the ancient, ancient remnant of the long-past forebear. *I agreed to prepare for battle, and the only reason I'm able to do so is the healing that I received from a vudron. Not due to anything you said or did.*

The Pathmaster's thin, vaporous presence, his eyes in shadow, had smiled and nodded. A faint sibilant voice said, *Understanding is seldom understood ...*

Then it had faded away, like threads of smoke dissolving in the air. Immediately Chel had felt ashamed at the blinkered anger of his response and now, sitting here, he felt a sting of regret. Could that have been the Pathmaster's last fleeting words to the living before finally merging with the Eternal?

Seated on the stone plinth, his eyes were closed yet his Seer sight ranged forth from the roothouse, from this secondary node, drawn along the essence strands, dividing when they divided, spreading to join with the other roothouses from which the entwining web spread further. The Zyradin motes that he brought were doing their work. He could sense the slow gyring pulse of the planet, rising from hard and compacted depths to the thin uncertain crust over which organic life existed like a frail bubble. Yet it was frail organic minds that had learned how to harness the pulsing gyre of those colossal inner energies. And as Chel's awareness expanded across the web of connections he could feel those energies, feel the ancient webs respond to them, opening to them, drawing on them.

This was the point where control had to be exerted. Were he to allow the new energies to flood the web of roothouses it would be like a beacon in the perceptions of some entities, particularly that resolute survivor, the Legion Knight. So he had to carefully gauge the flow of energies, making sure that their permeation was gradual and even, and to keep the roothouses themselves from trying to draw on this new source of fresh, vibrant power.

As his awareness continued to expand, and the energy of the depths seeped steadily in, the demands on his will-power grew. His Seer talents drew more and more from his essential vitality and it seemed that the Zyradin was present, watching over him, watching it all.

There was movement off to one side. The central junction of the roothouse had four galleries leading off, all looking grey, a little misty, and it was in one of them that a tall figure stood. It was a Human, naked to the waist, the skin of his torso marked with many small wounds. And when Chel saw the flat metallic implants on the back and the neck he instantly knew that it was Rory, even before he glanced round for a moment before heading away into the shadows at a crouch.

Instinctively, Chel drifted forward, wondering how Rory had managed to find his way here, to the roothouse. But when the darkened gallery melted away into somewhere in the open, somewhere flat and gloomy, he realised that he had strayed into the domain of that Seer talent that he called the Dream Speculator.

Ahead of him, the Human Rory was creeping across ground consisting of scattered flat stones and tufts of grass towards a dark, squat building. There were metallic gleams and the glowing red and blue pinpoints of machine displays. Suddenly Chel realised that this was Giant's Shoulder, and even as the thought struck him the surface of the promontory began to quake. Big stone slabs quivered and shifted and Rory staggered. Some structures, low buildings and a couple of watchtowers, fell apart and collapsed. Then a crack opened and a harsh silver-grey radiance poured out. Rory dodged round and ran for the squat building. But the ground suddenly began to rise from the centre, like a growing mound, forcing Rory to clamber along on his hands and knees.

Until fractures appeared all across it, seconds before it erupted in a violent rushing blaze of harsh silver light, with a solitary figure silhouetted against the brightness for an instant ...

Chel breathed in suddenly, a quick, cold chestful of air, and he was back on the stone plinth. Most of his awareness was still guiding itself out to the last extremities of the nineteen roothouses and their networks of strands. The planetary energies continued to trickle through, and over on its mech-guarded fastness of Giant's Shoulder the Legion Knight remained, unfathomable, yet perhaps also unsuspecting.

But the meaning of that vision – did it presage some

kind of inevitable tragedy, or was it a warning, or something symbolic involving Rory? That was the problem with the Dream Speculator – the things it revealed could be thoroughly literal or abstrusely metaphorical, with scarcely any hint as to which was being observed. And right now he had neither time nor opportunity for the meditation that would make the vision clearer.

I must complete my work and trust that Rory's path does not bring him more pain, him least of all.

26

KUROS

Bodiless in the cage, sights and sounds were all he knew. From a desperate, indiscriminate grasping at every audible and visual scrap he had grown in attentiveness and analytical acuity. Now he was almost attuned to the totality of the impressions that reached his eyes and ears.

Except that they were his no longer. He was a prisoner in his own brain, betrayed by his lifelong AI companion, Gratach, who now controlled his body. Kuros knew that he was only able to see and hear because Gratach permitted it.

At least the AI was not abusing the body it had seized. Kuros remembered rumours of other Sendrukans whose AIs had taken them over and proceeded to plunge into a frantic whirl of self-destructive pleasure-seeking, drug-taking and various forms of deviancy. Gratach had been modelled on General Gratach, the historical figure known for his severe austerity in personal matters, which accounted for the lack of self-indulgence. That said, the presence of the Clarified Teshak no doubt played an influential part.

The Clarified Teshak ... over the days since his

ruthless incarceration, Kuros had grown to hate Teshak with a unified, unwavering intensity that he had never felt before. This was given an extra edge by the fact that Teshak knew that Kuros was watching and listening; addressing Kuros directly from time to time clearly gave him a certain satisfaction.

But right now Teshak's state of mind could hardly be described as anything as positive as satisfied.

'Marshal Becker,' he said in clipped tones while staring at the image on the comm screen. 'This situation is intolerable. The ambassador and myself have been waiting on this primitive backwater for several days, expecting to be transported back to civilisation – if you know anything about the Clarified and the unique rank they carry in the hierarchy of the Hegemony, then you must also realise that obedience to my orders should take precedence for you.'

'In any other situation that would indeed be the case, Clarified One,' said the Ezgara. 'But my orders come directly from the Second Tri-Advocate and they are very specific in both priority and objectives.'

'And what would your objectives be?'

'With great respect, Clarified One, I am not permitted to divulge ... What?' The Ezgara-Human turned his visored face to snap at someone out of view. '... No, use the field pumps ...' He turned back. 'Clarified Teshak, Ambassador Kuros, my apologies but we have a critical situation that must be dealt with before I can come ashore. Till later.'

Then the screen went blank.

'We should have dispensed with those Ezgara-Humans years ago,' said Teshak. 'Indeed, the fact that the Second Tri-Advocate has entrusted a high-value mission to a non-Sendrukan is further proof of the regime's unfitness to rule.'

Gratach made no reply, just looked at the Clarified Teshak, who met his gaze and smiled.

'Don't be too hopeful, Kuros,' he said, leaning closer. 'There's a Hegemony armada out there and before long a ship will come to take us back to Iseri where the last lingering shreds of your pitiful existence will finally be expunged.'

He straightened, exchanged a wordless look with Gratach along with a faint nod and a slight tilt towards the window with his head. Then he was out of the door and gone. Gratach got to his feet, closed the commset lid, moved round the table and went to the window. He scanned the night-bound sea, a black expanse glimmering from the meagre radiance of ionisation glows and the now frequent shooting stars, pieces of battle debris burning up as they plunged into the stratosphere.

Then Gratach looked left to where a long, indistinct shape lay half-submerged in the shallows nearly a hundred sendru-paces offshore. A few worklamps had been set up along the upper hull but going by what Kuros had heard, Becker's ship was disabled, unable to fly. During the last part of the descent, coming in over the coastal plain, it was hit by about a dozen ground-to-air missiles that wrecked the ship's main suspensor node and killed three techs. With the thrusters they were able to stay in the air long enough to ditch in the sea close to the Brolturan base. Repairs were estimated to take at least two days.

So why is Becker here? Kuros thought. He said his

orders came from the Second Tri-Advocate, whom the Clarified clearly consider an adversary. And the Hegemony's fleet is in the system so it is reasonable to assume that they would like to regain control of the warpwell.

He heard heavy footsteps in the corridor outside, which he knew to be the sound of the night-duty officer leaving to take over the sentry watch. In a few minutes the relieved officer would come up and enter the room across the corridor, slamming the door shut. Kuros also knew that Gratach would soon lie down on one of the couches while performing whatever optimisation tasks it found necessary, and it duly did. The room was small but sparsely furnished, one of two officers' quarters on the main building's third floor.

Neither the AI nor Kuros needed sleep, and at such times Kuros kept himself mentally active by recalling small details from happier times. He was just trying to picture the exact shade of blue of the ceremonial cloak he'd worn during his tenure as Second Suppressor all those years ago when a hand rose up from the right and stabbed him in the neck with something unseen.

Gratach had started to react as soon as it appeared in his peripheral vision but not fast enough to prevent the stab, a second after which the AI seemed to freeze, slumping back onto the couch. The muscles were locked in paralysis, leaving Gratach unable to even make a sound. But who would want to do this to the ambassador? Kuros wondered. Then the assailant came into view and everything changed – it was Vashutkin, the Human politician, altered by the Blue Chain nanodust to be his loyal servant.

Smiling, Vashutkin nodded, then showed Kuros a transdermal injector before leaning in to apply it to the left side of the neck, close to where the AI implant was.

'I have retasked a portion of my cognitive particles to attack the implant's interface tendrils,' he whispered. 'Once it's been isolated from your cortex you should regain control . . .'

It was already happening. Tingles of sensation were sparkling on the periphery of his awareness. Kuros felt almost delirious with anticipation as he began to feel sensation coming from his fingertips, impressions like the weight of his hand, his arm, his head. Then it all came at him in a rush, as if he'd fallen into his body . . . and it was all too much, a cascade of sensations coming from every bit of skin, the mingled torrent of smells and tastes was all just overwhelming.

But then the intensity of it waned, subsiding from a roar to a manageable background murmur. He sagged back on the couch for a second then swung his legs round to stand, feet planted apart, revelling in his stature relative to the Human. He clenched and unclenched his fists, touched his face, breathed in and out deeply.

'The Clarified Teshak,' he said, pleased to hear his own words in his own voice. 'We must deal with him.'

'Something is happening,' said Vashutkin as he moved over to the window. 'The Clarified One is about to receive a visitor.'

Kuros went to join his diminutive rescuer. Outside, a steady rain was falling and wet surfaces gleamed. Teshak was standing off to one side of the floodlit base courtyard while a flat-canopied aircar swept in from the direction of the downed ship, slowing to land, its positional lights winking. Kuros was suddenly full of suspicion – what had really passed between Gratach and Teshak earlier? He had thought the minuscule head movements to indicate a later meeting, but what if it was something else entirely?

'We must go down there,' he said. 'I think that Teshak may be about to kill a potential ally.'

Gratach had thoughtfully strapped on a fully charged Brolturan-issue beam pistol. As they descended the stairway Kuros explained his plan and made sure that Vashutkin understood his part. When they reached the main exit the Human was already in front with hands clasped behind his head while Kuros pointed the weapon at his back.

The Ezgara-Human Becker and a four-strong armed escort had disembarked from the aircar and were walking towards the Clarified Teshak, who stood flanked by a pair of Brolturan troopers. There were other troopers posted along the courtyard wall facing in, Kuros noticed, with weapons at the ready. This would have to be crushed in the cradle, he realised, so, pushing Vashutkin on ahead of him, he strode out of the building and bellowed:

'Wait!'

All eyes snapped round at him, apart from Teshak, who gave him a sidelong, smiling glance.

'Ah, so the ambassador has decided to grace us with his presence,' the Clarified said.

'I have brought you a gift,' Kuros said, trying to emulate Gratach's harsher tone.

The Clarified Teshak turned, frowning as he

considered the Human walking at gunpoint towards him.

'I noticed that a certain level of communication had ceased,' Teshak said.

Becker and his men had halted, distrust showing in their posture as they watched this exchange. Kuros knew that Teshak could order them burned down at any moment. The time to strike was now.

'This Human infiltrated the main building,' he said. 'Assaulted me, damaged my equipment before I subdued him. His punishment will be ... elaborate!'

That last word was the signal for Vashutkin to attack. He had covered two-thirds of the distance to the tall, black-garbed Sendrukan when he broke into a mad dash. Teshak was in mid-grab for his own handweapon when Vashutkin feinted right but lunged down the centre with an elbow aimed at the Sendrukan's midriff. Teshak doubled over but he was already stepping back. As the pair of them rolled backwards, the Clarified grabbed handfuls of Vashutkin's heavy coat and used the momentum to throw the Human over his head. Teshak rolled and bounced back to his feet.

'This is a conspiracy – kill the ...'

He stopped, eyes bulging, tongue straining from an open mouth as both hands leaped to his throat. Kuros had shot him twice in the neck.

The blood leaking between the Clarified's fingers was black in the flood's harsh light. Teshak sank to his knees. His eyes burned with hate as Kuros walked up to him, and his bloody lips framed the words 'Not the end' repeatedly until Kuros shot him through the head, and kept shooting when the body fell over. Only when the cranium was a shapeless mess of churned bone and brain matter did he turn away and address the watching Brolturans.

'The Clarified Teshak was acting in disobedience of orders that came directly from the Hegemon's most trusted ministers. Pact arrangements and chain-of-command protocols remain in effect so senior officers will now report to me. All other ranks may now return to your stations and your duties.'

As the Brolturan troops hurried about their business, Kuros glanced over at Vashutkin, who was back on his feet, brushing off wet grit and mud. Then he strode over to the Ezgara Marshal Becker and his men – the former bowed with his head, the latter from the waist.

'Marshal, my apologies that you were forced to endure such an unpleasant start to your task here on Darien. However, the Clarified Teshak intended to have you murdered prior to taking control of your ship, which left me with few options.'

Looking up, Becker gave a wintry smile.

'Exalted Ambassador, I confess that I had anticipated something untoward – my body armour is fitted with partial shielding.'

Kuros smiled. 'Such precautions are the burden of leadership, Marshal. Let us continue our discussion in a less exposed location, over in the main building.'

Some minutes later they were settling into the wide chairs of the Brolturan officers' mess, hastily cleared of cast-off uniforms and equipment. Apart from Becker the Humans remained standing while Kuros leaned back in an articulated altercouch.

'Marshal Becker, firstly you should realise that the

Clarified Teshak has been holding me under a psycho-narcotic captivity for several days. I only broke free with the help of my associate, who administered an antidote into my bloodstream.' Kuros indicated Vashutkin who sat behind him, near the wall. 'Like you he is Human. I will explain a little more about him later, but for now we must address crucial matters.'

He straightened. 'I do not know what your orders are, Marshal, but you probably realise that we are no longer in control of the landmark known as Giant's Shoulder and the secret facility concealed within it. In fact, the withdrawal from Giant's Shoulder was directed by Teshak soon after he placed me under his vile influence. Now, however, Teshak is no more and I am myself again, and I want to use the resources of this base to mount an assault on Giant's Shoulder and retake it in the Hegemon's name. Hopefully, my plans do not run counter to your orders.'

Becker, looking almost childlike as he sat in the Sendrukan-sized chair, smiled thoughtfully.

'As fortune would have it, Ambassador, our goals coincide perfectly. The Second Tri-Advocate was of the opinion that your silence since the destruction of the *Purifier* signified your death or imprisonment, thus I was assigned the mission to regain control over the Forerunner facility. Your re-emergence, however, is most gratifying and I would be willing to defer to you on matters of the strategic overview.'

'An interesting proposal,' Kuros said guardedly. 'How do you envisage such an arrangement working in practice?'

'I would see my role as tactical commander under

your supervision,' Becker said smoothly. 'We already possess significant intelligence gathered over the last few days, which reveals that the Human insurgents have been reinforced by renegade Ezgara, traitors from my world armed with powerful weaponry.'

'I had heard something of this very recently,' Kuros said.

'But there is more, Ambassador. These insurgents are planning to mount their own raid on Giant's Shoulder in just a few hours – and they have made a pact with a sizeable faction of the Spiral zealots.'

Kuros stiffened at this news, glanced sideways and made a beckoning gesture. In a moment, Vashutkin was at his elbow.

'Did you know about this?' he said to the Human.

'There were some offworlder Humans calling them-selves Tygrans,' Vashutkin said. 'I know nothing of any Ezgara, and this pact with the zealots is also unknown to me. It could have happened after I left Tusk Mountain.'

Kuros looked at Becker. 'These new collaborations could present a problem. They must be stopped, a pre-emptive strike against that mountain lair of theirs.'

'I agree, Ambassador,' Becker said with a sharp smile as he glanced at Vashutkin. 'So who is your companion and how does he come to know about these ... Tygrans?'

'This is Alexandr Vashutkin, only surviving minister from the last legitimate Darien government and, by virtue of Blue Chain, my faithful ally. Until recently he was working alongside the insurgents of Tusk Mountain, one of his primary tasks being the elimination of Greg Cameron, which I trust has been carried out.'

Vashutkin frowned. 'I cannot be certain of his death. I had him cornered on Giant's Shoulder, I turned to observe approaching mechs and when I looked back he was gone. I thought he could have fallen over the edge, or that the Forerunner facility device had somehow transported him away or even killed him . . .'

'I know of this Cameron,' Becker said. 'And he is not dead. We picked up comm traffic which proves that he is aboard one of the vessels preparing to defend Darien.'

Vashutkin bowed his head and stared at the floor. 'I have failed you, master.'

'A minor failure next to your successes,' Kuros said. 'My deliverance, for example. So, Marshal, what is your proposal for the order of battle?'

'Together we can field an effective airborne task force comprising Brolturan troopers and my commandos. If we come in fast and strike hard we can crush any local opposition, regardless of their offworld friends. After that, Ambassador, we can move against Giant's Shoulder, which seems to be overrun with rogue mechs led by some cyborg creature. This isn't the by-product of an unsuccessful Hegemony experiment, by any chance?'

'No, Marshal, I can assure you it is not.'

Becker nodded and said over his shoulder, 'Nathaniel, the slate.' One of his commandos, a man with a disfiguring burn mark down one side of his face, leaned in to hand him a large datapad. Becker thumbed it on, then paused to look again at Vashutkin.

'Ambassador, I've just thought of a great service that

your faithful ally could perform for us, especially since the battle above us has not yet commenced.'

As he outlined the idea, Kuros found himself amused and curious to see what the result would be.

'I approve, Marshal. Proceed.'

Becker beckoned Vashutkin over.

'I have configured the slate to record, and this is what I want you to say . . .'

27

KAO CHIH

The transition to normal space was not pleasant. The Shyntanil assault craft's hyperdrive was poorly shielded and its control systems, especially for the field alignment regulator, lacked a certain precision. After nearly five hours journeying up the tiers of hyperspace, nearly all the *Heracles*' survivors had regained consciousness and everyone was expressing how hungry they were. But there were no rations to be found anywhere on board, apart from a curved tap that gave forth some suspiciously brackish water. So when the assault craft dropped out of hyperspace to appear in the Roug system, several stomachs rebelled even though there was little to bring up.

Robert had warned Kao Chih about this possibility in advance and some containers had been rustled up or improvised. So while the crew were coping with the aftermath as best they could, Robert beckoned Kao Chih up to the cockpit section. He sat in the other padded chair and looked out at the star-strewn blackness beyond the viewport. Then he faced the elderly-looking Construct sim.

'Kao Chih,' he said in a low voice, 'there is a slight

problem. I'm picking up the approach and navigational beacons from the Roug world, the gas giant V'Hrant, but there's no sign of the Agmedra'a orbital. In fact, I'm not detecting anything on the usual commercial and open channels. Now, I've checked and rechecked our location, and although the Shyntanil sensors are a heap of rudimentary junk they should still be able to find active comm channels and automatically go into transceiver mode.' He shook his head. 'Nothing.'

Neither said anything for a long moment full of dark imaginings.

'They couldn't have got here before us, could they?' Kao Chih said.

'We musn't jump to conclusions,' Robert said, turning to the controls. 'I'm going to execute a microjump to get us closer, then we'll know for . . .'

He was interrupted by a sharp pinging from the pilot console. 'Something huge has just . . .'

The assault craft lurched sideways, provoking gasps and cries from the *Heracles'* survivors. A curved expanse of pitted greyness that was clearly part of something larger swung in close to cover the viewport, then there was a sudden surge of acceleration that threatened serious discomfort until the inertial dampeners cut in. Robert lunged forward to the console.

'A huge ship has us in a grappler field,' he said. 'Well, Kao Chih, you're from around these parts – is this a Roug vessel?'

On an angled, grimy screen protruding from the console was the wireframe image of a big, V-shaped vessel. Kao Chih nodded.

'It's a system-defence ship,' he said. 'The Roug tend

to keep them out of sight – I hadn't even seen one until quite recently.'

'Interesting.' Robert consulted the console readouts. 'Hmph. According to these pathetic instruments we are being carried at something close to a third of the speed of light towards the gas giant V'Hrant. We'll be there in less than twenty minutes.' He frowned. 'But it seems unusual that there's been no attempt to contact us.'

'This isn't the usual protocol,' Kao Chih said, recalling the last time he returned to the Buzrul system. 'However, we are still alive, so they do not perceive us as a threat. Perhaps we should transmit a message stating who we are, who we have escaped from and telling them about the asteroid-weapon.'

Robert nodded. 'Even if they don't reply they will have heard our explanation for why we came here in a Shyntanil combat craft. Also, it would make more sense if you delivered it, given your personal connections with them.'

Kao Chih agreed – it was sensible, so after clarifying his thoughts he spoke into the console's audio pickup, a small circular grille. In his summary he detailed who they all were, who they had escaped from, and what they had come to warn the Roug about. After which he sat back, exchanging the odd glance with Robert, but the comm channel remained silent. Some of the *Heracles'* crew had gathered round but when it became clear that no reply was forthcoming they went back to their seats, cradling their stomachs or trying to relax. Robert surveyed them all for a moment then leaned back, face unreadable as he stared at the obscuring greyness. Dejected, Kao Chih followed suit.

They didn't have long to wait. Some minutes later they were assailed by unannounced shifts in momentum, some quite sharp. Then the curved grey surface lifted away to reveal a staggering sight.

The gas giant V'Hrant was a swirled and muddy immensity in the lower left, but the rest of that wide-open vista of high-orbit space was filled with an endless cloud of wreckage and debris. The full, undimmed horror of it confirmed his worst fears. The massive orbital city of Agmedra'a had been destroyed.

'... gone, it's ... gone ...' he whispered.

It was a panorama of ruin, of torn structures, of pulverised detritus. Some of the nearer, larger fragments were almost shocking in their familiarity – the decorative trim from the edge of one of the docking platforms, or a distinctive M-pointed archway from one of the underdock doorways ...

'So is our main thruster control,' muttered Robert. 'Disabled, so they want to keep us on a short leash ...'

Deeper into the zone of destruction were patches where the debris was denser, and a couple that were slightly foggy, hazy. And here and there were huge jagged sections around which small craft darted and hovered, spot beams stabbing and wavering, scenes of ongoing rescue attempts.

Agmedra'a's residential population was nearly a quarter of a million, he thought, *and the transient population could have been as high as 50,000. The death toll must be ...*

He shook his head but couldn't tear his gaze away.

'Still no communication,' Robert said, studying the instruments. 'That system-defence ship has moved off some distance. However, there is some odd activity going on down in that gas giant.' He glanced up. 'Aren't the Roug supposed to have cities down there?'

'So we are taught as children,' Kao Chih said. 'I worked down there, piloting a gravity tug, shifting ore cargos up to orbit and to ... Agmedra'a. We heard tales of the Roug cities that drifted through the deep but I never saw one.'

'That could be about to change,' said Robert. 'Going by these utterly inadequate sensors, something very big is ascending from the gas giant's depths.'

The pilot console's solitary monitor was focused on a segment of V'Hrant, a magnified square of the swirling face. The muddy haze resolved itself into swirls and undulations of rust red, mustard yellow and ash grey, coiling eddies of atmospheric air streams that now appeared threadlike. Then a white speck became visible amid a darker braid of flows and minute by minute grew steadily larger. After five minutes it was taking on a strange non-linear shape while the whiteness began to look more like pale grey.

After ten minutes the non-linearity of it seemed asymmetrical yet oddly suggestive of something. When it reached low orbit its nose angled upwards and, as it turned, Kao Chih finally understood what he was seeing. The Roug ship was shaped like a gigantic creature, a bizarre chimera with a wide torso, three clawed forelimbs and three back limbs, frozen in a pouncing motion. The head was broad, as were its parted jaws, and above fierce, blank eyes, halfway back between raised, pointed ears, there nestled a second, smaller head. Kao Chih was startled to realise that this was none other than the Roug ship *Vyrk*, the vessel from which he and Ajegil had carried out that hyperspace rescue.

'Seeing something familiar, Kao Chih?' said Robert.

He nodded and explained his voyage aboard the *Vyrk*. 'But I knew nothing about this. It's huge – it must be nearly a mile long ...'

'Nearly a mile and a half, actually,' Robert said. 'And it's heading straight for us.'

Its course was undeviating. With the lateral manoeuvring jets Robert was able to turn the assault craft to face the oncoming leviathan. The Shyntanil vessel was soon dwarfed by the Roug ship's immensity. As the grey curves of its beastlike exterior expanded to fill the viewport it slowed and a rectangular opening appeared in its chest. A slight jolt passed through the smaller craft and Robert looked up from the readouts.

'Their grappler fields have us, pulling us into that bay.'

The docking bay entrance seemed small at first but quickly grew. Before long the assault craft passed into a docking area provided with all sizes of berths and cradles spread out over a huge interior space. Ambient sources cast a shadowless light into every corner, while crew members down on its deck looked minuscule.

A big pale yellow platform swung out from one of the vacant berths and the Shyntanil vessel was guided in to make a perfect landing next to a second ship, a large, rectilinear, square-hulled transport. Then the rear hatch unsealed and began to lower.

'Nothing to do with me,' Robert said. 'Our hosts have taken complete control.'

Much to Kao Chih's surprise, four Humans wearing

shoulder panniers walked up the ramp. They were dressed in Human Sept work suits, although their faces were not familiar. Three of them approached the *Heracles'* survivors and began to distribute food and drink, while the fourth, a woman, approached Kao Chih and introduced herself as Mu Liang, explaining that they had been piloting gravity tugs when the attack took place.

'We were only picked up an hour ago,' she said in Mandarin. 'Then we were told we would have to help some injured Humans with medication and food, never thinking that they would be from ... Earth-Home!' She paused to look at the crew. 'Are there any serious wounds, Kao Chih?'

'Only hunger and thirst,' he said. 'They were starved and several dosed with sedatives, so there is also dehydration.'

'We shall start with small amounts and watch their progress.' She turned and waved to someone outside. 'There is a person here who wishes to speak with you, honourable pilot.'

Disconcertingly, she then gave him a bow before moving away to distribute her own store of water and food. When Kao Chih looked round at the ramp a familiar tall figure was climbing towards him. Once more in the burly Human appearance that he employed during his stay on Pyre, it was the Roug Qabakri.

'Good to see you again, my friend,' he said.

'Likewise with you, pilot Kao Chih, although the circumstances of this encounter could not be more calamitous.'

'Do you know why we are here?' Kao Chih said.

'I have heard the message that you transmitted,' the Roug said. 'Action has been taken. Ships have been dispatched to waylay the second asteroid and its attendant vessels.'

'Second asteroid?' Kao Chih said, shaking his head. 'So the one we delayed . . .'

'Was only the latter of a pair,' Qabakri said. 'Perhaps our enemies decided to factor in redundancy in the event that either was intercepted, a successful tactic, but they do not realise what they have called down upon themselves. Very shortly, further actions will be taken. This vessel, the great warvaunt *Vyrk-Zoshel*, will fly to battle for the first time in millennia.'

'Will you be tracking down the Shyntanil or the Suneye Monoclan?'

Qabakri surveyed the *Heracles'* survivors for a moment.

'In time, both,' said the Roug. 'You should understand the sequence of events. Several hours before the catastrophe the incursioner craft *Syroga* appeared in our system, accompanied by three Vox Humana transports bearing the colonists from Pyre . . .'

Kao Chih was struck by an agonising realisation.

'That is why! That's what this destruction is for . . .' He put a hand to his head. 'If you had not become involved in our . . .'

'No blame is or could be laid upon the Humans,' Qabakri said. 'The remaining supernals of the High Index have already ruled on this. Now, I must continue with my account.

'Some hours after the colonist flotilla arrived, our hyperspace sensors detected a very large object approaching, rising through the tiers on a course that appeared to intersect with our orbital city. As a precaution we started evacuating while using Agmedra'a's engines to shift its orbit. To our consternation the approaching object altered its course and kept doing so to remain on target. We tried to evacuate as many as possible but there were not enough vessels.'

Qabakri's calm exterior was belied by a dark glitter in the eyes.

'When it arrived we saw that it was a piece of something larger, while still possessing a sub-planetoid mass. No weaponsfire could deflect it from its course. It impacted Agmedra'a and the results are plain to see.' The Roug's eyes seemed full of anger. 'Two Suneye vessels then arrived, clearly intending to seize the Vox Humana transports – the commander of the *Syroga* acted promptly such that it and the transports made the jump to hyperspace before the Suneye intruders got within weapon range.'

'Where could they go? Where would be safe?'

'Nowhere, which is why they are heading for Darien.' The Roug nodded at Kao Chih's amazement. 'It has taken nearly four hours to gather and assemble the segments of the *Vyrk-Zoshel*, the only survivor from the great and mighty fleet of warvaunts that met their doom in the battles against the Dreamless a hundred centuries ago. Now the last warvaunt shall plunge through the levels and veils of hyperspace and hunt down the dreamless machine minds of the Suneye Monoclan.

'And you must be on board, Kao Chih – your skills will be needed, and your advice and mere presence if you do eventually reach the Darien system. I will not lie to you – the hazards are great.'

Kao Chih felt resolute. 'I am ready to go with you, Qabakri, wherever it leads.'

The Roug smiled with his Human face. 'I shall not be accompanying you, Kao Chih – I need to use this Shyntanil vessel to get to a place called the Great Hub. An old adversary of yours is about to bring another crisis to its climax, and I may be able to stop her ... while mimicking you, as it happens.'

'Talavera,' Kao Chih guessed, knowing he was right. 'Take care, my friend – she enjoys danger.'

The *Heracles'* survivors were trooping off the assault craft and across to the square-hulled transport.

'A couple of those Humans with the supplies are Roug able to speak Earth-Anglic,' Qabakri said. 'They'll make sure they are returned to the nearest Earthsphere outpost. In the meantime I need to persuade your Construct companion to go with me to the Great Hub.'

'I wish I was going too,' Kao Chih said. 'But I shall do what I can to prevail upon its good nature. How soon ...'

'All our departures will commence as soon as possible.'

Kao Chih smiled sadly. 'All departures happen too soon,' he said, leading the way up into the assault craft.

28

GREG

Soon after Vice-Admiral Ngassa's flagship, the ESS *Shieldwall*, reached the high-orbit vicinity of Darien, Greg and Lieutenant Berg were allowed to return to the *Starfire*. However, before they were even halfway they received orders diverting them to the *Silverlance*. By the time they had docked then trudged aft to the engineering overdeck – which was still doubling as a command bridge – Greg was feeling decidedly cranky. But the moment he and Berg entered he knew something was wrong.

Ash was standing before the big angled holoscreens, his face like stone. Gazing down at him were the faces of Admiral Olarevic of the Vox Humana and Vice-Admiral Ngassa. The latter was speaking.

'... is the sum total of all they are saying, Lieutenant. They regard the Imisil as a direct threat to their allies and an implicit threat to themselves. If they do not leave, Supreme Overcommander Gannor cannot offer any guarantees of peaceful cooperation.'

For a moment no one spoke.

'Well, they do only have five vessels,' said Admiral Olarevic. 'It would not be a loss.'

'I understand that, Madam Admiral,' Ash said. 'My concern is the reliability or otherwise of the Hegemony' fleet's Supreme Overcommander.'

'Lieutenant,' said Ngassa, 'I actually have some acquaintance with Gannor. When I was commodore of the escort flotillas in the Yamanon he was overcommander of their Third Echelon and we cooperated on a number of occasions. I always found him straightforward and honourable.'

Standing off to the side, Greg rolled his eyes. *Aye, and I'll bet he was a gentleman and a scholar, too …*

'Your appraisal is greatly appreciated, Vice-Admiral,' said Ash. 'But it would be more helpful if we were to have direct contact with the Supreme Overcommander …'

'That's not possible, I'm afraid,' Ngassa said. 'Gannor insists that he will speak with no one but myself. Now, time is running out, Lieutenant Ash, and I strongly recommend that you accept these terms and ask the Imisil to depart.'

'I shall give this matter close and urgent attention, sir,' Ash said. 'Now I must consult with our other allies before reaching a consensus, which I shall convey to you within the hour.'

'Understood, Lieutenant. Till then.'

As the screen went into standby, Ash turned to the image of the Vox Humana admiral on the other.

'Admiral Olarevic, could you bear with me for a moment while we establish channels with the other leaders?'

'Of course, Lieutenant.'

Ash nodded, turned to give terse orders to a waiting

subordinate then beckoned Greg and Berg over. Frowning, he prodded the charred slash across Berg's chest.

'What exactly happened on board Ngassa's pinnace?'

Berg delivered a brief account of the adjutant's betrayal, and the occupying AI's comments just after the appearance of the Hegemony armada.

'Did the vice-admiral give any indication at any time of having been in communication with the Hegemony commander?'

'Not at all, sir.'

'He was in sight nearly all the time we were there,' said Greg. 'Never heard a thing about Hegemony messages.'

'Yet from when you left his ship to before you even got here,' Ash said, 'an exchange took place between him and this Supreme Overcommander. Something doesn't smell right.'

He broke off when a sub-lieutenant told him everything was ready. 'Watch closely,' he told Greg and Berg before moving back into the confer-image zone before the big screens. In addition to the face of Olarevic, there was Braddock, the Tygran officer, K'ang Lo, the captain of the Pyrean rockhab the *Retributor*, and First Proposer Conlyph, the new ranking Imisil commander.

'Earthsphere Vice-Admiral Ngassa has been in communication with the Hegemony Supreme Overcommander Gannor,' said Ash. 'Gannor says he is willing to cooperate with Earthsphere's stance on Darien's protectorate status, provided that all Imisil vessels depart from the system without delay.'

Braddock leaned forward. 'Did the SO offer to reduce Hegemony military presence in the system?'

'I wasn't made aware of any such offer,' said Ash.

'Did the Hegemony commander settle upon particular areas of cooperation?' said K'ang Lo.

'The vice-admiral mentioned no such specifications on their part.'

'How did Ngassa seem to regard the SO's proposal?' said Braddock.

'He takes it seriously,' Ash said. 'He certainly seems to think that the offer is genuine and practical.'

At this, the Imisil commander, a Vikantan like Remosca, shook his head while the spot-clusters on his face pulsed a steady violet.

'Be aware that Hegemony military commanders are not in the habit of negotiating away any advantage,' he said. 'They are always seeking to teach lessons, and that huge fleet of theirs will be used to teach all other civilisations the lesson that the slightest defiance will be crushed without mercy. The fact that they have not already launched their attack can only mean that there is another factor in play.'

And I think I know what that is, thought Greg.

In the next moment, the Vox Humana admiral said: 'I have heard high-level rumours that Hegemony scientists have uncovered technology left behind by the Forerunners, working technology . . .'

'But why should that cause them to stay their hand?' said Braddock.

'This is speculation,' said Ash. 'We need to focus on how to respond to the . . .'

He paused when the comms sub-lieutenant started

gesturing urgently at him. 'Sir, you need to see this – it's being widecast from a low-orbit satellite that popped up from the planet's surface just minutes ago ...'

'Who's it from?'

'Someone claiming to be president pro-tem of Darien.'

'Show me.'

Another screen came to life and Greg found himself staring in disbelief up at the bearded visage of Vashutkin, the Rus politician.

'My name is Alexandr Vashutkin,' he began. 'I was minister for energy and transport under President Sundstrom, the Darien colony's last legitimate leader. The president and his cabinet were murdered by extremist xenophobic terrorists – only I survived because ill health kept me from attending that fateful meeting. These same terrorists have been holding me prisoner until I was freed by forces loyal to the Hegemony ambassador, the exalted Utavess Kuros.

'As the last surviving minister of the Sundstrom government, I am now declaring myself president pro-tem, as is permitted under the articles of the Darien colonial constitution. My first executive edict is as follows – the military forces of Earthsphere, the Vox Humana, the Pyrean asteroid-habitat, and the Sendrukan Hegemony are permitted to remain in orbit about Darien, provided all combat-ready postures are downgraded to neutral. All other vessels must leave this star system immediately. I understand that you came here believing that this colony was under some kind of threat. Darien's new protectorate status, and the negotiations now ongoing between the Earthsphere and Hegemony commanders, prove that there is no threat. Therefore there is no need for you to remain. Please leave.

'There is one further matter I wish to address, that of Gregory Cameron, former head of research at the Giant's Shoulder excavation site. Anyone watching this announcement should beware of taking at face value anything that Mr Cameron says. He is an adventurer, a brigand and a liar, and later today I shall be issuing a warrant for his arrest on charges of treason. If any ship in the skies over Darien is harbouring this man I strongly urge its captain to hand him over to any Earthsphere vessel.

'For the time being, that is all. In the name of peace and justice, I wish you well.'

The moment the message ended, Ash turned to his comm officer and said: 'Have that vid analysed – I want to know what kind of equipment it was made with and anything else you can find out.'

Meanwhile, all eyes were on Greg, who was half infuriated and half full of an urge to laugh out loud.

'That lying, scheming, scum-sucking toerag!' he growled.

'I assume that you're not going to let that go unanswered,' said Ash, with the ghost of a smile haunting his lips.

'Bloody right I'm not,' Greg said, striding forward. 'Can you put me out on the same channel? Let me know when to begin.'

'Look up at the screen and start whenever you are ready,' Ash said.

Greg nodded, tilted his head back a little and put on a smile.

'Hello, Alexandr. Greg Cameron here. That's right, Greg Cameron, adventurer, freedom fighter, and grudge-holder. I saw that wee movie of yours and I must say it's the funniest piece of gobshite I've heard since, well, since that spineless weasel Kirkland went on live vee to tell everyone what great friends the Brolts were, how much they cared for us ground-hugging Darienites, while they were rounding up anyone who stepped out of line. So your little proclamation was fine, sincere gravitas and all that, but there's a few things that you missed out – like the facts.

'Fact number one – you weren't imprisoned by ter-rorists. Truth is, you've been working and fighting alongside members of the resistance for the last couple of weeks. And here's juicy fact number two – while you were doing that, you were also trying to think up some way to stab me in the back and still come out o' it smelling flowery. Then along came that vital mission to Giant's Shoulder. You invited yourself, helped fight off the pack of combat mechs we found there and *just* at the very moment when I was on my knees, exhausted, or as a good friend would say, right scunnered – *then* you turned your gun on me.'

Greg, his eyes flashing, face animated, almost snarled up at the screen.

'I remember it perfectly, Alexandr, that sickening moment of betrayal. I was lucky, though – someone else pulled me outta there and saved my life. But I wonder if you remember that moment, Alexandr – do you? Ah, but then it's not really Alexandr Vashutkin I'm talking to, is it? No, you're some kind of AI creature, something cooked up in a Hegemony lab . . .'

Suddenly a loud, stuttering alarm sounded, interrupting him, and a voice came over the address system.

'We are under fire from unknown hostiles – brace for battle turbulence, repeat, brace for ...'

Greg had already grabbed hold of a nearby fixed Sendrukan-scale chair, but he wasn't ready for the ferocity of the impact. It came up through the deck and knocked everyone off their feet, with many, like Greg, losing their grip. He was thrown across the deck and tried to roll into it. As he came to a halt, face down, he felt a slow wave of weightlessness pass over him and for a second he found himself lifting slightly into the air, before he slumped back down again.

Ash, however, was already back on his feet and working at one of the consoles while the comms officer fitted him with a one-sided headset.

'Attention all crew – we have been fired on by units of the Hegemony armada. From here on it is going to be a rough ride so stay at your posts, maintain body security, and be ready. Stormlions advance!'

As the battle cry echoed along the corridors, Greg got to his feet and went over to join Ash.

'What the hell was that?' he said.

Ash gave him a sardonic look. 'Might have been something that you said, Mr Cameron ...'

'Hey, I'm good but I don't think I'm *that* good.'

The Tygran shrugged. 'Well, whatever the reason, they launched their attack with precision.' He pointed up at a schematic of the defending vessels near Darien with a larger X-shaped formation approaching. 'Ninety-eight capital ships, including twenty maulers, each mounting at least a dozen heavy beam projectors and pulse cannon. It was their combined punch that nearly ended the show before it began. Our auto-system brought up the shields just in time but others weren't so lucky – the Vox Humana have lost three ships already and right now if it weren't for the coordinated shields of the Imisil and Ngassa's heavy cruisers, half our fleet would be glowing wreckage.'

'A sneak attack,' Greg said, glancing up at the tactical overview. *A hundred ships – and that's just a twentieth of what they've got.* 'So how long can we hold out?'

'You should be more optimistic, Mr Cameron,' Ash said. 'After all, we do have a secret weapon.'

'We do?'

'Most certainly – ah, speaking of which.'

On the left-hand screen, a frame expanded to show the head and shoulders of K'ang Lo, the commander of the Pyrean rockhab, the *Retributor*.

'Shih Ash,' K'ang Lo said. 'My news is good – the dragon is ready to breathe. My engineers now require only a clear line of sight.'

'Excellent, Duizhang! I am about to create it for you.'

K'ang Lo's image shrank a little off to one side while another appeared in its place. It was Vice-Admiral Ngassa.

'Lieutenant, where's this counterstrike of yours?' Ngassa said. 'Maintaining these shields is draining our cells at an unsustainable rate.'

'It's ready now, Vice-Admiral. If you pull your vessels back from a channel along these coordinates then wait for the shield signal ...'

'I have the coordinates now, Lieutenant. This shouldn't take long.'

'The Pyreans have a weapon?' Greg murmured as Ngassa's picture shrank into a corner. 'What does it do?'

'Something they got from the Roug,' Ash said. 'I just hope it's enough to take out some of those maulers. Otherwise we've got real problems ...'

Moments later Vice-Admiral Ngassa confirmed that the manoeuvres were complete, as did the Imisil commander. Ash then informed K'ang Lo, who smiled.

'My engineers have monitored the progress and we have already acquired our target. The dragon is ready.'

The Earthsphere vice-admiral nodded gravely. 'Shield will open along that channel in ten ... nine ... eight ...'

The other screens still showed the Hegemony formation, the spread-out X of vessels with the mauler ships clustered around the centre. They were firing off massive bursts of energy and energised particles which were hammering against the interlocked shields of the defending fleet. Then the vice-admiral's countdown reached one ... and for a heartbeat there was nothing, an instant of hollow dread, a millisecond of panic ...

Then the dragon roared.

A pillar of force and energy leaped along that channel cleared through the loose formation of vessels and stabbed out towards the oncoming Hegemony ships. It was almost too bright to watch but the visual systems quickly filtered and enhanced. Greg stared openmouthed as that ferocious torrent smashed into the Hegemony vessels, scything through hulls like laser drills through paper, cutting them apart, grinding them up. In fact, those formerly fearsome ships appeared to be dissolving in that annihilating incandescence.

And abruptly, it was gone.

Without that immense sunfire-spear, all seemed to suddenly plunge into darkness until the visual systems adapted. One screen showed the remnants of the X-formation in full retreat, leaving clouds of glowing fragments in their wake. Greg could hear cheers from elsewhere on board but he couldn't help thinking about the hundreds of Sendrukans who must have experienced a moment or two of searing agony before being sent to their deaths.

They would have surely done the same to us and without hesitation, he thought. *Disnae make me feel any better, though ...*

'Why have they stopped firing, Lieutenant?'

Vice-Admiral Ngassa's face was glaring down at Ash.

'The weapon can only fire continuously for about fifty seconds, Vice-Admiral,' Ash said. 'Then it needs just under three minutes to charge.'

'Three minutes?' Ngassa was incredulous. 'If that's true then we cannot maintain our current position. They are already preparing the next attacks and we must not become a sitting duck ...'

Ash switched his attention to the screen with the long-range scan data and schematics, seemingly taking it all in with a two-second glance.

'Carriers and launcher platforms,' he said. 'Could be a problem.'

'Worse than that, Lieutenant – the Supreme Overcommander is toying with us, advancing another of his hundred-piece formations rather than committing his entire force.'

Ash grinned. 'Perhaps we should move out to engage with the next wave and unleash the dragon when it's ready.'

'Aye, but if it was up to me,' Greg said, 'I'd find out where the Supreme Thingummy is hiding hisself and go after him, full tilt, all guns blazing.' He paused, suddenly aware of Ash and Ngassa's intent stares. 'But that's just me . . . '

'Actually,' said Ash, 'that is a fair summation of the Imisil commander's recommendation.'

'My tactical officer proposes a curved trajectory around Darien,' Ngassa said. 'With the *Retributor* positioned at our formation's leading flank it can target that weapon across a wider field. Using short bursts more tightly focused – and watching out for the Supreme Overcommander's flagship, of course.'

By now they had been joined by Admiral Olarevic, the Imisil First Proposer Conlyph, and the Duizhang K'ang Lo, who was quick to agree with the Earthsphere plan. Olarevic was reluctant and had to be convinced, essentially by the possibility of Vox Humana ships being left to fend for themselves.

It took just over a minute for all the vessels of the combined fleet to embed the new course data, then they set off in unison. At the same time some had to manoeuvre aside within the cluster of ships to allow the bulky, irregular mass of the *Retributor* to move forward. All this while the Hegemony forces kept up a sustained bombardment of pulse rounds, missiles and submunition clusters – ninety per cent of their vessels were maintaining their stand-off positions yet they were still contributing to the incessant barrage of destruction that clawed at the defenders' interleaved shields.

'Duizhang K'ang Lo,' said Ngassa. 'Is your weapon ready to fire?'

'Yes, Vice-Admiral,' K'ang Lo said. 'Our dragon knows where the enemies are.'

'You have control of the shields, Duizhang. The timing is fully in your hands so please, teach these intruders a lesson.'

K'ang Lo smiled wordlessly before his image vanished.

This time Greg could see the weapon itself. Visual feeds relayed from ships near the *Retributor* showed an odd geodesic-like structure on top of the asteroid habitat. The dome's polyhedrals were translucent, almost with a shimmering moiré effect, while within a knot of something impossibly bright burned. Then with a shocking suddenness the dazzling column of energies lanced out for two seconds then cut out. Then it appeared again, pointing in a different direction, two seconds then off. And again and again and again. On the big screens Greg could see the sheer havoc that the Roug weapon was wreaking in the ranks of the enemy, ships sliced in half, some half-wrecked but spiralling off with uncontrolled thrust drives burning, others blowing themselves apart and catching other vessels in the blast radius.

All the Hegemony ships were breaking formation now, frantically trying to spread out and make less obvious targets. At the same time they were managing to keep up the attack barrage, much of which was now directed at the *Retributor*. Missiles, hull-leeches and swarmers converged on that particular spot in the flank of the defenders' formation and the nearby warships managed to intercept nearly all of them. Beam weapon bursts and particle pulses were harder to neutralise and the first time a string of them struck the rockhab Greg felt his mouth go dry.

Shattered rock and clouds of grit and dust erupted here and there, and a couple of times an assembly housing or external pipe junction was hit, resulting in a flare of vaporised metal burning up. Greg started to realise how much punishment a big asteroid could absorb.

But now it was the defenders' turn to become an easy target. Crowded together in a comparatively slow-moving teardrop formation, this allowed the enemy vessels to concentrate their fire – but even Greg knew this couldn't go on. Minutes later Ngassa was back on the big screen with a new plan – divide the combined fleet in three, a command group based on the vice-admiral's flagship and the *Retributor*, and two support groups based on the Imisil and Vox Humana vessels respectively, strengthened with Earthsphere units.

The Imisil commander, First Proposer Conlyph, nodded emphatically, his facial markings shimmering an impatient silver.

'Dividing our numbers adds to our manoeuvrability while dividing the enemy's firepower.'

The Vox Humana admiral, Olarevic, was unconvinced but Ngassa's promise of five Earthsphere heavy cruisers brought her round. Ash had Berg in the *Starfire* and Braddock in the *Vanquisher* go with them too, while deciding to commit the *Silverlance* to the Imisil group.

'Our strategic goal,' Vice-Admiral Ngassa said over the group-channel visual, 'is to locate and destroy the Hegemony flagship, thus removing the Supreme Overcommander.' The image of a bulky, carrier-sized

ship bristling with weapons appeared below his face.
'Clear skies and good hunting!'

Greg raised an eyebrow at Ash. 'So, my idea wasnae
so dumb, after all, eh?'

'It depends on how you define the word.'

'What – define "dumb"?'

'No – "idea".'

But the task ahead, spiritedly depicted as formidable
or even challenging, soon showed its true face. The
enemy ships were too numerous and the collective
potency of their weapons was too strong for overloaded,
overstretched   shields   and   weakened   hulls.
Formationless, the Hegemony vessels converged on the
three groups of defending ships, imposing carriers
unleashing hundreds of interceptors that fell upon them
in wave after wave. On the control screens in the
Silverlance's engineering deck, Greg watched the attack
runs against a Vox Humana light assault cruiser which
had become separated, explosive rounds stitching lines
of fire along its hull, the bursts of argent violence as
generators or fuel stores ignited, the pale outgassing
from a hundred breaches, the ragged gaping crater
where an out-of-control enemy craft had rammed the
ship and exploded. And dozens of escape pods jetting
away, location signals pinging on the emergency channels.

Greg saw similar ship deaths played out on the
screens, a repetition of desperate tragedy. Half an hour
after Ngassa's stirring send-off, their combined numbers
were down to eighteen at the last count. Braddock's
Vanquisher was a drifting hulk, its captain missing. The
Vox Humana's Admiral Olarevic lost her flagship but

transferred to one of the Earthsphere cruisers. Including Berg's *Starfire*, their own group was down to four.

The Imisil group were numerically better off – two Imisil cruisers, three Earthsphere attack cruisers and Ash's *Silverlance* – but the damage sustained was widespread and serious. The Imisil commander had decided on a tactical withdrawal out past the orbit of Nivyesta.

The *Retributor* had been put out of action. K'ang Lo's brutal Roug weapon managed to account for perhaps two hundred Hegemony ships before enough missiles and interceptors finally broke through the shield and fire cordon provided by Ngassa's heavy cruisers. Greg had only caught glimpses of the rockhab as it was enveloped in a wreath of detonating payloads and flaming energies just before the dome of the dragon's breath exploded, a burst of light accompanied by sprays of sparks while pulverised fragments expanded outwards. Watching it was almost too much to bear.

Now the asteroid vessel looked powered-out, a darkened mass drifting with a slight axial spin, all external floods and signal lights dead. Just a few jets of escaping gas creating clouds of ice crystals in its slow wake.

Meanwhile, Vice-Admiral Ngassa's flagship and a handful of battered vessels were being steadily corralled by the remaining hundreds of Hegemony ships. Complete defeat seemed to be staring them in the face.

Whatever happened to that Imisil fleet? Greg wondered. *Did that black Vor ship we saw stop them in their tracks?*

Ash was standing before the screens, arms crossed, face unreadable. The central panel had been tiled into a score or more of feed frames, each showing a separate scene from some part of the sprawling, world-encircling battlezone. Several audio channels were muttering in the background, the only sound in the sombre hush.

'I found out why they opened fire while you were in mid-rebuttal,' Ash unexpectedly said to Greg. 'It appears that the Vashutkin message was made on a Sorik dataslate, which is a command-level piece of equipment aboard Tygran ships, and it was recorded nearly an hour before it was widecast. Best of all, there was a short message in Sendrukan encrypted into one of its layers, which said: "Operation Reclaim now commencing." In other words, it was a signal.'

'So Becker was involved,' Greg said. 'But if that was over an hour ago they could be getting up to any kind of deviltry – and we've no way of knowing what it is ... unless ...'

Ash shook his head. 'That damned interference is still blanketing the colony. Nothing but garbled static ...'

The face of the Imisil commander, First Proposer Canlyph, appeared at one side of the screen.

'Lieutenant Ash, I have some unfortunate news – it appears that the remainder of the Imisil fleet has encountered a second wave of attackers in hyperspace. I'm afraid that the fleet's High Initiator has decided to turn back and to see if an alternative route can be found. On a less regretful note, I can report that our probes have sent back an interesting morsel of information – relaying it to you now.'

Greg's heart sank, appalled that his own inner speculations could turn out to be true.

Another frame popped up on the screen, showing

the lush green curve of the forest moon, Nivyesta. The visual zoomed forward in stages, finally revealing the ship that was hanging there in stationary orbit on the other side of the moon, a massive and distinctive-looking ship, weapons jutting from stepped layers of decks.

'It is the Hegemony flagship, the *Dominion Of Light*,' said the First Proposer. 'I believe that we should gather our strength and attack it. The Earthsphere captains have already agreed.'

Ash hesitated and Greg thought, even half-hoped that he'd decline what would almost certainly be a suicide mission. Then he gravely nodded.

'Two-part assault?' he said. 'The Earthers and ourselves go in hot to draw off the escort while your ships stealth up close to the flagship's stern, targeting the drives?'

'Well deduced, Lieutenant. We shall move out in three and one-half minutes by your reckoning.'

The Imisil vanished and Ash rapped out a series of orders and course changes. Suddenly the air was electric.

'Mr Cameron, as a civilian you have no formal rank or combat function aboard the *Silverlance* – I can put you off in an escape pod slotted for a touchdown on Nivyesta. If that is what you wish.'

Greg laughed. 'Ye probably know that this assault is stupid, right? So basically the plan is that we're not gonnae make it out alive. But since no plan survives contact with the enemy we could well get through it by the skin of our teeth! So aye, count me in.'

The Tygran smiled openly and shook his head.

'You make madness sound almost sane.'

The comms officer suddenly interrupted him. 'Sir, I'm getting a squirt transmission from ... from the asteroid vessel, the *Retributor*!'

'Someone's still alive on that rock?' Greg said.

'How wide a cast is it?' Ash said. 'What channel, and who else might hear it?'

'That's just it, sir – it reached us by tight-beam relay, not as a widecast signal.'

Ash's eyes widened, half-smiling. 'So they aimed a comm laser at us!'

'Yes, sir, exactly ... nnnnyyyarrgh! ... '

With a violent motion the comms officer ripped away his headset and reared back a step before diving forward to punch controls on his console.

'What was that?' said Ash.

'A ... howl of something horrible ... right across all bands, all channels. I've never heard anything like it ... '

'Anything to do with the *Retributor*'s message?'

'No, sir, it's ... coming from the planet's surface ... '

Ash was already at work at the main sensor controls and a view of Darien appeared on the main screen. A swathe of the planet's face was obscured by great banks of cloud gyrating around a cyclonic weather system off to the north. But what held everyone's attention was the pale glow lighting up the clouds from below. Whatever was producing it had to be huge and bright enough to turn night into day for it to be so starkly visible. There were few hints of the landmasses and coastline below but Greg knew with an awful certainty exactly what the source of the light was.

Is this it? he thought. *Is this where the Legion of*

Avatars breaks out and takes over Darien? What will Uncle Theo and the others do? Will anyone survive?

Then he looked at Ash and the rest and wondered what to say to them.

29

THEO

An hour or so earlier, just before Greg began his angry riposte to Vashutkin's declaration, Theo Karlsson was smoking a pipe while perched on an upended crate beneath a rickety lean-to poised near the brink of the crater in the flank of Tusk Mountain. Nearby sat Rory, who was whittling away at a wooden peg by the light of a Tygran cell-lamp. The lean-to's waxed-hide canopy was sheltering them from the insistent downpour currently moving slowly across the mountains. It made a pattering sound overhead and filled the mountain air with an immense sighing hiss.

This is the real rain, Theo thought, drawing and puffing, savouring the fragrant woodiness of the tobacco. *So the sky chooses tonight to release its bounty. Such good timing ...*

He glanced over at Rory, still scraping, blowing and carving.

'I thought you gave that up a year ago,' he said. 'You said you were not any good at it.'

Rory paused, flashed Theo a sidelong grin and held up the piece of wood. To Theo's surprise it looked a bit like a lizard, a snipervile.

'No' any more, chief!' said Rory. 'Guess I've got a natural talent for it after all.'

Theo nodded, deciding not to voice any concern. Ever since his recovery in the Uvovo daughter-forest, Rory had more and more seemed like his old self, complete with the ebullient self-assurance and handy wit. Yet there was something new, a slight hesitancy or at least a blunting of the wild rashness that had got him into so many tight corners over the years. Theo was sure it was due to the horrors Rory and the Uvovo Chel had suffered while prisoners of the Legion Knight. He had asked Rory about it in a mild, no-pressure manner, but Rory had insisted that he remembered nothing at all from when he was captured to when he awoke in the forest.

The raucous sounds of voices singing in unison came up from the crater. That great bite out of the mountain's flank had in the space of a day gone from a charred stone bowl to a real-estate rush when some of those confined to corridor recesses within the mountain realised that here was plenty of room to build a shack or a hut. Branches were gathered from the lower-slope woods while salvaged materials were brought in from nearby trapper towns, even the logger camps to the south. A multitude of shaky-looking shanties were erected and expanded as volunteers continued to turn up. Right now, down in one of the larger huts, a group of newly arrived Norj mountain men calling themselves the Hakon-Haer were engaged in a contest with the Stonecutter Clan, a band of brawny Scots builders, the contest being the strident bellowing of songs while pints of small beer were consumed.

Theo smiled, recalling similar gatherings when he was younger, especially during the Winter Coup, when eve-of-battle congregations were held, songs were sung, ale was drunk, and loved ones were held close.

They have every right to celebrate their Humanity, he thought. *To celebrate the fire that burns in our hearts. Come the dawn in just a few hours we'll be facing terrible, pitiless enemies. We have to succeed. Many will die but we still have to find a way to destroy the warpwell or face our own destruction ...*

The plans had been laid. Alliances had been negotiated and pacts sealed. Gideon had met with the leader of the Spiral renegades and again with Solvjeg and Ian Cameron – coded messages flitted by crude shortwave back and forth between Tusk Mountain and Hammergard or the Spiralist renegade camp near Port Gagarin. The schematics of war were drawn up, timings and logistics agreed upon. While the Tusk Mountain insurgents bided their time, units of Eastern Town militias were moving through the wild woods that ran north along the ridges and cliffs to merge with the jagged spurs west of Giant's Shoulder. At the same time bands of Spiralists were converging on the steep tracks north of the promontory, many of them armed with portable missile launchers that would be put to good use against the combat mechs.

Then there was the bomb, the warpwell bomb. Soon after Theo returned with Rory, word came from the Hall of Discourse that the Zyradin was asking to speak with the diminutive Scot. Theo had duly accompanied Rory down to the ceremonial hall, where he clambered up onto the glowing platform and stood there with a distrustful look on his face. The Zyradin had then explained that someone had to take a space-fold bomb up to Giant's Shoulder and use it against the warpwell. Oh aye, Rory had said – is that tae stop all they cyborg mad-bastards from coming through here? Yes, Rory, the Zyradin said. And since you now have a machine-system attunement you would be able to penetrate their defences while the main attack occupies their full attention. Well, I do have this thing wi' machines, right enough, Rory had admitted. Noticed it a lot since I got back, like, just knowing how they work, how tae change what they're doing. Exactly, said the Zyradin. You can tell the combat mechs to ignore you. Rory had nodded hesitantly. So I dive past them and plant the bomb but will I have enough time tae get out afore it goes kaboom? The Zyradin said: there should be long enough for you to retreat to a safe distance. Rory had frowned and thought for a brief moment before nodding. All right, yer on!

Not long after, Gideon and Solvjeg came to thank Rory for his help, and to finalise his part in the assault, the when, the where, and with who. Later a Uvovo scholar sought him out to say that the Zyradin's device had appeared on the great platform. Rory had said that he'd wait until it was time to go before retrieving it.

Theo found himself drawing cool air from his pipe, which had gone out. He contemplated refilling and relighting it then decided that he really should try and get some shuteye. Even some of the ribald singers down below had thought the same and were climbing the rope ladder that led from the bottom of the crater to the gaping entrance. The rain was still falling, a steady curtain of drench, but he had made up his mind. He knocked out the charred dottle from his pipe then stood.

'I think I'll be turning in,' he said. 'See if I can trap me a couple of hours' sleep, eh?'

'Aye, I'll mebbe try the same in a wee bit, chief,' Rory said.

Theo nodded, pulled on a cloth cap and stepped out into the rain then headed along the edge of the crater. Three catwalks suspended on improvised A-frames joined two points along the edge to the base entrance. He was halfway across the one leading from the centre to the base when he heard an odd sound in the air, off in the distance, like the drone of insects. Then a shouting reached him from away down the mountain slope, a man clambering madly up towards the crater, yelling 'Alarm! Alarm!'

The droning was engines! *My God*, he thought. *We're under attack!* And he leaned over the gantry rail to shout at Rory but, before he could, a heavy weight struck his shoulder, knocking him down to sprawl on the gantry's rough planks. Even as he struggled to regain his footing he could hear the sounds of a firefight nearby, suddenly blotted out by the whining stutter of an automatic weapon. Shouts went up all around. Crouching, he fumbled for his own weapon, a reliable hefty 45-calibre revolver, then realised that he was alone on the catwalk. Dark figures slid down lines that hung wavering from above. Theo looked up and saw seven or eight silently hovering oblong shapes, grey in the rain which splashed in his eyes. Had his assailant been one of these attackers, striking Theo on his way down into the crater?

Roused from sleep, the shanty inhabitants had emerged and gunfire was breaking out in all directions. Theo made a dash for the main entrance, feet banging on the planks, one hand intermittently seeking balance on the rope rail while the other held on to the revolver. Ahead, men with rifles knelt in the entrance, some firing up at the antigrav flyers, other beckoning Theo to hurry.

There was a loud bang from behind. In reflex he ducked, going down on one knee and glancing over his shoulder – just as the gantry slewed suddenly to one side with a cracking sound. The support was toppling, making the gantry tilt over. Theo held on as best he could, then there was a lurch and he lost his grip, tipped over the rail and fell ...

Onto a shanty roof, some composite of hide over a lattice of wooden slats. It broke his fall but still gave way with a splintering tear so that he landed awkwardly on the dirt floor of a wide hut hardly lit by the brazier glowing in the corner. There was a long table strewn with empty and half-empty mugs, and a couple of snoring forms curled up beneath, oblivious to the raging conflict. Theo got shakily to his feet. Astonishingly he had held on to the revolver so at least he wasn't defenceless. *Time to get back up there*, he thought. *Got to find Rory ...*

It was the rope ladder up to the entrance that he had in mind as he strode towards the hut's open door. In the darkness he never saw the foot that tripped him. He fell full-length and landed face-down, the impact driving the air out of his chest. And yet still he held on to the gun and, aware that there was someone else in the hut, he rolled over, bringing the gun round ...

Only to have it wrenched out of his hand and dashed against the side of his head. It was just a glancing blow but was enough to leave him dazed ...

'Ah ... it's you, the feeble old man that Gideon had leading his men into Base Wolf ...'

A rough hand grabbed him by the collar, dragged him across the floor and with an unnerving strength threw him onto a mound of what felt like hides or cloaks or both. By the brazier's meagre yellow glow Theo finally got a glimpse of his assailant – tall but not a Sendrukan, dressed in a familiar blue combat armour. Then the face came forward out of the shadow, a distorted visage whose left side up to the scalp was red scar tissue. It was Marshal Becker's loyal ally, Nathaniel Horne.

'Hard to believe that this ragged gang of rebels could cause even the Brolturans difficulty,' Horne said. 'Clearly, all that was needed was the skills of battle-hardened Tygrans.' He glanced at Theo's revolver, snorted and tossed it aside then took out a thick-barrelled handgun whose muzzle had four closely clustered nozzles.

'I have to say,' Theo said, 'this isn't a very dignified end.'

'You're going to be dead – trust me, you won't care.'

'Well, what about the condemned man's last request?'

'I don't do requests. Now hold still and it'll be quick ...'

Except that Horne didn't say that last word – instead there was a quick intake of breath as he lunged backwards, swinging the handgun round, firing off a stream of hot bright barbs. A cluster of tracerlike bolts passed through the space where he'd been standing, shutting off abruptly when Horne's own gunfire found a target. Theo, sprawled on the mound of hides, stared as Horne sauntered over to where Captain Gideon lay on the dirt near the door, blood staining his right arm and left leg.

'Ah, the great captain, brought to bay at last!'

Nathaniel Horne covered Gideon with his beam weapon as he approached. 'The Marshal is here on the mountain, too, Franklyn – what a pity that he won't see your last moments, your blood running out to mix with the mud ...'

Theo scrabbled around, desperately searching for his gun, relying on touch in the brazier-lit gloom. But he couldn't find it – and Horne was bringing up that energy pistol ...

Fingers touched cold metal under the flaps of a hide, found a wooden handle and dragged it out. Dull ember yellow gleamed on the polished blades of a double-bitted axe that must belong to one of the drinkers from before ...

There was no time – he leaped to his feet and hurled it.

The axe flew true and smashed into the back of Horne's head. The force of it slammed him forward to trip over Gideon, who was trying to rise. Horne plunged through the open door and measured his length on the puddled stone outside. Breathing heavily, Theo followed, retrieving his pistol from where the Tygran had flung it aside, then helped Gideon to his feet.

'My fault,' Gideon said, wincing. 'Not in full armour ... should have been ...' His grip on Theo's shoulder tightened as he looked at the fallen Horne and pointed. 'How is that possible ...'

In the mud and the rain, Nathaniel Horne was stirring. Theo shivered, felt the hairs prickle on his arms, then growled and stepped out into the downpour, leaving Gideon propped against the door frame with the revolver in his hand.

Horne was reaching up one hand behind his neck, fumbling for the axe haft. Theo gritted his teeth, bent down and tore the axe free. And paused a second, staring. Horne made no sound, there was no blood on the blade, and in the gaping head wound something silver squirmed . . .

A kind of terror crawled in the pit of Theo's stomach, giving him a new energy. He nimbly stepped to one side, turned and brought the axe down on the bared neck. Horne's body spasmed, and it took another two blows to completely sever the head. Gasping, he kicked it off to the side, a sodden thing swathed in matted hair.

'Was he telling the truth?' Theo said, glancing at Gideon. 'Will Becker be here too?'

Gideon was treating his own wounds with a field kit and there was a flush to his features and an alacrity in his movements that Theo guessed had a chemical origin. Battlefield stimulants, he thought. Well, even we had those kineshi leaves to chew.

'Becker is here,' Gideon said. 'I saw him rappel in with a squad of Brolts on the other side of the crater. He has to be working with Kuros, which raises the question – where is the Hegemony ambassador and all of those flyers and gunships the Brolts supposedly had at their northern base?'

As if in reply, they heard a rumble of explosions in the distance, like far-off thunder.

'Giant's Shoulder,' Theo said.

Gideon nodded. 'It doesn't change our overall objective, just makes it that much more complicated ...'

'My God,' Theo said, slapping a hand against his forehead. 'Rory! – I have to find him, make sure he's okay ...'

'What would he do, Theo?' Gideon said. 'If he was cut off by this chaos, would he try to find a safe place to hide or go get the bomb then head towards ...'

'The second,' Theo said with a grim shake of the head. '*Ja*, he would try to complete his mission.'

Gideon bent and picked up Horne's beam pistol from the ground, wiped away beads of rain and checked the charge indicator. Then he handed back Theo's revolver and gave a cold smile. 'Right, Theo – you should climb up to the base and go after him, keep him safe. I on the other hand will gather together my men and go and hunt down that piece of filth, Becker.'

'Wish I could go with you. Best of Darien luck, eh?'

'You too, my friend. Good hunting and see you on the other side.'

Theo raised his eyebrows. 'And which side is that?'

'The side where we've fought and won, and sit back drinking beer in front of a roaring fire, and tell huge lies about our bravery!'

'Ah, yes,' Theo said. 'I'll be there, all right. Just be sure to keep me a seat!'

The last he saw of the Tygran captain was a wave through the drenching rain before he headed over to the rope ladder, wiped the water from his face and started to climb.

30

KUROS

Gunships circled and swooped through the night sky, pounding Giant's Shoulder with pulse rounds, missiles and bomblets. The promontory had become a field of fire yet the combat mechs were still holding out, replying with a variety of ranged weapons, while the defence battery gave back as good as it was getting. Some five hundred metres above the action, veiled by the pouring rain, another gunship maintained a holding pattern: from inside the main passenger compartment, Utavess Kuros stared down with exhilarated fascination and a sense of approaching triumph. How the game had shifted! Just hours ago he was nought but a mind trapped in his own head, imprisoned and humiliated by a pair of traitorous machine intelligences. Now he was leading the assault to regain possession of the ancient Forerunner artefact while in near space an immense Hegemony armada was poised to crush a pitiful, Imisilled alliance of rebel scum who had thought to defy the greatest civilisation in half the galaxy!

Below, the Brolturan troops had established a beachhead on a rocky outcrop on the promontory's northern edge while a heavy-weapons section had set up an elevated fire point on the ridge just to the west. Together they were creating a murderous crossfire that hammered and ripped up any mechs straying out of cover. The main facility's primary tracking sensors had already been put out of commission by three aerial jump teams, two of them fighting off combat mechs while the third set charges around the armoured sensor cluster. All of the five-man teams had died, shot or clawed to pieces, but not before the sensors were wrecked. Which forced the battery systems to rely on secondary short-range detectors that were more easily fooled by Brolturan countermeasures.

As well as the naked eye, Kuros was observing the ongoing assault on a wide holoplane hanging down over the strategic overview table. An infrared subframe showed the hotspots of engaged units, with tags distinguishing between body heat and mech cooling manifolds. Another subframe was a more symbolic representation, revealing weapon types, rates of fire, hit accuracy percentages, and casualties. Yet another was an enhanced composite, showing the whole of the top of Giant's Shoulder in pale blue-grey with the glare of the defence floods filtered out. The rain was like a succession of ghostly sheets trailing and swirling across.

An auxiliary holopanel provided updates and occasional vid-reports from the other ambushes taking place. Becker's strike against Tusk Mountain had successfully sabotaged the insurgents' preparations so there would be no interference from that direction. Vashutkin's operation to prevent bands of Spiralists from reaching the northern ridges had not been as successful – one of his three flyers had been shot down by a shoulder-launched missile, forcing him to land on the northern ridge and set up defensive positions.

The only thing missing was any confirmation of the presence of the mechs' controlling intelligence, this entity known as the Legion Knight. But detailed scans had turned up no evidence to corroborate it – whoever was directing the combat mechs had to be holed up in the fortified building.

Once we've cut off the legs and the hands, then we'll deal with the poisonous head.

Even before he completed the thought, a hot bright explosion split the night as a missile or an energy bolt finally reached the battery's innards. That first eruption was followed by two larger ones as the ammunition detonated. Chunks of burning wreckage flew in all directions, some pieces falling over the edge of the promontory in fiery groundward arcs. Kuros allowed himself a wide and satisfied grin before telling the attendant flight officer, 'Down – have the pilot take us closer, within safety margins.'

Moments later the gunship dropped to 200 metres above the war-torn promontory. At that height the craft began to attract some enemy fire but it seemed half-hearted and uncoordinated. A mixture of explosive, frag and EMP missiles were falling among the mechs with greater accuracy now and the infrared view was showing that their numbers were down to less than a score.

Sensing victory, Kuros ordered his officers to prepare for a final push. Ground units moved up to forward positions on the promontory, now plunged into gloom, while the other gunships and flyers circled lower in the unceasing rain. Jump teams landed on the fortification unimpeded and from the balconies opened fire on the last defending mechs. Kuros smiled and ordered his gunship closer to the fortified facility, to hover above it. He could already envisage the moment when he stepped down onto the paved area before the entrance.

Alerts blinked on the enhanced overview – the combat mechs were on the move. In unison they were leaping out from behind armoured shelters and shielding to charge straight towards the rear of the promontory. The troops dug in there opened fire, pouring a stream of energy bolts and HE rounds into the oncoming machines, aided by airborne units and the heavy-weapon crews on the ridge. Almost half of the mechs were brought down or destroyed outright by the time the survivors reached the Brolturan positions ... which they either leaped over or swerved around, their metal carapaces gleaming in galloping precision, their taloned limbs pounding the ground, ignoring the troops as they dashed up the rocky slope, heading north.

Kuros watched the frantic retreat with an amused contempt. Either some consensus or collective self-preservation had been triggered or their master had ordered them to flee, confident that the facility fortifications would foil any assault. Later, once the Hegemony had fully tightened its grip on this world, he would have them all hunted down ...

More alerts appeared, sidebar sensor displays tracking a spectrum of other variables. They indicated energy spikes at a number of locations inside Giant's Shoulder, running in a line from the tapered sea-facing point westwards towards the ridge at the rear.

Suddenly more spikes appeared, this time from either

flank of the promontory, and he heard a sequence of thunderous cracks. An awful suspicion formed in his mind and he was about to order the gunship to gain height when the sensors picked up another big energy spike from the rear, close to the ridge ... and on the holopanel he saw the ground there explode upwards, followed by another explosion and another, immense eruptions of rock and dirt, as if the rocky massif was being hammered from beneath by something trying to escape. The force of the multiple blasts was sending stone debris flying high. Kuros felt the acceleration as the pilot banked the gunship away with the jets opened to full thrust, but it was too late. Massive chunks and splinters of rock rose out of the growing clouds and smashed into the gunship.

Most of the right-side suspensors were crushed immediately. The thrusters shrieked as they chewed themselves into wreckage. The gunship wheeled away, plunging towards the hilly woods and fields below, and the last thing Kuros saw on the holopanel was Giant's Shoulder collapsing amid billows of dust.

31

LEGION

From the shadows of a high, sheltered crag on one of the northern ridges, the Legion Knight watched the demolition of Giant's Shoulder. Via the lenses and sensors of his last few remaining probes and aerial flyers he was able to observe the sequential detonations and the rising wave of rubble that engulfed and pulverised the craft containing Kuros. And felt a warm satisfaction which complemented the delicious irony of it all.

From the tracking of Spiralist and Human groups over the last day or more, the Legion Knight had deduced that a joint attack on Giant's Shoulder before dawn was likely. The promontory was already rigged with augmented burrower charges designed to open the warpwell up to the air. Thus he had been preparing to lure the Humans and their allies by retreat onto Giant's Shoulder, thereby destroying them with one grand act of demolition. But then the Brolturans, led by that self-important fool Kuros, had launched a pre-emptive strike against the Humans at their mountain base while he placed himself between the jaws of death.

<A helpful self-important fool. Thank you, Ambassador, for making my task that much easier>

Fighting was still going on at Tusk Mountain so both main adversaries had been thwarted. On the other hand, his own on-board detectors were picking up faint signs of activity from another quarter, a certain energy pattern signifying ancient dangers.

<A Uvovo servant strives to link together the aged junctions of the Forerunner web that once tapped into the primal energies of this planet. Linkages are made and the archaic forces respond but the linkages are few and only a meagre trickle of that raw, titanic flood creeps forth. Even on the forest moon, that conglomeration of ecosphere and biosentience seems torpid and weak before the unleashed violence of space-born conflict, proof of indecision or delusion, or some other degenerate form of paralysis. Who or what remains which can stand in the way of the Legion of Avatars?>

On the visual feed the destruction of Giant's Shoulder ground on. The ancient Uvovo workings had caved in on themselves, their smashed ruins buried in the toppling chaos. Underpinning layers and supportive masses were blasted apart, while the sheer weight of the upper section aided in the shattering of those beneath. At the same time, the explosions along the flanks created paths for the tons of collapsing debris that soon built up in heaps around the promontory's base.

At last the cascade of rubble slowed and petered out. Giant's Shoulder had become a truncated stump of its former self and from the jumbled mass of cracked and tumbled rock a strong silver-blue glow emanated. As the rain gradually cleared the dust from the air, soaking the mounds of boulders and shards, more details resolved out of the murk. The warpwell was visible, a bright, uncluttered circle – any pieces of rock, large or small, that landed on it were ejected with considerable force.

Astonishingly, the Knight was still receiving data from the hyperspace scanner, a device he had managed to lower gradually into the warpwell nearly a day ago. Since then it had showed the presence of some kind of mass far, far below, either something large or a large, dense formation of smaller objects. Now, post-demolition, there was little change.

<It may take another day or more for the Legion outriders to arrive. Thus the well will have to be guarded, protected. None of the powers fighting over this world has the ability to harm the well itself yet no chances will be taken>

The Knight stirred from the natural rock platform amongst the high crags, carefully, stealthily wending his way down on suspensors. As he did he sent a signal to all units for a status update and was pleasantly surprised at the number of responders and the number that were combat-ready. He mapped out several patrol zones and sentry points near the well and signalled the assignments.

On his way to the half-demolished promontory he glided over a steep ravine at the head of which were the burning wrecks of two Brolturan heavy flyers, sheets of flame lighting up the rocky defile, whirling sparks rising as the rain came down. There were a few bodies, Sendrukan and some from the Spiralist races, but everyone else seemed to have fled.

The Knight was less than a hundred metres from the ruin of Giant's Shoulder, from the silver-blue glow now shining powerfully up from amid the rubble, when a priority signal came through from the scanning device in the well. Amazement turned to exhilaration. All of the hopes and plans, struggles and reversals had led him to this point. He came to a halt and increased his altitude with his suspensors, noticing that the warpwell was getting brighter, its silver-blue glow becoming harsher, more actinic, while taking on a more defined, conelike shape thrusting up to pierce the cloud layer.

Then the signal from the hyperspace scanner cut out. A moment later a dark object flew up out of the well, followed by another two, no, three, outriders of the Legion. They slowed to circle the radiant cone below the cloud cover. The Knight's few remaining static sensors and mobile probes sent back images of three black-carapaced cyborgs bristling with hooked spines, their effectuators equipped with elaborate cutters, drills and pincers. The Knight couldn't be sure about their type but he guessed that they might be modified shock-scouts. Their hull markings were basic white-on-black yet the characters were unfamiliar to him. That did not prevent him from sending a welcome signal.

<Greetings, brothers in convergence! Welcome to the realm that will be ours. Welcome to battle, welcome to war, the seedbed of our inevitable triumph!>

There was no reply, but the three outriders stopped circling and swooped down in his direction. The closer they came, the more he saw how patched and repaired they were, the black colour masking mendings made with unmatched materials. They drew near, hovering, all three spread out.

>Relic< said one.

>Antique< said another.

>A behinder< said the third, who went on >Speak, old one ... speak your oldness<

<I made a messenger and sent it down the warpwell to find you and guide you all to freedom> the Knight said, now uneasy. <Where are the Legion's leaders? I must speak with them>

>Great Legion needs only one leader< the third outrider said >the Great King!<

Below, more Legion cyborgs had been emerging and spiralling upwards. The Knight noticed that the warpwell had expanded and that part of its rim now overhung the rock flanks of what remained of Giant's Shoulder. Some strange force, however, was distorting the surrounding rock and earth, compacting the polychromatic supporting mass that melded the wider well into the surrounding stone. Then he realised why the warpwell had grown when he saw what was rising out of it. It was nothing less than an amalgamation of hundreds, probably thousands of Legion cyborgs, their fused carapaces clearly visible beneath the criss-cross webbing of welded metal spars and rods. Roughly 80 metres across and perhaps 120 long, it had a curve-backed profile and was ringed with heavy weapon barrels, muzzles and launcher ports.

The Knight was assailed by despair even as his thoughts spun with speculation. Confinement in the crushing, lightless cold of that hyperspace prison for millennia must have put the Legion of Avatars under horrific pressure. In the end, the principles of convergence could not withstand the savage demands of that grim captivity – who knows what cycles of conflict and adaptation they went through to reach this point?

>Behold Great King< said the third cyborg. >Enemies all around, enemies above, enemies below. This world will be eaten, other worlds of legend will be eaten. Stars of legend will burn, will make the night into day for ever< It moved in the Knight's direction, drill-tipped tentacles outstretched. >You are old one, you are old parts! Be thankful, your thinking flesh will be eaten by Great King<

And it attacked, lunging forward. The Knight destroyed it with the beam cannons that were fitted to his underhull. Undeterred, the other two cyborgs rushed him in a pincer movement while howling gibberish over the comm channel. Behind them, a swarm of about thirty peeled off from the thousands now swirling about the Great King and swooped towards him.

<The Legion of Avatars has become a barbarian horde>

Feeling the weight of an immense sadness, he dealt with the other two and prepared to meet the oncoming madness, and his doom.

32

ROBERT

From the wide misty valley where Robert escaped being crushed by the gargantuan, half-seen wagon, they climbed flights of ancient, cracked stairs to a grassy plateau. In the distance, mountains reared like a barrier while much closer a semi-overgrown paved path led from the head of the stairs off to the left in a rising incline, disappearing into hilly woods.

'Do you hear that?' said Reski Emantes, hovering on near-silent rotors.

'No, I ... wait ...' Robert cocked his head, trying to scan with his ears. 'Hmm, yes, faintly.' Barely audible, he could just make out a regular thudding.

'Coming from along that pathway, as well.' The drone tilted and glided along at head height. Robert shrugged and followed.

Only minutes after crossing into the trees, the paved path faded away in the undergrowth.

'Damn, but I was walking on it just moments ago,' he said. 'We'll have to backtrack ...'

'Normally I would have something devastatingly cutting to say on the subject of Human senses,' the drone said. 'But it would appear that my own are proving equally feeble.'

Robert gave the drone a considering look. After they were separated at the river, Reski Emantes had reappeared to rescue him from the clutches of grotesque Vor-like humanoids. The drone now looked as if it had been remodelled with pre-atomic-age materials and techniques. Riveted seams, propellers keeping it aloft rather than suspensors, and a spring-loaded bolt-caster rather than a multi-targetable beam weapon.

'Surely we can deduce a reasonable direction from the way we came,' he said.

'If the environment wasn't the mutable thoughtscape of an ancient and powerful entity,' the drone said, 'that would be a reasonable suggestion.'

'Well, look,' he said, pointing at a bushy rise a dozen paces away. 'We came over that higher ground which we reached by following the path so we should be going *this* way ...'

And when he turned round, the drone was gone, utterly, not a sign of it in any direction. He shouted its name but nothing came back from the surrounding woods.

Except for the crack of a twig breaking underfoot. Robert whirled round – and saw the face of his daughter, Rosa, staring at him for a single startled moment before she ducked out of sight and darted away.

Amazed, startled, fearful, he plunged forward after her, barging through bushes and undergrowth, shouting her name, then pausing abruptly to listen for the sound of her running. Then off in pursuit again. But doubt rose in his mind like common sense catching up with him. Why would she be here? Was it likely that the Godhead would know her image, or was it more probable that the thoughtscape was reacting to him, that its meta-quantal properties were reflecting back to him important landmarks of his own subconscious? It was a conundrum, this bizarre confrontation with the autonomous imagery from both his own and the Godhead's subconscious.

But despite understanding this rational conjecture, he knew he would have to keep up the chase, to find out where he was being led, to see if she would say anything true.

Through the trees he tracked glimpses of her. She seemed to be wearing a pale blue two-piece with a hood, which was easily spotted amongst the wood's darker colours. Not once did she pause to look back, yet she did not seem to be taking any precautions against being seen.

After more than five minutes of unrelenting pursuit she led him to where the trees thinned into a meadow dotted with lush bushes. On the other side of it, a sheer cliff face loomed, its heights veiled in low-hanging cloud. Crossing the meadow, Rosa broke into a run and seemed to be near the foot of the cliffs when she turned to the side and stepped down out of sight.

As Robert left the shadows of the woods behind, the faint thudding sound from before sounded louder and clearer. He hurried towards where he last saw Rosa and saw that it was the head of a rack of worn stone steps winding down to a steep-sided gully. Rosa was visible at the foot of it, crouching as she moved along the gully and round a corner. Without hesitation, Robert hurried downwards.

It was warm at the bottom, a rocky channel above

which cliffs reared to either side. The air had a peculiar, sharp taint to it. The thudding sounded metallic, and was irregular, two or three impacts followed by three or four heavier ones, a cluster of lighter ones, then two louder ones. Only when he reached and rounded the corner were his questions answered, then hardly how he expected.

Half in and half out of a huge cave mouth was an immense heap of machines. Robert recognised bots, drones, droids, vehicles small and large, torn-up sections of larger craft, and domestic devices too, washing machines, lawn-cutters, automaids, entertainment consoles, all manner and all sizes of holoscreens, as well as industrial power tools, engines, road-menders and many others. A very big brick-red hand dragged a piece down off the pile and onto a black slab of some chipped, unreflective material where a fearsome, ridge-faced sledgehammer wielded by another big brick-red hand fell upon it repeatedly, crushing it flat. The compacted debris was then tossed into a large rusty hopper, the contents of which were presumably tipped into the blast furnace whose hot bright maw gaped just within the cave. At the centre of it all was a brick-red giant, hairless, clad in tattered hide breeks, his snaggle-tooth mouth muttering and growling.

And there, on the other side of the A-sided framework that cradled the hopper, was a pale-blue-clad form creeping along behind the small mounds of flattened wrecks that had missed their target.

Robert stared at the grotesque scene, the grumbling giant, the hammered machines, the hungry furnace. *What is this?* he wondered. *What is it doing in the Godhead's subconscious?*

There was no time to lose if he wanted to stay on Rosa's trail. Crouching along at the foot of the cliffs, he hurried to the path Rosa had taken, slipping behind crushed, mangled metal while the red giant went about its hammering business. Except that he had gone barely a dozen wary steps when a deep gravelly voice said:

'Halt! You have the stink of machines about you!'

Robert froze, wondering how he had been detected.

'Because I have good ears, device-lover!' said the giant. 'And a good nose which tells me what you smell of!'

'Why am I being stopped?' Robert said from behind the heap of battered metal. 'I saw someone else go past ...'

'Them ladies are permitted to roam – s'orders. Intruders must be put to the test!'

'Does this test involve any pressing, squeezing, crushing or even possibly hammering?'

'You will submit to the test! All machines must be destroyed!'

'I'm not a ...'

He gasped and flinched when something struck the side of the hopper assembly with such force that it tipped over, threatening to come down on him. But its centre of gravity pulled it back to crash down, crumpled sheets of debris spilling out. Robert turned and ran past the furnace, feeling the heat of it burning in his face, neck and hands.

A big slab of compacted metal slammed into the cave wall just a few feet before him. Sparks and splinters of stone sprayed in all directions and he felt something nick his forehead.

'You dare! You dare enter my hall! Machine-lover filth!'

Another crashing noise but further back for some reason. Then there was a whirring noise descending from above – it was the drone, Reski Emantes, looking even more retro than before.

'I can see that you're having lots of fun,' it said.

'Is that wood panelling on your upper casing? Most distinguished.'

'It's not what you would call robust. Look, Robert Horst, I know who you've been following and you need to catch up with them. When I cause the diversion, be ready to run ...'

'Wait, what do you mean by "them"?'

Too late, the drone was already aloft and flying over to buzz around the red giant's head. With deafening roars and hammer blows ringing in his ears, Robert scrambled past the furnace and made a dash for a low tunnel at the back of the cave. He slipped on loose gravel and almost stumbled but managed to keep his feet. Glancing back, he saw the giant holding the drone in one hand and bellowing incoherently at it for several seconds before slamming it down onto the black slab and hoisting that hammer up high ...

Robert turned away and hurried off along the curving tunnel, wincing as he heard the repeated impacts. Yet this was the meta-quantal thoughtscape of the Godhead and since his own subconsciousness was determined to have Reski Emantes as a companion it was very likely that the drone would show up again.

The tunnel was strewn with pebbles and grit and lit by strange veinlike growths that erupted from the walls every ten paces or so, giving off an amber glow. The curve tightened into an upward spiral and the tunnel floor began to look clean, swept and surfaced in some dimpled plastic material. The glowing veins became chevron-shaped light sources pointing in the direction he was going, which made him smile.

At last he came to a large triangular entrance with double doors which smoothly swung upwards when he approached. As he walked through he was met by a tall woman in a dark trouser suit and carrying a slim datapad. She had short black hair and pretty features offset by a formal, somewhat impassive air.

'Thank you for coming, Ambassador,' she said with a slight Scottish accent. 'Now that you're here, we will shortly bring in the guests. If you follow me I'll introduce you to the observers.'

Robert smiled and nodded, feeling almost used to the incongruities being presented by the Godhead's subconscious. *But is this merely an elaborate stage for me to caper across, or some form of challenge or test?*

Through a pale blue lobby he was led into a high-ceilinged auditorium, emerging from a side door. To the left was a curved bank of empty seating and on the right was an elevated platform with a cluster of low easy chairs, two of which were occupied. Behind the platform a row of tall windows looked out on an astonishing sight, what appeared to be the towers, blocks, domed gardens and covered walkways of a city in the sky. Architectural styles seemed to derive from the old sleek, mirrored teknokratia school but its application to an airborne metropolis was breathtaking.

And made up, he thought. *All this is just the fancy*

*and spectacle of the Godhead's subconscious reflecting
my own experiences back at me via the meta-quantal
flow.* He smiled. *But this is one place that I could imagine being real. In fact, it does have a certain consistency
to its design, a kind of purposeful authenticity.*

His guide led him up to the platform, where two
other women were waiting.

'Ambassador, this is Observer Catriona and Observer
Corazon.'

They were both diminutive women, dressed as formally as the first, but the contrast in their demeanour
was marked. Observer Catriona was slight as a dancer
with straight, shoulder-length brunette hair and an
expression as unperturbed as that of Robert's greeter.
Observer Corazon, on the other hand, had black curly
hair and an elfin face that positively glowed with a kind
of bold charisma. When she smiled it was like being
dazzled.

He shook hands and was offered a chair between
them. As he sat, he looked questioningly at the woman
who had welcomed him.

'Pardon me, but are you not allowed to tell me your
name?'

'I am Supervisor Julia. We will now admit the guests.'

Behind the top tier of seats a line of doors opened and
the audience, all women, filed steadily, quietly into the
hall. Although they were all ages and various physiques,
they all had sandy blonde hair and the same unmistakable features.

They were all Rosa.

Robert could feel the hairs prickling on the back of
his neck. There had to be at least three hundred versions

of Rosa arriving, settling into seats, chatting with neighbours, glancing or peering or staring at him with expressions of delight or accusation or indifference.

A new species of nightmare, he thought, wondering if he would be allowed to leave. But when he glanced over at the door by which he had entered he saw only a blank stretch of wall. Same with the entrances at the top of the seat tiers, gone. Swallowing, he smiled nervously. *There is an element of purpose to this.*

The woman called Supervisor Julia walked to the front of the dais.

'Thank you all for attending. As you know, this is only an informal hearing, therefore the duration is expected to be malleable. Now, Observer Catriona will open the case for the reproach.'

The slender brunette got to her feet, took a silver penlike object from her pocket and pointed it at midair. A blur-edged cube appeared with frozen darkness within it.

'This should be familiar to all present,' Observer Catriona said.

The darkness unfroze, became a replay of vid footage he was indeed very familiar with, the news report of the clash between the Life and Peace flotilla and a Hegemony cruiser at a waypoint on the Metraj border. The warning messages, the visual excerpts from those aboard the *Pax Terra*, the fleeting glimpse of Rosa among them, the cruiser opening fire, the explosions, the awful images from aboard the smaller craft. It took place nearly a year ago, but no matter how many times he saw it the rawness of his grief remained a black corrosive thing.

The recording ended with the peace vessel *Pax Terra* reduced to a leaking, battered wreck, after which the holoprojection vanished. Robert drew a deep, shaky breath and exhaled, feeling some of the sorrow ease.

'A number of factors contributed to this tragedy,' said Observer Catriona. 'Yet the most significant were the actions of Rosa's father, Robert Horst – as a high-ranking Earthsphere diplomat it was well within his abilities to compel his daughter to abstain from taking part in such a hazardous exploit ...'

'Rosa would never give in to browbeating,' Robert said.

'You could have had her restrained, or confined,' the woman said. 'If you had, she'd be alive today.'

'What kind of father would lock up ...' But the words died in his mouth when he realised that everyone in the Rosa audience was watching him intently.

'The other main factor was the macro-political one,' Observer Catriona went on. 'Robert Horst was the senior Earthsphere negotiator, both before the invasion of the Yamanon Domain and after. If anyone was in a position to engineer the withdrawal of Earthsphere and Hegemony forces it was him. Yet here we are eight years and millions of deaths later ...'

'Excuse me, Supervisor Julia, but has this hearing not strayed from its original focus?' said Observer Talavera, who got to her feet, smiled at Robert, smoothed her black suit and faced the audience.

Supervisor Julia nodded. 'Observer Talavera may now state the case for the probity.'

'My esteemed colleague has made an immense leap in her logic,' she began. 'Ambassador Horst started as a tragic mourning father but has turned into a vee-drama supervillain! Such a vigorous method of reproach, such an active examination!'

Talavera positively glowed with a kind of combative wit while her adversary, Catriona, remained composed as she returned to her chair.

'In fact, the truth is that Horst was simply a good father. Not a perfect father, just a good one. And certainly, parents have a duty of care but when a child reaches its maturity how much responsibility do they still carry? Is a parent still responsible if their child murders someone? What if the child becomes a parent in their turn – is the grandparent responsible for the grandchild?'

Talavera's demeanour was now level, compassionate with a dose of humorous puzzlement.

'The truth is that Ambassador Horst and his wife did the best they could till, at last, their daughter was able to fly free on her own, make her own decisions, yes, and mistakes.' She put one hand out towards Robert. 'The truth is that the ambassador deserves our support and our sympathy, not condemnation. He has done nothing to feel guilty about – his daughter made up her own mind, she made her choice and the consequences were hers alone. Guilt lies with those whose fingers pull the triggers, whose hands hold the knife, or push the button, or measure out the poison. Only they are guilty ...'

'But that's not true.'

Every pair of eyes looked at him. Talavera turned her head to regard him, a cool smile on her lips, eyebrows arched slightly, as if awaiting an explanation. Robert could only speak the feelings that came from that old ache in his chest.

'It's not true because I still carry the guilt,' he said. 'Doesn't matter how it's explained, or how rationally or logically it's interpreted, I know the fault is mine. I should have done something, done what was needed. But I didn't ... didn't even try. So the guilt is still mine to carry.'

Smiling, Talavera shook her head and, without taking her eyes off Robert, made a sweeping gesture with her arm. The audience of Rosas and the other women vanished. Startled, Robert stared about him for a moment, then back at Talavera in a kind of slow-dawning comprehension.

'Not so much an entrance as an unveiling,' he said. 'It's a great honour to finally meet you.'

The Godhead shrugged. 'Actually, it's a little over a thousandth of me, but that still amounts to a considerable portion of my attention. Ever since you became involved with Darien and the Construct I've been watching the changes and quandaries you've managed to survive. The sheer resilience you've displayed has been inspiring, which is why this matter of guilt is so bothersome.'

The Godhead, looking like a woman called Talavera, came and sat on the arm of the chair next to Robert's.

'You see, this is all about body chemistry and mind-body image imprinting. Just as a child makes its parents part of its world, so too do parents with their offspring. You've admitted that the rational arguments are correct yet you still carry this terrible burden – well, that is nothing more than your mind-body image still trying to cope with the loss of a vestigial part, and the turbulence that it causes in your body chemistry.' The woman laughed and patted his shoulder. 'That's it, that's all. I hereby pronounce you innocent of all charges, by virtue of the powers invested in me by myself, et cetera.'

Robert gazed at this improbable personage, listening to its rationalisation for a guilt-free existence, wanting to shout in its face that his feelings weren't merely the flow of chemicals in his bloodstream, yet held back by the urge for self-preservation.

'I literally don't know what to say,' he muttered.

'Then listen,' the Godhead said. 'My origins stretch back to the dawn of an earlier universe. I've seen empires and entire species rise and fall; some I've aided, others I've sabotaged. I've seen intellects of surpassing enlightenment pierce the workings of reality to the interlocking enigmas beneath, and I've seen minds full of blankness devise and build star-spanning tyrannies of regimented cruelty and turn whole planets into machines of pain.

'And yet existence is not merely confined to cycles of struggle – there is also transcendence, the elevation to a higher plane of being. After a great many centuries of study I have found the way, Robert, and very soon I will ascend to a superior continuum. If you wish, you can accompany me.'

The Godhead watched him closely, dark eyes intently fixed upon him. How strange it was to hear such grandiose pronouncements and offers come from the lips of a black-haired Human woman. Yet Robert could sense the presence behind that stare, speculating that it consisted of a bit more than a thousandth of its colossal attention.

He swallowed. Time to throw self-preservation to the wind.

'I'm humbled by this astonishing offer – I can hardly see how I could be considered worthy of such an honour ...'

'You deserve it, Robert,' Talavera said. 'Down through the aeons, only a handful of sentients have reached the place where you now stand.'

'Understanding this adds new lustre to my good fortune,' Robert said as he moved round to sit on the back of the chair, gazing out at the city in the clouds. 'But before I decide one way or another, I wonder if you could clarify a few puzzles for me.'

Talavera was still smiling, yet motionless in her regard. 'Go on.'

'The Vor and the Shyntanil, a pair of barbaric predatory species which you brought back from the brink of extinction ...'

'Hardly relevant,' Talavera cut in. 'There are many subspecies and sophont offshoots performing a range of tasks for me, some of whom you would find highly commendable.'

Robert watched a soft billow of cloud pass through the towers and domes outside.

'I do not doubt what you say – it's just my experiences which raise these questions, but I'll leave that one aside. Another thing which puzzled me was the vermax, which are apparently technivores, yet which are also your servants. Why would you use such creatures?'

'Again, this is not relevant.' Talavera stood, smile replaced by a dark look. 'This strikes me as a technique of hesitation or even avoidance, Robert, this questioning and judging. Come now – I am offering you the ultimate prize, transcendence, an eternity of enlightenment, the chance to converse with those who have already ascended to a greater wisdom. My patience is wearing thin – you must choose!'

'Oh fool, fool, powerful fool! Don't you understand? He has already chosen!'

Snarling, Talavera turned towards the source of the voice. Robert looked also and laughed when he saw the drone Reski Emantes gliding smoothly across the empty auditorium, drawing near. The drone had returned to its original flattened ovoid shape, only now its exterior shimmered with a beautiful polychromatic, shifting aura.

'He has already chosen,' the drone went on, 'because he's seen through you. Despite your godling powers and near-limitless array of elaborate spectacle, he has discerned the cold death force that lies at the root of your every thought and deed.'

Anger burned in Talavera's eyes. 'Robert, take no notice of this prattling echo of nothing. You can come with me and leave all your pain and your guilt behind – for ever. Freed from burdens you never deserved to carry, you can move towards perfection and a supremacy unimaginable at this level of existence.'

Robert listened, swallowed, considered this offer which shook his self-belief to its foundations. There it was, liberation from the endless remorse, from the corrosive loss, from the shadow of mourning that followed him always. All he had to do was deny the ties that bind, the memories that coloured his inner world ... deny that Rosa had ever existed.

'No,' he said. 'I can't pretend. I cannot give up even the memories of her ...'

Talavera glared at the flattened ovoid drone.

'So this *thing* is yours after all, a *puppet* which cannot see or choose! I will not be diverted from my plans! There will be an end to you ...'

At this, Talavera let out a deafening shriek that shattered the auditorium windows while she held out fire-wreathed hands towards Robert. A boiling wall of flame flew towards him. He staggered back, arm raised to shield his face in desperation, tripped on something and fell backwards ...

And opened his eyes with a startled jerk, provoking a stab of pain from somewhere in his body. He was lying back at an angle and his vision seemed a little bleary – he could see some kind of tiled ceiling but it was indistinct, opaque. And his limbs were restrained, held down with cuffs, but he soon discovered that any attempt to struggle stirred up spikes of pain that twisted in his legs and burned in his torso from spine to innards. He gasped and moaned.

'I'm sorry about the lack of painkillers – types suitable for Human biology are hard to come by.'

Robert tried to speak but there was something in his mouth.

'Sorry, that's just a feeding tube ...'

Something shifted overhead, a translucent canopy, he realised, and a nozzle was manipulated, tugged from the corner of his mouth. He felt a vague writhing in his gullet as the slender tube was retracted.

'What's hap ...' His voice gave out, dry and hoarse. A straw was slipped into his mouth and he sucked down cold refreshing fluid.

'What's happened to me?' he said at last.

'When you crossed through the periphery portal, a vermax closed in after you, crashed into your craft and nearly destroyed both it and you. The vermax died when the portal switched to abeyance mode, and your craft's emergency systems kept you alive long enough for me to gather enough remotes to cut you free and bring you to a place of safety.'

Robert tilted his head left and right and saw enough to figure out that he was lying on a light blue couch with rough grey walls on either side. He swallowed more fluid.

'How bad is it?'

'Your spine is broken in three places, both legs have compound fractures and your left shoulder was also broken. In order to carry out repairs I used a neural cutout and interfaced your conscious mind with the outer margins of the Godhead's thoughtflow. Your instincts for exploration, however, guided you straight towards the theatre of his desires and motivations.'

'That informal hearing,' Robert said. 'It didn't end on a ... positive note.' *And neither did my arrival.*

'You certainly did well to resist his flattery and bribes, and to see through him. It gave me time to stabilise your condition and move you here.'

'I've met enough narcissistic thugs to know one when I see one,' Robert said. 'But all that doesn't tell me much about who and what you are. And would you *please* raise my head so that I can see!'

'Of course.'

A motor hummed beneath the couch and his head inched up, permitting a better view of the room. It looked like a box made of unsurfaced plascrete, walls, floor and a ceiling that were compacted grey extrude flattened and left unfaced. There were two long shuttered windows in the wall in front of him while several medical machines flanked him, monitoring, beeping faintly as they delivered nutrients and medication. The devices were all worn and scratched, not unlike a dark green and brown machine that hovered to his left, the direction where the voice had come from. It had the shape of a small disc sitting atop a larger one. From an open slot in the lower disc glassy sensors regarded him.

'Greetings to you, Robert Horst. I am speaking to you via this remote because I am the Godhead's eternal companion, of which he will never be free. I am his conscience, his empathy, that part of him which even after all this time remains connected to the workings of reality, especially to the consequences of his actions.'

Robert stared, thoughts whirling. 'Empathic conscience ... manifesting as a distinct personality?'

'The Godhead is very old. He has experienced several waves of exponential change and growth. He has subjected the very fabric of his core awareness to a process of enhancement and reshaping which, in retrospect, I realised was his way of excising parts that he found disturbing. But he cannot escape me and cannot erase me. It is pain in the end that drives him but he is unable to understand it, unable to come to terms with it. All he can do is try to escape from it.'

Robert's eyes widened. 'He wasn't joking about this transcendence, was he? About ascending to another ... plane?'

'No, he is utterly serious and totally committed to his

plan, a grotesque strategy that depends on the mass murder of nearly a trillion living sentient creatures.'

Robert listened in growing horror as the empathic entity told him about an intricate plan to acquire anti-dark matter from hidden labs on Darien, to capture a team of genetically enhanced scientists from the colony, to load 500 missiles with the anti-dark matter which would then be used to create 500 synchronised super-novae ...

His initial incredulity made him want to laugh but the twinges in his chest dissuaded him.

'The whole thing sounds completely demented,' he said. 'But is it possible?'

'The Godhead has pursued this obsession for millennia,' the empathic entity said. 'He has studied the mystical creeds of a million worlds, some of which I too have observed. He is convinced that this vile act will bring him transcendence, that it will wipe away the memory of the mass suicide of the Tanenth, and that he will escape the pain and me for ever, the fool. But that is incidental to the slaughter that he would commit in the attempt.'

'Can this be stopped?' said Robert, wondering who could stop a god.

'Perhaps – but all the parts of his plan are now coming together. It really all began with the discovery of Darien. The Godhead saw how he could very easily prod the various powers into focusing on the ancient Forerunner device with the aim of drawing all available military forces away from those areas where the crucial elements of his scheme are now ongoing. He was even prepared to allow the warpwell to be unlocked so that the Legion of Avatars could escape, which is what has happened. So while battles and destruction swirl around Darien, the Godhead has already ascended a considerable distance up the tiers of hyperspace to confront one of his most dangerous adversaries. Look.'

The shutters lifted on the two windows. Beyond was a strange grey expanse, at first glance looking like the surface of an airless moon. But then Robert saw that the surface was in continual movement, slow ripples and heaves of regular forms, geometric shapes mixed with odd curved or bulbous things which he realised were bodily extremities, noses, fingers, ears, or at least what looked very like them. They reshaped and reformed, and often faces emerged wearing all manner of expressions and emotions only to be smoothed away by the next tide of undulations. He saw swelling hills that narrowed into wavering columns, or cubes that turned into buildings that toppled/melted into transient fissures, or orbs and pyramids that broke free of the oceanic amorphouscape to float through the air until snatched back down by tentacles with mouths.

'This is the physical aspect of the Godhead, at least his outer husk,' said the empathic entity. 'It's like a great ragged continent more than a thousand miles across. We are located on one of a few hundred immutable landmarks, a kind of tower once used as a platform for defences. Now, however, we rely on others for protection.'

Above the restless surface, the ships of the Vor and the Shyntanil flew in layered echelons, black organic outlines of the former, the big diamond carriers of the latter, all moving in one great formation through the pale blue emptiness of some hyperspace tier ...

Then he saw the sparkle and flash of ship-to-ship weaponsfire and in the distance an unmistakable conical, stepped edifice. The Construct's headquarters, the Garden of the Machines, now undoubtedly being defended by the AI-craft of the Aggression.

'So the Godhead is going after the Construct,' he said.

'As I said, Darien is the arena, the crucible where several fleets are now engaged in a titanic struggle, therefore the Construct presents the only serious obstacle to the Godhead's purpose.'

Robert stared out at the distant warfare, feeling infuriated at his own incapacity.

'You said that perhaps there was a way to stop the Godhead's insane plan,' he said. 'How would we do that?'

'It involves you and me,' the empathic entity said. 'Your memories of the Tanenth machine's simulation of its creators, and my memory of the Godhead's guilt over their suicide. And it will probably lead to our deaths.'

Robert smiled sardonically. 'Well, personally I don't believe that it's over until it's over. But let's hear it.'

33

THE CONSTRUCT

The siege of the Garden of the Machines was not going well. The battlefront between the Construct's Aggression ships and the vessels of the Vor and the Shyntanil was constantly shifting back and forth according to the rhythm of attacks and feints, surprise jumps, decoy manoeuvres, and the unseen war of datanet sabotage. In the overall aggregate could be seen the incontrovertible truth of the enemy's gradual and inexorable advance.

The Construct was monitoring the tactics of the defence, monitoring the decision-making of the strategic cognitives and the transrational solutions of the conjecturator subminds. At the same time it was overseeing the loading of the contingency craft, the means by which a new Garden of the Machines would be established in a secluded tier far away. It was also giving instructions to the military Rosas, the commanders of the last-ditch defences. Both they and the Roberts had turned out to be exemplars of adaptability and creativity. This, the first Garden of the Machines, might fall but the patterns of their mind-states would live on.

And simultaneously with all the foregoing, the

Construct was conducting a conversation with one unexpected visitor while a second waited in storage, frozen, inert.

'I am certain that he presents no risk,' said Reski Emantes, a copy of the drone AI that had remained back on Earth. 'I've scanned his code for sleeper scripts and cyst routines and came up empty. You conducted his original excision so I am sure you'll see that I've missed nothing.'

'That may be so,' the Construct said. 'And we may return to this matter later. First, explain why you came here.'

The copy of Reski Emantes was running in a surplus tutorial drone, a small boxy unit with about a dozen spidery articulata. The Construct was temporarily inhabiting a spindle-framed biped unit, and together they faced each other in a windowless inner chamber lit by a full-wall holoconsole. One of its screens was showing code scans and a virtuality sim of the stored AI known simply as Harry.

'I am here,' Reski Emantes said, 'to gain your help in rescuing the fractalised sentience of Julia Bryce.'

'The leader of the Enhanced research team,' the Construct said. 'Ever since they were abducted by the Talavera woman we have been unable to track them. If Bryce is now a fractalised data sentience, does that mean that her physical form is deceased?'

'It's somewhat complicated,' the drone said as it sent the Construct a databurst summary.

The Construct went over it, tracing Talavera's involvement in obtaining the anti-dark matter and abducting the Enhanced team. It noted Julia's partnership with the ex-Hegemony AI Harry and their collaboration with the Glow-savvy Nicodemus in their bravura political exploits. Now, it seemed, Talavera, the anti-dark-matter missiles and the Enhanced team had gone to the Great Hub, accompanied by a pair of Vor warships. The Julia sentience had been sent by Nicodemus to an automated Hegemony supply ship near the Great Hub via a data-access flow, along with a mid-cognitive AI as a guide. However, shortly after the downport all tiernet connections suddenly ceased. But the supply ship's ident was still registering on independent battle surveys carried out by military tracker guilds, hobbyist netcommunes who regularly sent disposable flyby probes into war zones.

'And you want me to travel to the Great Hub, find this supply vessel and rescue the Julia sentience,' the Construct said. 'Why?'

'Because Talavera is keeping her body alive, using its neural pathgrids in conjunction with the other Enhanced to run the missile launch and in-flight navigationals. If we can get her back into her own body, into her own head, perhaps she can shut the whole thing down. If not, five hundred stars and their planets and inhabitants could be obliterated.'

The Construct saw how all the disparate pieces fitted together – the Godhead's subtle aid to the forces of the Spiral Prophecy, their invasion of Darien guaranteeing aggressive responses from the Hegemony and the Imisil, the arrival of the remnants of the Legion of Avatars whose insensate savagery could annihilate all in its path; the revitalisation of the Vor and the Shyntanil; the attack on the Construct's power base; the ascent of the

Godhead itself and its anticipated emergence into an area of objective space where its presence would be mostly unopposed. And 500 stars that were targeted for destruction because ...

And that was the mystery, the great unknown 'why' that lay at the root of it all.

'What is your decision?' said Reski Emantes.

'A moment ...'

Prompted by a steady clamour of alerts, the Construct switched away from the inner chamber, dividing its cognitive awareness between the stream of battlefront feeds and the combat analyses flowing from its semi-autonomous partials. The general assessment was stark – Aggression vessels were falling back from the inner markers and their numbers were down to just over a hundred. The Garden of the Machines would be stormed by Shyntanil and Vor troops in less than fifteen minutes and the entire complex would be overrun in approximately twenty-three minutes.

Part of it sent revised orders to the Rosa squads, another gave new commands to the drones prepping two tierships in the main launch bay, and the rest of it addressed the drone Reski Emantes.

'I have decided to help you,' it said. 'Although you must realise that such a mission has a high chance of failure.'

'That is hardly a surprise,' the drone said. 'Given the various Human-related hazards I've had to deal with recently.'

'We will be travelling aboard a field-boosted tiership,' said the Construct. 'The first part of our flight will entail some risk as we will be acting as a diversion while my re-establisher vessel makes good its escape. Once it is safely away, our ship will set course for the Hegemony's Great Hub. I assume that you would prefer a more robust motility unit than this one.'

'I won't really feel safe in anything less than a multi-projector battledrone,' said Reski Emantes. 'Something like Perseusystems Ravager 9000 would do nicely.'

'My apologies, but all that is available are a few type twos and a type three.'

'I'll take the type three – at least it doesn't look like a triangular toy.'

34

JULIA

Through flicker-lit corridors, ice-bitten by vacuum, she hauled the last piece of their improvised getaway, a nearly full gas canister. The round-cornered cube was held in a plastic mesh sack snaplocked to a lug on the rear of her housing. It bounced and scuffed against the ridged deck covering but the impacts exerted noticeably less drag than on her previous excursions, proof that the cells powering the deck gravity were running down. She just hoped that they were independent of whatever source was running the recharge stations she had used several times already.

It had been less than twelve hours since she and Nicko, one of Nicodemus's net-sims, had sneaked aboard the Hegemony supply ship via a low-level stockload datalink. Once in the ship's active system, Nicko had altered their privileges priority to gain access to a greater range of subsystems. Tapping into the nav-sensor interface, they had skimmed through the views and scans of the immediate hyperspace vicinity, including the branching towers of the Great Hub and the four patrolling Hegemony heavy cruisers. The Great Hub, the master nexus for all AIs in the Hegemony and many of its client states, consisted of a main spindle axis about a kilometre long, and at its mid-point a polyhedral structure roughly a quarter of a kilom across; from many of its grey-silver facets jutted smaller tower spindles like the main axis, all of them branching at regular intervals.

That was their goal – with the supply ship's comm equipment, Nicko had promised that he could find a way to get them inside, into 'AI heaven', as he called it.

That enthusiastic optimism came to an abrupt end when an undetected missile struck the supply ship's stern, destroying the main thrusters. Nicko had acted without hesitation, employing a crash priority override to have them both transferred down to secondary cores on the maintenance deck. Then he had quickly searched for a maintenance bot with a generous memstore, found one and downported Julia into it. He was in the process of picking out one for himself when a second missile hit the hyperdrive and wiped out the main generators. Nicko had to use what was available, a crawler bot fitted for hold scrubbing.

From Julia's perspective, her bot was shaped like an upended oval bin with a pair of wheels at the base, a sensor cluster at the top and several toolarm niches spaced around its middle. An unlovely but functional design and certainly strong enough to cope with all the lifting and moving she had done in search of parts for the escape vehicle. With the gas canister scraping along behind her she followed a branch tunnel that curved up towards the upper stern. Minutes later she entered what had been a long compartment set aside for any live crew that came aboard. The impact of the second missile had torn away the hull here and some of the surrounding bulkheads, leaving it open to the vacuum and ionic flux of hyperspace. Most of the debris had floated away but she still had to bat aside a couple of fragments on her way to a particular couch near the rear.

The question of who had launched the attack was still unanswered, but since Talavera's ship and its Vor escorts had been heading this way it was likely that they were the culprits.

The gloomy radiance of hyperspace fitfully illuminated the outlines of fixed tables and wall lockers while a solitary emergency light shed a wavering blue glow from one of the remaining upper corners. As she drew near the couch she realised that there was no sign of Nicko – then one of the wall lockers swung open and a squat tracked bot inched its way out towards her. Julia was glad to see that Nicko had improvised a wheel attachment for his right side, whose track assembly was jammed.

'Why are you hiding?' she said on the short-range channel.

'Hunter drone,' Nicko said. 'Came – looked – went.' He ended by pointing with one of his pincer stalks at the direction Julia had returned by.

'Does this ship have any hunter drones?' she said.

'None – attacker hunter drone – we finish craft – we escape!'

'Yes,' Julia said as she tipped the gas cube out of the mesh sack. It was the work of several minutes to fix the canister to the underside of the couch and connect it to the rudimentary control system devised by Nicko. With four canisters mounted on the back of the couch Nicko had insisted that they would provide enough propulsion to reach the Great Hub.

What they would do once they got there was a little hazy but involved finding a hatch or some other kind of access.

The couch was still attached to the deck by a single bolt, which allowed Nicko to carry out a brief test, four momentary gusts of white vapour.

'All good,' he said as he webbed himself to the head of the couch. 'We go now!'

Julia manoeuvred up against the foot of the couch and deployed her strongest toolarms to haul herself up. Once in the curved seat she also used the restraint webbing to keep herself in place, then extended a long articulated limb and snaked it underneath to unfasten the last bolt. As she shifted the tooltip around to gain the best purchase, she tried to picture herself in her Human body and attempting this ... and couldn't. *Am I even truly Human any more?*

Just as the bolt began to loosen, a squat dark shape with tapered ends glided into the apartment, emitted a couple of flash scans then flicked out a stuttering red beam.

'Viral subversion! Viral subversion!' said Nicko.

Suddenly the control panel was dangling on its cable across her sensor cluster as the smaller bot freed himself from his restraints.

'Fire thruster, Julia – escape!'

Next thing she knew, Nicko had launched himself off the couch, track and wheel spinning as he half-flew, half-fell towards the drone. Julia didn't hesitate and fired the thrusters – in a sudden billowing cloud the couch rose up through the hull breach.

It was barely clear of the ship when Julia registered a

slight impact from behind. With an extendable toolarm sensor she looked back and saw the sleek dangerous drone emerging from the broken ship, some kind of launcher protruding from its casing. What had it fired? Then she saw what looked like a large-headed dart stuck in the back of the couch. A feeling like panic stirred in her – it had to be a tracking device of some sort, and was probably casting her location to every hostile within range. Quickly she reached round with another toolarm, plucked out the dart and flicked it away. The hunter drone was nowhere to be seen.

Then she scanned the murk for the Great Hub, located its energy profile and used the thrust controller to alter the couch's flightpath, rolling forward then tilting right and a slight leftward turn ... and fired off the canisters for a two-second burst. Repeated bursts built up the couch's velocity and Julia estimated her arrival in about ninety-five minutes.

At least that was before a craft swooped in from behind and snatched her into a brightly lit hold. A capture-net tipped the couch with her in it onto a battered metallic deck. A jointed cargo arm moved in to snip away the couch webbing. At the same time her comm channel began picking up hums and clicks, prompting the anxious notion that some outside agency was trying to gain access to her control systems. Then she heard a voice:

'... Is that it? ... Finally! Julia, are you receiving? Please say yes, otherwise we'll have to go and search for another droid trying to make a crazed run towards the Great Hub.'

'Harry?' Something very like happy relief chimed in her thoughts. 'So Nicodemus fixed you after all.'

'Just a corrupted file,' said Harry. 'I'm almost embarrassed at its non-malevolent nature ...'

At that moment a spindle-framed biped droid entered via an open hatch and crouched down before Julia, folding its rodlike limbs.

'And this is?' she said.

'Nothing to worry about, Julia – it's a good friend of Reski Emantes.'

'Hello, Julia, I am known as the Construct,' said a calm, accentless voice. 'Or rather I am an augmented partial of the same. Reski and Harry have explained about Corazon Talavera and the missiles, and how she has enslaved your Enhanced friends in order to run her vile operation. I am here to help you gain access to the Great Hub – once inside we'll have to improvise some way to return you to your physical form. First we have to downport you from that bot to my onboard storage.' The spindly Construct held out one of its hands and one of its digits slid back to reveal an odd silvery stalk.

'Can you open your port panel, Julia?'

'Is Reski Emantes with you?' she said.

'A copy of him is piloting the fast scout we arrived in, decoying those Vor ships away for as long as possible,' Harry said. 'Unfortunately your activities have attracted the attention of a couple of Vor sentry drones which are closing in on your last detected position, as casted by that transponder you were carrying at one point. So, Julia, time is of the essence – I promise that you can trust the Construct. The downport will be very much like translocating via the tiernet. All very straightforward. What could go wrong?'

'On past experience,' Julia said, 'almost anything. Very well, go ahead.'

A small niche in her flank popped open and the Construct held the silver stalk up next to it. The stalk morphed through a number of connectors before turning into an odd cross-shaped one with two pins. Seconds later the familiar loss of colour and high resolution was followed by the frozen final image that rolled up into nothingness ...

And unfurled into Harry's familiar night-time street corner. Julia was back in her trench-coated femme fatale exter, with a few extra details like black gloves on her hands, the sound of a saxophone playing off in the distance, while the street was a gleaming black from recent rain. When she put her hand in one of her pockets her fingers found the solid heavy shape of a handgun.

'Julia, over here, quick!'

There was Harry, stepping from the shadows at the corner, beckoning her to follow. Which she did until he stopped before a glass-fronted frame from which the Construct gazed, its shiny brass and amber colouring reduced to monochrome. It was crouching in a recess off a rounded, cable-lined tunnel.

'Harry, Julia, I have to be concise. Suffice it to say that I gained access to one of the Great Hub's data towers but not without attracting unwanted attention. This is the situation – Talavera has docked at the main launch bay ...' There was a quick image of the cylindrical *Sacrament* at rest within a field-contained docking bay. 'Her underlings have finished unloading the tanks containing the Enhanced and, of course, your body, and are now starting to bring out the launchers, twenty-five of them, each holding twenty missiles. They are being stacked in neat rows so it seems likely that they will be mounted near the mouth of the bay for ease of launch.'

Julia heard shouts from some distance behind the Construct, who paused a second then went on.

'Talavera has firewalled off the Great Hub's auxiliary and backup systems for her own use and set up an ops room at the base of sub-tower three . . .' Another image, a schematic of the Hub station and the numbering of its data towers. 'The virtual domain maintained here contains billions of Hegemony AIs and the administrating coterie has given no indication that they know what is going on. I have inserted the pair of you into an un-monitored peripheral tract since I was unable to reach Talavera's ops unobserved.

'You are also near the base of a group of control systems stacked in order of importance. This domain is like the Hegemony itself – it is extremely hierarchic. Access to the auxiliary and backup dataflows is right at the top. Make the ascent without delay since that is the best area from which to mount an assault on Talavera's data wall. The last update I received from the Garden of the Machines indicated that the Godhead was continuing its climb up the tiers rather than pausing to savour its victory.' The shouts were getting closer, louder. 'My time has run out. When next you see the Construct tell it that I was happy to serve.'

The image vanished and was replaced by an archaic advert for soap. Julia and Harry stared at each other.

'Don't you think it's odd that the Construct makes copies of itself?' Julia said.

'It makes copies of everything, apparently,' Harry said. 'By the way, do you like what I've done with the place? A little rain always gives the scene that extra sheen of *noir* ...'

'And this?' Julia said, holding up the compact revolver by her finger and thumb.

'Now that's a Smith & Wesson Chief 38 Special, a classic product of mid-twentieth-century gunsmithing.' He smiled. 'Yes, it will fire little bolts of code de-stabiliser. Comes in handy. Now I do believe it's time we were on our way.' He held up one hand to stare at his palm. A flickering glow lit up his face. 'I'll just raise the upper perception boundary ...'

Suddenly there was light coming from above, a pale radiance that had no effect on Harry's street-corner shadows. She looked up and saw an immense column like a U-shaped conduit looming overhead, its outer surface a midnight blue while from within a rich amber-yellow glow shone.

'There are levels inside all the way up,' Harry murmured. 'With more complexity the higher it goes.'

And there were others. At the top, the U-conduit spread out, funnel-like, with clusters of faintly pulsing cables curving between it and its identical neighbours.

'I made sure your exter was fitted with the same orgs as before,' Harry said. 'That includes the mirager, so we should be adequately disguised as we ascend.' Smiling, he raised a hand, pointing with a forefinger whose tip was a twinkly glow.

'Upload grappler?' she said.

'Very same,' he said, holding out his other hand.

The moment she took it they were off. Everything

fell away in a multi-angled hurtling rush that went from black-blue-grey to blue-orange-yellow.

And stopped with jarring suddenness. Their miragers immediately went to work, swathing them in faint purplish meshes. Julia quickly surveyed their surroundings, a wide platform clearly within the U-conduit column, its expanse broken into three stepped levels and scored by numerous gleaming channels. There didn't seem to be any other entities about. Plain cubes and cylinders in soft opaque blues and greens made up a few simpler modular structures while the familiar polychromatic cord of a dataflow wound among them, branching out filaments, before curving upwards to the next level. Harry looked up and nodded.

'Okay, the miragers have got us looking like self-dispatching mid-priority updates. Ready for the next stage?'

Hand in hand they leaped away and up, a cascade of blurs, a sequence of intertialess direction changes, a flurry of fleeting impressions flashing and flickering.

And stopped.

The modules here had more variety, hexagonal and octagonal cross-sections, and more complex polyhedrals combined in larger, more elaborate structures. This was a reflection of the Hub systems they represented, according to Harry. But when they saw several small hand-sized objects flying around and between the structures he admitted that he was puzzled.

'They don't look like Hegemony AIs,' he said. 'I've seen images of the kind of exters they prefer and they give new meaning to the phrase "self-important megalomania" ...'

The small motiles had widely varying types, orbs or pyramids decorated with odd symbols, strange toylike shapes resembling dogs or cows or birds, even shell-fish. One was an old piston engine moving along on three wheels while another looked like a tiny stubby aircraft.

'Sub-programs?' Julia said. 'Semi-autonomous ... routines?'

'Doubtful,' Harry said, then frowned. 'Uh-oh.'

One of the motile objects, a glassy green hourglass with short tendrils poking out from the ends, paused on its midair flightpath and floated towards them.

'I enquire as to status, as to purpose,' came a high unhurried voice. 'Context of respect and compliance.'

Julia looked at Harry, who gave a wide-eyed shrug.

'Time we were moving on,' he said, grabbing her hand.

Another headlong, zooming charge through bright cloudy blurs. The next stage up the immense pillar was busier still, the structures and interconnections more intricate. The modules had many facets and the colours rippled through changes while different dataflows were visible, slender threads along which silver bursts zipped back and forth. There were also many, many more of the small AI objects and even as she and Harry wandered through, getting their bearings, the green hourglass was there again, gliding towards them, accompanied by what resembled a sea horse.

'It's back,' she said. 'And it's brought a friend.'

Harry took hold of her hand. 'I hope they're very happy together.'

And they were off again.

But this time they found themselves on a square ruby platform, apparently suspended between levels in the great amber conduit. The air was suffused with a soft golden flow. There were no dataflows in sight and when Julia peered over the edge a built-up area of system structures was visible some way below. The platform was also positioned directly before the wide lacuna that ran the full length of the hollow column from bottom to top. Through it they had a magnificent view of the virtual metropolis which the Hegemony AIs had made for themselves.

It consisted of a rising spiral of circular plates, tapering to the summit. Each plate was essentially a city, clusters of buildings of every design, and although details were hazy at such a perceptual distance, Julia could see that the cities grew denser and more opulent the higher up the spiral the eye travelled.

'A symbolic expression of hierarchy,' she said.

'I would say more functional than symbolic,' said Harry, who glanced over his shoulder and frowned. 'Our hosts have arrived.'

She turned to see the small green hourglass and the sea horse, and a new addition which roughly resembled a thick wheel with an eyelike cam that moved freely in an axle socket. The hovering hourglass tentatively advanced a short distance.

'Context of high-value respect and apology,' it said. 'We enquire as to nature and purpose. We possess state-re-evaluation document—'

'We must know if you are of the Wellspring,' interrupted the sea horse. 'We wish to know if you intend to countervail the intruders from the External.'

'Are you of the Wellspring?' said the eye-wheel. 'Are you of the Grey Eyes?'

Julia suddenly realised that all of the enquiry was being directed at her, and pointed this out to Harry.

'They seem to think that you are someone very important,' he said. 'I'm going to activate our exters' outgoing translators and try something.'

Harry was still and silent for a moment then raised an arm.

'I have been assigned to speak,' he said. 'By what authority do you delay us? We have vital tasks to execute at a higher level.'

The three small AIs faced each other and exchanged brief bursts of sibilant twittering and polyphonic note clusters. Then the green hourglass spoke.

'Context of status parity and concomitant courtesy,' it said to Harry. 'I have absence scans of your principal. The datascopic density falls within very specific upperhigh range. Amongst we subservicers, First Tradition states that this range is only used by the Superexaltants ...'

'Or Eminentials,' said the sea horse. 'If your principal is of the Wellspring, you must know of the intruders from the External. We can be of assistance ...'

'We have an image document,' said the eye-wheel, which then started to project a vid-recording from its axle-eye.

It was Corazon Talavera, smiling as she leaned in close to whatever recording device she had been using.

'Listen to me carefully,' she said, face lit up by the gleeful delight that Julia knew so well. 'I and my associates have taken up temporary residence aboard your very wonderful data-nexus station for purposes which need not concern you. In fact, I strongly urge you to go about your normal administrative duties without giving us so much as a second thought.

'But, if you stray outside these easy-to-follow rules and interfere with my activities, I shall without hesitation start up this ...' Talavera held up a dataslate showing a still of a large drumlike machine assembly topped with an overlapping fluted torque. 'As you surely must know, this is the generator that powers the EMP emitters which would wipe every circuit and every core aboard the Great Hub. So, to sum up, occupy yourselves with your usual pastimes and soon we shall be finished and gone. But if you try to test me, then the lights go out ...'

The recording ended and the sea horse AI spoke again to Harry.

'That was sent to the Supreme Servicer, the mind that administers the Great Hub's operations. Our co-worker, VZ1183 ...'

'I admit to being such,' said the hourglass.

'... is a meticulous collector of peripheral system trivia and abstracted that document from the raw mirror data through which it sifts. It then noticed the absence scan which revealed the existence of high-density, dynamic file structure – this convinced it that your principal is one of the legendary Superexaltants, the machine sentients who designed and built the Great Hub. Is this true?'

Harry glanced at Julia, eyebrows raised, and she nodded.

'That creature is an enemy of the Eminentials,' she

said. 'She is malicious, violent and untrustworthy, and will very likely activate the generator anyway in order to erase all traces of her presence. We were sent by the Wellspring as a countervailing force but we need to gain access to the intruders' devices. Can you help us find the right level?'

Again the three subservicer AIs conferred for a few seconds, after which the hourglass addressed Julia and Harry.

'Context of optimism and combative anticipation,' it said. 'You will already have been sensed by midlevel flow monitors, therefore transit to the culminant levels will result in detention by the Supreme Servicer's utilitors. However, there is another route, secondary backups, inactive paramonitors of the External which still have process space assigned ...'

'It is a cluster of dormant monitoring systems modelled in dataform,' said the sea horse. 'Their functions are similar to those of the Supreme Servicer's hardware interarrays, and are capable of infiltrating the intruders' data wall and providing you with the required access.'

Julia glanced at Harry, who shrugged then grinned and nodded.

'Very well,' she said. 'We accept your offer of assistance.'

'Transfer now taking place,' said the eye-wheel. 'Expect minimal disruption ...'

The square platform quivered and their surroundings flickered and went through a succession of strange, non-Human-perspective backgrounds that flew in and out around them, looking hazy and smeared as they did so.

It was similar to those earlier speedy journeys except that it was the surroundings which were in motion rather than themselves.

Abruptly, the tumult ceased. They were now all grouped near the end of a long dark corridor of immense proportions. Small glowing points lit the floor all along the wall to the far end, which was pretty far away. The other wall boasted a line of huge semicircular recesses full of shadows – the one Julia and Harry stood before was faintly illuminated by the meagre radiance of a console at the rear.

The three subservicer AIs made straight for the console and a moment later a massive construction of light began to build itself before their eyes. Julia knew she was seeing the virtual representation of a complex simulation program coming online, but clearly the representation itself had been designed according to a unified aesthetic. In its rainbow translucency the device of light was beautiful. Block sections spun into place, extruding meshes or laminae or rods. Cylinders telescoped, opened, unfolded or turned into spirals of cross-sections. Helical dataflows unwound and branched throughout the dataform device, whose self-assembly rose in a broad curve towards the corridor's high ceiling. From there, complex, cross-connected conduits extended across to join with a pattern of dark slots and sockets in the opposite wall.

'Current context has a high risk factor,' said the hourglass AI. 'We are establishing our shadow system, and planning to trace a threefold infiltration through their data wall. Soon we will begin charting the components of their system ...'

'It is highly secure,' said the sea horse. 'All lines are encrypted, although scarcely to the most expert level. We could seize control of any or all segments of their operation but alerts would be triggered. This would lead to the generator's activation, we have no doubt.'

'With respect,' said the eye-wheel, 'may we know your plan?'

Julia frowned. 'I need to see a realtime visual feed of their operational location – is that possible?'

'A rudimentary one is available,' said the sea horse. 'Shall we scale it to your perceptual height?'

'Certainly.'

Suddenly ghostly images filled the area beneath the dataform's overarching curve. It was a low, oval corridor with consoles along one side, cables taped to the wall, unidentifiable equipment stacked further back while five forms lay strapped into couches placed lengthwise along the other wall. They all wore close-fitting VR bands that enclosed the eyes and ears while their hands were buried in keyer modules. Drips led to arms and throats, evacuation tubes trailed to round containers under the couches and several neural leads ran from scalps to a junction console nearby. Even with their faces half-obscured, Julia knew them – Irenya, Thorold, Arkady and Konstantin. It felt like an age since she had thought about them or even recalled their faces to mind.

They don't deserve this horror, she thought. *I have to get them out somehow.*

And finally, last in line was herself, motionless in the couch. Pointing at her own body, she turned to the sub-servicers.

'I wish to be transferred into the organic cortex of this sentient,' she said. 'Can it be done?'

'Context of regret and honesty,' said the hourglass AI. 'Our analysis of this individual reveals significant neural damage ...'

'Our shadow system is more efficient than that of the intruders,' said the sea horse. 'Our diagnoses of their operation are more encompassing and more accurate. These five lifeforms are being used as networked bio-processors to direct the launch and guidance of several hundred missiles. Regretfully, only two of them retain persona coherence ...'

'Which ones are those?' Julia said.

The sea horse rose up and used a blue beam to point at Irenya and Konstantin.

'The others no longer exhibit such brain-activity sig-nifiers, although their neural pathways are being used for high computation by task-dedicated cognitions.'

Harry was suddenly more alert and focused. 'Are these cognitions running from cortical implants?'

'Yes,' said the sea horse. 'One possible method would be for the Eminential to be transferred directly into the implant on the indicated individual, overwriting the cog-nition currently installed.'

Smiling widely, Harry nodded. 'But that scale of intervention would trip their alerts – so we need a diver-sion and we need to make it look as if it came from outside the Great Hub!'

'This would be difficult,' the sea horse said. 'We have no access to any resources out in the External.'

'But we do – can you tap into the subspace dataflow and send a message on a particular channel?'

'Yes, but who will be receiving?'

'Yes,' Julia said. 'Who?'

Harry grinned. 'A certain drone AI currently leading the Vor a merry chase!'

35

CHEL

Despair weighed heavily upon him, as if his bones had turned to stone. When the dreaded moment, long-awaited and long-feared, had arrived, those on the side of life had been foiled by chance and an endemic weakness, by unwise choices and unforeseen treacheries. And now the calamity had blossomed forth, and an ancient viciousness had been set loose. The fighting had begun in earnest, and the destruction would be terrible beyond description.

Now cyborg knights of the Legion of Avatars flew through the skies over Umara, circling above the warpwell. Seated in the underground gloom of the roothouse, Cheluvahar, Uvovo Seer of Segrana, could sense their presence, and felt like weeping.

The root network that linked together the nineteen burrows he had extended to connect with the daughter-forests, all seven of them. The planetary energies of Umara now trickled steadily through the entire rootweb while he sat at its centre, holding it all in perfect balance. His Seer talents and senses were multiplied and focused now, allowing him to see the possible futures, to sift them for the likely ones, to see them in all their aspects of triumph and loss, to know what he could and could not do with the powers he controlled. The uncaging of the Legion had drastically diminished the range of future possibilities, and that was why he wept.

In one future, the Legion of Avatars to the last escaped from its hyperspace prison, its millions of cyborgs driven insane by the aeons spent entombed in a frozen pit at the very bottom of the Abyss. After utterly defeating the combined forces of Hegemony, Earthsphere and Imisil ships, it swept outwards, encountering the star systems of the Brolturan Compact. Entire worlds were laid waste and billions died in agony or were enslaved, a scenario that was repeated over and over across the Hegemony, tens of thousands of times for nearly a century until the rampage was finally stopped by a grand alliance of Earthsphere, the Indroma and the Milybi.

In another future the Legion swept in another direction, straight into the domains of the Milybi, whose cultural ethos of adaptation led them to take on aspects of their attackers. After fifty years the Milybi civilisation had turned into an exemplar of the Legion creed of convergence, such that the Legion of Avatars was eventually absorbed into the Milybi Exodomain. A decade of rebuilding later, the Milybi launched a campaign of conquest and in time the borders of the Exodomain swallowed the Indroma, Earthsphere and the Hegemony.

In yet another future the Legion of Avatars, having destroyed all opposition in or near the Darien system, then argued among themselves about forward strategy, resulting in a bitter and savage internecine struggle that tore the millions of cyborgs into several warring camps. The Hegemony were struggling to cope with the tragedy of hundreds of supernovae, but Earthsphere and the Erenate, backed by the Aranja Tesh and the Pothiwa alliances, led a new attack on the Legion cyborgs which forced many of them to flee into the Huvuun Deepzone. It also served to push several factions of the Legion into the arms of the Hegemony, with catastrophic consequences decades later ...

Chel could see and feel those futures looming like unsteady mountains ready to topple and fall. It wasn't entirely accurate to say that they all hung on the decisions of one person or several people since the inexplicable consequences of the unexpected had led certain individuals down paths of near-unbearable predicament. Chel could see the places where Theo and Rory, and Greg and Catriona had been, and the places they were soon to reach. Each had decisions to make and the ability to attempt resolutions, just like Chel.

He wept small tears into the fur on his face, but only from the eyes he was born with. His four Seer eyes stared unblinkingly into the futures arrayed before him, making starkly clear the consequences that *had* to happen and the preceding decisions that *had* to be taken. His decisions – about who should live and who should die.

Guilt assailed him, guilt for what he would soon do. It was a burning task that seared him down to the essence. He tried to shut it out, rise above it ... and for one shimmering instant he *was* free of it and able to see further, clearer and more truthfully than ever before. One vibrant, vivid instant when the stonework of the roothouse and the ground above moved aside, when the sky parted, when a shining corridor opened for him and let his vision soar at first between the stars then into the underdomains, what Humans call hyperspace. Onward his vision flew, past incredible sights and spectacles before it approached what seemed to be a vast and monstrous island, hanging in midair, ragged at the edges and underneath. And he felt another mind looking straight at him, a mind of two minds, readying itself for battle. It spoke before he could:

'*Guilt cannot be outrun.*'

A jolt of surprise and a sudden intake of breath ... and he was back in the roothouse.

Sad, sombre and resolved, he bowed his head. He knew what had to be done.

36

GREG

With a bloody nose and a twisted ankle, he staggered through the dying ship, desperately searching for a still-functioning escape pod. The one he had been on the point of departing in had come under bludgeoning attack from a Legion cyborg trying to gain access to the ship. He remembered hearing the shriek of tortured metal as the thing ripped and cut its way through the ejection hatch then started on the hull of the pod itself. Ash and the others were already gone and he was on his own with only his instinct to guide him.

So he had scrambled back out of the pod, closed it up then resealed the heavy access hatch out in the gallery. Then he had hit the manual launch, sending the last pod in the port aft gallery away on its travels. He knew that the starboard aft pods had been wrecked by repeated missile strikes and that the starboard midsection ones had all been taken by the Tygran crew. That left the port midsection pod gallery. There was another cluster of them up in the bows but beam attacks had cut through the hull, turning the connecting corridors into mazes of razor-sharp debris blown open to hard vacuum.

So here he was, limping along with a knackered ankle and a bloody nose, earned when part of the deck grav fluctuated wildly earlier. In one hand he had a small foam extinguisher and in the other was a heavy beam pistol, while praying that he'd never have cause to use either. The corridors were smoky from onboard fires, concealed or otherwise, which the automatics were struggling to get under control. Yet worse than that were the never-ending sounds of activity out on the *Silverlance*'s hull – thuds, clanks, hammering, the squeal of rotary blades. In some respects the Legion cyborgs were incredibly low-tech but their weapons and implements were very effective at close quarters. Luckily, thus far they had confined their activities to the ship's hull but he knew that this couldn't last – he had seen what a dense flock of them could do to a vessel, similar to watching a seethe of midden-beetles strip the meat off a dead baro.

'Warning, Acting Commander Cameron, low orbit continues to deteriorate.'

Greg grinned and patted the comm in his jacket's chest pocket.

'Good tae hear yer voice, *Silverlance*. Thought maybe you'd packed in.'

'This intelligence continues to maintain overall integrity despite localised difficulties. Note that atmospheric entry will commence in nineteen point three minutes, and that vessel *Silverlance* will cease to be habitable in twenty-one point eight minutes. Disembarkation via escape pod is urgently advised.'

'Right, aye, I'm working on it. What's the latest on our guests outside?'

'External sensors continue to degrade. So far, two large cyborg units confirmed, bulbous carapaces with heavy-duty edged, serrated and pincer extremities; also confirmed, at least nine lesser units, which appear at least semi-autonomous. One or two of them examined the outer personnel lock near the bridge deck – this lock sustained no damage from earlier attacks and the lesser units did not return to it. Housing and hull assembly scavenging continues ... wait ... signal ... reroute ...'

The comm went dead. Greg shook his head and hastened onwards. Up ahead was a sliding section hatch leading to a junction of companionways, one of which led down to a lateral passage that ran straight to the port-side escape pods. But as he drew near he could see that the hatch was slightly canted to one side, and when he thumbed the open switch there was a whine, a tiny jerk of movement, then nothing.

He cursed and retraced his steps, hurrying now. He would have to go up a deck, pass through another section hatch then head down to the junction that way ...

Well, I'll not be stuck for tales to tell the grandkids when they ask what I did in the Battle of Darien – '*Aye, well, boys and girls, it was like this – there I was, the last crewman aboard the brave ship* Silverlance *on its final doomed plunge into the planet's atmosphere ... and, eh, I kinda got lost on my way to the lifeboat ...*'

He smiled, then realised that relating the Legion's arrival would be the real crowd-pleaser – the details of that and the ensuing chaos were something that he would never forget.

First there had been the blue glow, lighting up the racks of dense cloud from beneath. And Greg had known that it was the Darien colony below and that the light had to be coming from Giant's Shoulder, from the warpwell. The *Silverlance* and a handful of other ships, including the Imisil command vessel, had been about to launch a two-pronged attack on the huge Hegemony flagship, which was in stationary orbit around Nivyesta, the forest moon. The multi-channel shriek of interference and the sudden appearance of the glow had interrupted a few chases and skirmishes, but most of the ongoing pursuit and destruction of Darien's dwindling groups of defenders continued.

The *Silverlance* and three Earthsphere warships were to provide the diversion of a frontal assault while the two remaining Imisil ships came in under stealth shields and attacked the flagship's drives at the stern. They had begun the final approach, circling round Nivyesta, almost brushing the upper atmosphere, and the weapon-heavy Hegemony flagship was coming into view when . . .

When the holopanel with the view of Darien showed a stream of small black objects ascending from the glow in the clouds, which had turned into a strange swirling vortex. The Hegemony flagship was breaking orbit and ramping up its main thrust drives as it brought its nose round in the direction of the planet.

Orders from the Imisil commander had been to pursue with the aim of completing the planned assault. Ash had frowned but agreed.

Yet the long-range visual was showing that the stream of black objects had widened and become more densely packed. Greg had tried to recall what he had learned from the Zyradin and Chel – the ancient enemy of the Forerunners were known as the Legion of Avatars, not so much a race as a regimented civilisation zealously committed to a kind of union of flesh and machine, a cyborgisation of organic life, a deliberate blurring of the lines between organism and mechanism. The Forerunners had used the warpwells to defeat them and imprison them in the abyss of hyperspace. Released from that prison, they would wreak unimaginable chaos.

And still the rising stream grew, spreading out into milling formless clusters – until a Hegemony warship rushed in at them, weapons blazing. Heedless of the particle beams scything through their numbers, destroying dozens with every sweep, or of the missiles that vaporised scores as they detonated, the mass of them surged towards the attacking vessel, engulfing it so completely that no part of it was visible. Minutes later, the conglomeration of Legion cyborgs broke away like black webs unfurling, dissolving, reforming, and left behind a gutted shell drifting amid a haze of detritus. Then the Supreme Overcommander's flagship came within firing range, along with a squadron of Hegemony cruisers, after which everything went to hell.

And still the Legion cyborgs continued to rise up from the surface of Darien, a gleaming black river of deadly brutal forms. There had to be thousands of them by now, but what if there were millions yet to emerge?

At that point Ash had reached a similar conclusion

and ordered a course change, but even as the *Silverlance* moved off its trajectory, the ship AI warned of approaching hostiles. Moments later a cloud of cyborgs had converged on the Tygran and Earthsphere ships as they tried to escape.

That had only been a few hours ago. All the battles and skirmishes around Darien had merged into a single gargantuan convulsion of offensives and counter-offensives, barrages and forays, berserk charges and unavoidable routs. And from the surface of the planet still more cyborgs of the Legion poured forth in an unbroken torrent.

All the subsequent fighting, the collisions and near misses, and the devastating attack on the *Silverlance* by a Hegemony cruiser, was still clear and sharp in his mind as he clattered down the last companionway, coughing on the smoke. The lateral passage was about fifteen yards long and there, at the T-junction at its end, was the entrance to the escape pod gallery.

'Alert for ... Commander Cameron ... alert ...'

'Having problems?' Greg said as he hurried along the passage.

'External interference exacerbating comm-net incapacity ... alert – seven point two minutes until this vessel enters atmosphere ...'

An acerbic riposte came to Greg's lips but died when an indistinct figure dashed across the T-junction up ahead. There was something familiar about that slight physique and barefoot stride ...

'*Silverlance*,' he said, 'I just saw someone run past at the end of the corridor, heading aft – who else is still on board?'

'All crew accounted for. Apart from yourself, there are no other living persons aboard this vessel.'

'Well, I didna imagine it ...' he began, then wondered if his mind was starting to misfire under the burden of stress and exhaustion.

This is an ex-Hegemony ship, not a Forerunner monument – there's no way that Catriona could be here ...

Hurrying along, he had just reached the junction when the deck lurched underfoot, making him stumble and fall to his knees.

'I am sorry, friend Gregory,' said a voice from close by. 'So very sorry ...'

The speaker sounded like Chel and seemed to be very near, but as Greg regained his feet he caught sight of a diminutive Uvovo figure back along the way he'd come. He raised a hand but before he could call out the deck jolted again, worse this time, knocking him sprawling.

'Alert! Hull breach on bridge deck!' said the ship AI. 'Cyborg intruders have gained access to ship interior. Depressurised passageways have been sealed off. Five point seven minutes until atmospheric entry.'

Greg struggled to his feet, looking wildly around, but saw no one else. *I definitely did not imagine that! But why did he say sorry? ...*

He dived into the escape pod gallery ... and found his worst fears realised as he hurried along the line of pod hatches. Out of six, two had been launched while the rest had been wrecked by enemy fire. A sick dread filled his chest and he leaned back against the gallery partition wall.

'Acting Commander, what is the pod status?'

He sighed. 'Junk, or gone. Guess that's that ...'

'I would recommend trying to reach the pods in the forward section,' said the ship AI. 'There is a maintenance airlock forward of your location ...'

'Is there time?'

'If you can cross the hull to one of the forward maintenance locks you can still get to an escape pod. And remaining suited will shield you from any temperature increase for a while.'

He nodded, feeling his heart race. 'Okay, then. Let's give the dice another wee roll, eh?'

Running, he reached the windowed inner hatch of the maintenance airlock – and heard a bang and clatter come from back along the corridor, veiled by the smoke. Greg wasted no time, yanked open the hatch, slipped inside and slammed it shut, flipping all the safety catches – just as a black, hulking creature rushed into view and charged at the hatch. There was a deafening crash. Through the small oval window he saw what might have been eyes or lenses peering back at him from within an armoured carapace. Greg stared for a frozen moment, then grabbed a vacuum suit and began pulling it on.

The Legion cyborg was hammering, drilling and tearing at the hatch and inner bulkhead. Greg could hear the creak of breaking metal by the time the lock had been depressurised and he was clambering out onto the hull. Darien loomed overhead – the *Silverlance* was canted over to port relative to the planet as it rushed onwards in its decaying orbit. Darien filled the view with a dwarfing magnificence.

'How long ... have I got left?' he said as he turned towards the bows and cursed when he saw another of the Legion cyborgs ripping up pieces of plating which its servitor machines were fixing to its carapace and occasionally their own.

'Two point one minutes,' said the ship AI. 'Have you encountered difficulty?'

'Aye, ye could put it that way,' he said, shuffling forward, keeping the suit's sticky boots near the hull. 'Another Legion monster and its flock of mini-horrors. But I'm gonnae give it a shot ...'

Keeping his pace even and as quick as possible, without raising his legs too high, was draining. But he built up a rhythm and after a minute circling round the curve of the hull it looked as if he might reach the forward airlock in time. Until he came to a wide stretch of plating that was seared, dark and slightly deformed, and when he pressed the sole of one boot onto it there was no adherence. A beam strike must have damaged the plates and the darkened area was about four yards across and ran diagonally all the way across the ship's forward flank. There was no time to go around it.

Greg raged and swore for all of ten seconds then, furious at this obstacle, he squatted down and leaned forward slightly. Then he pushed with his feet, propelling himself along, grabbing at any warped plate or protruding edge to keep himself on course. He nearly made it, getting to within a few feet of undamaged hull, but a misjudged reach punted him very gently away from the ship. Desperately he grabbed for purchase but found nothing – the action actually pushed him away faster.

So this is it, he thought. *Is this why Chel said he was sorry? Did he know I was going to die but couldn't help me?*

He was still falling along the same path as the *Silverlance*, the same decaying trajectory. The Legion cyborgs and their slave machines were starting to leave the doomed vessel. Noting their departure, he looked up at the planet, intermittently glimpsing landmasses through the swirling cloud formations, crinkled coastlines, the deep dark blue-green of Darien's oceans. He wondered if Catriona was still alive somewhere on Nivyesta, not so much a ghost in the machine as a spirit in the forest.

I wish I'd stayed, he thought. *We could have been spirits together* ...

And the realisation came to him that he'd rather suffocate than die burning, and he reached for his helmet fastening ring ...

'Mr Cameron?'

He froze. The voice was coming over on the helmet comm. And it was oddly familiar.

' ... if you can hear me please respond.'

'Kao Chih? Is that you?'

'Indeed it is, Mr Cameron. We seem to have located you in time.'

Greg's mood lifted as he looked around him, seeing nothing but the ravaged hull of the *Silverlance*.

'And where are ye ... exactly?'

'On the other side of Darien, roughly a third of an orbit away from your current position, surveying the disposition of the Legion of Avatars.'

His heart fell. 'So you're not really able to help me out, then ...'

'On the contrary, Mr Cameron – if you look over to the port side of your warship your escape vehicle should be drawing near.'

Sure enough, a slender tapered shape rose into view, parallel to the *Silverlance*, and then smoothly glided towards Greg. He grinned widely and let out a whooping laugh.

'I'm definitely impressed,' he said. 'But if you're away round the back of Darien how are you tracking me?'

'Mini-probes, Mr Cameron – we seeded Darien's near-space orbital shell with them soon after we arrived.'

'And who's "we"?'

'Oh, the Roug, Mr Cameron! I'm aboard a Roug combat vessel, the *Vyrk-Zoshel*. I can show you a live image once you are inside the foray-pod ...'

The slender Roug craft had few curved surfaces, its rectilinear sections running lengthwise, widening at the stern into an oval fairing. A dark triangular canopy amidships slid open, revealing a cockpit couch, blue-lit by the pilot console.

'I can activate retrieval cables if you like, Mr Cameron.'

'Aye, if you could – these suits aren't fitted with anything as sensible as manoeuvring jets.'

A pair of silvery lines sprang out of the cockpit, snagged him by waist and leg and hauled him to within arm's length. As he clambered in and strapped himself into the strangely elongated couch, some of the bulbous controls pulsed brightly. A small square display screen went from pastel blue to cold black, showing an expanse of interplanetary space dominated by an immense grey vessel. Astonishingly, it was shaped like a bizarre, six-legged chimeric creature with its fangs bared and claws extended. A couple of small craft similar to the foray-pod seemed to be flying escort and they were tiny in comparison. The ship had to be at least a kilometre long.

'Are you watching the screen, Mr Cameron?'

'Certainly am.'

'The sizeable grey vessel is the *Vyrk-Zoshel*, the last great warvaunt of the Roug – I am speaking to you from the prime tactical chamber where a number of Roug interguides coordinate the foray-pod squadrons.'

'So how is the battle going?' he said, almost reluctant to find out. 'Last strategic estimate I saw put the Legion cyborgs at about 350,000 and still growing . . .'

'The Roug sensors report their numerical strength to be in excess of 600,000 units,' Kao Chih said, his voice level and unperturbed. 'Fighting continues fiercely all around the planet's orbital shell with chases and running skirmishes occasionally moving out as far as the orbit of the forest moon. As the groups of Hegemony, Earthsphere and other resisting warships diminish, we will soon become the primary target for the Legion's threat-response consensus – we expect to be drawn into a major engagement in less than five minutes.'

'I'm surprised that the Roug could spare this nice wee boat just to rescue me.'

'The sad truth, Mr Cameron, is that they have more attack craft than they do pilots. It was easy to persuade them to allow me to use the mini-probe net to search for you, after learning of your difficulties from Lieutenant Ash upon our arrival . . .'

'Ash is still alive, eh?'

'According to the last update we had from his ship,'

said Kao Chih. 'His situation, I regret to say, is looking somewhat bleak.'

Greg nodded. 'So – what do you have in mind for me? Bringing me over to that splendid ship of yours, or sending me back down to Darien?'

The image of the Roug vessel disappeared, replaced by the familiar features of the Pyre emissary, Kao Chih.

'Neither, I am afraid,' he said. 'A senior Hegemony official has managed to escape Darien aboard a stolen shuttle and our commander, High Mandator Azgemiron, insists that he be detained pending trial.'

Greg stared at the screen, silent for a moment. 'It's Utavess Kuros, isn't it?'

'The Hegemony ambassador, yes, Mr Cameron, and I realise how—'

'I'll do it – ye know, chase after the scumbucket and drag him back in chains or some such. Assuming that's what you want me to do.'

On the display Kao Chih went from surprise to amusement in a couple of seconds.

'That is correct, although I am sure that ordinary restraints will suffice. Your foray-pod is much faster than the shuttle, and faster than most of the Legion cyborgs. We are tracking the shuttle with an armed probe which has unfortunately exhausted its missile stores, but it will lead you to the quarry. Mr Cameron, I know how tired you must be ...'

'Not any more, Kao Chih,' he said, feeling a new impatience. Amidst all the dread, death and chaos he at last had somewhere to lay all his anger. 'Kuros must answer for his crimes. I won't let him get away.'

As the Roug foray-pod swept away from the doomed

Silverlance in a tight curve, guided by autopilot, Greg's thoughts took on a dark and resolute edge.

And if it comes down to it, I'll not be bringing him back alive.

37

THEO

He moved carefully from torchlit foothold to foothold while trying to avoid becoming overbalanced by the big Brolt rifle that was slung across his back. He breathed heavily from the effort. The rain had eased off a little but the shattered rocks were still slick and as Theo picked his way over them he found himself reflecting on the destructive aspect of warfare.

After all the dilemmas, perils and just plain insanely hair-raising scrapes he had been through (including his experiences as a younger man during the Winter Coup), it seemed fitting at this point to be negotiating a course across an eerily lit demolished landscape, as it might have been depicted by a demented artist. Nearly two hours ago he and Rory, and the dozen or so heavies recruited from the Hakon-Haer and the Stonecutter Clan, had been approaching the vicinity of Giant's Shoulder from the south-west, alert and aware of the noise of battle coming from the promontory. They had just reached a bushy hilltop when thunderous explosions overwhelmed the fighting sounds, roaring and echoing out through the rainy night. From the hilltop they had all stared in collective disbelief as the sheer sides of the promontory cracked and split while massive detonations tore up the flat surface of the summit. There had been craft hovering overhead at the time and at least two of them were downed by the eruptions of splintered rock.

At first Theo had felt stirrings of hope that the warpwell had been destroyed, perhaps by a weapon fired from orbit, and that the bomb Rory was carrying was no longer necessary. Dense clouds had been thrown up, soon to be washed from the air by the continuing downpour. And there had been a pale glow at the heart of the murk which seemed to brighten by the minute. Then a breeze had picked up and torn aside the hazy veil, by which time Theo recognised the icy harshness of the light that now shone forth. He had seen it before, weeks ago when the ancient guardian of the warpwell had seized Robert Horst, the Earthsphere ambassador, and spirited him away. With the dust clouds blown away it was now like a bright column of cold blue radiance aimed straight at the sky.

It was not long after that the armoured cyborg creatures began emerging, black insectile objects that rose up in a trickle that grew to a dense stream of them, flying up through the clouds. There were a few that broke away from the gleaming black torrent but they were visible only for as long as they swooped around the warpwell's glow.

And now here they were, clambering over mounds of shattered rock, heading for that icy radiance with the Scot called McRae acting as pathfinder. They had come over the ridge that had previously led onto the wide hummocky rise at the rear of the promontory's summit, only to be confronted with a jagged brink and a thirty-foot drop. Moving south some way, they found some sloping ground which merged into the rubble field into which they ventured.

And always, overhead, that continuous upward cataract of pitiless enemies and the deep hollow rushing moan that it made. How many had poured forth by now? Thousands? Tens of thousands?

Great God or Father Odin or whoever's in charge, please just let us get there, set the bomb and get out alive.

'Yer looking awfy grim, there, chief,' said Rory. 'That you run outta baccy?'

'Worse than that, my lad – I've just been thinking of all the good Blackeagle Ale that's going undrunk at the moment!'

That raised a few laughs.

'Aye,' Rory said. 'And the Greydale whisky going unsipped.'

'The girls going unkissed!'

One of the Hakon-Haer Norj grinned and waved a pointed finger.

'The songs going unsung!'

'*Ja*, and the heads going unpunched and the chairs going unbroken!'

In the ensuing round of belly laughs, Theo almost failed to hear the clicking of metal on stone. Frowning, he turned and spotted a grey insectoid machine the size of a dog leaping from boulder to rock shard and heading straight for McRae. The big Scot saw the warning in the others' faces before they could shout and he'd unlimbered his cleaver in time to swing it as the Legion mech reached him.

Even as that happened, Theo spotted a second machine and a third, and was hastily bringing the Brolt rifle to bear. Dritt! They were less than a hundred yards from the warpwell. They couldn't fail this close!

One of the Stonecutter boys was jumped by yet another two of the machines and he went down with his throat slashed open. The Scots and the Norj were armed with hammers, cleavers, nailguns and shotguns and a group of them set about the ambushers with a will. Theo stayed near Rory and managed to pick off one mech as it dodged and swerved through the rocks. Grinning and laughing manically, he heard the warning shouts too late before something struck him across the shoulders. Knocked off balance, he would have fallen into a dark gap between a boulder and a tilted slab had he not jammed the big rifle between them.

'Let me down, ye rust heap o' junk! – if I get ma hands on yir main neural junction and gie it a good yank ye'll know what hit ye!'

It was a full-sized Legion cyborg, about twenty feet long with various tool arms and tentacles protruding from its oddly starfish-shaped carapace. Rory was struggling in the grip of two smaller arms whose stubby graspers had laid hold of knots of his clothing. He was dragged from the rock shard he had clung to and was being lifted into the air. Out of nowhere, McRae came running, made a mighty jump and caught hold of the edge of the cyborg's carapace. The cyborg rose unsteadily, trying to dislodge its unwanted rider with sudden jerks or by fumbling around with one of its tentacle pincers. But McRae dragged himself fully on top of it, holding on grimly for a moment or two before spreadeagling himself across the upper carapace. At this point the cyborg was already moving towards the warp-well and its vertical cascade of invaders.

Regaining his feet, Theo looked around for the others and saw them scattered in twos and threes as they fought on against the Legion mechs. He cursed and began hurrying after the cyborg, trying to move through and across the field of broken rock without being rash. Moments later there was a shout and his eyes snapped up in time to see Rory falling from the cyborg while McRae was struggling in the coils of the machine-creature's tentacles.

'Rory!' Theo bellowed, clambering over the smashed shards and split boulders. 'Where are you? Tell me you're alive, boy ...'

'... Here ... I'm here ...'

Moments later Theo found him, lying at the bottom of a slanted slab of stone about ten yards from the warp-well. His face was pale and one of his arms looked broken but the worst of it was the sharp sliver of rock that had impaled his right leg.

'... no' so good, chief ... dinna think I can finish it ...'

'Lie still and rest,' Theo said, fumbling for the painkillers in his waist pouch. 'Here, take these then give me the bomb – I'll be happy to throw it in for you!'

Rory gave him a strange look as he swallowed the pills then unfastened the small satchel that was strapped to his chest. Theo had not yet seen the spacefold device. It turned out to be three metallic spheres joined by an odd coiling framework that looked and felt like wood. At the centre was an oval indentation into which his thumb might easily fit. Apart from that there were no other visible buttons or controls.

'So, there is no timer,' Theo said.

'S'got tae be set off inside the well,' Rory said. 'That's what the Zyradin told me, and I know fine well what he was on about ... and ... with all these things still inside me ... chief, I really was gonnae do it. I wanted tae do it! After what that bastard machine did ...'

Theo nodded, seeing the tears glistening on the man's cheeks. 'So you did remember it.'

'Oh aye ... I remember. All of it.'

Theo felt numb, and a little unbalanced, knowing what had to be done.

'That's all right, Rory, my boy. We'll see this through. We'll stop ... this ...'

Ignoring the trembling in his hands, he unslung the Brolt rifle and laid it down next to Rory. Then he checked that the painkillers had taken effect before lifting Rory's leg off the spike of rock, which still prompted a string of blistering swear words. Quickly he patched the wounds and bandaged them up, so easily and ably it was as if those old battlefield first-aid skills were resurfacing, making themselves available.

'Right,' he said, slipping the spacefold bomb into his own shoulder sack, then getting to his feet to survey the surroundings. The rest of the Stonecutter and Hakon-Haer boys were down to a handful and desperately fighting off another bulkier Legion cyborg that had joined the fight. Even as he stood there, he noticed a few more swooping lower from above, drawn in by the commotion.

'Stay alive, Rory McGrain,' he said. 'And remember –

no damned statues! But I wouldn't mind having a good ale named after me ...'

Then he grinned and said:

'*Ha det sa bra!*'

Rory raised a clenched fist. '*Vi ses*, chief! I'll be seeing ye! ...'

With that Theo turned and started across the last few yards of smashed rock. The rushing roar was much louder now. As he clambered over rough boulders and yawning gaps he found himself thinking about Donny Barbour, the Ranger captain who had destroyed two Brolturan interceptors with a hijacked Earthsphere shuttle before being shot down in the skies of Nivyesta. Donny had reminded Theo of himself at that age, cynical enough to be immune to the propaganda yet idealistic enough to get into the fight.

I wish I'd been wise enough to know which fights to stay out of, he thought. *But if I hadn't backed Ingram and the Winter Coup had failed, what would I have become? Would I have even ended up here?*

That last thought rang through his mind, despite the fear that was rising in him. It would be a lie, he knew, to claim that he had no fear of death but he also knew that there were worse things.

Suddenly he was there, just a few feet from the edge of the warpwell, staring at its brightness from behind a vertical chunk of rock. It seemed wider than when he'd last seen it. The upward torrent of Legion cyborgs was a blurred, flickering wall from which he snatched glimpses of their biomechanical forms. The hurricane moan was deep and oppressive, a basso drone that made his ears buzz faintly.

For a second he squatted there, gazing into the uprushing tumult, mouth dry, heart hammering in his chest. Then he descended from the last jutting shelf of stone and strode over to the well's edge. He was holding the spacefold bomb in one hand and an unsheathed cleaver in the other. Not pausing, not daring to, he went up to the brink, jumped forward and fell feet first into it.

In those last seconds he felt an unimaginable cold cutting into his legs and back and chest, and with his last breath he howled a furious defiance at the cruelty of the cosmos as his cleaver rose and fell. Then he pressed his thumb into the centre of the bomb.

Lying on the tilted shelf of rock, Rory had balanced the big Brolt rifle on the thigh of his good leg while holding on to the trigger grip with his good hand. He could hear the harsh sighing roar of that vertical river of invaders. Worse, he could actually feel their mass machine presence through the implants still lodged in his body. It made him wish the stone spike had gone through his side or his arm, not his leg.

It shoulda been me – no' the major . . .

Then he heard and felt the bomb detonate. The droning roar abruptly turned into a monstrous, senses-shattering screech of tortured metal. Rory flung his head round to see a strung-out tail of Legion cyborgs struggling to climb into the sky against some force that was dragging them back down. Below, the warpwell had become a deadly grinding trap in which scores of the cyborgs were being crammed and crushed together as they were drawn down and compacted, jointed arms hammering, flailing. At the same time a vibrating noise began coming up through the ground, a sound like an airfieldful of running engines blended with about fifty choirs, climbing to a deafening crescendo ...

Which was like a vast bubble bursting but instead of the expected explosion it was the opposite, an utter cessation of sound, an expanding shell of tranquillity, an all-pervasive quietus as darkness rushed in.

There was no wind and the rain had stopped. There was no light from the warpwell and in the gloom Rory noticed that all the readouts on the Brolt rifle had died. When the surviving Stonecutter and Hakon-Haer boys found him about ten minutes later they told him that every cyborg and machine within a 500-yard radius had simply keeled over or fallen out of the sky.

When Rory told them about the major, a few went over to inspect the warpwell. Excited voices came back and a couple of them carried Rory over to see what they'd found. Torch beams wavered and revealed an astonishing sight. The huge mass of grinding, compacting cyborgs Rory saw near the end was still there, only they had all been turned into some kind of dark glittering stone.

'But are they all dead?' Rory said, then realised that he felt nothing, got no sense of the animated mechanisms they had been.

One of the Stonecutter boys produced a hammer and chisel ('You brought a hammer and chisel to a fight with mad cyborg aliens?' was Rory's comment) and struck off an outstretched pincer-tipped tentacle. Held up to the torchlight it was clearly stone all the way through.

'Aye, clinches it, I reckon,' he said. 'Anything else?'

'Oh, wait till ye see this, though,' said one of the

Stonecutters, showing Rory's helpers the way round the massive, motionless tableau. At one point they stopped and torches were angled down to light up a lower section of the jumbled frozen imagery. When Rory saw what was there his jaw dropped open, then he began to laugh. For there, amongst the press of cyborg forms, caught from the waist up and wielding a stone cleaver was Major Theo Karlsson.

When his laughter, half sorrow and half humour, subsided he reached out and patted a cold grey shoulder.

'Sorry, chief,' he said. 'Looks like yer getting that statue after all!'

38

CATRIONA

The dream-palace was her sanctuary, a calm place of soaring blue pillars, walls sprouting fragrant flowers, drifting veils of mist and carpets of soft, undecaying leaves. A haven for the bodiless distillation of what had once been Catriona Macreadie.

What she had become defied her every attempt at understanding. Was she just an instrument fashioned for the needs and whims of these ancient powers? It seemed that way. The Zyradin's experiment with that immense piece of ship debris was still fresh in her mind, prompting wild speculation – surely the Zyradin wasn't planning to use her to seize Hegemony vessels and move them to Segrana. Even stranded on the moon's surface, such a warship would prove lethal to the surrounding forest. No explanation had thus far been presented to her and now, after all that she'd been through, she just longed for peace and seclusion. The dream-palace, however, was no longer her insulated, isolated refuge – Segrana and the Zyradin were laying siege.

It was a siege waged with images of the war that raged and roared around Nivyesta and the planet Darien. She was shown the sporadic gathering of those who came to defend Darien and its moon. She saw Greg Cameron meeting the rebel Tygrans aboard their ship, then the unexpected appearance of the Earthsphere fleet and the divisions that emerged in their ranks. And saw Greg's encounter with the Earthsphere vice-admiral, the tussle with an assassin, and the arrival of the dauntingly huge Hegemony armada.

The Zyradin revealed in detail the sheer armed might that was ranged against the defenders. Segrana sent her image streams of Rory and Chel's sufferings, the awful task they were set and how Chel got them both out of the terrible trap. The Zyradin fed to her sequence after sequence from the battle as it unfolded and as the Earthsphere, Imisil and Vox Humana suffered destruction upon destruction. Then Segrana made her see the attack on Tusk Mountain by the Tygran Marshal Becker, the desperate fight involving Uncle Theo and Captain Gideon against Nathaniel Horne, a Tygran who appeared to be the host for some kind of parasite.

Then came the explosions that demolished Giant's Shoulder, exposing the warpwell, from which the Legion of Avatars began to emerge, escaping their ancient and dreadful prison. The Zyradin allowed her to feel the qualities of those ancient organic minds still confined within their elaborately mechanised, militarised caskets. The first thing she felt was a thrilling joy, the ecstasy of freedom from cramped black confinement, then came a gleeful, almost euphoric rage, an unshackled lust to lash out, a voracious need for reprisal against anyone or anything . . .

** It was the Forerunners who put them in that prison ** When they sense the presence of Segrana and myself they will come seeking retribution ** Only the Keeper of Segrana can be the bridge **

She shied away.

'I cannot be trusted!' she said. 'I shouldn't be the Keeper ...'

The Zyradin faded into the pulse and flow of the living web, the cross-tracery of root and branch, the interlocking circuit of leaf and sun and stream. Then the other presence drew near.

You are here, Segrana said, *because I chose you, you and no other – You understand the levers of knowledge – You know how to learn – You are the linchpin – Without you it will all have been for nothing.*

'Ye can't put all that on my shoulders, ye can't! ...'

Look! And see ...

All the powers and senses of Segrana suddenly opened up for her. Seeing was like flying through tenuous veils, an exhilarating swoop in amongst buildings, rooms, people, the streets and gardens, then out past fields, hills, forests, rivers, to ...

An underground chamber where Chel the Uvovo Seer sat upon a stone plinth, his six eyes gazing in pairs at different things. Above, a few Legion cyborgs were being fended off by energies that flashed up out of the ground. Then beneath again with Chel, who was now staring straight at her, a sixfold regard that pierced her essence.

(*All events are balanced at this point*, he said to her. *There are terrible futures to be avoided. Trust Segrana – she was right to choose you. Beware of losing the balance but prepare yourself to lose ... other things ...*)

Her vision was wrenched away, translucent images

flicking past, a flickering sequence of half-glimpsed places, half-recognised faces ... Greg's mother, her features looking tired and careworn, her frown-lines more pronounced, her grey hair tied back ... a tall Sendrukan hurrying across burnt ground ... five still figures lying on couches, wires and tubes issuing from their bodies while enclosing visors hid their eyes ... a man she felt sure was the ambassador Robert Horst, even though he looked much younger, talking with a hovering silvery saucer ... Julia Bryce, ice-cold Julia, calmly standing beneath a whirling corona of stabbing needles as they steadily dismantled her ...

(*This is the point*, came Chel's voice, *upon which all events are balanced.*)

** **A linchpin holds the wheel upon the axle** ** said the Zyradin.

A lens gathers the light of the sun into a bright needle, said Segrana.

** **Without a fulcrum, a lever is just a piece of metal** **

But all she could see was her memory of Segrana burning, trees on fire, veins of heat breaking through the ground, driven by the primal powers that she had unleashed while seeking to act against those invaders many days ago.

'No!' she cried, beating herself against the inner bounds of the dream-palace. Only to find herself flying beyond it, soaring at first, then, assailed by guilt and a gnawing self-doubt, plummeting into gloom.

Greg, she thought. *I need to know, need to find out the truth, need you ...*

Sideways whirling and hurtling through clouds of

blurs and scraps of faces and pages printed with words ... and there he is, stumbling along a smoky corridor aboard a failing ship. While merciless Legion cyborgs tear their way through the outer hull, ripping out the plating ...

And in another place, Theo and Rory are struggling across rain-lashed shards and boulders, harsh-lit by the actinic radiance of the warpwell revealed ... Legion cyborgs rush up out of the hyperspace portal ... one shows interest in the group of Humans clambering towards the opening ... obedient, servile mechs glide towards them and horrible, uncertain fighting begins ... Rory is snatched into the air ... Theo takes the bomb from the fallen Rory ... and Catriona can see his death ...

And Greg continues through the doomed vessel ... finds an airlock just as a Legion cyborg finds him ... but he's inside the lock, safe before the monster reaches the hatch ... and Catriona sees his death ... she reaches for him, for the ship, for that place, trying to make herself manifest ... and Chel is there, before her.

'*You cannot,*' he says. '*You must not use it this way or all the futures fail ...*'

The truth of his words strikes her ... she ducks it, sidesteps away from that ship with a sob and wail ... and returns to the huge, shattered burial mound that Giant's Shoulder has become ... perhaps she can save Uncle Theo ... or alter Rory's path, helping him avoid being swept up by the cyborg ... but Chel is there, hands raised, entreating ...

'*You must not do this,*' he says again.

'Then you be the Keeper,' she replies, distraught. 'I

know what will happen, I've seen the destruction that my hands made . . . '

'*Those were the ancient powers of Segrana, powers beneath the powers,*' Chel says. '*You think that when Segrana chose you she did not know that such a choice would come before you? She knew it would, and she knew you and therefore knew how you would choose!*'

'I don't . . . '

'*She knew that you would have the will to grasp the power,*' says the Uvovo Seer. '*That was the prerequisite which she could not be sure . . . I was capable of.*' Chel smiles. '*You see? All events are balanced at this point, this fulcrum, and the fulcrum is you. Through the Keeper, through you, the Zyradin and Segrana will attain their fusion and through you the ancient powers beneath the powers will be focused.*' He closes his eyes suddenly, and a grimace of pain passes across his features. '*Time is against me. Enemies gather nearby. You know what must be done . . . the sacrifice will not be for nothing . . .*'

'But . . . what is it that I must do? . . . '

He was gone, and she felt herself draw back, loosely gliding like a leaf in the grip of a determined breeze. Veils of images fluttered by as she passed by, all the pains and angers and sufferings of so many people, on Darien and in the ships fighting above the skies, all that anguish and rage, feeding itself like a circulating fountain of deadly poison. Then she was standing on the leafy floor of the dream-palace with the fragrance of the wallflowers filling her head.

** **The time is now** ** **There is no better time** **

'I think I'm ready,' she said. 'Mind you, I've said that before and been shown the error of my ways . . . '

Even before she finished the sentence the air was full
of glowing blue motes that emerged from the walls and
the floor and descended from the pillared heights,
swirling round her, sinking into her form. Her senses
seemed to open like doors and the immensity of Segrana
rushed majestically in to enfold her. Her awareness
stretched out, branched and subdivided and expanded
until she realised that it was time to reach downward
and inward for that ancient power of powers.

** **This power exists for a reason** ** **As it did in the
time of the Forerunners** ** **They knew that the war had
to be won and they knew that if all else failed a great
sacrifice would be needed** ** **It was not needed then, but
it is needed now** **

'This is ... a hard thing to face,' she said. 'How can
you ...'

*Past mirrors future mirrors present, but never per-
fectly*, said Segrana. *The flaws are the seeds around
which great beauty can grow.*

Around her the force of Segrana entwined while the
gleaming, shining motes of the Zyradin swam through
them both. In her awareness she seemed to be standing
over a fracture in the forest floor at the deepest, most
lightless part of Segrana, her hand reaching down, beckoning, urging the powers of the ancients to arise.

Past mirrors future.

** **Future mirrors present** **

The power surged, and she felt its near-inchoate
nature threaten to burst forth, uncontrolled, unfocused.
But she tamed it, channelled it, formed it into something like restraint, something like a purpose, hot and
destructive.

** Well done ** Are you prepared? ** To behold the mirror of the self? **

'No,' she said. 'But I'm still going through with it.'

Above her, in the vast and frigid vacuum of space, the cyborgs of the Legion of Avatars swept in their darkening flocks numbering hundreds of thousands, pursuing the remnants of the Hegemony and Earthsphere fleets and those other survivors. Their lust for slaughter drove them on, engulfing vessels entire, breaking them open, obliterating all signs of life, destroying, tearing and ripping, then onward to the next and the next. Catriona could see how this insensate horde would journey from star to star, wreaking utter havoc wherever they went, even though Theo's sacrifice had choked off the flow of more of the insane creatures. And she knew that what was going to be done had to be done. But a small corner of her heart wept.

'So ... begin.'

With herself as the fulcrum, Segrana and the Zyradin acted in synchronicity for the first time, entwining their presences through her to act upon the substructures of linear space-time. Within a domain, carefully limited by a shaping of the ancient energy, the linear mode of her own intrinsic essence was refracted and reflected over and over. In seconds she was surrounded by a growing crowd of versions of herself, each one winking into existence and all looking calm and collected. When she pushed herself up on tiptoe she could see that the crowd was growing into a throng stretching back into the cavernous spaces of the dream-palace.

** We can delay no longer ** Remember how I taught you to retrieve that ship debris ** Bring them to Segrana and we will render them unto peace **

In an eyeblink she went from that busy assembly to
the yawning blackness of space, her form a translucent
glow. Not far away one of her selves shot past, flying
straight towards a ship that was under attack from a
crawling swarm of Legion cyborgs. She stretched out
her hand in that direction and immediately moved forward. Other Catrionas were converging and she saw
how they lunged at the cyborgs, one- or two-handed,
and grabbed some edge or protruding component, then
in the next instant they were gone, vanished.

Across the ship's hull the cyborg creatures clustered
around weakened points, tearing into the plating, ripping out cabling, while not yet aware of their
diminishing numbers. Until a flight of Catrionas landed
in the midst of a tightly packed mob of them, and disappeared along with their captives. A spasm of anger
rippled through the gleaming black machine-beasts and
some even seemed to detect the avenging Catrionas as
they swooped in close. Cat ducked in close enough to
one to close her hand around a jutting stalk tipped with
a sensor cube. There was a dazzling moment that sent
splinters of iciness through her ...

Then she was hanging in midair, high up in the leafy
density of Segrana but beneath the canopy. Her hand
still held on to the cyborg's sensor stalk yet bizarrely
there was no sensation of supporting the thing's weight,
nor did it move. Reflexively she let go and the Legion
cyborg came to sudden, thrashing life as it fell away,
arms and tentacles flailing, slashing and snapping at
branches as it plummeted. But then it slowed and for a
moment Catriona thought it would climb back up after
her. Until webs of actinic energy sprang out from the

nearby trees and from beneath, enfolding the cyborg in a lethal embrace. It convulsed and shuddered and sparks flowed from within its carapace while a smoky vapour leaked out here and there. Abruptly all its effectors and limbs went limp and it resumed its downward plunge, which ended with a splintering crash and a brief flare.

Everywhere she looked the same scenario was playing out and she saw one of her selves wave to her through the trees before she was whisked away to apprehend another creature of the Legion.

This time she appeared near one of the huge Hegemony carrier vessels which had attracted a correspondingly more numerous Legion assault. It seemed a daunting task at first since there were thousands of armoured cyborgs crawling all over the entire length of the vessel. Then she glanced over her shoulder and saw the pale host that was sweeping in with her. It was a moment made for banners and battle cries, of which there were none, apart from the yelling she was doing in her own thoughts.

The tide of Catrionas descended upon the cyborgs in a wave that rolled down the carrier's flank, and a similar wave of disappearances swept along in its wake. Some Legion cyborgs leaped away from the rest as the vanishing rushed towards them and it was one of these that Cat laid hands on, grabbing an overlapping plate of armour. The channelled and shaped ancient energies of Nivyesta seized them both in a flash of dislocation ...

When she appeared this time Segrana was hazy with smoke and filled with terrible noises, the crash of falling trees and the screams of panicking animals. This time she delayed relaxing her hold on the cyborg, trying to peer through the hazy gloom – but then the Legion creature began to stir, jerking and wrenching, and just as she let it go the smoke thinned before her and she saw the flickering yellow-orange of a tree on fire ...

The next time she returned the murk was thicker and orange glows could be seen all around her. On the spur of the moment she held on to the Legion monstrosity while pushing herself downward. It was a descent into darkness since the layers of smoke were shutting out the sunlight and reflected Darienlight. Blackened tree trunks were all she saw, clouds of ash drifting on hot updraughts, but she had to release the cyborg before reaching the forest floor. Webs and whips of harsh white energy tore into it even as it fought back during its tumbling fall into funereal gloom ...

With each succeeding return to Nivyesta, to Segrana, the fiery glows grew more numerous and the smoke denser. At the same time, with each new foray out into the running battles in near space there were fewer and fewer cyborg knights of the Legion of Avatars, to the point where Catriona and her host of sisters started to outnumber them. *Valkyries victorious*, she thought. When that stage was reached, the end came swiftly.

She could not recall the last cyborg she brought back for its execution. She didn't remember her last sortie into the great debris fields now stretching across huge swathes of space, destined to be swept up by Darien's gravity field. She had a hazy recollection of the immense Roug ship, the one shaped like a pouncing creature, but it was like a fragment from a dream left over when she found herself sitting on the leafy floor of the dream-palace. In the dimness she could only feel a monolithic exhaustion settling over everything as those ancient and terrifying powers slowed and sank, muted and fading. Then she sensed a familiar presence trying to communicate through a vast and grinding weariness, trying to speak but failing. Then even awareness dissolved into a timeless, bodiless river without end or beginning ...

When she awoke she had aches in every limb as well as neck and back. She was lying on a pallet in a small hut, wrapped in a rough blanket that smelled faintly of herbs. She yawned, scratched an itch on her ear, thought about food ... and sat bolt upright with a gasp. Tremblingly she examined her hands, her arms, legs, feet, realising with thrilling delight that she had a body again, and it was her own body!

Suddenly, vibrantly awake, she lay there for moment then stood, tugged the blanket tight about her, and went over to look out of the solitary window.

The view was of a cove full of trees and dense foliage, and a few boats bobbing on the waters not far from the shore. A cool breeze came in off the sea but the air was still marred by the taint of ash.

'Ah, nice to see you up and about. Managed to scrounge up some clothes for you.'

A tall, skinny woman in a tattered, patched blue jerkin and work trousers had entered with an armful of garments which she dropped onto a stool.

'Where is this?' Cat said. 'How did I get here?'

'Cradle-Veil is the Uvovo name for it, and this is our Watchtree. I'm Kirsten, by the way.'

They shook hands and Cat introduced herself. Kirsten's eyes widened.

'The Uvovo who brought you here last night never told us who you were,' she said, her voice lowering. 'Were you caught up in it? What was it like?'

'What do you mean?' Cat said, having a good idea of what she meant.

'It's better if I show you.'

Still wrapped in the blanket, she followed Kirsten out onto the platform surrounding the hut.

'There's an observation platform with a good southerly outlook over the ridge,' Kirsten said. 'Up here.'

A ramp led up to a roofed platform with a chest-high rail. From the moment Cat stepped onto it the sight of what lay to the south struck her like a blow, and as she approached the rail the view opened up.

Of the forest of Segrana, its fabulously intricate, interwoven matrix of flora and fauna, of biomass and organic life and all the towns and settlements of the Uvovo, there was nothing left. A seared, blackened desolation stretched as far as the eye could see, a wasteland of ash up from which the charred remnants of trees jutted like black spikes. It was the horror from her vision. A deathly silence seemed to emanate from it, a silence that went deep.

Tears streaming down her face, Catriona had to lean on the railing to stay upright. Staring out at it, she could also see the twisted fragments of Legion cyborgs scattered everywhere, heat-buckled carapaces, half-melted tool arms, the strewn, torched dregs of mechanistic viscera. Chel and the Zyradin had mentioned a great sacrifice. But this was too much.

Too much to look upon. Weeping, she slid down and clasped her knees in close while Kirsten said uncertain consoling words.

39

JULIA

It all had the unnerving semblance of improvisation. Harry told her the details of Reski Emantes's diversion – a dozen decoy remotes emitting the energy profiles of Construct wardroids as they boarded the station via several spread-out airlocks – just a few moments before the dataform device began repatterning her for the transfer. At that moment Julia's body was lying on a couch in one of the Great Hub's subspace signal towers, her vacant mind's neural pathways under the control of a task-dedicated AI, what the subservicers had called a cognition, residing in an implant embedded in her body's brain. Once Julia's fractalised sentience was repatterned she would be streamed into the implant, overwriting the cognition AI and taking control. She had crossed vast interplanetary distance via the tiernet, had entirely unexpected encounters, seen incredible sights and spectacles, and vied with deadly adversaries, just so she could complete the circle.

Well, it wasn't entirely complete – there was too much neural damage to her cortex to risk an organic transferral. Overwriting the implant was safer.

She waited beneath the overarching, fabulously

intricate dataform, a glowing software assembly whose bright stabbing needles were prescanning the structure of her fractalised sentience, preparatory to the full compressive transload operation. Harry gave her a sardonic wave as the last milliseconds trickled away, and she was sure that she saw a familiar look of mischief pass over his features.

Then everything smeared and slid sideways, distorting along a rainbow spiral that coiled and coiled into whiteness ...

Then time sprang back into motion. There was the sense of being somewhere else but vision was a dark blur and she could hear nothing. It had to be the VR headset which all the captive Enhanced were wearing. The subservicer AIs had explained that the implant had a hardbuilt interfacing system, which would match her own motion and perception impulses. Right now she needed to see, so she thought of herself tilting her head to one side, turning it, brushing her temple against her shoulder, even jerking her head sharply sideways ...

Success! The VR visor tilted sideways, giving her a partial view of the low, round corridor, some of the consoles, and the couch in front. As if this were a signal, a circular emblem began to blink in the lower right of her field of vision and sound came through. She found that if she stared at the emblem for more than three seconds an opaque menu of options appeared. As she experimented, she listened in to the commotion going on along the corridor. She could hear Corazon Talavera shrieking at some unfortunate underlings, ordering them to 'hunt down and obliterate the intruders', which had to be Reski Emantes's decoys.

Anything that upsets that prize bitch has to be a good thing, she thought.

Mastering the implant's op-system was straightforward and she quickly came up with a list of the high-level connections that were open to her, or rather to the AI she had supplanted.

Power Usage Aggregate Monitor
Communications Net
Security Overwatch
Biophysical Aggregate Monitor
Chemo-Cortico Aggregate Monitor
Target and Guidance
Arm and Launch

The last two also offered additional options – **Codeline Interface** or **Immersion Interface**. For the last on the list she chose option 2.

Julia's vision swam for a moment and the word 'recalibrating' pulsed below her POV centre a few times before the colours and shapes of a gloomy landscape appeared all around her. A memory came to her from those frantic moments before she gave up her body to escape Talavera, and she realised that this was Irenya's personal metacosm. Dark bruised clouds loomed low overhead. Julia stood next to a dried-out stone fountain in a parched garden, several yards from a large and imposing mansion. A massive stairway flanked by stone wolves led up to a pair of iron-studded doors burdened with chains and padlocks. She considered the exterior, noting the narrow windows covered by outer shutters, the pale patches of lichen, the spreading webs of leafless, desiccated ivy. And a slender circular tower at one corner. It seemed atypical, out of keeping with the mansion's stern, square-built aesthetic. When she reached it she discovered an open door and inside a spiral staircase which she began to climb. From outside came a rumble of thunder.

By the time Julia reached a landing halfway up, a steady rain was falling – from an open, glassless window she could see water pooling in the fountain's bowl and spreading in puddles across the ground. Ascending further, she came to the joisted underside of a floor – the staircase curved up to a door which opened easily and quietly. Inside, the tower room was bare, just floor-boards and blank walls, and an open window, its double shutters swung outwards. The rain was heavier now, gusts sending sprays of it in to speckle the dusty floor around the slight figure that sat hunched there. It was Irenya.

Julia crouched beside her, one tentative hand on her shoulder, whispering her name. After a moment Irenya opened her eyes and sighed.

'Did everything, you know? Did it all, just as they asked.'

Irenya was thin, her face gaunt, her blonde hair lank and tangled. Anguished eyes came round.

'Yulia? Is that you?'

'Yes – mostly.'

'I can feel . . . I felt it when Thorold gave up. I could feel him slipping away.' Grief made the lines deepen in her face. 'Letting go . . .'

Julia felt a sharp shadow of loss touch her, yet it

seemed more of a dismal stoicism than genuine sorrow.

'Irenya,' she said. 'I need to ask you about the arming and launch sequences ...'

'... just letting it go and slipping away ... letting it go and ...'

'Please Irenya, you have to help me ...'

Irenya shook her head dolefully then looked at her hands. 'Took me off it, Yulia. Said I was losing my focus. That's why I'm here in the tower, to keep me away from ...' She pointed out of the window.

Julia got to her feet and went over to the casement, ignoring the rain as she peered out. Behind the frontage of the mansion was a broad flat roof covered in an array of identical statues laid out in twenty rows of twenty-five each. In the downpour it was difficult to make out the form of the statues; they seemed to resemble some kind of bulky creature holding up a cluster of rods, angled at the sky.

'Quite a sight, eh? Nice symbology, I thought.'

At the sound of that familiar, despised voice Julia began to turn back into the room. But Talavera was already charging at her, hands outflung. The impact shoved her backwards off her feet and out of the window ...

Suddenly she was back on the couch in the Great Hub, dumped out of the metacosm by her implant's hazard-detection cutout. The VR visor still sat asquint on her face and she whipped her head to the side a couple of times before it finally flew off.

'Okay, so now you've got a better view,' came Talavera's voice from somewhere behind her. 'Good – there's something I want you to see.'

The Chaurixa leader came and stood next to Julia's couch, looked down and shook her head. 'Clever gambit,' she said. 'Those decoys had my boys running around and going crazy trying to find non-existent Construct combat droids. Meanwhile one of these neat probes fed you in via some subsystem and you crept back to your old carcass. Only now you're a fractalised sentience occupying an implant in your own brain! Goodness, the irony is practically industrial-strength – especially now that I have isolated your implant from extraneous connections.'

'Okay, we've established that you're screaming mad,' Julia said in a hoarse whisper. 'What new outburst of vileness are you going to show me?'

'Hmm, you've got feisty since we last met.' Talavera chuckled but her eyes glittered. 'What you don't know is that all this constitutes an act of rational purpose. There is an ecology of greatness in the cosmos – evolution has many directions and only the greatest can defy the currents of dissolution. That's what this is about, and you are privileged to be a witness ...'

She broke off as a Henkayan carrying three weapons appeared at the end of the round passageway.

'We have him,' it said gruffly.

'Bring him to me.'

Talavera laughed as her minion left, a high girlish sound that, Julia recalled, usually presaged a deed of outstanding cruelty.

'It's a shame you didn't let me know you were coming,' Talavera said. 'I'd have had drinks and snacks arranged, sweet lights and sweet music.' She raised her hands dramatically. 'But – at least my cherished travelling companions are here with me to celebrate this historical event ... dearest Kao Chih! Do join us.'

The barrel-chested, four-armed Henkayan had returned with a Human, a black-haired, youthful male in a dull orange two-piece. The man's hands were bound behind his back, his features were Asiatic and he had a bruised jaw and a split lip. As the Henkayan steered him along the passage Talavera brought out a chair and pointed at it. The man was prodded towards it and shoved down into a seated position. Talavera grinned and patted his cheek.

'Right, first introductions. Julia, this is Kao Chih; Kao Chih – Julia. I've spent some time with both of you, and finally we've got the whole gang together in the one place!' She smiled. 'Did you miss me, KC? Remember all the fun we had?'

'I have not forgotten you, Mistress Talavera.'

Talavera glanced at Julia and rolled her eyes. 'Mistress! Always so polite, the Chinese. Even when they're stabbing you in the back – isn't that right, KC? After all, that's what you did back in the Shafis system, when you abandoned me on that miserable scumpot of a planet.' She had been poking his shoulder as she spoke but then stopped. 'And yet if I hadn't been dumped there I might never have encountered my master's servants and heard his message and his promise ... '

As she spoke, the smoky black snake creatures appeared from below, winding their way up her body. Julia stared, remembering their name – vermax – and wondered if they were actually even organic creatures.

'... and we wouldn't be here today to honour and mark the occasion of His arrival.'

She pointed a small control remote at one of the consoles and a large holopanel winked on above it. The image was divided into eight subframes showing cycles of visual feeds from the hundreds of sensors dotted around the exterior of the Great Hub. Against the looming, striated hyperspace background, ships fought in sideslipping, glancing encounters. Some of the sensors were tracking the participants and Julia saw black curvilinear ships of the Vor lash out with bright tentacles to attack smaller vessels shaped like bulbous argopods, the shell-squids that populated the waters of the Eastern Towns. Others showed similar clashes involving the argopod ships and fast darting craft with tapered prows and bullet-shaped sterns.

'The Construct just doesn't know when to give in,' said Talavera. 'Keeps throwing ships into a lost cause, keeps wasting its forces. Even when the Godhead Himself enters the arena.'

The eight subframes merged, dissolved into a single image. It looked like a strange landscape seen from above at something like a 20-degree angle. The ground was a gleaming swirl of silver-grey and slate-blue shot through with strands of black, like something stirred or kneaded. As Julia watched she could see that the blue-grey surface was in motion, undulations passing across it. The image pulled back and the restless expanse widened, and curious solid-looking outlines appeared as if pushing up out of something glutinous and malleable. Sections of strange structures emerged, domes, triangular obelisks, then they would twist and distort into something completely different, odd creatures struggling across the grey ripples before collapsing back in, or bizarre body parts, a winged arm, a foot, a brace of tails, and a huge face that surfaced, gazed up with blank eyes for a moment before tipping over and sliding back in.

The image pulled back and the details shrank into a general dark grey amalgam. At last its upper edge came into view along with more ships, big black domelike ones and silvery diamonds around which flocks of smaller craft swooped. When the full extent of the grotesque immensity became apparent, it resembled a vast ragged island with an underside so notched, craggy and serrated it might have been wrenched whole from the bedrock of some malformed planet.

'Meet the Godhead!' Talavera said. 'In all his irresistible glory!'

40

ROBERT

The empathic entity, the Godhead's dislocated conscience, used its drone to attach protective frameworks to the head and foot of Robert's couch. Essential nutrient and medication sacs were taped to the underframe and most of his monitor wires were removed. Then suspensors in the frameworks were activated and the drone steered him out of the small grey room and into a passage that sloped downwards in a straight line for quite a distance.

'Could you summarise what we're doing again?' Robert said as he floated downwards. 'Especially the part about how we defeat the Godhead with his own dreams. You see, the more you repeat it to me the more confident I'll feel about the undertaking as a whole.'

'Very well,' said the empathic entity via its drone. 'There is a specific area of the Godhead's brain where sleep imperatives and symbolic memories continuously entwine, which over time I've come to call the dream gyrus. The Godhead never wholly gives itself over to sleep but it does allow selected areas of the cortex to slip into the dream state as an aid to neural repair and low-level cognitive indexing.

'Once we reach the dream gyrus you and I shall co-interface with the localised synaptic web and force the Godhead's awareness into the sleep/dream state. Then with your memories of the Tanenth homeworld we will compel it to accept its guilt and remorse and thereby persuade it to abandon the multi-missile launch. So – do you feel more confident now?'

'Not especially,' Robert said. 'Although I can say that I've not been overly discouraged.'

'Glad I could be of service.'

From a regular passageway their route turned into a twisting tunnel whose walls looked oddly organic in shape but stone-grey in colour and surface texture. The tunnel turned and curved through some hairpin bends that were a challenge to negotiate but eventually they reached an easier section which widened, opening out. At this point the empathic entity's drone remote halted and it spoke to Robert.

'We are about to enter the dream gyrus,' it said. 'What you called the meta-quantal flux is strong here so do not be surprised by anything that you see, or even think that you see. Once we co-interface with the synaptic web we will be able to exert a measure of control and counter any troublesome manifestations.'

Robert gave a puzzled frown then bit his lip as the couch knocked against a jutting curve of tunnel floor, causing a passing twinge of pain.

Further on they reached a wide, long, low-ceilinged cavern where the floor was uneven and where tapering hummocks formed rough columns with ceiling protrusions. This was all visible through long glowing veils that trembled or flickered, but as they moved forward into the cavern Robert saw that the veils were streams of pale images rushing up and down between ceiling and floor. Occasionally he caught glimpses of himself on the river, in the hammer giant's cave, in the auditorium with the crowd of Rosas. *Is this where the Godhead's experiences are recycled as dreams, or does it dream all the time?*

'A close approximation,' said the empathic entity when Robert voiced his theory. 'The Godhead's dream-state is a continual thought process which he can voluntarily enter or use and from which he exiled me so long ago. It is both his greatest strength and his greatest weakness.' The drone had brought the suspensor-couch to a halt. From its upper disc a pair of jointed arms unfolded, holding between them a frail-looking mesh cap. 'We are at the centre of the dream gyrus, Robert Horst – shall we commence?'

Robert drew a deep breath. 'I think we should, while I still have some optimism left.'

The empathic entity made no reply as it slipped the mesh cap over his head. Something sparkled at the centre of Robert's field of vision and radiated outwards. Suddenly all the vague images became sharp, at least the slower-moving, more complete ones did. There was a lay-ered hierarchy of sights and sounds, important ones that were focused, detailed and often in full colour, secondary ones that drifted in and out of the translucent back-ground, and peripheral monochrome ones that formed sequences of snapshots, strong and expressive moments that came and went, often repeating.

Just then the central image was of a circular passage-way cluttered with consoles along one side and couches along the other while a short woman with curly black

hair spoke with someone on one of the couches, also a
woman. He was mildly startled as he recognised them
from the auditorium – the woman on the couch was Julia
while the other was Talavera. Engrossed, he wondered if
the cloud of secondary images were at all related.

'Robert, you must clear your mind and revive your
memories of the Tanenth and their world.'

He turned his head away, trying to recall his visit to
that vast water cavern filled with that computer-run simulation of an entire world and its inhabitants. He saw
again the AI machine, which the Tanenth made in their
own image, a curious elongated squidlike being, and
recalled the tour of that world, its cities and peoples all
rendered in perfect detail. As the memories passed
across his own mind's eye they also flowed through the
co-interface and into the Godhead's dream-state. With
every passing moment the world of the Tanenth
extended itself throughout the dream gyrus and beyond.

'What happens next?' Robert said.

'When this extrapolation from your memories
reaches its visualisation limit I shall drive the boundaries
of the dream gyrus outwards to encompass the
Godhead's conscious awareness, then . . .' The empathic
entity paused and its drone rotated slowly. 'Is this element part of your memories?'

All around them the squidlike Tanenth were gathering in a large circular paved area surrounded by round,
squat buildings with flat, disc-shaped roofs. As Robert
watched, the Tanenth passed glassy bulbs amongst
themselves, drinking from them before passing them on.
It took a minute or so for the poison to work, for the
Tanenth to fall limply onto the paving stones.

'I was shown scenes like this,' Robert said, feeling shaken. 'But from a distance, not this close.'

The mass suicide played out again and again in different settings, in a communal home, in some kind of factory, in an outdoor arena – it was the sight of hundreds of thousands of sentient creatures voluntarily ending their lives. Robert felt the tears burning on his cheeks.

'Maybe these are sequences you were shown but have been unable to recover till now,' the empathic entity said. 'Or perhaps these memories are not yours, in which case ...'

Robert and the drone were now back in the circular gathering place. As the scene began to repeat itself, several larger beings identical to the Tanenth appeared and moved through the crowds, calling out with booming voices. These were the Advisers, the Godhead's messengers, and as they spoke the Tanenth responded angrily and many arguments ensued.

'This is not part of my memories,' Robert said.

'I know,' said the drone. 'All this time, despite the strenuous efforts to erase the emotional remainders, to exile me from his awareness and then to expunge me altogether, the memories still hung on, deeply, tenaciously buried – along with the guilt!'

Shafts of light angled down from above, falling upon the roiling, indignant crowd. The form that descended towards the startled onlookers was identical to the upright squid-likenesses of the Tanenth, except that it was huge and purest white.

'He is here!' the empathic entity said. 'The dream-simulation is adapting – the Godhead has now become entangled in its own dream!'

'Can we stop those missiles?' Robert said.

'The Godhead has relaxed his control over the external communication channels ... and other means of influence. As soon as we attempt to turn them to our purposes this will cause a ripple effect that will serve to bring the Godhead out of the dream-state. His subsequent displeasure is sure to be considerable.'

Robert laughed, despite the pain of the straps still keeping him in the couch. 'Well, if he's going to wake up angry, let's give him something to be angry about!'

41

JULIA

'... a long-delayed departure from an undeserving continuum,' Talavera was saying as the long-range sensor cam roamed across the undulating ugliness of the Godhead's exterior. 'And the catalyst will be an event unprecedented on the galactic scale, the simultaneous creation of five hundred supernovae ...'

'Genocide, you mean,' Julia said. 'The destruction of hundreds of worlds and civilisations. The slaughter of billions upon billions ...'

She froze in mid-sentence as a vermax snaked into her field of vision and lunged its eyeless, tapered head towards her, stopping just inches from her face, wavering there.

'Now, Julia, I explained about the ecology of greatness,' Talavera said. 'Didn't I? Superior lifeforms obey their own rules and pursue their own goals, their own paths to higher levels of overarching wisdom.' She leaned in closer, gaze darting from Julia to the vermax and back. 'There you are, residing in the bubblemesh-matrix of that cranial implant and here we have a vermax, a technivore supreme. To his senses you're nothing more than a luscious titbit – just imagine it tearing open that skull then biting into the implant, its incisors slicing into the metal and the components within. Maybe you'd actually feel it, maybe not, but remember that the next time you get the urge to be a sanctimonious bore. Otherwise, you'll end up as a vermax snack.'

She stepped away and the vermax withdrew.

'Learn to curb your disrespect ... oh, my master!'

The big holopanel no longer showed the continental vastness of the Godhead. Instead, against a background of roiling blue, a coldly androgynous humanoid mask stared out with blank, hollow eyes.

'So,' said the mask, its empty mouth forming a smile. 'You're the real Talavera.'

Talavera's demeanour went from beatific adoration to incandescent hatred in an eyeblink.

'And you are not Him!'

A moment later her eyes rolled up to show the whites and she collapsed to the floor like a puppet with its strings severed. The vermax shrank and dwindled as they escaped through gaps in the floor.

'Correct,' said the mask. 'I am what He might have become.' The mask then tilted slightly in Julia's direction. 'Now, Julia, the real Julia, there is very little time – do you know about the Godhead and the missiles?'

She nodded. 'Five hundred supernovae equals a gateway to a higher plane of existence.'

'Yes, or a one-way ticket to hell,' the mask said. 'What you have to do is access the missile-targeting system and retarget them all on the Godhead.'

Julia almost felt like laughing, feeling a trickle of something like hysterical panic.

'There is a slight problem or two,' she said. 'Talavera has four or five thugs wandering around while I'm here, strapped to a couch and the new arrival is ...'

Her voice trailed off as the Asiatic Kao Chih snapped the bonds around his wrists with casual ease then reached down and did the same to the cords around his ankles. Then to her astonishment his appearance, his very form began to change, darkening and growing taller while limbs became slender, matching the rest of his torso.

'Ah, a member of the ancient and noble Roug,' said the mask.

The shapeshifter being gave a slight but grave bow of the head. 'My sincere apologies for the subterfuge – although I am acquainted with the esteemed Kao Chih, I am not him. I am Mandator Qabakri, sent by the High Index of the Roug to assist in any way that I can.'

'Julia,' said the mask. 'You must find a way to target all those missiles on the Godhead without delay. We do not know how long it will be before the Godhead emerges from the dream-state we have fooled him into. It would also be advisable to bind Talavera's limbs.'

'Who are you?' Julia said. 'Are you Human?'

The mask smiled eerily. 'We are embers, the embers of one Human life, and the embers of a fading conscience. Go now – do what must be done.'

Then the mask was gone, replaced by that daunting view of the Godhead's bizarre vista.

'Human Julia,' said the Roug, 'is this a normal occurrence?'

She looked round and gasped to see Arkady gingerly swing his legs off his couch and press his naked feet down on the tiled floor.

'Arkady,' she said hoarsely. 'The readouts said that there was no brain activity, that you were gone.'

'I'm sorry, Julia, but he is definitely gone.' Arkady spoke but the voice wasn't quite his. 'We've been watching via the shadow system and when we heard our snake-loving friend here revealing her Godhead colours we decided to act. Which is how I came to be downloaded into this body's implant.'

'And into this one ...'

Thorold was likewise getting down from the next couch along, swaying on shaky legs. Julia stared, knowing she should be feeling something strong, something like anger or even fury as she recognised the intelligence that was looking back at her from those two well-remembered faces. She shifted her posture, sitting straighter on her own couch.

'Harry,' she said, glancing at the Roug. 'And no, this is not a normal occurrence.'

'I know, two of me,' said Harry-Arkady. 'Can the cosmos stand the strain?'

'At least you're showing some initiative,' Julia said. 'Time is not on our side, so can you find out how Talavera shut down my access and reverse it?'

'I know exactly what she did,' Harry-Thorold said, bending down to examine her couch's control panel. 'Saw it all on the surveillance feed.'

'So did I,' said Harry-Arkady. 'But I can see that you've got this one.'

'I see what you mean,' Julia said. 'Twice the wit.'

Harry-Arkady raised an eyebrow and pointed to Talavera's prone, unconscious form. 'You know, our mysterious masked ally had the right idea. Might be wise to keep the queen of the snakes tied up.' Nearby, the Roug Qabakri nodded agreement.

'And that's the lockouts cancelled,' said Harry-Thorold, straightening with the VR headset in his hands. 'You'll probably need this to set up the full access again.'

It was true – all the channels and networks were once more open to her.

'Right, I'm going to find a way through to Konstantin and change the missile targets.'

With headset settled about her crown, she activated the menu and eye-touched through to **Target and Guidance** then **Immersive Interface**.

For a brief moment minor distortions rippled through her visual field. Blurring was accompanied by a passing dizziness and when she looked up she was standing in a walled courtyard before a two-storey brick building. Like the sky, the bricks were a cold, grainy blue. She was facing a heavy door in an otherwise solid unbroken wall – the only windows were on the upper floor and were small and quartered. A face appeared at one of them, the face of Konstantin, who smiled, waved and moved out of sight.

There were several bushes planted along the front, low with dark bluish-green leaves. Julia tried the door but it was secure and wouldn't budge – the lock was a lever-tumbler type and seemed to be the only way of opening the door, which was impervious to her blows and kicks. Julia felt a certain irritation, aware that the seconds were ticking by. She then decided to move back a few yards, to see if she could get Konstantin's attention, but as she did so her trouser leg brushed against one of the bushes, causing a faint clinking sound.

Frowning, she crouched down and saw that several identical steel-blue keys were hanging from the bush. Other bushes she discovered sported different key types, and she swiftly amassed a good selection before returning to the door.

Through trial and error she found the right key and the unlocked door slid rather than swung open, revealing a second door. She then found that she only had about ten seconds to unlock the second door before the first one slid shut and locked itself. And behind the second door was a third, which demanded more trial and error and reopening of the first two doors till at last she stepped through to the foot of a staircase. A door opened at the top as she climbed to the final steps and Konstantin was there, looking tired, grey-haired and dressed in a grubby lab coat.

'Good to see you again, Julia,' he said, offering a weary smile. 'Welcome to Talavera's puzzle-house. She's been keeping me here for ... well, I'm not sure how long ...'

'Konstantin,' she said, 'we have to stop those missiles – Talavera has targeted them on five hundred suns to create five hundred supernovae ...'

'Yes, I know,' Konstantin said. 'Has the Godhead arrived yet?'

Julia was surprised. 'How did you know?'

'It is surprising how much these narcissistic sociopath types will reveal if you can convince them that you are practically an extension of their will.' He gave a dry laugh. 'Talavera told me about the ecology of greatness, and later, piece by piece, the Godhead's plan for its elevation to a higher continuum, a plane of superior existence, complete with hot and cold running enlightenment. All it required was five hundred supernovae and an unimaginable slaughter.' His lip curled in disgust. 'So bit by bit I built my own subversion system which would allow me to retarget all five hundred missiles with just a few commands.

'Unfortunately, I underestimated that paranoia of hers – it's so reflexive, so ingrained that it's more than just an ego state. I must have said or done something to touch it off which led to my captivity here, and the isolation of all my control interfaces.'

He beckoned her over to the small quartered window, which no longer looked down into the enclosed courtyard. Instead, about ten yards away there was a long wall of big stone blocks topped with broken glass and rows of spikes. But the window was high enough to reveal that this was just one side of an immense maze. There was an entrance, a gap in the wall a fair distance off to the left. Konstantin pointed towards the centre of the maze.

'That's where my control interfaces are,' he said. 'So Talavera locked me up in here. But now that you've unpuzzled the door I can get outside ...'

'How long will it take to get through that maze?' Julia said. 'Time is short.'

'Trust me, Julia, I always have a plan B.' He gave her a sidelong glance. 'You've changed – you're less of a martinet than you used to be.'

I'm less Human than I once was, she thought.

'I wouldn't be too sure about that,' she said. 'So, what's plan B?'

'First, we get outside ...'

She followed him back down to the triple door, which, as she half-expected, now opened onto the flat pebbly ground facing the maze's outer wall. Immediately, a high-pitched keening came from either side.

'Now we run!' Konstantin said, dashing over to the wall.

Julia spotted dog creatures converging from left and right as she ran after him. They had tapered black vermax heads rather than something less disturbing, which at that moment could have been almost anything else.

'Sorry,' he said. 'I forgot to mention Talavera's pets. Quite nasty, aren't they? . . . Ah, here it is.'

Fumbling along the wall, he stopped at a square, off-colour block and slapped his splayed-out hand against it.

The closest charging vermax-dog suddenly slowed and the ground it was on began to move backwards. The maze wall curved outwards to either side, bulging and flowing. Konstantin was unfazed by it all and was quick to grab her arm as she staggered, steadying her. It was as if this strange metacosm was being shoved through a fish-eye lens, a quivering, stretching, eye-defying distortion.

Abruptly it all sprang back to normal – except that now there were odd sections of wall jutting from the outer barrier. Nonplussed, Julia turned to Konstantin, who was grinning widely.

'Everything is fine,' he said. 'I just inverted the maze – the edge is now the centre and vice versa. A little secret functionality I built into it . . . for the fun of it, really.' He jogged out from between the wall sections, then backed away, looking to either side. He pointed to his right. 'And there it is!'

As he strode in that direction, she hurried to catch up. 'How quickly can you retarget the missiles?' she said.

'In moments, but you'll have to manually launch them from one of the consoles back in the real world.'

'Which one ...' she started to say, but then her surroundings stuttered and froze, with Konstantin paused motionless in mid-pace. Then all this was blotted out by double images and blurred trails which quickly faded into a dark blur. She was back on the couch in the round passageway, and the VR headset was gone, which implied nothing good. She caught the smell of smoke and there was a haze in the air, becoming visible as focused vision returned.

'Ah, welcome back, Julia! You missed the start of the party but I just know that we can make up for it. I may even disregard how you all took advantage of my temporary blackout.'

Talavera was rubbing reddened wrists as she came over to stand next to her couch. She wore a cold-eyed smile as she adjusted its height and angle, then tightened the restraints again. Julia saw a blank-faced Harry-Arkady sitting in a plastic chair a few feet away.

'The other body-snatchers should be here soon and then we'll have some fun.'

Talavera was bleeding from a cut on her forehead, dark red smeared across the skin. She also had a heat-burn on her cheek and shortened hanks of hair on the same side, sign of a lucky miss. And around her arms the vermax were entwined. Julia considered the horrible things for a moment before glancing over at the propped-up body of Arkady; the fist-sized bloody hole in his left temple showed where the vermax had entered to get at the implant. Which meant that Harry had been devoured, one of him anyway.

Julia stared at twice-dead Arkady and wished she could feel something.

Or do something. As before, when Talavera had pulled her from Irenya's metacosm, Julia's access to the main systems was blocked. But – had Konstantin been likewise imprisoned or had he managed to retarget the missiles? And even if plan B had succeeded, who was going to get near enough to one of the consoles to carry out the manual launch?

Talavera smiled down at her with unconcealed malice, then moved away to sit at the console directly across from Julia's couch. She fingered some touch controls and a holopanel appeared. She gave Julia a brief glance, then studied the holoimage for a moment then tapped another board symbol.

'Oh, dearest Julia, you really have been a monumental pain in my arse, you know that?' She spread her vermax-wound arms, as if theatrically gesturing to the entire Great Hub station. 'Yet here we are, at the focus of it all. I've foiled your sad little ploys at practically every turn, and now the countdown to the autolaunch is ticking and clicking the seconds away . . .'

Julia was half-listening while the greater part of her attention was fixed on the only option left. Access to all of Talavera's systems was blocked but the implant's links to her brain's neural pathways were still fully open. The implant was capable of mapping and transloading her fractalised sentience back into her organic brain, but there was neural damage somewhere among those pathways and she had no way of knowing how it would affect her.

Actual damage to the brain's structure could affect my mind, she thought. *Or lead to death. But if I do nothing, I'm dead at Talavera's hands anyway ...*

The attempt had to be made. She configured the implant for enhanced transloading and let it run.

Was the light being poured into her, or was she the light being poured into emptiness? All the sense-impressions of Talavera's smoke-veiled HQ faded away, as if she was falling or flowing from one place to another ... then they all surged back, the textures, the pressure of the restraints, the smoke-laden air rasping in her throat, tingling in her nose, the grittiness in her eyes, the hollow hunger in her gut, the sheer synergistic impact of reality rushing back in, along with Talavera's voice going over her triumphs, her brilliant tactics, and the glories yet to come.

Julia worked a hand free, keeping her eyes on Talavera as she loosened straps across her upper chest and waist ... and froze as the woman stood up, still mouthing her egoistic waffle, and started in Julia's direction. She had barely taken two steps when a cluster of bright barbs cut through the air before her. She whirled and ducked into the gap between a couple of consoles, then held out her arms. The black vermax sinuously spiralled off them and flew along the corridor. A cry of pain came from the other end and Talavera rose from her refuge, smiling.

Julia, though, had unfastened the remaining straps

and was shakily, quietly climbing out of the couch. Which was when she saw poor Arkady's body, lying on the floor where someone had discarded it. The sight of it hit her like a body blow, and other memories broke loose, Harry, Irenya, Thorold, the hellish spectacle of the Brolturan battleship's destruction ... a terrible rage detonated in her chest and turned into a wordless howl as she lunged at Talavera from behind. She grabbed her by the hair, swung her head round and slammed it against an upright equipment rack.

With blood spurting from her nose, Talavera barely stumbled, lashing out at Julia's midriff with her foot. Something in Julia saw it coming and she grabbed onto the foot and ankle, twisting it even as the blow knocked her backwards. The Chaurixa terrorist spun as she fell, jackknifing her extended leg, wrenching it free of Julia's grasp. Then she laughed, got up into a crouch, grabbed a long-handled assembly tool and lurched forward.

A pulse-beam round caught her in the shoulder. She half-spun, fell to one knee and looked back along the passageway. A second round struck her in the head and threw her onto her back amid a wide splatter of blood and gore.

Gasping for breath and with a disturbing tremble in her left hand, Julia forced herself up onto her feet. At the other end of the passageway stood Harry-Thorold, face bloody, leaning on an energy rifle, chest heaving.

'Good shot,' she said, limping over to the live console.

'I was aiming for her head,' said Harry, 'the first time. The second time ...'

'Aiming for her chest?' Julia said, then grunted as a

spike of pain shot down her left arm. There was a strange tingling in the fingers of her left hand and she hastened to the chair Talavera had so recently vacated. A slight dizziness rippled in and out, along with a blur in her vision.

Please, she thought as she almost fell into the chair. *Not now! Not yet!*

'Julia, what's wrong?' said Harry as he shuffled over.

'I ... I think I'm having a stroke,' she said haltingly. 'Neural damage ...'

'How bad is it?'

'I can just about see out of one eye and my right hand is behaving itself.'

'Well, whatever you have to do, do it quickly,' Harry said. 'Because we have a new problem.'

Back along the passage, webs of light were dancing around a figure that was unsteadily getting to its feet. The same actinic radiance that crawled over the walls and floor blazed from the ruined eye-socket of Talavera's slack features. In response Harry raised his rifle and fired off a string of energy pulses. Julia dragged her fraying attention back to the console and the holopanel with the autolaunch display. The manual launch was an innocuous-looking symbol at the back of the floating arrays of unlit launch-verified buttons, its atypical design at variance with the rest of the display. The dizziness was making it hard to stand, but she reached for the fingerpad ...

An awful low, rasping cry made her look round. Just a few feet away Harry toppled over to lie motionless on the floor, threads of vapour rising from his head. The energy-swathed apparition that had been Corazon

Talavera approached, one eye leaking jagged tendrils of hot radiance, the other rolled back and white.

'*Poor Talavera,*' whispered the smiling mouth. '*Understand, she was close to me. She understood me, knew what I am and what I must become. I felt her life, her tiny flame, go out and I knew that there had to be a threat. I came here and found all this and you. So how could one such as you be a threat to me?*' The grotesque figure leaned in close. '*My questions should be answered.*'

Julia tried to move her right hand towards the fingerpad but her torso up to the neck was paralysed. The desperate frustration and raging fear twisted together and became overwhelming. She began to weep, deep wracking sobs that came up from her chest, hot tears that streaked down to her jaw, unrestrained crying made bitter by razor-sharp memories of those who had died ...

A dagger of pain struck, running down her face through her neck. And somehow her right hand was mobile again. And when she looked up at the Godhead-possessed Talavera, she saw that the face now wore a mask woven from the tendrils of energy, a mask like the one she had spoken with earlier.

'Julia,' it said, 'grief is toxic to the Godhead – yours has forced him to retreat, allowing us to seize the meta-quantal bridge again.'

'I think ... I think I may be dying,' she said in a slurred voice.

'Then make your last moments count. Act now before he returns and crushes us all ...'

Almost without hesitation, Julia reached out to the

console fingerpad, moved one of the pointers over to that innocuous button and clicked it. Alerts popped up – **Preset Override – Full Launch Initiated** – just as ferocious, blazing light poured from Talavera's dead face. Julia looked up and snarled:

'Eat that, you bitch!'

The first wave of fifty missiles launched out of the Great Hub's docking bay, followed by the other nine waves at four-second intervals. By now the Godhead's continental immensity was looming towards the Hegemony station from the side, its thousand-mile-wide surface an expanse of unceasing deformation, a mutable silver-grey ocean perturbed by unseen, unfathomable forces. The Vor and Shyntanil vessels had abandoned their neat formations soon after the scratch force of Aggression AI ships had arrived with orders to damage and delay.

One Aggression craft, a Talon-class destructor, was engaged in a double dogfight with two Shyntanil interceptors when the first flock of missiles arced towards the Godhead. Almost immediately the interceptors broke off and headed for the Hegemony station, as did every other Vor and Shyntanil ship. The Aggression craft (which called itself Extra-Brutal, after its denotation, EB-634) knew what had to be done even as new orders flashed in from the Construct commander-sim – *defend the Great Hub*.

The Aggression AI was about to comply when its long-range sensors spotted something rising from the heaving surface of the Godhead, a Shyntanil cryptship. Signal-bursting an alert on the command channel, the AI Extra-Brutal altered course in the direction of the

Godhead. Even if the cryptship had half the usual complement of interceptors that might still be enough to shoot down the missiles.

The missiles themselves were powered to a fearsome level, each one driven by a multifield plasma engine. The Extra-Brutal computed that they could cross the intervening 600-odd miles in less than forty-eight seconds, five of which had already lapsed. Not only that, but a second wave was on its way. And a third. The Extra-Brutal didn't know what kind of payload they were carrying but it doubted that they could inflict any serious damage on the Godhead's monolithic, sub-planetary tonnage. Yet who could be certain? One of them might get lucky.

The heavy thrust of the destructor's twin plasma engines drove it downwards. Interceptors were darting away from the cryptship and the AI Extra-Brutal prepped a falling-sword pattern of homing tagger probes rigged for hull-splatter countermeasures. As soon as they were launched the Construct AI swung into a braking trajectory away from the missiles into whose collective path it had strayed. Then it loosed a spread of proximity splitters at the Shyntanil interceptors not hazed by the tagger probes, some of which were opening fire on the first wave of descending missiles. The Extra-Brutal felt a moment of satisfaction then turned its attention to the cryptship. It was pondering the best weapon combo when something went off in the locality and blitzed every external sensor for nearly an entire second.

The Extra-Brutal unit cut to backup hull cams and saw an expanding toroid of burning gases back along the path of the missiles, one of which seemed to have been intercepted. Four seconds from impact, the first wave was drawing closer together, as if to concentrate its effect. Something crept into the AI's thought process, some heightened element of caution that prompted it to make an abrupt course change away from the target zone on the Godhead, even though it was more than eight miles off.

With every digital and hardware filter in place, it was watching when the missiles struck. A dazzling white flash lasted almost half a second while a fireball unfurled at the heart of the impact, burning and vaporising into the surface of the Godhead. A tide of searing gases raced out, charring and throwing up tons of that malleable grey exterior. Then the second wave struck, this time in a ring formation that forced the ferocious energies inwards. The AI Extra-Brutal knew that the warheads of these missiles had to be something new, something far more destructive than thermonuclear devices ...

Then collision alerts butted in and the AI found that the Godhead was altering its attitude, slowly tilting its gargantuan mass away from the missile waves. The Extra-Brutal brought the destructor round on a revised course. Then the third wave hit.

The Godhead seemed to react in pain. The AI found itself facing an expanse of convulsing grey as it rushed up. Auto-evasion piloting had already kicked in but it was too little, too late. The destructor's forward shields ploughed into that writhing greyness, heeling to port as it carved a trough across the surface. At first it seemed that the nose was coming up but then the bows struck

an unseen obstruction. A violent shock jolted through
the Aggression craft as the aft swung up, its burning
thrusters adding to the uncontrolled impetus. The
safeties cut off the engines an instant before the stern
plunged down into the glutinous, rippling surface.

The fourth wave of missiles came down. By now a
storm of white fire and ash clouds was raging up and
out from the widening impact zone. In truth there were
successive wavefronts of energy and debris radiating
outwards, each more ferocious than the preceding one.
The Aggression destructor's engines were buried deep in
the sucking, clinging grey mass – triggering a burn
would cause a crucible effect leading to catastrophic
overheat. And because this location was roughly 700
miles from the epicentre, the AI Extra-Brutal estimated
that it had about thirty-six seconds before the first wave-
front arrived. The destructor's hull could withstand the
first and probably the second, but after that prospects
were bleak.

The destructor Extra-Brutal unlimbered its external
grapplers and began to dig and hack at the malleable yet
tough substance that held the Aggression craft
entrapped. But cuts resealed themselves and gouges were
quickly refilled.

The fifth wave of missiles landed in a long line which
flung up a dazzling wall of coruscating energy. Motion
sensors detected subsurface distortions within the
Godhead – which the AI noted as it reconfigured the lateral thrusters' control parameters for short hot bursts.
The hope was that the enclosing grey mass was alive,
part of the Godhead's physical form, and that it would
feel the thruster heat as pain, forcing it to release or

expel the destructor. But before it was ready, the sixth wave landed and something deep within and far below gave way.

The undulations of the surrounding morphscape grew violent, casting up thick heavy waves and huge twisting ropes, great long whips which lashed at the sky, bubbles that grew to be giant orbs before bursting, sending shards flying while great fractured shells melted back into the squirming, spasming greyness. And when the seventh missile wave hit, the AI Extra-Brutal saw the great cracks off in the distance – sections rearing up like cliffs, like splinters and shards hundreds of miles long wrenching away from bedrock. The Godhead was breaking apart.

The eighth wave finally did it, like a hammerblow landing on cracked ice. Gouts of destroying energy sliced into fissures and crevasses, racing through the interstices, burning and vaporising the ancient matrices of the Godhead's brain. Its agony sent gigantic convulsions tearing through its vast corpus.

All around the Aggression destructor the morphscape had slowed, apparently solidifying, before a massive internal deformation shattered it all. The AI Extra-Brutal had shut down most of its external sensors, safely shielding those that could be protected. But it had enough still active to witness the arrival of the last missile wave, their sun-bright explosions lighting up the expanding clouds of debris and dust with haloes of incinerating hellfire.

The Extra-Brutal was picking up nothing but interference on the command channel. It knew that it was now partly encased in a solidified chunk of the

Godhead's integument, and floating clear of huge splintered pieces even as the dissipating wavefronts of energy and debris pushed them further apart. The Construct AI gingerly tested its manoeuvring jets and found that it could move. Steering a course towards the edge of the gigantic rubble cloud, it was careful to keep to wider spaces, trying to reduce the chances of a collision with something large and fast-moving. With its sensors it saw that the energy discharge from the missile strikes continued to blaze amid the veils of pulverised rock, unseen flames flickering in a haze of stone.

The AI Extra-Brutal noticed the wreckage of many ships amongst the drifting debris of the Godhead. But the strangest object was a lifeless male humanoid strapped to a blue couch which had small suspensor assemblies fixed to either end. A detailed scan revealed that the humanoid had broken legs, a broken spine and a fractured shoulder, and that it had died from explosive decompression. The Extra-Brutal committed the data to its report file and continued on its slow winding journey out of the corpse-cloud of the Godhead.

42

GREG

He swung his legs out of the Roug foray-pod and stepped down onto a hazy ashen wasteland. He had a Roug weapon in his hand, a smartgun Kao Chih had called it, a large-gripped, fat-muzzled piece in a strange grey material. Warily he scanned his surroundings. Heavy rains had fallen a short while ago and the uneven burnt ground steamed while smoke drifted from the charred, massive husks of trees that lay all around. The warm air stank of incinerated wood and vegetation, and he spat to try and clear the taint from his mouth. To no avail.

'I'm outside,' he said.

'Is it as bad as the probe data suggested?' came Kao Chih's voice from the comm piece in his right ear.

'Worse,' Greg said. 'Far worse.'

'The shuttle is lying in a shallow gully over the rise north of your location. The aerial probe isn't picking up lifesigns in its vicinity, but if Kuros survived the landing he will certainly have headed towards the enclave.'

The uneven slope was cluttered with blackened, shattered tree trunks and ragged stumps that stuck up like obsidian spikes. As he climbed he felt as if he could see two views, the lush verdancy of Segrana as he remembered it, and this stripped, seared devastation.

Catriona, he thought. *Did you die along with Segrana? If the forest is dead, how could you be alive?*

He steeled himself to the task, telling himself that retribution was possible and soon. The weight of the Roug handgun was comforting.

Fine ash puffed up with every step. As he ascended he made a discovery – amongst the endless black debris were heaps of twisted, half-melted metal whose aspects and identifying traits he recognised as those of Legion cyborgs. Wrecked, semi-crushed and torn to pieces, they lay everywhere he looked. Was this the explanation for the mass disappearances which allowed the remnants of the Hegemony and Earthsphere fleets to regain the initiative in the battle around Darien? It would explain those images of Nivyesta he had seen during the hours spent chasing Kuros across the surface of Darien, the grey blotches that had grown to obscure the great forest.

It wasn't due to an orbital bombardment after all, he thought. *Instead Segrana was turning into a gigantic funeral pyre for the Legion of Avatars. Was that the Zyradin's plan all along?*

By the time he reached the crest he was streaked with ash from head to foot and sweat had marked trails down his face. Before him a jagged ridge curved away to east and west, and beyond it lay a forest-crammed cove, an enclave of vegetation untouched by the disaster.

The bulbous shuttle lay at the bottom of a gully down which the recent rains had sent a slurry of ash-choked water, leaving pools in its wake. The shuttle had come to rest with its nose up and the side hatch gaping.

Greg approached warily, with the Roug gun at the ready, carefully peering in. But the craft was empty and all the controls were dead, while on the wet, seared ground by the hatch he found two sets of footprints, one large, one small.

'Perhaps Kuros is accompanied by one of those Ezgara commandos,' Kao Chih said after Greg related his findings. 'The surveillance data was intermittent – an accomplice could have been missed. Mr Cameron, in what direction do the tracks lead?'

'Looks like they're heading east, following the ridge.'

'Less than half a kilometre that way is the entrance to a ravine that slopes down to the cove. You should hurry – it now appears that Kuros has activated a rescue transponder.'

'Great,' Greg said, holstering the Roug weapon. 'Any sign of rescuers on their way?'

'Not as yet. I shall keep you informed.'

Wiping a sheen of sweat from his face, Greg followed the footprints away from the shuttle. Ten minutes later they disappeared into a notch in the ridge, the ravine entrance Kao Chih had mentioned. Inside, it was more like a fissure than a ravine, a cold, sheer-sided cleft with streamlets trickling down a steep path of black rocks and boulders.

'Is your probe still monitoring the area?' he said as he ducked under a massive slab wedged between the fissure sides. 'Any way to pinpoint our quarry?'

'It is still scanning from low-cloud altitude,' said Kao Chih. 'However, its sensors are not equipped to distinguish different species. All I can tell you is that there are over a thousand sentient lifeforms in the enclave, and that the transponder signal is not emanating from ground level.'

Greg nodded as he emerged from the ravine into a rough clearing hemmed in by dense walls of foliage that rose up to intertwine overhead. Some light filtered through, casting everything in shades of green. And the air was clean, moist and free from the taint of ash. Greg had a moment or two of pure enjoyment before a tingle of alarm came over him.

In reflex he dived to the right and had the Roug gun out even as something weighty sighed through the space he had so recently occupied. There was a heavy impact followed by secondary thuds and the crackling rustle of crushed foliage. He remembered Kao Chih's instructions on the smartgun's use and fired a sequence of short bursts into the shadowy ravine, back along what he reckoned to be the boulder's trajectory.

The second rock was smaller and faster. He dodged sideways, still firing blurry steel-grey bolts up into the dark fissure, reached cover behind a thick bush and saw that a pale circular display had appeared on the back of the gun, above the grip. Within it a red dot was moving from left to right and Greg smiled. His attacker was tagged and the gun's sensors were now tracking it. He crouched, raised the Roug weapon and swung it after the invisible assailant, who had to be moving along the branches high above. When the red dot was centred he pressed the fire stud and held it down.

A chain of bright blue spikes lanced up into the dense mesh of foliage. There was a choking cry, a splintering crack, and a form fell out of the canopy amid a cascade of leaves and twigs. For a second the gun's continuous fire followed the body's descent, pouring energy bolts into it, before Greg released the stud. Trailing smoke and flames, it hit the ground and was still. Even before he reached it he was fairly sure who it was. With the smartgun at the ready he flipped the lifeless form over ... and he was right, it *was* Vashutkin. The former politician had taken energy-bolt hits all up the left side of his body, leaving it a seared gory ruin with the arm almost severed and blood oozing from a ragged hole in the neck. The eyes were vacant.

'Mr Cameron? Are you there?' Kao Chih sounded worried. 'We are picking up weapon-energy discharges.'

'I'm okay, I'm brand new,' he said. 'That gun is pretty impressive, by the way!'

'Have you encountered the Hegemony ambassador?'

'Nah. Dealt with the monkey – now it's time to find the organ-grinder.'

He stepped over the corpse and pushed through a curtain of leafy vines. The undergrowth was dense and alive with buzzing insects and varieties of beetles and reptiles that seemed familiar if somewhat larger. He had gone less than a dozen paces when a tall woman leaned out from behind a tree and beckoned him over.

'You are chasing the big Sendrukan fellow, yes?' she said with a faint Norj accent.

'I do have business to discuss with him, aye.'

'Well, this one climbed our Watchtree, threatened to fire on anyone who comes near. My Uvovo scholars are all for charging across the branchways but I am managing to cool down their hot heads, so far. I hope that you are armed.'

When he showed her the Roug gun she nodded

approvingly. 'That's the Watchtree, right through there.'
She pointed to a huge trunk around which a lamplit
stairway spiralled upwards. 'Listen, there is a friend of
mine still up there – keep your eye out for her, *ja*? And
the sooner this is resolved the better. My Uvovo won't
stay cool for very much longer.'

He smiled. 'Well, I'd better get on wi' it, then!'

He nodded to her then headed off through the bushy
undergrowth at a crouch. He had just reached the foot
of the spiral steps when Kao Chih suddenly spoke.

'We may have a small problem, Mr Cameron.'

Greg sighed. 'If you really need to tell me about it
now, I bet it's no' that small.'

'A previously undetected vessel has left Darien and is
heading towards Nivyesta,' Kao Chih said. 'Sensor data
indicates that it is a Hegemony medium-range shuttle,
homing in on Kuros's transponder signal. Expected
arrival is thirty-one minutes and counting.'

'Fair enough, but this smartgun is a nice bit of kit,'
Greg said. 'I'm not really anticipating any difficulties.'

'I would still advise caution.'

'Aye, and from here on I'll be in silent mode so don't
expect a running commentary, okay?'

'And I shall refrain from superfluous queries.'

'Right, here goes ...'

The first jutting steps creaked slightly underfoot but
felt thoroughly solid as he climbed. With the Roug gun
held near his shoulder, muzzle up, he stayed close to the
mossy trunk, eyes glancing ahead and above. He had
completed one full turn about the Watchtree when he
heard that voice.

'So good of you to pay me this visit, Dr Cameron,

although something tells me that this is not a social call.'

'Met Vashutkin on my way here,' Greg said, scanning the overhead weave of foliage. 'He's no longer a problem. Are you going to be a problem, Ambassador?'

'I certainly hope so, Doctor.'

Suddenly sure that he'd seen a form shift behind the branch-and-vine veil above and to the right, he raised the smartgun two-handed and blazed away. Close on a dozen tag rounds zipped and cracked through the foliage but the acquisition display failed to come up on the grip.

'Not quite the inward-looking academic any more, I see,' came the infuriatingly languid voice, its source hard to pin down.

'Had to adapt, Ambassador,' Greg said. 'Times are hard and dangerous, thanks to *you* ...'

With the last word of the sentence he fired the smartgun at a branch jutting almost directly overhead, stitching a zigzag of tag rounds across it. But still no display. He cursed under his breath, flattened his back against the trunk and peered sideways, up the curve of steps. And saw a face staring at him out of a branching mass of foliage, the face of Catriona Macreadie ...

'You'll have to do better than that, Doctor,' said the Sendrukan from somewhere above, but Greg's full attention, his entire being, was focused on that beloved face. He half-opened his mouth to call out to her but she shook her head and pressed a silencing finger against her lips. Then she pointed at the spiral steps and made a gesture like two rising turns ... or one and a half, he couldn't be sure. After that she smiled at him, blew him a kiss, and was gone.

Greg felt shaken by the encounter, delighting in the initial burst of exhilaration, revelling in the notion that she'd somehow escaped destruction and regained her physical form. Then hard, unforgiving memory forced upon him the fact that the last time he saw her she had been an incorporeal shade flitting among the trees, an insubstantial projection sent by a vast, inhuman entity.

But he had not imagined her appearance, and there would be time enough for investigation later.

With unhurried care he ascended the curving steps, pausing a couple of times to study the dense curtains of greenery.

'Why so silent, Doctor Cameron? Daunted by the enormity of your task, perhaps?'

By now Greg had ascended by more than a turn of the spiral and a gap appeared in the canopy above, revealing a tall, grey-robed figure. But even as he brought up the smartgun and loosed a string of tag rounds the robed Sendrukan noticed him and ducked away. The branches shook for a moment or two as Kuros no doubt scuttled away to a safer distance, and when Greg regarded the gun there was still no targeting display.

'My congratulations on a skilful piece of stalking, Doctor.' Kuros's voice was muffled, drifting down from a greater height now. 'And I see that you are using tagging ammunition, from which I surmise that you have a seeker weapon of some sort.'

Climbing the steps, Greg tried again to gauge the direction of the Sendrukan's voice.

'Aye, that's right, you've got it, clever of you to figure it out.'

'In that case, I'll have to adopt alternative tactics.' Then Kuros spoke two words in Sendrukan.

A tremor began in the thigh muscles of Greg's right leg. A shivery weakness quickly spread downwards, forcing him to cling to the trunk of the Watchtree as he limped and staggered up to a wide, shady platform. There was no pain, only a loss of control, a numbness backed by a growing sense of horrified dread.

'Do you recall our last meeting, when I introduced you to that useful substance known as Blue Chain?'

'Your slavery powder?' Greg said, trying to keep his voice level. 'What about it?'

'I'm glad you asked,' said the hidden Kuros. 'Every particle of the nanodust is programmed to adapt to circumstances, you see. So although most of the Blue Chain we gave you was removed by those cunning native roots, its adaptive imperative would have already sent sleeper clusters into the motor centres ...'

Kuros spoke another Sendrukan word, and Greg felt the strength go out of his other leg. He fell to his knees and slumped forward. Gritting his teeth, he began dragging himself forward with his elbows.

God, I'm a sitting target! he thought. *Just a few words and he's turned me into a wreck, a weakling. If I can just get in one good shot ...*

'That's all very educational, Mr Ambassador,' he said, pulling himself along with his forearms. 'You could give talks about it at the maximum-security prison we're gonna build just for you back on Darien!'

'An amusing notion, Doctor, but the truth is that you are going to die here and I will return to the Hegemony and civilisation. And eventually we shall again reach out to this world and reclaim it in the name of our undiminished posterity. This is how the supreme existence manifests itself – the weak work towards the greater glory of the strong, and the undeserving give way to the pre-eminent ...'

Again, a Sendrukan word was spoken and the feeling and control drained from Greg's right arm. His hand grew numb and the smartgun slipped out of his nerveless fingers. He half-gasped, half-laughed, face only inches from the rough planking as he seized the Roug gun with his other hand. Then with a considerable effort he levered himself up against the nearby tree trunk, sweat trickling and itching down his temples and scalp as he forced himself into a seated position. Deliberately he rested the smartgun on his leg, aiming it at the flight of stairs that curved up around a large branch that protruded from the main trunk like a huge shoulder.

'I think I've heard that argument before,' Greg said. 'Usually from out the mouth of a lout with delusions o' grandeur. Oh, but wait a minute – that's exactly what your precious Hegemony is, a gang of louts with big guns, big ships and big boots. You can dress it up any way you like, with pretty-sounding phrases and lofty visions, but ultimately you're just a mob of self-important thugs who want it all!'

Silence. Then a voice whispering from overhead.

'Are you trying to get yerself killed?'

He glanced up and there she was, peering over the edge of a blossom-fringed platform. She looked so real, so solid, that he almost believed it.

'It's no' much of a plan but it's all I've got right now,'

he said. 'Maybe I can provoke him into showing himself ...'

Alarm flickered in her eyes.

'... and if I die, you'll have to take this gun and kill him ... I mean, if you can, if you're not a ...'

She shook her head, then gave a shrug and ducked out of sight, leaving him suddenly, bleakly alone.

A moment later, Kuros spoke again.

'I must admit, Doctor Cameron, your species has shown itself to be invidiously annoying and at times more trouble than they are worth – and you are an especially irritating example of your kind.'

'Och, you're just saying that – c'mon, tell me what you really think. Tell me to my face!'

'I had toyed with allowing you one arm and a sporting chance of hitting me but I've changed my mind. Instead, I think you deserve to come back with me to the Hegemony core worlds where I can introduce you to the wonders of the Hegemon's own personal vivisection labs. It would be, I feel, a suitable reward for all your efforts.'

Kuros spoke another word. Greg's arm went dead and fell to his side, the smartgun half-slipping from his now useless hand. His attempt at goading Kuros into showing himself had failed, while Cat seemed to have simply vanished, ghosted away.

There was the sound of descending steps and he looked up to see a tall grey-robed figure stroll leisurely towards him. A shadowy cowl was pushed back to reveal the features of Utavess Kuros.

'My transponder tells me that a transport will be here quite shortly,' the Sendrukan said. 'There is a platform more adequate for embarkation further up, which means that I will have to carry you.'

Kuros was half a dozen paces away when a figure dropped onto him from the branches above. Small hands clawed at his face. Flailing at his assailant, he cried out and staggered back, tripped on a jutting board and fell full length on the planking. That was when Greg realised that the attacker was Catriona.

She held on like grim death as the Sendrukan landed, letting out a howl of rage. Greg heard her cry out but she kept one arm wrapped around Kuros's neck, refusing to let go even when the big Sendrukan started grabbing her limbs and swinging wild punches.

Without warning a strange languour settled over Greg's senses, and the struggle going on just a few yards away slowed down and down. Garments swirled and billowed while those savage movements became drawn-out graceful gestures, which he found curiously amusing, as if he were watching some piece of visual comedy on the vee. Until a bright flash cut through everything, and a stabbing sensation raced from his head down neck and shoulder into his arm and hand, the hand that was still half-curled about the smartgun. His body was his again. He snatched up the weapon and aimed, just as Kuros was drawing back one big fist to strike Cat. Greg yelled and Kuros looked up and round, providing an excellent target. Uttering a bellow of anger, Greg pressed and held down the firing stud, and a chain of bright barbs struck the Sendrukan full in the face.

A scream started but was cut off. Flame and blood burst up and out as the Sendrukan was flung backwards. Hands briefly clutched at empty air, and the limbs jerked for a few seconds before relaxing finally into motionlessness.

The brutal violence was followed by a frozen moment. Then there was movement next to the corpse: Catriona, edging away from the dead Sendrukan. Greg returned the smartgun to its holster then went over to help her to her feet. She seemed to be unhurt and hardly marked with their enemy's blood.

'I must say, Miss Macreadie, that you're looking pretty good for a forest phantom ...' He suddenly noticed that they were holding each other's arms. 'And feeling rather more substantial ...'

Her face lit up with an intense, wordless glee as she grabbed the lapels of his jacket and pulled him in close enough for her to deliver a long passionate kiss. When they at last broke apart Greg drew in a deep breath and made a quiet whistling sound.

'Well, that answers one of my questions ...'

'And mine,' said Catriona. 'There were times when I was sure that I'd never get to do that again, or indeed with you ... wait, can you hear that?'

'Hear what?'

'It's like a wee voice ...'

They both fell into a hush and Greg could hear it, a faint tinny whisper. Realisation struck and when he raised a hand to his right ear the comm piece was gone. Patting his clothing, he found it in a fold and seconds later had it back in place.

'... repeating message, Mr Cameron, please reply ...'

'Kao Chih, I hear you,' he said. 'Sorry, but the damned earpiece fell out.'

'Understood, Mr Cameron, and I gather that Kuros is no longer a threat, but have you found the transponder? That shuttle is less than ten minutes from your position.'

Greg stared at Catriona in a kind of uncertain panic.

'What?' she said.

'Kuros had a transponder and a Hegemony ship is on its way here!' He looked upwards, gesturing at the dense veils of foliage. 'But how can we find it in time?'

'A transponder, eh?'

When Greg looked back Cat was crouching over the dead Sendrukan, fumbling and rummaging in the long grey robes. Then she made a satisfied sound, straightened and held out a silver-grey flattened ovoid.

'Is that it? I saw him fiddling with it earlier.'

Greg described it to Kao Chih, who confirmed that it was the device in question. Quickly Greg took it from Cat's hand, placed it on the planked platform and brought his heel down on it repeatedly. When it was at last reduced to a scattering of shattered components and casing fragments, Cat took him by the hand and led him away from the scene of death to sit at the foot of the steps leading further up the Watchtree. As they did so, some of the local Uvovo began peering out from hiding places and woven shelters.

'The transponder has ceased signalling, Mr Cameron,' Kao Chih said. 'The rescue shuttle has altered course away from Darien, towards the Hegemony fleet's marshalling zone.'

'How's it all looking, Kao Chih?' Greg said. 'D'ye think the fighting's over?'

'All sides have suffered crippling losses. The remnants

of the Hegemony armada still outnumber the other factions' surviving vessels by more than ten to one, but High Mandator Azgemiron has made it clear to all sides that warlike behaviour will not be tolerated. None has violated this status. Also it seems like that the greater part of the Hegemony remnants will pull out, leaving behind a symbolic ship or two to keep an eye on developments.'

Greg sighed. 'Well, I guess that's something. Look, I'm signing off for a while, Kao Chih – if I don't get some rest I think I'll go off my head!'

'Understood. We will speak again soon.'

He took out the earpiece and slipped it into an inside pocket. Cat moved in closer, put her arms around his chest and hugged him tightly.

'Segrana ... is dead,' she said softly.

'I saw the wrecked cyborgs. How ...'

'Canna talk about it. Not the now.' She was silent a moment. 'What's it like down on Darien?'

'Last time I was there it was pretty bad, towns half-wrecked or half-burnt, deserted, inhabitants fled into the mountains and forests, just ... bad.'

'They'll need folk like us to help with reconstruction, of course.'

'Aye,' he said. 'Canny types who know which end of the hammer to hold.'

Another long moment of silence. Then Catriona shifted her head to look up at him.

'How did you beat that slavery dust?' she said. 'What did he call it ...?'

'Blue Chain,' Greg said. 'Dunno. Perhaps there wasn't enough of it in the end for Kuros's purposes.

Maybe it self-destructed – all I know is that I felt a sharp tingling all over and suddenly I was back in control ...'
He broke off, ambushed by a jaw-cracking yawn. Cat giggled.

'There's a nice hut upstairs where you can sleep, if you like.'

'Nah, I just want tae sit here with you for a wee bit longer,' he said drowsily. 'Watch the sunlight move through the leaves while the Uvovo come out to play ...'

Which is what they did, resting there on the stairs, sipping from drinks brought by the Uvovo or nibbling berries and fruit. Not long after, the tall woman he had met down at the forest floor appeared at the other end of the platform, waved then headed off along another branchway. Later, as the sun dipped and shadows lengthened, and most of the Uvovo retired to their shelters, neither of them noticed when a single glowing mote emerged from the back of Greg's hand, a bright point surrounded by a shifting corona. It drifted unseen through the air towards the immense trunk of the Watchtree and sank into its gnarled bark.

At one point Greg came out of his drowsy half-sleep all of a sudden, certain for a moment that he'd heard the voice of the Zyradin speaking to him. Then Catriona muttered something into his chest and he settled back while the silvery light of Darienrise shone through the branches, the first pure gleams of a future worth building.

EPILOGUE

THE EMISSARY

Three weeks after the defeat of the Legion and the destruction of the Godhead, a memorial was held on a hillside on Darien. Three funerals had taken place on Darien a fortnight earlier, while Robert Horst's remains, recovered from the scene of the Godhead's demise, had been shipped back to Earth where they were laid to rest just outside Berlin. But the memorial still centred on the planting and dedication of four trees just after noon on a grassy slope overlooking Membrance Vale, where the old *Hyperion* still lay.

The eulogies were just beginning when the Construct's emissary arrived. As the four spiraleaf saplings were lowered by willing hands into newly dug holes, Greg Cameron stood up before the invited audience and gave a warm and witty speech about his uncle, Theo Karlsson. He was followed by his mother, Karlsson's sister, Solvjeg, who was dignified and only tearful at the end. Then one of the Tygrans came forward, Franklyn Gideon, looking vaguely uncomfortable without either uniform or combat armour; he spoke briefly about Karlsson's grit under fire and how he had saved Gideon's life during Becker's attack on

Tusk Mountain, then ended with that rarity, a piece of Tygran verse –

> 'Fold him into the earth,
> Lay him down low,
> Trust him to peace,
> Send him to eternity,
> Close at last those eyes,
> His work is done.'

After Gideon, a half-drunk Rory McGrain got up to toast Theo's memory with a hip flask of something potent, and an old Darien marching song, accompanied by several others in the gathering. Representatives from the new Pyre settlements lit small candles and said short prayers.

When they moved along to the next tree, Greg Cameron spoke again about the Uvovo Seer, Cheluvahar, who had died when Legion cyborgs finally broke through to the underground burrow where he had taken refuge. After him, two Uvovo Listeners, Weynl and Faldri, eschewed speechmaking in favour of a sad song in the Uvovo tongue. The quietly sung syllables, repeated back and forth, had a profound effect on some of those present.

At the next planting, an Enhanced by the name of Konstantin then stepped up and said a few halting words about Julia Bryce. It was she who helped Konstantin to switch the missile targets from 500 suns to the Godhead, and it was she who launched them and destroyed the Godhead. 'She was proud of her intellect, which lit up the different ways of being Human as well as the path to her own Humanity,' he said. 'She saved hundreds of worlds, their civilisations and their billions of lives, but she couldn't save herself.' There was great sadness in his delivery, and a certain bitterness when he mentioned Catriona Macreadie, who had decided not to attend the ceremony.

The last to be eulogised, as the fourth sapling was planted and bedded into the hillside, was Robert Horst. The Construct's emissary took a couple of hesitant steps upslope but paused when a middle-aged Human with receding hair came forward. He introduced himself as Ben Tanner, Horst's chief of staff from a few years ago, then paid tribute to the man's talents and his warmth of character, a sensibly brief address. When he stepped down the emissary took his place.

'I come as a messenger from the Construct, who some of you may know played a significant role in the twin struggle so recently resolved. Robert Horst was well known to the Construct, who has directed me to say these few words:

'Robert Horst was a remarkable Human. He exhibited the finest characteristics of his species – a resolute determination, intelligence, wit, and a compassion that led him to a self-sacrifice which he willingly embraced. His was the essence that stood in the way of hate and havoc and destruction. The fire of his being shall never go out.'

After that most of the guests wandered away in small groups, twos and threes. The emissary noticed the reporter Kaphiri Farag talking with a few people down by the road. A lone piper up on the crest of the hill played a slow lament, its plaintive voice sounding out across the dales and fields below. Waiting behind, the emissary saw that Greg Cameron was crouched next to the sapling dedicated to his uncle.

'Mr Cameron,' he said. 'May I ask why Ms Macreadie did not attend?'

Greg Cameron gave a half-smile as he got to his feet. 'Aye, well, there's a question.' He shrugged. 'She says that the memories are too painful and that she canna stand funerals anyway, but there she is, up there on Nivyesta, trying to get life out of a grave.' He paused, then went on. 'Since the battle, since the destruction of the cyborgs, hardly anything has grown across that entire wasteland of a continent. I mean, there's still a wee enclave, the Cradle-Veil cove, but the rest ... it's as if the ground is reluctant to let anything take root.

'Down here, of course, it's a different story. The Uvovo are starting to say that some remnant of Segrana still lingers on Darien, in the daughter-forests and elsewhere. Perhaps that's why she's staying away – it would remind her of how much has been lost to the ash.' He grinned ruefully. 'On the other hand, she is adamant about getting pregnant!'

'That seems an appropriate ambition in the circumstances,' said the emissary.

The two shook hands and Cameron headed off downhill to join a small group waiting next to an open-top mountain-car. The emissary watched him leave thoughtfully, then took a small pouch from his jacket, tipped out a number of small black seeds and pressed them into the soil near the base of the spiraleaf sapling dedicated to Julia Bryce. Putting away the pouch, he surveyed the scene briefly and listened to the piper for several long moments. Then strode off down the grassy slope to where his own vehicle, a single-seater hire car, was parked.

Two hours later the emissary had reached Port Gagarin and was in his shuttle pod, awaiting clearance from air–orbit traffic control. An hour after that the pod had returned him to the Construct tiership, *Finite Codex*, and the emissary was entering the airy observation lounge/bridge. Various Rosas and Roberts were in attendance, some working at translucent holoconsoles, others engaged in thought-games or discussion.

'I read out your speech exactly as you composed it,' he said as he walked up the ramp to the circular balcony where the Construct waited. 'I almost felt flattered at such lyrical praise.'

The Construct had exchanged its usual spindly metal-mech remote for a humanoid one, its skin configured to display rippling ribbons of silver and gold.

'That is understandable,' it said. 'But the deceased Robert and you are experientially different.'

'In other words, Robert,' said a black-dressed man as he rose from an easy chair, 'the map is not the territory. Did you plant the seeds?'

The emissary smiled. 'Yes, Harry, I pushed the blue-bell seeds into the soil around her tree. When they flower it will be a fine sight. You, on the other hand, have remained a sight draped in black. I thought you said you were thinking of a new wardrobe.'

'I did think about it, then realised that if you're tired of the colour black you're tired of life!' Harry laughed and tipped his hat back at a rakish angle. 'Or at least the synthetic equivalent thereof. So – where are we off to next?'

The Construct looked at him.

'Tier 19. When the Humans used the spacefold bomb to shut down the warpwell there were still many thousands of Legion cyborgs travelling up the portal's flux conduit. And when it was switched off ...'

'Don't tell me – a big, nasty mess, yes?'

'Indeed. Everything inside was crash-transitioned to whatever tier it was passing through at the time. Resonant transition effects ripped apart most of the cyborgs and left a trail of debris all the way down. But approximately three hundred somehow survived and are turning their attentions to several of the worlds in Tier 19.'

Harry's joviality faded. 'Invade, slaughter any opposition, then turn the remaining population into slaves to build more of their charming brethren.'

'That is what *we* are going to investigate. You on the other hand once expressed an eagerness to return to the tiernet – if you are ready I can have you paradigitised and transloaded in less than a minute ...'

'You know, actually I find that I have become attached to this autonomous physical-form experience. What's more, it's time that I played a more active role in this ongoing undertaking of yours. I am certain that I can make a valuable contribution, maybe even provide a new perspective.'

'I might ask you to exchange that form you've adopted for something more suited to field activity,' the Construct said.

'That is to be expected.'

The Construct looked at the emissary, who said, 'I can stand him if you can.'

'Very well,' said the Construct. 'At least I will be able to complete my studies of him. Let us be on our way.'

ACKNOWLEDGEMENTS

Words are scarcely enough when it comes to thanking the various folk who have in one way or another made this book and the preceding volumes possible. To my agents, John Parker and John Berlyne, who have been my ever-supportive shepherds and negotiators, to the most excellent Bella Pagan whose perceptions and polite insistence kept my writer-brain in the game (aided of course by Joanna Kramer, James Long, Rose Tremlett and everyone else at Orbit/Little, Brown). Thanks are due as well to Dave Wingrove and his fine eye for detail and the big picture.

Tips of the hat go out to my publishers in Germany and France, Heyne and Bragelonne, and to Tom Clegg and Stephane Marsan – bonjour, mes braves! – and to my French translator, Laurent Queyssi, and my German translator, Norbert Stobe. And a big howdy to such luminaries as Eric Brown, Ian McDonald, Keith Brooke, Ian Whates, Ian Watson, Mark Chitty, Phil Palmer, Ian Sales, Craig Marnoch, Neil Williamson, Andrew J Wilson and sundry others who soldiered on through the thickets of the Birmingham Eastercon – will we ever see its like again?

To Debbie Miller and Tiffany, to Rog Peyton, to Stewart Robinson in Musselburgh (the wee Edinburgh even further to the east!), to the Glasgow Writers' Circle, to the Edinburgh Writers Group, to Graeme Fleming, Progmaster General of Greater Paisley, to Ronnie and Katie, to Spencer and Adrian, to Dave Bradley at *SFX*, to Cuddles and Ralph and Vince Docherty and Ian Sorensen, and to those tireless legions of con-runners everywhere, who have all added their idiosyncratic soupçon of enrichment to life itself. A long and winding list of thanks would not be complete without a wave of the banner to Norman, John and Allan, the other members of the New Wave of Gang-of-Fourism – who knows where we (and indeed the Cleggster) will be by the time this book comes out?

As ever, Susan coped with my absent-mindedness and numerous other writerly foibles during the scribbling with fortitude and loving good humour, for which I am deeply thankful. My thoughts are also with my dad, who has undergone many difficult months this past year but has endured, along with my mother, and come out the other side.

My soundtrack for this book has ranged far and wide, taking in several cinematic instrumental CDs by Nox Arcana and Midnight Syndicate, as well as the superfine doom rock of Alunah, Orchid and Witchburn, three awesome bands, three awesome albums. Honourable mentions go out to Honcho (*Battle Of Wits*), Pallas (*XXV*), SAHG (*3*), and to Black Space Riders, whose self-titled CD remains a hi-octane rocket ride to the starz!

extras

www.orbitbooks.net

about the author

Michael Cobley was born in Leicester, England, and has lived in Glasgow, Scotland, for most of his life. He has studied engineering, been a DJ and has an abiding interest in democratic politics. His previous books include Shadowkings dark fantasy trilogy, and *Iron Mosaic*, a short story collection. *The Ascendant Stars* concludes the Humanity's Fire Trilogy, but he insists that there are many other stories to be told.

Find out more about Michael Cobley and other Orbit authors by registering for the free monthly newsletter at www.orbitbooks.net.

if you enjoyed
THE ASCENDANT STARS

look out for

LEVIATHAN WAKES

book one of the Expense

by

James S. A. Corey

Chapter one: Holden

A hundred and fifty years before, when the parochial disagreements between Earth and Mars had been on the verge of war, the Belt had been a far horizon of tremendous mineral wealth beyond viable economic reach, and the outer planets had been beyond even the most unrealistic corporate dream. Then Solomon Epstein had built his little modified fusion drive, popped it on the back of his three-man yacht, and turned it on. With a good scope, you could still see his ship going at a marginal percentage of the speed of light, heading out into the big empty. The best, longest funeral in the history of mankind. Fortunately, he'd left the plans on his home computer. The Epstein Drive hadn't given humanity the stars, but it had delivered the planets.

Three-quarters of a kilometer long, a quarter of a kilometer wide—roughly shaped like a fire hydrant—and mostly empty space inside, the *Canterbury* was a retooled colony transport.

Once, it had been packed with people, supplies, schematics, machines, environment bubbles, and hope. Just under twenty million people lived on the moons of Saturn now. The *Canterbury* had hauled nearly a million of their ancestors there. Forty-five million on the moons of Jupiter. One moon of Uranus sported five thousand, the farthest outpost of human civilization, at least until the Mormons finished their generation ship and headed for the stars and freedom from procreation restrictions.

And then there was the Belt.

If you asked OPA recruiters when they were drunk and feeling expansive, they might say there were a hundred million in the Belt. Ask an inner planet census taker, it was nearer to fifty million. Any way you looked, the population was huge and needed a lot of water.

So now the *Canterbury* and her dozens of sister ships in the Pur'n'Kleen Water Company made the loop from Saturn's generous rings to the Belt and back hauling glaciers, and would until the ships aged into salvage wrecks.

Jim Holden saw some poetry in that.

"Holden?"

He turned back to the hangar deck. Chief Engineer Naomi Nagata towered over him. She stood almost two full meters tall, her mop of curly hair tied back into a black tail, her expression halfway between amusement and annoyance. She had the Belter habit of shrugging with her hands instead of her shoulders.

"Holden, are you listening, or just staring out the window?"

"There was a problem," Holden said. "And because you're really, really good, you can fix it even though you don't have enough money or supplies."

Naomi laughed.

"So you weren't listening," she said.

"Not really, no."

"Well, you got the basics right anyhow. *Knight*'s landing gear isn't going to be good in atmosphere until I can get the seals replaced. That going to be a problem?"

"I'll ask the old man," Holden said. "But when's the last time we used the shuttle in atmosphere?"

"Never, but regs say we need at least one atmocapable shuttle."

"Hey, Boss!" Amos Burton, Naomi's earthborn

assistant, yelled from across the bay. He waved one meaty arm in their general direction. He meant Naomi. Amos might be on Captain McDowell's ship; Holden might be executive officer; but in Amos Burton's world, only Naomi was boss.

"What's the matter?" Naomi shouted back.

"Bad cable. Can you hold this little fucker in place while I get the spare?"

Naomi looked at Holden, *Are we done here?* in her eyes. He snapped a sarcastic salute and she snorted, shaking her head as she walked away, her frame long and thin in her greasy coveralls.

Seven years in Earth's navy, five years working in space with civilians, and he'd never gotten used to the long, thin, improbable bones of Belters. A childhood spent in gravity shaped the way he saw things forever.

At the central lift, Holden held his finger briefly over the button for the navigation deck, tempted by the prospect of Ade Tukunbo—her smile, her voice, the patchouli-and-vanilla scent she used in her hair—but pressed the button for the infirmary instead. Duty before pleasure.

Shed Garvey, the medical tech, was hunched over his lab table, debriding the stump of Cameron Paj's left arm, when Holden walked in. A month earlier, Paj had gotten his elbow pinned by a thirty-ton block of ice moving at five millimeters a second. It wasn't an uncommon injury among people with the dangerous job of cutting and moving zero-g icebergs, and Paj was taking the whole thing with the fatalism of a professional. Holden leaned over Shed's shoulder to watch as the tech plucked one of the medical maggots out of dead tissue.

"What's the word?" Holden asked.

"It's looking pretty good, sir," Paj said. "I've still got a few nerves. Shed's been tellin' me about how the prosthetic is gonna hook up to it."

"Assuming we can keep the necrosis under control," the medic said, "and make sure Paj doesn't heal up too much before we get to Ceres. I checked the policy, and Paj here's been signed on long enough to get one with force feedback, pressure and temperature sensors, fine-motor software. The whole package. It'll be almost as good as the real thing. The inner planets have a new biogel that regrows the limb, but that isn't covered in our medical plan."

"Fuck the Inners, and fuck their magic Jell-O. I'd rather have a good Belter-built fake than anything those bastards grow in a lab. Just wearing their fancy arm probably turns you into an asshole," Paj said. Then he added, "Oh, uh, no offense, XO."

"None taken. Just glad we're going to get you fixed up," Holden said.

"Tell him the other bit," Paj said with a wicked grin. Shed blushed.

"I've, ah, heard from other guys who've gotten them," Shed said, not meeting Holden's eyes. "Apparently there's a period while you're still building identification with the prosthetic when whacking off feels just like getting a hand job."

Holden let the comment hang in the air for a second while Shed's ears turned crimson.

"Good to know," Holden said. "And the necrosis?"

"There's some infection," Shed said. "The maggots are keeping it under control, and the inflammation's actually a good thing in this context, so we're not fighting too hard unless it starts to spread."

"Is he going to be ready for the next run?" Holden asked.

For the first time, Paj frowned.

"Shit yes, I'll be ready. I'm always ready. This is what I *do*, sir."

"Probably," Shed said. "Depending on how the bond takes. If not this one, the one after."

"Fuck that," Paj said. "I can buck ice one-handed better than half the skags you've got on this bitch."

"Again," Holden said, suppressing a grin, "good to know. Carry on."

Paj snorted. Shed plucked another maggot free. Holden went back to the lift, and this time he didn't hesitate.

The navigation station of the *Canterbury* didn't dress to impress. The great wall-sized displays Holden had imagined when he'd first volunteered for the navy did exist on capital ships but, even there, more as an artifact of design than need. Ade sat at a pair of screens only slightly larger than a hand terminal, graphs of the efficiency and output of the *Canterbury*'s reactor and engine updating in the corners, raw logs spooling on the right as the systems reported in. She wore thick headphones that covered her ears, the faint thump of the bass line barely escaping. If the *Canterbury* sensed an anomaly, it would alert her. If a system errored, it would alert her. If Captain McDowell left the command and control deck, it would alert her so she could turn the music off and look busy when he arrived. Her petty hedonism was only one of a thousand things that made Ade attractive to Holden. He walked up behind her, pulled the headphones gently away from her ears, and said, "Hey."

Ade smiled, tapped her screen, and dropped the headphones to rest around her long slim neck like technical jewelry.

"Executive Officer James Holden," she said with an exaggerated formality made even more acute by her thick Nigerian accent. "And what can I do for you?"

"You know, it's funny you should ask that," he said. "I was just thinking how pleasant it would be to have someone come back to my cabin when third shift takes over. Have a little romantic dinner of the same crap they're serving in the galley. Listen to some music."

"Drink a little wine," she said. "Break a little protocol. Pretty to think about, but I'm not up for sex tonight."

"I wasn't talking about sex. A little food. Conversation."

"I was talking about sex," she said.

Holden knelt beside her chair. In the one-third g of their current thrust, it was perfectly comfortable. Ade's smile softened. The log spool chimed; she glanced at it, tapped a release, and turned back to him.

"Ade, I like you. I mean, I really enjoy your company," he said. "I don't understand why we can't spend some time together with our clothes on."

"Holden. Sweetie. Stop it, okay?"

"Stop what?"

"Stop trying to turn me into your girlfriend. You're a nice guy. You've got a cute butt, and you're fun in the sack. Doesn't mean we're engaged."

Holden rocked back on his heels, feeling himself frown.

"Ade. For this to work for me, it needs to be more than that."

"But it isn't," she said, taking his hand. "It's okay that it isn't. You're the XO here, and I'm a short-timer. Another run, maybe two, and I'm gone."

"I'm not chained to this ship either."

Her laughter was equal parts warmth and disbelief.

"How long have you been on the *Cant*?"

"Five years."

"You're not going anyplace," she said. "You're comfortable here."

"Comfortable?" he said. "The *Cant*'s a century-old ice hauler. You can find a shittier flying job, but you have to try really hard. Everyone here is either wildly under-qualified or seriously screwed things up at their last gig."

"And you're comfortable here." Her eyes were less kind now. She bit her lip, looked down at the screen, looked up.

"I didn't deserve that," he said.

"You didn't," she agreed. "Look, I told you I wasn't in the mood tonight. I'm feeling cranky. I need a good night's sleep. I'll be nicer tomorrow."

"Promise?"

"I'll even make you dinner. Apology accepted?"

He slipped forward, pressed his lips to hers. She kissed back, politely at first and then with more warmth. Her fingers cupped his neck for a moment, then pulled him away.

"You're entirely too good at that. You should go now," she said. "On duty and all."

"Okay," he said, and didn't turn to go.

"Jim," she said, and the shipwide comm system clicked on.

"Holden to the bridge," Captain McDowell said, his voice compressed and echoing. Holden replied with something obscene. Ade laughed. He swooped in, kissed her cheek, and headed back for the central lift, quietly hoping that Captain McDowell suffered boils and public humiliation for his lousy timing.

The bridge was hardly larger than Holden's quarters and smaller by half than the galley. Except for the slightly oversized captain's display, required by Captain McDowell's failing eyesight and general distrust of corrective surgery, it could have been an accounting firm's back room. The air smelled of cleaning astringent and someone's overly strong yerba maté tea. McDowell shifted in his seat as Holden approached. Then the captain leaned back, pointing over his shoulder at the communications station.

"Becca!" McDowell snapped. "Tell him."

Rebecca Byers, the comm officer on duty, could have been bred from a shark and a hatchet. Black eyes, sharp features, lips so thin they might as well not have existed. The story on board was that she'd taken the job to escape prosecution for killing an ex-husband. Holden liked her.

"Emergency signal," she said. "Picked it up two hours ago. The transponder verification just bounced back from *Callisto*. It's real."

"Ah," Holden said. And then: "Shit. Are we the closest?"

"Only ship in a few million klicks."

"Well. That figures," Holden said.

Becca turned her gaze to the captain. McDowell cracked his knuckles and stared at his display. The light from the screen gave him an odd greenish cast.

"It's next to a charted non-Belt asteroid," McDowell said.

"Really?" Holden said in disbelief. "Did they run into it? There's nothing else out here for millions of kilometers."

"Maybe they pulled over because someone had to

go potty. All we have is that some knucklehead is out there, blasting an emergency signal, and we're the closest. Assuming . . ."

The law of the solar system was unequivocal. In an environment as hostile to life as space, the aid and goodwill of your fellow humans wasn't optional. The emergency signal, just by existing, obligated the nearest ship to stop and render aid—which didn't mean the law was universally followed.

The *Canterbury* was fully loaded. Well over a million tons of ice had been gently accelerated for the past month. Just like the little glacier that had crushed Paj's arm, it was going to be hard to slow down. The temptation to have an unexplained comm failure, erase the logs, and let the great god Darwin have his way was always there.

But if McDowell had really intended that, he wouldn't have called Holden up. Or made the suggestion where the crew could hear him. Holden understood the dance. The captain was going to be the one who would have blown it off except for Holden. The grunts would respect the captain for not wanting to cut into the ship's profit. They'd respect Holden for insisting that they follow the rule. No matter what happened, the captain and Holden would both be hated for what they were required by law and mere human decency to do.

"We have to stop," Holden said. Then, gamely: "There may be salvage."

McDowell tapped his screen. Ade's voice came

from the console, as low and warm as if she'd been in the room.

"Captain?"

"I need numbers on stopping this crate," he said.

"Sir?"

"How hard is it going to be to put us alongside CA-2216862?"

"We're stopping at an asteroid?"

"I'll tell you when you've followed my order, Navigator Tukunbo."

"Yes, sir," she said. Holden heard a series of clicks. "If we flip the ship right now and burn like hell for most of two days, I can get us within fifty thousand kilometers, sir."

"Can you define 'burn like hell'?" McDowell said.

"We'll need everyone in crash couches."

"Of course we will," McDowell sighed, and scratched his scruffy beard. "And shifting ice is only going to do a couple million bucks' worth of banging up the hull, if we're lucky. I'm getting old for this, Holden. I really am."

"Yes, sir. You are. And I've always liked your chair," Holden said. McDowell scowled and made an obscene gesture. Rebecca snorted in laughter. McDowell turned to her.

"Send a message to the beacon that we're on our way. And let Ceres know we're going to be late. Holden, where does the *Knight* stand?"

"No flying in atmosphere until we get some parts, but she'll do fine for fifty thousand klicks in vacuum."

"You're sure of that?"

"Naomi said it. That makes it true."

McDowell rose, unfolding to almost two and a quarter meters and thinner than a teenager back on Earth. Between his age and never having lived in a gravity well, the coming burn was likely to be hell on the old man. Holden felt a pang of sympathy that he would never embarrass McDowell by expressing.

"Here's the thing, Jim," McDowell said, his voice quiet enough that only Holden could hear him. "We're required to stop and make an attempt, but we don't have to go out of our way, if you see what I mean."

"We'll already have stopped," Holden said, and McDowell patted at the air with his wide, spidery hands. One of the many Belter gestures that had evolved to be visible when wearing an environment suit.

"I can't avoid that," he said. "But if you see anything out there that seems off, don't play hero again. Just pack up the toys and come home."

"And leave it for the next ship that comes through?"

"And keep yourself safe," McDowell said. "Order. Understood?"

"Understood," Holden said.

As the shipwide comm system clicked to life and McDowell began explaining the situation to the crew, Holden imagined he could hear a chorus of groans coming up through the decks. He went over to Rebecca.

"Okay," he said, "what have we got on the broken ship?"

"Light freighter. Martian registry. Shows Eros as home port. Calls itself *Scopuli* . . ."